NEW YORK REVIEW BOOKS
CLASSICS

D0441636

LITTLE REUNIONS

EILEEN CHANG (1920–1995) was born into an aristocratic family in Shanghai. Her father, deeply traditional in his ways, was an opium addict; her mother, partly educated in England, was a sophisticated woman of cosmopolitan tastes. Their unhappy marriage ended in divorce, and Chang eventually ran away from her father—who had beaten her for defying her stepmother, then locked her in her room for nearly half a year. Chang studied literature at the University of Hong Kong, but the Japanese attack on the city in 1941 forced her to return to occupied Shanghai, where she was able to publish the stories and essays (collected in two volumes, *Romances*, 1944, and *Written on Water*, 1945) that soon made her a literary star. In 1944 Chang married Hu Lancheng, a Japanese sympathizer whose sexual infidelities led to their divorce three years later. The rise of Communist influence made it increasingly difficult for Chang to continue living in Shanghai; she moved to Hong Kong in 1952, then immigrated to the United States three years later. She remarried (an American, Ferdinand Reyher, who died in 1967) and held various posts as a writer in residence; in 1969 she obtained a more permanent position as a researcher at Berkeley. Two novels, both commissioned in the 1950s by the United States Information Service as anti-Communist propaganda, *The Rice Sprout Song* and *Naked Earth* (the latter now available as an NYRB Classic), were followed by a third, *The Rouge of the North* (1967), which expanded on her celebrated early novella "The Golden Cangue." Chang continued writing essays and stories in Chinese as well scripts for Hong Kong films, and began work on an English translation of the famous Qing novel

The Sing-Song Girls of Shanghai. In spite of the tremendous revival of interest in her work that began in Taiwan and Hong Kong in the 1970s, and that later spread to mainland China, Chang became ever more reclusive as she grew older. Eileen Chang was found dead in her Los Angeles apartment in September 1995. In 2006, NYRB Classics published *Love in a Fallen City*, an original collection of her short fiction. The following year, *Lust, Caution*, a film adaptation of Chang's 1979 novella, directed by Ang Lee, was released.

JANE WEIZHEN PAN has collaborated with Martin Merz on translations of many works by contemporary Chinese writers. She first encountered Eileen Chang's work as a high-school student in China and has been a devoted reader of her writing since. She is based in Melbourne, Australia, where her research focuses on early Chinese translations of English classics.

MARTIN MERZ studied Chinese at Melbourne University and later received an MA in applied translation in Hong Kong. He moved to Asia in 1980 and has worked in greater China ever since. In addition to his co-translations with Jane Weizhen Pan, he translated the modern Peking opera *Mulian Rescues His Mother*, which was performed at the Hong Kong Fringe in the early 1990s.

LITTLE REUNIONS

EILEEN CHANG

Translated from the Chinese by
JANE WEIZHEN PAN *and*
MARTIN MERZ

NEW YORK REVIEW BOOKS

New York

THIS IS A NEW YORK REVIEW BOOK
PUBLISHED BY THE NEW YORK REVIEW OF BOOKS
435 Hudson Street, New York, NY 10014
www.nyrb.com

Library of Congress Cataloging-in-Publication Data
Names: Zhang, Ailing author. | Pan, Jane Weizhen translator. | Merz, Martin
  translator.
Title: Little reunions / by Eileen Chang ; translated by Jane Weizhen Pan and
  Martin Merz.
Other titles: Xiao tuan yuan. English
Description: New York : New York Review Books, 2018. | Series: New York
  Review Books classics
Identifiers: LCCN 2017036350 (print) | LCCN 2017041597 (ebook) | ISBN
  9781681371283 (epub) | ISBN 9781681371276 (alk. paper)
Classification: LCC PL2837.E35 (ebook) | LCC PL2837.E35 X53613 2018 (print)
  | DDC 895.13/52—dc23
LC record available at https://lccn.loc.gov/2017036350

ISBN 978-1-68137-127-6
Available as an electronic book; ISBN 978-1-68137-128-3

Printed in the United States of America on acid-free paper.
10 9 8 7 6 5 4 3 2 1

CONTENTS

TRANSLATORS' NOTE

THE MANUSCRIPT

Eileen Chang completed *Little Reunions* in 1976 and sent the six-hundred-page handwritten manuscript to Stephen Soong and his wife, Mae Fong Soong, her close friends who later became her literary executors.

Sixteen years after completing the still-unpublished *Little Reunions*, and a few years before her own death, Chang wrote to the Soongs to discuss her will and mentioned she was contemplating destroying the manuscript. However, there were no further discussions along those lines, and in 2009, fourteen years after her death, *Little Reunions* was finally published in Hong Kong, Taiwan, and China.

We have worked from a photocopy of the manuscript she posted to the Soongs in 1976, a copy of which is also archived at the Central Library in Hong Kong. The manuscript differs only slightly from the Hong Kong edition, in that some characters are deliberately written slightly larger, or physically to one side. We have attempted to typographically reproduce these differences in the translation.

TITLE OF THE NOVEL

The Chinese title of the book is a play on 大團圓, literally "big reunion," the reunion of a family at a traditional Chinese festival like the Lunar New Year. A secondary meaning is the happy ending of a novel or a drama.

Chang had something else in mind when she chose the title 小團圓 ("little reunion"). In a letter to Stephen Soong dated August 13, 1991, she explained:

> My life is like a stalk of bamboo with its nodes marking the intervals of my mother's comings and goings. When I was a child, every interval was four years long. There were a total of four intervals. Then came a five-year-long interval. The end of that interval was the reunion in Shanghai with my aunt because of the war in Hong Kong. There were a number of little reunions.

The title of this novel is commonly rendered as *Little Reunion*. While the Chinese title, 小團圓, does not provide any indication of singular or plural, for this translation we decided to render the title as *Little Reunions* to reflect Chang's musings on her life.

KINSHIP TERMS AND OTHER NAMES

To describe members of the large, extended family in *Little Reunions*, Chang employs the complex Chinese kinship system that distinguishes relations according to lineage, age, generation, and number. And so, for example, Nineteenth Mistress and Third Aunt are actually the same person, as Julie's third aunt is the younger sister of her father who ranks nineteenth in her own family. In many cases, Chang provides no names, only the hierarchical position of a character. We have followed her designations as closely as possible, while endeavoring to reduce the burden to the English reader. For further clarity, readers can refer to the character list at the back of this book.

Chang also created other names for many of the characters in her novel, the meanings of which quickly become lost if simply transliterated. And so Euphoria reveals far more about the third mistress of the House of the Euphoric Moon, than Ai Lao San or Old Third Ai. Thus we have avoided transliteration where possible.

ROMANIZATION

Little Reunions is set in an era that predates the pinyin system of romanization by several decades. We have chosen to use the Wade-Giles romanization system that was current at the time of the story. This approach is also consistent with Chang's own style. She mostly used the Wade-Giles system in her English writings, including *The Fall of the Pagoda* and *The Book of Change*, the two semiautobiographical novels she completed in the 1960s.

For place-names, the postal romanization developed by the Imperial Post Office in the early 1900s is used unless established names already existed in English.

ACKNOWLEDGMENTS

We owe immense debts to many friends and colleagues for their help and encouragement during the course of the translation and editing process.

In particular, Roland Soong, Chang's current literary executor, who provided us with a copy of her handwritten manuscript; the scholar Tom Fung helped solve literary puzzles in the novel and pointed out errors in our early drafts; the writers Su Tong and Emily Wu answered our questions about dialects; Yuan Ze, an expert on Chinese costume history, gave invaluable advice on translating Chang's detailed descriptions of clothing and fashion; Wang Jun, a journalist and a dear friend, helped track down historical names; the late Pang Bingjun who assisted with poetry; and librarians of the Chinese Collections team at the National Library of Australia offered generous assistance in locating reference books.

We also wish to thank Jeffrey Yang, Edwin Frank, and the rest of the staff at New York Review Books for their patience, wisdom, and support.

LITTLE REUNIONS

I

ONLY THE somber mood of troops waiting in the dawn before battle can compare with the morning of final exams, like the rebel slave army in *Spartacus* silently peering through the predawn mist at the Roman troops maneuvering in the distance—surely the most chilling moment in any war film—everything charged with anticipation.

"Rain. It's like living by a burbling stream," Julie wrote in her notebook as her thirtieth birthday approached. "Hope it rains every day so I can believe your absence is due to the rain."

On the night of her thirtieth birthday, Julie contemplated the moonlit balcony from her bed. The concrete balusters, like overturned stellae, lying in ruins, were bathed in blue moonlight. Moonlight of the late T'ang dynasty of a thousand years ago. But for Julie, thirty years already felt too long, weighing heavily on her heart like a tombstone.

There is one good thing about being older, Julie often thought—no more exams. And yet she never stopped dreaming about exams. Nightmares, always nightmares.

The alarm clocks went off followed by the sound of flushing toilets reverberating through the building. Bebe and a classmate lay on beds separated by a partition, taking turns peppering each other with questions. Their voices sounded normal when asking questions but instantly turned timorous when being questioned themselves. Their chants of naming bones were painful to listen to. Bebe had to repeat the previous grade.

Julie returned to her small room after her morning ablutions. She had forgotten to switch off the Z-shaped desk lamp. The spherical cream-colored glass lampshade was still glowing against the dusty blue sea outside the window. It looked surreal. Julie shivered, as if she'd been pricked with a pin, and quickly switched off the lamp.

Julie's mother worshipped Western-style schooling, and indeed some middle-aged women of her generation were now attending primary school for the first time in their lives. After assiduously studying the regulations of Julie's school in Hong Kong, her mother learned that boarders were required to bring nothing but a desk lamp. She spent three Chinese dollars to buy the lamp from Sincere Department Store, one of the most prestigious shops in Shanghai. The lamp could easily have been broken en route to Hong Kong, but she had packed it in Julie's suitcase nonetheless.

The war in Europe had thwarted Julie's plans to study abroad. Hong Kong was the only alternative. The exchange rate at the time was three Chinese dollars to one Hong Kong dollar. Julie thought it a waste of money, but by then the money had been spent so it was too late for regrets. The costliest part was the yearlong preparatory course, taught by members of the joint student recruitment team of Oxford, Cambridge, and the University of London. It goes without saying that the tuition fees were exorbitant.

"I'm going downstairs now," said Julie to Bebe, as she pushed open the swinging doors that were just like the old-fashioned saloon doors in a Hollywood western.

"When did you go to bed last night?"

"Early." At least she would have a clear head.

Bebe was fiddling with something inside her sleeping bag. Her family had mailed her the sleeping bag even though they once had lived in Hong Kong themselves and were fully aware of the sub-tropical weather. Her mother was worried that Bebe would throw off her blankets in her sleep and catch a cold.

Finally, Bebe pulled a lamp out of the sleeping bag. It was still switched on, shining brightly.

"Were you reading under the blankets?" asked Julie. She was puzzled because the dormitory did not have a lights-out rule.

"No," said Bebe, grinning. "It was cold last night." She had used the lamp as a hot-water bottle. "The sister would have a fit if she found out." Bebe switched off the lamp and clipped it back onto the iron bed frame above her head.

"Are you prepared?" she asked.

Julie shook her head. "No, I don't even have good notes."

"Are you serious, or are you just saying that?"

"It's true!" said Julie. Noticing a smile of disbelief on Bebe's face, she casually added, "I'll still probably pass."

But Bebe knew that for Julie it was never just a matter of passing.

"I'm going now," said Julie.

She walked downstairs carrying her dip pen, inkpot, and exercise book. In a school populated with offspring of rubber-plantation tycoons, Julie stood out as the only student who did not own a fountain pen. It was a sight to behold, her carrying an inkpot everywhere she went.

The sisters who supervised the dormitory were attending morning mass in the small chapel set off from the hall. Julie could hear the murmur of Latin prayers from the staircase. The sound had a soothing effect on her heart, like pouring oil on troubled waters, and for a moment her thoughts stopped churning, she wasn't about to throw up, but then the urge to throw up came back more strongly than ever.

A strong aroma of cocoa drifted through the halls, the sisters' morning brew awaiting them in the kitchenette. Julie quickened her pace and scampered down the terrazzo steps. The refectory was in the basement.

It's crowded today. Her heart sank. Most of the seats at the pinkish faux-granite-topped long tables had been taken. The local students could go home at the end of the day but they chose to board because the school was quieter than their homes, and they could concentrate better on their studies. Too much happening at home every day.

Each girl had five or six "mothers" who enjoyed equal status and addressed each other as "sister," a common feature of wealthy Hong Kong households.

The girls usually were chauffeured home every other day of the week as well as on weekends. But today they had all come. The refectory was filled with a gaggle of ornamented beauties and much hubbub. No wonder Mr. Andrews had commented that a handful of Cantonese girls is much noisier than a dozen students from northern China.

Julie shivered again.

"*Say lo! Say lo!*" cried Sally in Cantonese. "Alas, alas! I'm doomed." She was bouncing in her chair, and her shoulder-length curls, tied with the most fashionable gold-striped wide plastic ribbons, bounced in concert. She was wearing a thin light pink wool cheongsam printed with light blue puppies and parachutes. Sally was not a petite girl— she had an ample bosom—but was ever so childish. "I'm doomed for sure! Elizabeth, *nei dim ah*? What about you?" she asked. "I'm just waiting for the end."

"*Say lo! Say lo!*" the crowd echoed. Even the two overseas Chinese first-year students from Penang were wailing "*Say lo! Say lo!*" One of them paced around while fidgeting with the little gold cross dangling in front of her chest. The other flapped her hands nervously. But their voices were not as loud as those of the local girls and did not sound sincere at all, so no one believed their claims of being doomed.

"Hey, Emma, remind me of what happened in 1848," pleaded Sally. "Apparently, Mr. Andrews always asks questions about 1848."

Once again, Julie felt as if she'd been pricked with a pin. She winced.

The basement was in fact on the ground floor. Because of the subtropical humidity, houses located on the hilltops had very tall foundational pillars and in effect were built on artificial hills. No one lived on the ground floor, which usually served as the garage. With minor alterations, however, the garage was converted into a refectory. And when the garage doors were wide open, the refectory faced out to the sea.

Julie placed her inkpot and stationery on an unoccupied table and chose a seat facing the sea.

A feast before the battle will at least provide enough energy to fill up the exam booklets. Each student was issued an exercise book with a blue cover, though Julie usually requested two extras because she filled up three in no time at all, wearing her knuckles down to the bone in the process.

To prepare for the English exam Julie could easily memorize *Paradise Lost* from cover to cover. After all, no one can outdo the Chinese when it comes to memorization. Westerners do not encourage rote learning unless there's a good reason to do so. But Julie simply had to find a way to force teachers to give her the highest marks ever awarded and make sure they would feel guilty if she didn't receive the top score.

What could possibly be on the exam today?

The condemned prisoner eats a last meal. The sky is always blue when the prisoner enters the execution ground cruelly trussed up in front of a surging crowd of spectators.

As she ate, Audrey read a book that was balanced on her lap. She was Shanghainese but here the lingua franca was either English or Cantonese. Mainlanders shunned speaking Mandarin and Shanghainese in public, as it seemed impolite and suggested they had something to hide. Julie knew Audrey's surname was Sun but didn't know her Chinese given name.

Audrey looked up from her book and saw Julie. "Where's Bebe?"

"When I came down she was about to get up."

"We're not going to wait for anybody today," declared Audrey sternly. Her pretty doe eyes and heart-shaped face were framed by an upwardly fluffed coiffure.

"Has the driver arrived?" a voice asked in Cantonese.

Ruby entered in a rush, hesitated a moment, then sat near Julie. Everyone was aware that she would not sit with Jenny. The two girls who had transferred from the mainland were not on speaking terms. Julie only knew their English names. Ruby's hair was cut very short. A pair of gold-rimmed spectacles adorned her rosy, round face. She was a large girl and usually wore a blue cotton gown, the trademark of the national schools in China known for austerity and patriotism.

Jenny was from the remote northwest of China and wore her hair braided in two pigtails. She had a pretty oval face, but her yellow skin reminded people of desert sands. She always wore a blue cotton gown as well, though a few months after arriving she bought a bright blue wool overcoat with red and white specks. She wore it indoors and even at mealtimes.

"When I wear this coat, I look like a Victoria University student," she said, mocking herself. "And when I don't wear it, I don't look like a Victoria University student."

Before long, Jenny's coat began to exude a strong odor of garlic, discernible even when it was hanging on a coat hook. This was rather mysterious, because although the sisters cooked rustic French dishes, they respected the wishes of the majority and did not use any garlic, nor did Jenny ever buy food for herself.

Jenny was quite frugal, but she subscribed to a newspaper because the dormitory only provided the English paper—the *South China Morning Post*. Ruby also subscribed to a newspaper, which she eagerly devoured every day after classes. Occasionally Jenny would pound the table and, standing with one foot on a chair, slap her knee and whoop when news of territory lost or recaptured was reported. The place-names she shouted out suggested the war had probably reached Hunan Province. Her tone of voice and gestures resembled an old man's. Perhaps she was influenced by her father in her enthusiasm for news about China, even though she often said he wanted her to be in this peaceful environment so she could concentrate on her studies.

One day after class, Julie and Bebe were dawdling downstairs, waiting for food to be served in the refectory. Sister Thérèse, a Cantonese nun, was ironing clothes. Bebe set a cotton print tea cozy on her head like a Napoleonic military hat, and pointing at Sister Thérèse, sang a line from Gilbert and Sullivan's opera *HMS Pinafore*:

Refrain, audacious tart, your suit from pressing.

Bebe's double entendre was intended to put an end to Sister Thérèse's ironing and badger her to go upstairs and light the gas heater for the bath.

"*Ah-Bebe, Ah-Bebe,*" Sister Thérèse called out, in the Cantonese manner of adding "Ah" before a first name.

Also in the room was Marie, whom Sister Thérèse called *Ah-Malee.* Marie was a Cantonese girl sent from an orphanage overseen by the convent to work as a maid in the school. Marie was tall and skinny with yellowish skin and wore a pair of black-framed glasses.

Marie twittered in a low voice, pleading with Bebe to ask Ruby and Audrey on her behalf if they wanted her to do some washing for them. She wanted to make a little pocket money to buy pictures of saints and purchase fabric to make a cape for the statue of the Virgin Mary.

Bebe told Julie that Marie had already accumulated quite a few likenesses of saints.

"She's happy," said Bebe in Marie's defense. "She knows that everything will be taken care of, so she doesn't need to worry. It's not easy to get into a convent. You have to pay some money, like a dowry, as if you are married to Jesus."

Marie pestered Bebe to ask Ruby then and there, but eventually gave up and went upstairs to ask Sister Henri for the key so she could heat the bathwater. Bebe went with her.

Julie was reading a novel. Her eyes strayed from her book and skimmed over the newspaper Jenny was reading. Jenny caught her glance. She smiled and slid a sheet of the newspaper toward Julie.

Julie felt a little embarrassed. "I don't read newspapers," she said. Then, in an attempt to defend herself, added, "Except for the movie advertisements."

Jenny continued to smile but did not respond.

"Soeur Thérèse . . . ," A voice in French pierced the silence from upstairs.

Jenny was folding the newspapers scattered about on a dining table in the large, dimly lit refectory. She picked up one newspaper and glanced at the headlines. "This is traitorous!" she suddenly bellowed, and began to tear the pages apart.

Ruby jumped up and extended her heavy arms across the table to rescue her newspaper. The cuffs of her blue coat went up to her elbows and the shape of her bulging bosom was obvious even though covered by her sack-like coat. But she was not fast enough. The tug-of-war ended with the newspaper being torn apart.

It happened too fast for Julie to react, even though she was sitting next to Jenny. It took a while for the words to sink in, just like a lightning bolt arriving faster than a thunderclap.

"Don't you dare defame the Peace Movement!" barked Ruby, in a husky masculine voice. Julie was surprised to hear Ruby speak in Mandarin like that. Ruby's Mandarin was not bad, though she had a discernible accent. But she sounded different because she was ordinarily a quiet girl, and like most people, when she spoke English she spoke softly.

"Traitor newspaper! It's all claptrap!"

"That's my paper! Don't you dare tear it!"

Jenny raised her eyebrows in a fury. She folded the newspaper, attempting to tear it further but failed because the bundle was now too thick. In an instant, Ruby snatched away half of the paper. Jenny continued to tear her half. Ruby was about to hit Jenny but then hesitated. Instead, she grabbed what she could of her newspaper and stormed out.

Julie related the drama to Bebe, and through Bebe, it became a talking point among the girls. The reason for the incident was revealed later when Audrey learned that Ruby was the niece of Wang Ching-wei, who had played an important role in the Peace Movement since the 1930s and was considered a traitor by many for his collaboration with the Japanese.

In British Hong Kong, the niece of Wang Ching-wei was not as worthy of attention as the niece of Sir Robert Ho Tung, an influential Hong Kong businessman. And there were two of *his* nieces in the school. But Audrey, being Shanghainese, had a different perspective. Ruby was a regular visitor to Audrey's room. Once Julie passed

Audrey's door and saw Ruby wrestling with Sally on the bed. Ruby was something of a tomboy and delighted in competitions of strength.

The dormitory rooms were divided by thin wooden boards into three cubicles, one bright and two dark. Audrey occupied a dark cubicle so she usually kept the swinging doors open to let air and light in. When Julie walked by her door late at night, she often saw Audrey studying while holding a skull in one hand like a soccer player holding a ball. Wrapped in a royal-blue quilted satin bathrobe, her hair draped over her shoulders, and a skeleton standing behind her in the dim light, Audrey looked like a witch as she mumbled her lessons to herself.

Jenny had a regular visitor from her hometown. His complexion was dark and he was quite short and skinny. He wore a Western suit and had black-framed spectacles. On first seeing him, most people would instinctively avert their eyes, as though to avoid embarrassing a disabled person. Jenny said he was her father's friend.

Once, after he had left, Sister Henri asked in jest, "Jenny's Mr. Wei has gone?"

Jenny stopped on the staircase, turned her head and giggled. "Mr. Wei is a married man, sister."

But henceforth Sister Henri continued to refer to the man as Jenny's Mr. Wei. The only other person who was part of this general category was Audrey's Mr. Lee, a classmate to whom she was practically engaged.

Jenny had stayed with Mr. Wei's family for several weeks, temporarily changing her status to a day student. She explained that Mr. Wei's parents, both of whom lived in Hong Kong, were especially fond of her. They prepared hometown cuisine for her and spoiled her terribly. It was unclear whether their daughter-in-law had not accompanied them to Hong Kong in the first place or had already returned to their hometown.

After that, Jenny was invited to stay with the family every once in a while. She maintained cordial relations with the residents of the dormitory, and no one said anything about the matter. A month went by and she coyly commented, "This hometown cuisine has made me quite plump."

"People from her hometown are very important to her," commented Bebe. The northwest of China was indeed far away, but Bebe was implying that Jenny was a small-town girl.

"She's just like a character in a Chang Hen-shui novel," joked Julie, "with her pigtails and blue cotton Chinese gown...."

Having grown up in China, Bebe had watched many Chinese movies and local operas. She understood the reference and smiled.

But it was hardly appropriate for a character from a Chang Hen-shui novel to move into the Wei household. Considering Mr. Wei's appearance, there must be some sort of plot afoot. Who knows what the nuns were thinking, and Sister Henri continued her teasing about "Jenny's Mr. Wei."

Hong Kong people had always regarded northerners as barbarians from beyond the pale of civilization. Jenny and the Wei family were not Catholics so there was no point in being overly concerned, and in any case, the two families were on friendly terms. Besides, the arrangement presented the school with a modest saving of meal expenses, which was just as welcome to the school as was the local students returning home every two or three days.

Julie was the only student who didn't return home, even for the summer holidays, thereby saving on travel expenses. The previous year Sister Luke had told her that the dormitory could not be kept running just for one student. She would take Julie to the convent where she was to teach two classes of English in the convent primary school. Julie would be provided with food and board there. Of course, this was because her marks had broken all records, but it was still a generous offer.

One afternoon, before Julie had moved to the convent, Sister Henri called out from the ground floor, "Julie, someone is here to see you."

Sister Henri was talking to a guest who was leaning on the balustrade outside the refectory. It was Julie's mother. Julie approached, smiling politely, and mumbled, "Second Aunt." Luckily Sister Henri did not understand the appellation, otherwise she would have thought this family even more peculiar than she already did. Julie's uncle—her father's eldest brother—had no daughter of his own, so there was a verbal agreement that he adopt her. Consequently, Julie called her birth parents Second Aunt and Second Uncle, and since childhood found this arrangement liberating. Even her younger brother followed suit by calling their parents Second Aunt and Second Uncle. Julie followed her brother's lead by calling her adoptive parents Eldest Aunt and Eldest Uncle, not mother and father.

Sister Henri was aware that Julie's parents had divorced, but as the Catholic Church did not recognize divorce, she did not address Julie's mother as Mrs. Sheng or use her maiden name, Miss Pien—Sister Henri simply did not address her at all.

In the midafternoon sunlight Julie's mother appeared slightly haggard. Julie was momentarily stunned. Perhaps it was the new hairstyle—bouffant in the front and curled inward at the collar in the back—which made her appear thin.

Julie's mother dressed modestly in a teal green linen shirt and white canvas bell-bottom pants, probably because she was there to visit the school dormitory. After all, Julie was supposed to be an impecunious student.

That day Sister Henri seemed somewhat distant. On previous occasions when Julie's mother had visited, Sister Henri was most ebullient and even the usually stern-faced Miss Cheng, the administrator, was all smiles. Miss Cheng's nickname, Automobile, referred to her stocky torso that seemed to lack a neck and her thick-lensed spectacles resembling headlights. On previous occasions Miss Cheng had been chatty, making light of Julie's forgetfulness and imitating her pleading "I forget" in a squeaky voice.

Julie's father had only visited her at school once, when she attended the Liu Academy for Girls in Shanghai. Because Julie had not received a formal education, her mother first sent her to a school run by three women who were acquaintances of hers: a mother and her two daughters. They in turn had hired two teachers: an old man and Miss Lu.

Her father visited during morning calisthenics. A dozen-odd girls of all ages were exercising on the school grounds. Miss Lu had not changed and was still wearing a yellow-striped padded cotton gown. A whistle on a black silk ribbon dangled on her chest. She had shoulder-length hair, and wispy bangs sat above her dainty face. With one hand holding her whistle the petite Miss Lu ran in place, shouting in a high-pitched voice, "*Zuo jia, you jia, zuo jia, you jia . . .*!" The Shanghainese speak rapidly so "Left, right, left, right" becomes "Left foot, right foot, left foot, right foot."

Julie's father sported a white English pith helmet and wore hexagonal gold wire-framed spectacles. A breezy, light gray silk gown hung on his tall slender frame. He lightheartedly observed from the sidelines, perhaps standing a little too close as he seemed mildly embarrassed. After the class, Miss Lu did not come over to greet him. Several times when Julie was back at home, her father, reclining on his opium bed, asked all manner of things about Miss Lu and coyly inquired into her marital status.

Julie's mother always visited the school in the company of Julie's third aunt, her father's younger sister. Although her third aunt was no beauty, she followed the fashions of the day and was quite eye-catching. Bebe did not think Julie's mother was pretty, but Julie had never heard Bebe say anyone was pretty. "There are many women of your mother's type in Hong Kong," Bebe remarked.

Indeed, in Hong Kong her mother's appearance was quite ordinary because she resembled all the other mixed-blood Cantonese. Sister Henri was Macanese, shorthand for Sino-Portuguese Eurasian. She had large black eyes, long eyelashes, and plodded slowly as she walked, having filled out in her middle age. Racial prejudice meant Sister Henri could not rise beyond the third-highest position of the dormitory staff.

Sister Henri led the way to the refectory, which was deserted because of the summer holiday. It felt smaller than usual. Julie thought it a pity that not a single person was there to see her mother.

"Go upstairs and show her around," said Sister Henri, but refrained from accompanying mother and daughter, most likely to give them time alone to talk.

Julie did not ask her mother when she had arrived. It was certainly several days prior, but to ask would be tantamount to complaining of not being informed earlier.

"I arrived with Miss Hsiang and the others," said Rachel. "It came up at the mah-jongg table. We decided to travel together. Nancy and her husband wanted to go, too. Miss Hsiang wanted to go sightseeing. They all said, 'Let's go together.' It was decided, so I agreed to travel with them." She chuckled, feigning she had no choice in the matter.

Julie didn't ask where her mother was going. *She was clearly just passing through Hong Kong. Miss Hsiang had probably only ventured as far as Hong Kong for a holiday. Perhaps Nancy and her husband were on their way to Chungking. Many people wanted to leave Shanghai. Yet even before Shanghai had become the "Orphan Island" surrounded by a sea of Japanese forces, Rachel had lamented, "I'm stuck here in Shanghai and can't go anywhere."*

Julie was one of the reasons Rachel was stuck in Shanghai, and now after she had finally left Shanghai, there was a war in Europe. Where else could she go?

Julie did not expect her mother to reveal her ultimate destination. Thinking back, it appeared that even her mother's traveling companions didn't know, either, and she had obviously feared Julie would inadvertently spill the beans if privy to her itinerary.

While upstairs, Rachel briefly glanced into Julie's room from the doorway. "All right, then," she said. "I had to attend to a few things and thought I'd look in on your dormitory on the way."

Julie did not ask about her third aunt.

After they emerged from the refectory, Sister Henri came to see them out. The asphalt path became steeper as it wended down to the main road that traversed around the mountain. There were cream-colored concrete railings on both sides of the path. The sunlight had baked the red flowers in the blue ceramic flower pots, transforming them into little black fists, and had bleached the sea to a faded hue, like old blue linen drenched in sweat.

"All right, then," Rachel said in English, "you may come tomorrow. Do you know how to take the bus?"

"Where are you staying?" asked Sister Henri, it suddenly dawning on her to inquire.

"The Repulse Bay Hotel," Rachel answered hesitantly.

"Oh," Sister Henri responded nonchalantly, "that's a nice place."

The voices and countenances of the two women did not reveal what was on their minds. But as she walked beside them, Julie was mortified, knowing full well the Repulse Bay Hotel was the most expensive hotel in Hong Kong, yet her mother feigned financial hardship to take advantage of the convent and enable Julie to board for free over the summer.

The three of them continued down the hill.

"How did you come here?" Sister Henri asked to break the awkward silence.

"In a friend's automobile," Rachel answered. Looking away, she spoke rapidly in a soft voice, as though she did not want to discuss the topic further.

As soon as Sister Henri heard that she stopped in her tracks and did not continue down the path to see the visitor off.

Julie was reluctant to return to the convent with Sister Henri. She knew Sister Henri would not say anything to her if they walked back together, but she felt she really ought to see her mother along a little farther. Julie continued walking. She then realized that she would soon be able to see the road. If the car were parked on the nearer side she wouldn't be able to see it from her current position. Sure enough, a vehicle was parked on the other side of the road. But of course it could belong to the household opposite the convent. Julie stopped.

Perhaps it would be best, Julie thought, to stay on this spot smiling until her mother disappeared from view, though it still might appear that she was waiting to see who would open the car door for her mother if she had in fact arrived in that car. But if she immediately headed back, she might catch up with Sister Henri. After hesitating a moment, she turned and headed back. As she walked, Julie worried that Sister Henri would be watching her dawdle and think she was avoiding her.

Fortunately, Sister Henri was nowhere to be seen.

After that Julie went to Repulse Bay almost every day. One morning she came down to the refectory for breakfast. A parcel had been placed beside the solitary setting of a mug, a plate, and cutlery. She did not appear particularly excited. *Who could have sent the parcel? Perhaps it is a dictionary. It resembles the shape of one of those long narrow dictionaries, though it is a little too long.* Julie picked up the parcel and noticed some tattered, used banknotes visible where the yellow wrapping paper was torn. She was shocked.

"*Hai-m-hai nei ge?* Is it yours?" asked Sister Thérèse in Cantonese. "Someone's waiting for you to sign for it."

That much Cantonese Julie could understand.

A little old man sauntered through the open refectory doors. Julie had never seen such a shabbily attired postman before. In Hong Kong, postmen did not wear green and she did not recognize his uniform at all, except for the gray mailbag slung over his shoulder.

Cantonese men have unique features, and this old man resembled one in a classical Chinese painting, with a bony face and two thin wisps of black whiskers. The skinny man with long hair and particularly long eyebrows was the very image of longevity. He passed over the receipt and then the stub of a pencil with a look of immense self-satisfaction, as if he were saying, "If it weren't for me...."

Julie waited until he left and there was no one around before she carefully untied the hemp string. The parcel contained a large bundle of cash and a letter. The signature belonged to Mr. Andrews. He addressed her as Miss Sheng, and went on to say that he knew her application for the scholarship was unsuccessful, and asked that she permit him to give her a small scholarship. He said that if her results were maintained she would certainly be awarded a full-fee-paying scholarship the next year.

The parcel contained eight hundred Hong Kong dollars in total, and there were many tattered one- and five-dollar notes. *Perhaps Mr. Andrews did not write a check in case word got out and people gossiped.* To Julie the letter was a lifeline and she couldn't wait to show her mother.

Fortunately, Julie had been summoned to visit her mother that day, otherwise she'd have had to hold on to the news for another day or two. How would she survive that? It's not something you can explain over the telephone.

Heart aflutter, Julie felt as if she were flying in front of the bus like a colorful flag. When she arrived at Repulse Bay, Julie first told her mother about the money and then showed her the letter. The parcel, placed on the table in its original packaging, looked like a washerwoman's bar of soap. For Julie, these were the most precious banknotes in the world—she could not bear the idea of depositing the money in a bank and receiving different banknotes upon withdrawal.

Rachel read the letter carefully. "How can we possibly accept someone else's money?" she said with an embarrassed smile. "It must be returned to him."

"No, Mr. Andrews is not that sort of person," Julie muttered anxiously. "He'd be offended if the money were returned. He'd think . . . I'd misunderstood his intentions." She paused, then added, "We have no contact out of class. He doesn't even like me."

Rachel did not respond. After a while she mumbled, "Leave it here for the moment, then."

Julie folded the letter and slid it back into the envelope. As she returned the envelope to her purse, she felt uneasy, fearing it appeared she had fallen in love with Mr. Andrews. The bar of soap, that large yellow bundle all alone on the table, was very conspicuous, but Julie took pains not to look at it as she walked around the room.

Julie had thought she would be unable to endure staying silent about the good news for a day or two, but she had not anticipated the agony of keeping the news to herself for two days after she returned to school. She was afraid of going back to the Repulse Bay Hotel, thinking the money would still be there as long as she was not, since Rachel would not return the money to Mr. Andrews of her own accord. But then she thought it would be rude if she didn't write a thank-you note. Mr. Andrews might think the money had been lost in the mail—probably embezzled by the postman—since it had been so carelessly wrapped.

Julie knew the matter of the money wouldn't arise immediately upon her arrival. While she and her mother took afternoon tea as usual, Nancy dropped in. Nancy's olive complexion was perfect for sunbathing. Recently she had spent a lot of time at the beach and her skin had taken on a bronzed tan, the gleaming tan only rickshaw pullers have on their shoulders and backs, the tan only a few people can achieve by sunbathing. Complemented by her flaming-red lips and revealing outfit, she had a rather voluptuous appearance, despite her flat face and thin figure. Nancy greeted Julie with her customary enthusiasm: "Hi, Julie."

Nancy had bought Dr. Yang a wool cardigan and had come to show it to Rachel. If it was inexpensive, it would not hurt to buy a few more to sell back in Shanghai.

"Rachel, you lost a lot last night, right?"

"Oh that Mr. Pi had all the lucky hands," said Rachel, again in a tone suggesting she wanted to drop the matter. "Nancy, when did you return?"

"We came back early, before two o'clock. I suggested we come and look you up but Charlie was tired. What's this about you losing eight hundred dollars?" Nancy asked, smiling curiously.

At first Julie didn't pay much attention, though it did strike her as a little strange that Rachel seemed to stop Nancy in her tracks and change the topic of conversation. Julie didn't react when she heard the figure mentioned again—she was completely indifferent. And after Nancy left Rachel did not raise the matter of Mr. Andrews's money again. Best that it was not raised, Julie thought at the time, believing she had made a lucky escape. Only on the bus back to the dormitory did she begin to see the light.

What a coincidence! Exactly eight hundred dollars. If there is a god, like destiny, he plays tricks on people. It seemed absurd, but Julie realized something had come to an end. It was not something she herself had decided, but she knew it was over, that she had come to the end of a very long road.

Many years later, back in Shanghai, Julie wrote a piece that infuriated her maternal uncle's family because it obviously referred to them. Third Aunt was slightly amused. "Your second aunt *will* be upset when she comes back," she said to Julie.

"I am now completely uninterested in whatever Second Aunt may have to say about anything," Julie replied.

She then told Judy about the eight hundred dollars. "After that, I don't know why, but I simply didn't care anymore." This part she relayed in English.

Judy was quiet for a while. "You know," she said, putting on a conciliatory smile, "she did spend a lot of money on you."

Julie knew Judy thought her resolve was all because of the eight hundred dollars.

"I will definitely repay Second Aunt," Julie replied coldly, "no matter what."

Judy again fell silent, then chirped, "Miss Hsiang says it's not good to be resentful every day."

Julie felt embarrassed and smiled with a hint of surprise. Was Miss Hsiang referring to what she had observed in Shanghai? Or was it because she learned more about what she hadn't known after staying in the same hotel in Hong Kong and spending more time with Rachel? Julie wasn't sure.

Actually, the time Rachel and Julie spent together in Hong Kong was quite good, all things considered, almost as good as a second honeymoon. The first honeymoon took place when Julie was a little girl and Rachel returned to China for the first time after spending several years abroad. In Hong Kong Julie resumed her role as the young guest, always visiting around four or five for afternoon tea.

On Julie's first visit, Rachel wore a transparent egg-yellow nightgown. When a bellboy knocked on the door she suddenly clutched at her neck with open hands to cover her breasts with her arms as she shrank away. Julie was astonished. She had never seen her mother behave in such a discomposed manner. Nor had she seen her mother dressed so inappropriately. It was as if her haggard appearance had conquered her composure. By the time the bellboy entered the room to serve tea, Rachel had already retreated to the bathroom.

Rachel poured two cups of tea from the tall, slender silver teapot. "That friend of yours, Bebe," said Rachel. "I invited her over for tea. She had telephoned so I invited her to visit."

Rachel was referring to when Bebe returned to Shanghai over the summer break.

"She seems to be very capable. I'm sure she can help you, but you mustn't let her control you. That wouldn't do." Rachel articulated those last three words in a low voice through her thin, slightly pursed lips.

Julie knew that her mother was referring to lesbian love. She had often heard Rachel and Third Aunt gossip about women they knew who were extremely close, in relationships in which one was totally obedient to the other.

Julie's maternal uncle used to mock the two in-laws, Second Aunt and Third Aunt, for being lesbian lovers.

For Rachel, everything about herself is dignified and noble, but she is always cynical about other people, no matter what they do.

Once, Julie talked about her mother with Bebe, who concluded that Rachel was probably going through menopause, though she wasn't old enough yet, really. Later Julie thought of Rachel while reading D. H. Lawrence's short story "The Lovely Lady." The female protagonist was sixty or seventy years old. Not that she had a magic formula for eternal youth, though she did take care of her health. Her natural endowments made her look younger than her years. Her son was a paunchy, unmarried, middle-aged man. He always felt uncomfortable when he visited his mother. "In the lovely lady's womb he must have felt VERY confused." That line got Julie thinking about herself. *The ugly duckling is no longer young, and no duckling is as tall as I am. An ugly egret is more appropriate, and everything about it is ugly.*

A Eurasian day student named Angie happened to take the school bus down the mountain one day. She squeezed in next to Julie.

"Angie says you are beautiful," Sally told Julie later. "I don't agree, but I thought I ought to tell you,"

Julie knew that Sally felt the need to tell her that because she sensed Julie's lack of confidence.

Perhaps Angie's taste was unusual because she herself had an unusual appearance. She had the typical features of a Chinese girl— a petite frame and a flat round face. But she had the whitest of white Caucasian skin, as white as paper, with thick ink-black eyebrows, large light-blue eyes, and plump lips, thickly plastered with glistening cinnabar lipstick. It was all rather striking. But thanks to popular female characters in Hollywood movies with a similar appearance, Angie numbered among the school belles.

Julie didn't know if Sally had said the same to Bebe, but since Bebe never mentioned it, of course Julie wouldn't raise the subject.

After that, it was always a little awkward for Julie when she encountered Angie.

Bebe never ever commented on someone's looks, but whenever Julie said, "I love the name Katinka," Bebe would unfailingly reply: "I know a girl called Katinka." Of course the girl Bebe knew was unattractive, which sullied the name in Bebe's mind.

"I love the name Nora," Julie said on another occasion.

"I know a girl called Nora," Bebe retorted. The way she responded was more like an explanation of why she did not like the name.

Julie discovered that characters similar to her own mother were common in English-language novels. She told Bebe that both Florence, the mother in Noël Coward's play *The Vortex*, and Mary Amberley, the mother in Aldous Huxley's novel *Eyeless in Gaza*, bore a strong resemblance to Rachel.

"She really had affairs?" asked Bebe.

"No," said Julie, "she just wants to be loved."

Bebe immediately lost interest.

One day after finishing afternoon tea, Rachel went to the bathroom to change and put on her makeup. Miss Hsiang arrived. Julie called her Eighth Sister because she was low in seniority within the family clan, even though she was actually a generation older than Julie. Rachel had met Miss Hsiang at the mah-jongg table two years earlier. Miss Hsiang professed a family connection with her. It turned out she was a member of the Sheng clan. Owing to their shared experience of divorce, however, Miss Hsiang instantly claimed Rachel as her best friend, despite Rachel having had no contact with the Sheng clan for a long time. Miss Hsiang visited a few days later and gave a detailed account of her divorce. She candidly admitted her desire to marry again. She was in straitened circumstances, and her seventeen-year-old son lived with her.

After Miss Hsiang departed, Rachel called out from the bathroom in a long-drawn-out cry, "*Oh, Judy.*" Ever since Julie had moved in with them she was aware that something was amiss between Rachel and Third Aunt. But they were as intimate as ever that night when Rachel recounted Miss Hsiang's visit to Judy. Julie had gone to bed. She was surprised when she overheard the conversation in the bathroom. "As if all divorced women are the same," Judy groused on Rachel's behalf.

Rachel responded shyly in agreement and giggled lightheartedly. "That Kong family really is something!"

"That's right. I heard the young men of the house do not dare to venture into other rooms. Go into any room that should be unoccupied and you'd bump into people—in broad daylight."

When Miss Hsiang was married to the Kong household's fourth son she was a renowned beauty among the relatives, with a delicate round face and a high nose bridge, which was the standard of beauty at the time. Nowadays, Miss Hsiang was a little chubby and had a double chin. She wore her hair in the George Washington style, an unconventional, boyish look.

Miss Hsiang had not seen Julie for a year. She greeted Julie without perfunctory pleasantries, then turned to Rachel. "I just came by to see what you will be doing later on," she said, indicating she did not want to disrupt the conversation.

"Have a seat," said Rachel. "Julie was just about to leave."

"No thanks," said Miss Hsiang. "What are your plans for today? Will you join us for dinner, or do you have a prior engagement?" The corners of her eyes dropped when she spoke. She looked grumpy and her voice sounded hoarse.

Rachel paused. "We'll see. Anyway, we can catch up in a while at the lounge bar. The usual time."

"Very well, then," snapped Miss Hsiang. "See you later."

Occasionally Miss Hsiang spoke in this prickly tone, which she had acquired as a child from the concubines in the household. Prostitutes were accustomed to employing this sort of pouting to manipulate clients. Today, however, Miss Hsiang seemed to be overdoing things. *Just because it was rare for her to come to Hong Kong for pleasure, was she entitled to act up and rebuke Rachel for not accompanying her at all times?*

Julie had not asked Rachel how long she planned to stay in Hong Kong, but after several weeks without any word of her departure, Julie thought it was odd.

One day when Julie was leaving the hotel, Rachel accompanied her downstairs. The tailor and curio shops were located in a short T-shaped corridor above which was a vaulted glass ceiling. As Rachel window-shopped, two people emerged from around the corner. The two parties exchanged a friendly "Hello!" It was Miss Hsiang with Mr. Pi.

So Ambassador Pi was also in Hong Kong. They must have come together.

"Mr. Pi."

"Hello, Julie."

"We're just window-shopping," said Miss Hsiang cheerfully. "The things here are of course as exorbitantly priced as tiger meat."

"That's right. It's not worth buying anything here," said Rachel.

Then the conversation lapsed.

"Where are you off to?" asked Miss Hsiang to fill the awkward silence.

"Nowhere in particular," mumbled Rachel. "Just ambling about."

Miss Hsiang stood facing Mr. Pi, exchanging a few quiet words with him, and then, with a beaming smile, raised her hands to straighten his necktie. Ambassador Pi was well over sixty but still stood bolt upright. His receding hairline made his head look like a moon gate, his forehead appearing especially large. A pair of tortoiseshell-framed spectacles adorned his broad face that resembled a crab's carapace. There was not a trace of a smile on it.

That little possessive gesture startled Julie and she took pains to hide her reaction. She turned to snatch a glance at her mother and saw that Rachel pretended not to notice by looking into the shopwindow. The darkened glass pane reflected Rachel's lustrous features, and for a moment her former glamour returned, as she tenderly gazed into the shopwindow.

At that moment Julie came to a vague realization that Miss Hsiang's earlier outburst probably stemmed from an attempt to absolve herself of any blame. Rachel had incessant engagements that did not include Ambassador Pi or Nancy and her husband. Miss Hsiang frequently ended up paired with Ambassador Pi, so Rachel could not really blame her for snatching him up.

"Then we'll see you a little later at the lounge bar," said Miss Hsiang. Everyone nodded politely and dispersed.

Just as Julie was about to say, "I'll be going now," Rachel said, "Let's go for a walk—the garden here is wonderful." Julie was quite surprised that her mother actually wanted to go for a walk with her.

The garden was designed in a formal French style based on symmetry, with a narrow passageway paved with faux marble and bordered with holly trees pruned into the shape of goblets. Several roses were in bloom. It was very strange for Julie to walk next to her mother in the garden. Rachel probably sensed it too and suddenly started to talk of her own childhood. She began with the sort of homily she often gave after lunch when Julie was eight or nine years old.

"Thinking back, in the old days, it was just so.... Your maternal grandfather died while stationed in Yunnan on official duties. He was only twenty-four. It was one of those Yunnan miasmas. When the news arrived your maternal grandmother was embroidering on a high chair with First and Second Concubine. She fainted and fell to the floor, bringing the high chair down with her. Of the three wives, only Second Concubine was pregnant." Rachel always called her birth mother Second Concubine.

"No one in the clan believed any of the wives were with child. They wanted to divide up the property of a branch of the family without a male heir and demand a physical examination to determine if the woman was pregnant. How could that possibly be agreed to? The clan members made such a ruckus, insisting the pregnancy was fraudulent, threatening to drive the women out and burn down the house. Some of the menfolk, Hunan soldiers who had been with your great-grandfather, surrounded the house just before the due date and set up watches at the front and rear entrances to check everyone who came and went. They even kept watch on the roof.

"Finally Second Concubine gave birth to a baby, but it was a girl. A maid called Ling went out with a basket and bought a little infant boy from a Shantung famine refugee. She hid the infant in the basket and smuggled him into the house. The boy became the twin brother. Ling was terrified the baby would cry at a checkpoint when she came back—if her ruse had been discovered they would have shot her on the spot. On her deathbed your maternal grandmother ordered that Ling must be given special treatment, that she should be looked after for life. Your maternal uncle respected her wishes—he's always good to Ling."

At first Julie could not make heads or tails of the story. After a pause she asked, "Does Maternal Uncle know the truth?"

"No," said Rachel softly, shaking her head.

No wonder Third Aunt had once said girl and boy twins are rare. When Julie responded, "But aren't Second Aunt and Maternal Uncle twins?" Judy was quiet for a second, then, with a cagey smile, mumbled her acquiescence: Rachel and her brother indeed looked alike. But whenever people said that, Judy also smiled. *They are not as alike as identical twins, but girl and boy twins are apparently not really twins.*

"They grew more alike because they both suckled on Second Concubine's milk," said Judy. Julie later came to realize that Rachel had related this family story because she wanted to diminish the distance between mother and daughter and had let Julie in on one of her secrets. Moreover, being eighteen years old, Julie could be counted on to keep it secret.

Julie recalled seeing a maid called Ling in her maternal uncle's household. Ling was retired but occasionally visited her former employers, neatly attired in a black cotton jacket and trousers. Her age did not show on her round, fair-skinned face. *Come to think of it, she must have once been quite attractive, and probably flirted with those old Hunan soldiers to get through the checkpoint. How else would she have been able to take a basket back into the compound without being searched?*

Sensing Julie's intense interest in her story, Rachel immediately warned, "Now don't even think of suing Maternal Uncle to make a grab for family assets!"

Julie raised her eyebrows and chuckled. "Me? Why would I sue Maternal Uncle?"

"I'm just saying that maybe one day when you really need money you might think about it. In that Sheng clan of yours even siblings are capable of suing each other."

Mother has already envisaged her own daughter as an impoverished vagabond who one day would somehow find evidence in a scrap of folkloric family legend of infants being switched at birth in order to chase after her maternal uncle's rapidly dissipating assets.

They walked another circuit of the garden in silence then headed back.

Julie finally broke the silence and, with a distant smile, spoke. "I've always felt guilty that I have been such a burden to Second Aunt. Who can know what the future will hold? It is such a pity that someone like Second Aunt has had to waste all these years because of me."

After a short lull Rachel said, "I don't like you saying…"—

Julie thought she heard a slight pause after "I don't like *you*"—

"…as if I were some kind of superior person, aloof up on high. My life is over," lamented Rachel. "I've already thought it through and will leave all the remaining funds to support you." She then lowered her voice, continuing, "And just find a place for myself and be done with it." She spoke so fast the last few words were barely audible.

Rachel did not elaborate but Julie guessed she was referring to a longtime admirer like Lloyd, the English businessman. He was younger than Rachel, tall, with a red face and a long chin. Droopy eyelids framed his blue eyes. He habitually brayed with laughter before finishing what he was saying, rendering the rest of his words unintelligible and making him appear unsophisticated. He once invited Rachel and Judy to watch his team's water polo match, and they brought Julie along. The seating at the YMCA pool was very cramped. Julie remembered the summer dusk, the chlorine smell of the pool, the frills on Rachel's blue-gray gauze silk shirt, and Rachel's animated laughter.

As soon as Rachel spoke of marrying herself off, Julie could see in her mind's eye a gloomy entrance hall with an old-fashioned dark-wood stand with hat racks on both sides, a mirror in the middle, and a space for umbrellas beneath.

It was just like one of the houses that Julie had lived in as a child where she invariably felt like a guest, a young guest who felt uneasy standing in the hallway. But her childhood sense of security always revolved around her being a young guest.

Rachel's loathing of being dependent on others was now haunting her. Julie was careful to avoid displaying her delight. She quietly took in the news, but felt it was not quite right, as she did not think Rachel had made much of a sacrifice.

Evening fell.

"Very well, then," said Rachel. "You may go now. No need to come tomorrow. I'll telephone you."

The next time Julie visited, Rachel was doing her makeup in front of the dresser mirror and mentioned Judy for the first time. "I received a letter from your third aunt. As soon as I leave, boyfriends come out of the woodwork! As if I were holding her back. Really!" She sneered.

The relationship between the two of them is now very strained and they only live together to save money. But Mother is away from Shanghai now and gets angry if Judy doesn't miss her.

Julie didn't ask who her third aunt's boyfriend was. But soon after her mother arrived, Julie also received a letter from Judy. Obviously, at that time her third aunt did not have a boyfriend. The letter was still written in her usual cheerful tone. She referred to Bertrand Russell's aphorism "Pessimists say the glass is half empty, optimists say it's half full" and wrote, "I am now enjoying a half-full life."

Julie did not like what she said in the letter and therefore did not comment on it when she replied. In her mind, Second Aunt and Third Aunt would always be the same way she remembered them as she stood beside them as a child for the first time watching them dress up to go ballroom dancing. Rachel put on a pale pink knee-length beaded tassel dress with a fringe. Judy wore a black dress, and a blue velvet rose bloomed on her waist. Judy, a fair-skinned and curvaceous woman, had a pretty nose, though her teeth protruded and she wore glasses. Even at that time, in a child's eyes, they were no longer young. But the setting sun is always beautiful, and the younger generation should appreciate such memories by stepping back and not being in too much of a hurry to grow up. That was Julie's way of showing respect for the aged. "Youth have many long days ahead," was something Julie heard her mother frequently intone. But now it had become an excuse, everything was put off.

This time in Hong Kong it seemed that Rachel had decided to forego her incessant correcting of everything Julie did. After Rachel changed into her bathing suit at dusk, she said to Julie, "Come with me to the beach for a look around."

Is mother trying to show me how sophisticated people live? Julie felt it was her mother's last attempt before completely giving up on her.

As they walked side by side, Julie could not avoid the searing image of Rachel's white bathing suit from the corner of her eye. *Those pointy breasts look fake.* The photos of her mother taken at the beach in southern France always showed her fully clothed, with long pants and parrot-green woven sandals covering the insteps of her now unbound feet. *She still had to go into the water.*

Julie tried not to look at Rachel's white rubber sandals. They seemed too big for her. Women with bound feet often had sticklike legs, which would make their shoes look oversized. Of course, they stuffed padding inside their shoes.

They emerged from a small grove to a stretch of beach with light reddish-brown sand covered in a muddle of footprints. A couple splashed about in the water with their child; a whole family played with a beach ball together. They were either Cantonese or Macanese. Only Julie was wearing a long Chinese gown. As if that didn't attract enough attention, there were always the spectacles that Judy made Julie wear before heading to Hong Kong. Julie felt like she was dressed in a body glove that separated her from the sunlight.

"Look!" Rachel poked at a starfish with the tip of her toe.

The patterns of round nodules set between black ridges resembled the inlay of Southeast Asian black silver bracelets, though their squelchy pustules of silvery flesh were quite revolting.

"The worst thing about swimming is bumping into jellyfish—their stings hurt like needle pricks," Rachel added.

"Oh yes," Julie chimed in, "I saw them from the gunwales." On the boat to Hong Kong, she had seen school after school of jellyfish hovering in the water like yellow mist.

What on earth is this huge open space for? At least a dockyard could be built here to make some use of the land. Actually, as soon as Julie had disembarked from the bus, she excitedly imagined the scene that confronted her—thick clusters of Japanese jasmine shrubs beside the macadam road, like plump piles of green leaves on the ground, the sound of insects chirping at the end of the day, the scent of jasmine wafting through the air, and a line of vase-shaped white granite balustrades visible through the shrubs—surely this was like the seaside in southern France. But for some strange reason, whenever she was with her mother everything became dull.

"Let's sit here," said Rachel pointing to a white rock by the edge of the small grove.

Mosquitoes unleashed a ferocious attack. *Mustn't scratch the mosquito bites in public.* But in the end, she couldn't refrain from scratching her calf. "There are a lot of mosquitoes," she complained.

"They're not mosquitoes," Rachel corrected. "Sand flies. Tiny little sand flies."

"Their bites are terribly itchy. If I'd known, I would have worn socks." *Socks at the beach?*

Julie suppressed the urge to scratch for an eternity.

Suddenly a man surged forth out of the water. Against the backdrop of the ash-gray sea at dusk, the image was in that instant exceptionally clear: his torso rose from the water like a pure white stallion, a lock of dark hair clinging to the space between his eyebrows like a tuft of black on a white horse's mane. It was a slightly licentious image, perhaps because it triggered an association with pubic hair.

The man raised his hand high and called out a greeting. Rachel stood up, turned to Julie, and said, "Very well, then. You may go now."

Julie stood up and acquiesced to the command, but she did not want to appear to rush off in a hurry. She observed Rachel plodding unsteadily into the sea with her oversized white rubber sandals splashing the water. The person waiting for her in the sea was probably a young Englishman.

Was he the one who had driven Rachel to the school the other day?

Julie trudged back through the wooded area. *She has not yet left Hong Kong because she must want to have a bit of fun for a few days, one last fling before finding that "place" for herself. What a pity Rachel had tarried so long and now suddenly looks old.* Julie felt sorry for her. Would her suitor-in-waiting be disappointed when he finally saw her face-to-face?

When she returned that evening, Julie rang the dormitory doorbell. A searchlight on the other side of the harbor suddenly came on, illuminating the little cream-colored door canopy of the dormitory high atop the hill and two pairs of vase-shaped pillars. She felt she was standing inside the niche of a small shrine, bathed from head to toe in a blue mist. She froze, turning her startled half-smiling face to look across towards the Kowloon peninsula on the other side of the harbor.

The searchlight stayed trained on her. *What can they possibly think they have seen? Such stupidity.* She was bewildered. Finally, the beam of light moved away, like wide stripes drawn with chalk on the night sky by a lazy hand, sometimes crossing other stripes, sometimes staying parallel.

But it all happened in just a few seconds. A sister opened the door into the darkened entrance hall. It was like coming home after watching a sentimental movie, the same feeling of strangeness that she felt when returning to her childhood home: everything became smaller, shorter, and older. She experienced a sense of rapture.

On another day at Repulse Bay, Rachel again took Julie for a walk in the garden. "I want to tell you about something strange that happened," said Rachel casually, in a low voice. "Someone searched through my belongings."

"Who?" asked Julie softly, taken aback.

"The police, of course. And not just once. After they ransack my luggage they always put everything back in place. I told Nancy and the others but they don't believe me. Do you think I can't tell if someone has interfered with my belongings?"

"Do you know why?"

"Clearly it's because they see a single woman and assume suspicious behavior. They suspect I'm a spy."

Julie couldn't help but feel a flutter of pride. *Of course—they found Rachel mysterious; a black-haired Marlene Dietrich.*

"It's infuriating that these people are such cowards. The plan was that we would travel together, watch out for one another, and bring a little bit extra back with us to sell, because they are well connected and Dr. Yang is a medical doctor, after all. When you encounter this sort of thing you get to see what people are really like." She sighed as she broke into a bitter smile.

Julie was about to say that everything would be all right because she came with Ambassador Pi, but after she heard Rachel out she thought it best to keep quiet.

"You'd better not come for a few days."

That was after the incident with the eight hundred dollars. Not visiting for a few days suited Julie just fine.

On the next visit, Rachel was packing her bags. Julie passed things back and forth from the sidelines but felt she was unable to be of use so she might as well sit down and watch.

"Hey," said Rachel, suddenly grumpy, "help me press down on this." She was packing a sewing machine, tying ropes around it. Rachel wanted Julie to press down firmly on a knot, and then told her to let go. The sewing machine bucked like a steer and only with great difficulty was it subdued.

Miss Hsiang came and sat for a while. She was very quiet and spoke softly and slowly, as if she were terrified of offending Rachel.

"Miss Hsiang and her companion are not leaving Hong Kong," said Rachel after Miss Hsiang had left the room. "She has linked up with Mr. Pi. I suppose it's a good thing because she was looking for someone to marry. They plan to settle in Hong Kong."

Again, Julie did not ask Rachel where she was going. She must be traveling by sea. Rachel had only recently announced she intended to find a "place" for herself and now it appeared she was racing to put her words into action. Julie recalled hearing that Lloyd was in Singapore.

Rachel didn't mention the espionage incident again and Julie was afraid to ask, not wanting to provoke another tirade.

"In an emergency you can ask Rick for assistance. He's at your school. Do you know him?"

"Yes, I've heard of him. He teaches in the medical faculty."

"Don't bother him for no reason." She paused, then added, "Just tell him I'm your aunt."

"Yes."

Rachel clearly was not angry with Julie.

Was it because Nancy and her husband and Mr. Pi had made her feel so bitterly disappointed? Especially now that Mr. Pi had taken up with Miss Hsiang and seems to have abandoned Rachel. That didn't quite make sense. If she really was jealous of Mr. Pi and Miss Hsiang, she would never show it. And Miss Hsiang would be embarrassed to reveal that she was fearful of enraging Rachel.

So who was Rachel angry with? Could she be angry with the young man at the beach for not helping her? It was just a chance encounter with a stranger. You can't really blame him for not agreeing to vouch for her. Moreover, she didn't have to be questioned at the police station, it was just a secret investigation. And then there was Rick. It's not as if there were no Englishmen who could act as her guarantor, and Rick is a local university lecturer, though it was the summer holidays and he might be out of Hong Kong.

Julie did not attempt to find the answers.

The day of Rachel's departure Julie went to the Repulse Bay Hotel to say goodbye. It was raining heavily. The hotel bus overflowed with people. Julie didn't know if they were traveling with Rachel or just seeing her off, making up for their earlier coldness with exceptional warmth, chatting and laughing as they crowded around her.

Rachel broke away from the crowd to lean out the window and say impatiently, "Very well, then, you may go now," as if to suggest that Julie hadn't really wanted to come and see her mother off at all.

Julie stood at the bottom of the steps, smiling stiffly as she waited for the vehicle to leave. The bus pulled out and splashed water from a puddle all over her.

2

"THAT Bebe! She *still* hasn't come down," grumbled Audrey, looking at her watch.

"*Say lo, say lo,*" the two girls from Penang continued to yammer.

"*You* don't have to worry," said one of the Penang girls. "Your brother can help you study."

"Says who?" Rose shot back, smiling. "He has his own finals to worry about. No time to help me. He telephoned yesterday and asked, 'How's it going?'" Her almond-shaped eyes peered out from her fair-skinned round face.

Julie stuffed herself with milk and porridge, fried eggs, toast, and coffee, yet she still felt empty and unsettled. She had no one to lean on. She was hollowed out, like a bottomless pit.

Sister Thérèse was rushing around. "Ah Ma-lee!" she shouted as she headed for the dishwashing area in search of the girl from the orphanage. From upstairs came a cry in French, "Soeur Thérèse!" Then she responded in Cantonese, "*Lei le, lei le,* I'm coming, I'm coming," accompanied by muttered curses under her breath as she stormed up the stairs.

Several seniors, overseas Chinese from Malaya, sat at one end of a long table. All the female overseas Chinese students studied medicine. Otherwise, it would not be worth the risk to let girls travel so far on their own. It was generally accepted that only the medical faculty at Victoria University was any good.

Most medical courses ran for six years but here it extended to seven years. Moreover, students commonly needed to repeat a year. Some seniors were women in their thirties. Though they were all old hands at exams, today they remained particularly taciturn. The dinner table was usually a scene of lively talk and laughter. In-jokes and technical terms abounded, as did white lab coats. Julie couldn't understand the jokes of the Malaya students except for one story of a wicked classmate who removed a penis from a formaldehyde jar and tossed it on the road in front of the gate to the anatomy building. The seniors almost died from laughter.

"Rick is the worst." Julie caught this snippet of conversation one day, though she couldn't discern what made Rick so terrible. Their thick Malay accents were difficult to understand, and they dropped the word "man!" in every sentence, just like the original inhabitants of the West Indies, when they meant to call their interlocutors "brother." English-language shibboleths in British possessions spanned both the Atlantic and Pacific oceans, perhaps first propagated by sailors, then from the West Indies on to the American jazz milieu.

All the students ever talked about, apart from their classes and accidents during their internships, was rating their professors. The majority were rated "terrible." British professors have a tradition of humorous sarcasm that extended to making fun of students. The medical faculty was reputed to be the cruelest.

Bebe also said Rick was terrible, but when asked about it she pulled a long face, turned her head, and responded in English, "Awful." Rick taught pathology. Julie imagined his caustic tongue embarrassing the girls as they dissected cadavers. Especially such a feminine specimen as Bebe. Julie told Bebe that her mother knew Rick but did not mention she was instructed to go to him if she needed help.

One day, with no need to attend her first two classes, Julie strolled down the hill on a small path instead of taking the bus. After many days of spring showers the entire hillside was festooned with two different reds—the crab red and lilac pink of azalea petals on the ground, the trees still flushed with their bright blossoms. The sky was clear and the blue sea surrounded the hill, making the horizon seem to float in midair. The small houses of the neighborhood consisted of professorial residences.

As she passed a small bungalow, Julie saw a man sitting on a balcony railing, his back resting against a wooden pillar. He was small and handsome, with a pale face, and appeared to be in his twenties or thirties. Two callous, light-colored eyes, appearing almost transparent in the sunlight, cast an unseeing gaze in Julie's direction. She was startled for a moment. It was Rick; she had seen him before on campus, the back of his collar always wrinkled.

He had a bottle in one hand. *Drinking alone at ten o'clock in the morning?* Of course, all of the teachers drank. Julie had heard that the head of the English Department and his wife were both alcoholics. Sometimes, during the four-student tutorials held in their home, his wife, like a mother hen, could be seen in a faded floral dress beaming radiantly as she sailed by without looking at anyone.

Somerset Maugham's stories spoke of loneliness in the Orient and depression from life in a small town. In Julie's eyes, Hong Kong was a magnificent city, so there was no need for such nonsense, and she suspected it was all an act. Otherwise, how could this life of comfort amount to the "white man's burden"? Julie had not the slightest inkling of just how stifling life in that tiny social circle could be.

Mr. Andrews was also a drinker. His brick-red face betrayed his tipsiness, making him unpredictable. Everyone feared him. He had begun to put on weight. His low hairline ended in a widow's peak, under which perched thick, black eyebrows. Once, during a discussion in class about the coats of arms and markings of medieval knights, he asked Yen Ming-sheng, "If you could choose a coat of arms, what would it be?" Yen Ming-sheng was an extremely studious but rather short overseas Chinese student. Fidgeting with his wire-framed spectacles, he answered, "A lion."

In the midst of uproarious laughter, Mr. Andrews asked with a straight face, "And what sort of lion? A sleeping lion or a ferocious lion?"

China had once been likened to a sleeping lion. Yen Ming-sheng paused, then answered, "A ferocious lion."

The raucous laughter resumed, and even Mr. Andrews grinned a little. Julie, bent over her desk, laughed herself to tears.

During a tutorial in Mr. Andrews's office, Julie noticed a bookcase full of bound volumes of *The New Yorker*. "So many *New Yorker*s!" She giggled. She was surprised an Englishman would read an American magazine.

Mr. Andrews casually picked one out and passed it to her. "Would you like to borrow it? You may come any time to take some, even if I'm not in."

Julie was careful to return the magazines *only* when Mr. Andrews was out, and managed to read the entire collection in no time at all. Julie was a master of the surreptitious picking out of books. Her father bought slightly racy books, and although he didn't say so, he did not really want her to read them. While her father dozed on the opium bed, Julie would sneak over to the desk where his books were haphazardly piled. She would furtively choose one, read it, return it to the pile, and purloin another without ever being noticed.

Julie felt a letter of thanks for Mr. Andrews's scholarship would be sufficient, especially as he lived so far away, but Rachel insisted that she thank him in person. Julie had to arrange for her classmate Sally to accompany her, and they set out on two rickshaws. The journey consumed most of the day. Julie was very tense in front of Mr. Andrews and he quickly became impatient. He chatted a little with Sally before the two girls took their leave.

Sally often praised Mr. Andrews and expressed her outrage about the injustices done to him. "Actually," she fumed, "he should have been appointed chair of the department, but he can't even make it to professor and is still just a lecturer!"

Mr. Andrews was a graduate of Cambridge, which was apparently well-stocked with homosexuals and left-wingers. Julie sometimes wondered whether something like that had caused his colleagues to shun him. He was not married and did not live on campus in the housing allocated to professors, preferring instead to cycle the long distance to and from work. But then again, perhaps he found the atmosphere in the staff residential quarters stifling. He obviously liked Sally and often joked with her during class. England was full of aloof old bachelors who weren't necessarily homosexuals.

Mr. Andrews often wore a red tie. It was the red of old bricks, not a bright red. If he were a communist, one couldn't tell from his lectures, though he loved to ask questions about 1848, the year many small revolutions broke out in Europe.

Rumor had it that Mike, the Dean of the Arts Faculty, was a real operator. Julie took his class and concluded that this round-faced, silver-haired old man did not really like to read books and simply wasn't close to being an educated gentleman. He promised to be an impassable hindrance.

"*Say lo! Say lo!*" After finishing her breakfast Sally moved to Julie's side of the table. "Daphne, how are you doing? You don't look nervous at all."

The less Julie wanted to see of her, the closer Sally sat. She turned to Julie and pleaded, "Quick, Julie! Tell me something! Anything!"

"This time I really don't know anything, either." Julie groaned, putting on a forced smile.

Sally tossed her head around to face Julie. "Even *you* are saying that!" she blurted out. "You don't need to worry about—" Sally halted in mid-sentence, paused, then turned to Daphne. "*Say lo! Say lo!* I really am done for today!" she whined, rocking on her chair.

Sally certainly was no fool. But who else didn't know that Julie really had nothing to worry about?

One day Mr. Andrews asked questions no one could answer. He was about to give up when he impatiently called out, "Miss Sheng!" but Julie also grinned and shook her head. He paused, a little startled for a moment, then called on someone else, but a hint of annoyance could clearly be discerned in his voice. The class became silent for a moment. Students were very sensitive to this sort of thing.

The prediction Mr. Andrews made in his letter was correct: she did win a full scholarship. *But what if I do not do well in the second half of the year? How will Mr. Andrews feel if I don't live up to his expectations? That would be embarrassing.*

Julie wasn't able to concentrate on her modern history studies in the new semester because the closer to the present day history progressed, the more it resembled the daily newspaper reports.

Events in newspapers seemed perennially gloomy and dull. Besides,

Julie never believed what appeared in the papers because she was convinced there must always be an inside story.

Bebe also said that what happens in one's own life is much more important than big events on the world stage, the same way closer things appear bigger in drawings. The flowers in a vase on the windowsill in front of our eyes are much more substantial than the crowded scenes outside the window.

Finally, Bebe arrived at the refectory. She didn't have time to sit down, and stood as she hurriedly made a fried-egg sandwich to eat on the bus.

The gurney wheels rolled smoothly toward the operating theater. It was time for the scalpel to make the first incision.

The refectory table faced the blue-gray vista of sea and sky. Silhouetted humps of outlying islands floated in the mist like a family of large and small turtles. Several planes flew low, big and black. The duck-eggshell sky seems unable to support them. Suddenly: *Boom, boom*. Two thunderous explosions.

"Another drill," said a senior-year overseas Chinese student.

Julie saw a speeding car explode on the horizon. She couldn't tell if the water tower had been hit or the oil storage tanks had exploded, destroying the car on the road. In an instant, the car was gone. She felt overwhelmed with guilt. Mr. Andrews also had an old car, which he never used. He always rode his bicycle and waved with a smile whenever he saw Julie.

Then, *boom, boom, boom*—several dull thuds gently drifted across the sea.

While everyone gazed out, Sister Henri appeared from behind, her head lowered, hands hidden in her sleeves. Her big black eyes stared through her thick eyelashes at the students. Her large face was framed by a white collar that pushed up against a double chin.

"University Hall telephoned," she said calmly without raising her voice, "to say that the Japanese are attacking Hong Kong."

Commotion immediately broke out.

"Those were real bombs!"

"I was wondering why I hadn't heard about any drills today."

"Sister, sister, did they say where the bombing's happening?"

"Why wasn't there an air-raid warning?"

"Oh, no!" cried Sally. "My family holidayed on Tsing Yi Island over the weekend. I don't know if they returned yet. I'd better telephone them."

"You won't reach them," said Sister Henri. "Everybody is trying to telephone now. Sister Luke tried to call the convent but couldn't get through either."

"Sister, sister! Did the attack come from Kowloon?"

"Sister, sister! What else did they say?"

In the midst of the cacophony, only Julie was silent. She sat motionless and cold like a rock. Surging waves of ecstasy rose higher and higher as they lapped against the rock. She dared not move in case her happiness showed.

"The snake who slithered out of its hole knew all along," snorted Jenny accusingly. "As soon as the sister came in to tell us, someone already knew and left immediately."

The room suddenly fell silent. The girls looked around. Ruby was indeed gone.

The local girls all went upstairs to telephone their families. The rest wandered outside to watch. There were no more planes. The gardener was standing on a steep slope outside the railings, holding his hand to his forehead, a visor against the glare, as he looked out to sea. Flowers and shrubs had been planted on the grass slope. Lettuce growing in a plot of freshly plowed red soil looked like giant green rosebuds.

As she leaned on the iron railing, Bebe threw her head back to catch the fried egg that was slipping out of her sandwich.

"We'd better take all that white cloth inside," said Audrey pointing at the sisters' white headwear drying on a low wall. "They'll be visible from the air." Each piece of fabric stretched several square feet, starched stiff as a board and pasted onto thin panels edged with aluminum.

"Go back inside!" shouted Sister Henri, as she rushed out. "It's dangerous!" No one paid any attention. She then bawled at two Penang girls. Having graduated from a convent girls' school in their hometown and accustomed to obeying orders, the two girls leisurely wandered back inside, giggling.

"Gardener! Put the door panels back in place!" Sister Henri commanded. "You'll all be safest here on the ground floor." She then rushed upstairs to seek out the latest news.

As the gardener replaced the door panels most of the students had already returned inside. Sally sat by herself, sobbing. She had tried to telephone her family but could not get through. A senior implored her not to worry. The local girls were all packing upstairs, as their families had sent cars to pick them up. Ruby had been the first to call home and was the first collected.

Bebe entered from the back door to eat the oatmeal she had missed out on earlier in the morning. Julie sat down next to her. Sally went upstairs again to make a telephone call.

Several seniors bombastically expounded that it was just fine for the Japanese to attack now because Hong Kong was well prepared and Singapore was even more of a fortress. Reinforcements would arrive at any time.

"The King of Flowers says a bomb hit Deep Water Bay," said Sister Thérèse, rushing in to report the latest news. She held the slightly built old gardener in high esteem. He lived with his wife and child in a small hut with a cement floor at the back gate.

"Sister! There's no more butter!" whined Bebe in a plaintive voice. "Sister, come and see for yourself, the coffee is ice cold. Please bring another pot."

Sister Thérèse did not say anything as she stormed away bearing the coffeepot and the butter dish.

A downcast Jenny leaned forward. Her yellow oval face turned as dark as a clay statuette; her eyes, far apart on her face, stared down at the table in front of her.

The only light in the refectory shone through the panes of glass at the top of the door panels. The scene resembled a somber Dutch religious painting: huge, cream-colored square columns the girth of two people linking hands; students crowded around a long monastery table set on the bright red floor tiles, eating their last supper.

"Jenny has seen the most of . . . of war," said Audrey giggling nervously. Then turning to Julie, "There wasn't much to see in the foreign concessions in Shanghai, right?"

"Right."

Julie had lived through the two battles for Shanghai. She thought all she needed to do to survive was follow her father's instructions: Stock up on rice and coal, don't be too fussy about food, and don't go outside.

A senior suddenly asked Jenny, "So . . . what's war like?" She seemed a little anxious, perhaps worried she'd relate too much as she clearly knew the answer.

Jenny was quiet for a while, then replied softly, "It's all about fleeing, suffering, and starving."

A fresh pot of coffee arrived. After a momentary pause, the lively discussion around the table resumed. Bebe appeared glum and resentful as she continued to wrestle with her breakfast. When she finished, she said to Julie, "I'm going back upstairs to take a nap. Are you coming?"

As they walked up the stairs, Julie said, "I'm thrilled."

"That's terrible!" exclaimed Bebe.

"I know."

"I know you think it's not really terrible if you know it's terrible."

Bebe believed that it was better to be a hypocrite—at least a willingness to pretend to be virtuous was a kind of virtue. She loved to debate, but Julie could never be bothered to rebut her.

They headed toward the two small rooms with doors opposite each other at the end of a corridor paved with bright red tiles. Julie went into Bebe's room with her.

"I'm exhausted," declared Bebe as she collapsed on her bed and proceeded to pummel herself on her waist. Her spine curved too far upward when she lay supine, causing her lower back to hurt. "Call me when it's time for lunch."

Julie sat down on the chair. With tall windows on both sides, the tiny room felt like a glass bauble dangling high above the sea. Of course, the ground floor would be safest, but the atmosphere in the refectory was suffocating.

The glass bauble suspended over the sea awaited bombs from the planes to blow it to pieces.

Julie didn't like modern history, but now modern history was pounding on the door.

Bebe struggled with the sleeping bag beneath her. The brushed-cotton lining exuded the distinctive smell of India. "What are you reading?" asked Bebe.

"My history notes."

Bebe laughed mockingly at Julie for trying to repair the pen after the sheep are out.

Julie thought her good luck was too good to be true—it couldn't last. If classes soon resumed, then the final exams would proceed.

Suddenly at noon, a klaxon emitted a long, screeching blast, belatedly rescinding the air-raid warning.

Bebe received a telephone call after lunch. "A boy wants to take me to the movies," she furtively reported upon returning upstairs. "The cinemas are open for business as usual."

"Which film?"

"Don't know. But whatever it is, it will be worth the trek."

"Yes, to see what's going on in town."

"Would you like to come?" asked Bebe, as if suddenly struck by a pang of guilt.

"No, no," answered Julie quickly with a smile. "I don't want to go."

Bebe never disclosed the names of her suitors. It was always simply "a boy."

"Some boys visit brothels after they go out with their girlfriends," Bebe once told Julie with annoyed amusement. "Have you ever heard anything like that before?"

Julie never ever allowed herself to appear surprised. "It's entirely possible," she chuckled.

"Malayan boys are the worst," said Bebe on another occasion. "They all go out whoring."

"Indian boys are the worst. No matter how close they are to their girlfriends, they always go back to India to get married."

One day Bebe stormed in furiously. "Audrey says there's no such thing as love. Marriage is just about becoming accustomed to a man."

From the sound of it, Audrey did not love her Mr. Lee.

"What do you say?" asked Bebe. "Does love exist?"

"Yes, it does." Julie giggled.

"I just don't know," said Bebe loudly, as if to wash her hands of the matter. She turned around and sullenly tidied her desk.

On summer nights, groups of boys strolled up the mountain, stopping near the women's dormitory to parade around arm in arm, singing popular songs in unison. Occasionally they shouted the name of a girl in the dormitory, followed by a torrent of laughter. They mostly called out the names of the few local girls who had studied in English colleges, and Sally was the most frequent target, though sometimes they called out Bebe. Perhaps they emulated the Malayan boys' penchant for wooing with songs, but as a group activity it took on a jocular flavor, since they would be too embarrassed to undertake it alone.

"Those boys are singing again," smirked a girl in her room upstairs.

There was no musical accompaniment or vocal harmonies, but the singing in the distance at night sounded quite pleasant. Whenever Julie heard it, she felt sad.

Bebe went off to the movies the day war was declared. When she returned that night, the citywide blackout had been ordered and only a solitary white candle glowed in the refectory. But the nuns were particularly animated that day. They prepared deep-fried calf brains with deep-fried mashed-potato balls, and that afternoon two nuns took the bus down to the city to buy fresh baguettes. On their outings, the nuns traveled in pairs to protect and watch over each other, like police officers walking the beat.

"Who did you go to the movies with?" asked Audrey. "Was it Chan? It was, wasn't it? Ha! Groping his way to take you back up the mountain in the dark." She cackled, clapped her hands, and repeated herself in Mandarin, emphasizing *groping* to insinuate that something else took place in the dark.

Few people in the room understood Mandarin, and although Bebe maybe understood a little, she was more interested in gobbling down the food that Sister Thérèse had saved for her.

"You know, it was eerie with the blue lantern at the box office lighting up the dreadful darkness," said Bebe in a low voice to Julie. "And halfway through the movie, the air-raid siren went off but the show continued regardless. It was like something extra added to spice up the movie."

After supper both Audrey's Mr. Lee and Jenny's Mr. Wei turned up. To avoid suspicion, Jenny and Mr. Wei stood by a cluster of evergreens outside the back door, whispering to each other in the dim light emanating from the refectory.

Audrey and Mr. Lee stood silently next to each other in a corridor outside the refectory, leaning against a cement wall, arms crossed. Mr. Lee was a Malayan Chinese student. Fair-skinned with small eyes pointing up at the corners, he seemed underage, like a child actor in a Chinese opera. Mr. Lee's family was rich; they owned a rubber plantation.

People came and went, but Audrey just greeted them with a sad smile.

"Why don't you come sit in the lounge?" hollered Sister Mark, the elderly acting dormitory proctor. "Come on up, come on up!" she commanded, bending over the balustrade to peer down, and then ask, "And where is Jenny?"

Audrey just smiled, cheekbones protruding from her small pointy face. Her cheeks were flushed.

Bebe softly sang a tune from an Arthur Sullivan opera:

> A witch, a witch! Beware, beware!
> Or on a broomstick she may fly
> Up and up through the air!

That night, Julie learned from Bebe that the boys were clamoring to join the armed forces. Mr. Lee also wanted to sign up, but Audrey wouldn't let him go. The two of them quarreled.

All the medical students were to be dispatched to an emergency first-aid station outside the city, each group consisting of two male students and one female. The two Penang girls teased each other about which males they would like to be allocated, as if they were choosing who they'd want to be alone with on a desert island after a shipwreck.

It's like tying a lamb to a tree as bait for a tiger. And that thought must have occurred to Bebe, too. But they had to go or risk expulsion from the university.

Bebe had been a prefect at the English girls' school in Shanghai, making her an ideal choice for wartime volunteer work. At any time, she could be called upon to pack her things into a small bundle and head off, just like that. However, her thin little voice grew fearful, as timid as the morning she had prepared for final exams.

Only two liberal-arts students—Julie and Jenny—stayed behind. Julie didn't expect the dormitory to stay open just for them. She had heard that many students were going to Happy Valley that afternoon to report for duty as air-raid protection volunteers, for which they would be issued rations. "Are you going?" she asked Jenny. "Let's go together."

Jenny paused, then raised her eyebrows and broke into a smile. "All right, let's go together."

After lunch, Julie went to call Jenny but no one was there. She must have left first. Julie had never imagined Jenny disliked her so much.

Several hundred students marched off to report for duty, but Julie did not recognize a single one and did not bother to look for Jenny in the crowd. The procession was attacked from the air just as they were passing the Catholic cemetery at Happy Valley.

The cemetery lawn was as green as ever this winter. It sloped up to a lush hill speckled with ivory-colored tombstones rolling out to the horizon. Two yellow boards hung on either side of the simple cemetery gate and on each of them a line from a couplet was inscribed in green. The couplet read:

THIS DAY MY MORTAL REMAINS TO NATIVE SOIL RETURN
JUST AS ONE DAY YOU TOO WILL FOLLOW IN AN URN

That tone evoked the style of an overseas Chinese, with a hint of eerie humor in the face of death.

On the return journey, one of the boys lugged a burlap sack full of black bread issued by the Air Raid Defense Headquarters, one slice per person. Julie had never before tasted such delicious bread.

"I almost died in an air raid. A bomb landed across the street from us," Julie could hear an imaginary conversation of herself telling someone. But who was there to tell? Auntie Han? Judy was always indifferent and would not think much of it. Rachel didn't even come to mind. Bebe was always happy, and Julie's death would make no difference to her.

Almost blown up and there was no one she could tell. Julie felt a sense of desolation.

It was dark by the time Julie had made her way back to the dormitory. Sister Henri surreptitiously signaled to Julie, as though she had a lollipop just for her. "Mr. Wei came to pick up Jenny," she said to Julie as she neared. "We have to return to the convent because this dormitory is closing down. You may go to the American Methodist Episcopal Mission; they will take you in. It's very close to University Hall. Ask for Miss Donaldson."

The Episcopal Mission had a women's dormitory for female employees. Julie felt that it was unconscionable for the convent to shunt her off to a strange place just like that, though she was fully aware that the convent was bursting at the seams with very important refugees, who were, after all, co-religionists. Besides, she still felt pangs of guilt for boarding in the convent for free the previous summer, while her mother stayed at the Repulse Bay Hotel. That evening Julie went to see Miss Donaldson, the English spinster, who agreed to take Julie in, though meals would not be provided.

The building was an old run-down bungalow but there were plenty of vacant rooms. No doubt those who could find shelter with relatives had already left. Julie had a room of her own. It was very dark.

To her surprise, Julie encountered the Belle of Penang—Rose arrived at Julie's door to say hello. Her demeanor was a little awkward, perhaps worried that Julie would ask why she hadn't reported to the first-aid station. No doubt Rose's brother wouldn't allow it. He must have sent her here and arranged for Miss Chang, who was from the same town, to keep an eye on her. Miss Chang was forty or fifty years old and extremely cold toward Julie. At first Julie didn't know why but after a few days she discovered that everyone living there behaved secretively. Unless they met at the common bathroom, Julie rarely saw anyone. And when she did encounter people, they rushed past, heads lowered, and disappeared in an instant. In the gloomy light, they all appeared to be withered Cantonese women.

Some female missionaries were also staying with Miss Donaldson. They had hired a maid but the downstairs kitchen was always deserted and never appeared to be used. The thermos flask on the chest of drawers in the hallway, however, was always full.

A steady stream of high-sounding verbiage emanated from the Air Raid Defense Headquarters but no rations were ever issued. After Julie finished the few tinned biscuits she had brought with her, she turned to the boiled water. She had to be careful not to drink it all because she was afraid her host would be annoyed and cut off the supply if she used it up.

It soon became clear why everyone was being so secretive. They didn't know one another well and feared the awkwardness of refusing to assist when others ran out of food. Especially in a Christian mission it would not be right to turn people down.

Miss Chang must have warned Rose, which was why she had been avoiding Julie.

One evening after Julie had returned from her duties at the Air Raid Defense station and was busy fetching water to wash her clothes (at the time, strict water rationing was being enforced), a huge explosion went off, followed by a cacophony of voices. The seemingly empty building suddenly filled with people who gathered at the bottom of the staircase by the entrance to the hallway. Julie also went down to see what was going on.

"Shrapnel destroyed a corner of the roof," explained Rose with a startled smile. "They say it's dangerous upstairs."

Julie sat with the other people on the stairs, which were covered with a floral-patterned canvas.

"Rose, your elder brother is here," a voice called out. "Dr. Lin is here." The graduating class of medical students were addressed as "doctor" before actually qualifying to use the title.

"Goodness, brother, how did you manage to get here? We were just hit by shrapnel."

"It's dangerous here. I came to pick you up. Come, quick." Seeing Julie, a classmate who used to live in the same dormitory with Rose, he added, "Does your friend want to come with us?"

Julie immediately acquiesced. As she stood up, Julie saw Rose was about to speak but then hesitated—she couldn't really tell her brother that she had been trying to avoid Julie.

The three of them departed together. "Bonner Hall is safer," said Dr. Lin. That was the male dormitory.

They walked along a cross street to the main road that circled the mountain. Flaming-red poinsettia bracts blossomed on the large trees in the dusk. Suddenly, they heard the shrill screeching of flying shrapnel.

"Quick!" yelled Dr. Lin. "Run!"

The three of them held hands and bolted.

Eee-eee-o eee-aaa eee-aaa... The ear-piercing noise seemed to go on for a very long time. Julie felt terribly exposed, as if she were a net of flesh sailing in the sky to catch every single shard of shrapnel.

Dr. Lin, running between the two girls, dragged them along for all he was worth. Julie ran as fast as she could to keep up. *I mustn't endanger them.*

Eee-eee-o eee-aaa eee-aaa!

The shrieking sounds seemed to intensify.

They ran uphill. The road wasn't steep but it was a long stretch and Julie couldn't catch her breath. She felt as if a metal plate were pressing down on her chest.

Once they turned onto a small path on a grass slope, they were out of danger. After arriving at the men's dormitory, they sat down in the refectory and heard the sound of explosions far off in the distance. The dull thuds actually made Julie feel safe. Dr. Lin gave the girls a few copies of *Life* magazine to read. Later in the evening, after the bombardment ended, he accompanied them back to the mission.

The Air Raid Defense station was located in a library. The person in charge, a lecturer from the Engineering Department, was a skinny Cantonese man who had studied in England. He knew Julie's mother and third aunt, who had asked him to take care of Julie, so he requested that Julie be his secretary, a desirable indoor job.

"Can you type?" he asked, as he sat in front of a typewriter.

"No."

He frowned and continued to type a report with one hand.

He gave Julie an exercise book and an alarm clock, and instructed her to record the time of each air raid.

Julie didn't understand why that was necessary. *Surely the Japanese aren't so stupid as to make their next attack at the same time, as if reporting for duty.*

"Did you record the time?" he constantly asked her.

"Oh, no!" she replied, smiling sheepishly. "I forgot." She then glanced at her watch and estimated that five or ten minutes had passed.

Julie hid the novels from the library she was reading underneath the exercise book.

Eventually, Julie's negligence in recording the times of the air raids roused him to ask sternly, "Would you prefer to work outdoors?" His eyes betrayed a hint of teasing.

Julie knew that anti-air-raid personnel were also responsible for putting out fires. Poking around in bombed-out buildings where there might be unexploded ordnance carried the risk of having a limb blown off. "Yes," she replied, smiling ruefully.

Knowing, however, that Julie neither knew her way around Hong Kong nor spoke Cantonese, he didn't pursue the idea.

Feeeeeewwwwww! Another bombing raid. This time the explosion was rather distant. It sounded like the resonant, raspy thump of a small, open-ended iron barrel.

Feeeeeewwwwww! That was closer.

One day you escape alive from a firefight and the next day you get blown up, just like that.

Feeeeeewwwwww! As if all around the city large metal barrels were being knocked over and half buried under rubble.

FEEEEEEWWWWWW!

That one was very close. The floorboards shuddered and she heard the sound of glass shattering onto the ground.

"Machine guns will work, they can shoot 'em down!" Julie over-heard two boys talking about the two machine guns on the roof terrace above the library. She then realized it was the machine guns that attracted the planes circling overhead like flies to honey.

"You may go downstairs," said the anti-air-raid station chief. "I can man the telephone."

Julie smiled but shook her head to indicate she would not leave, even though she was only there reading novels. Now the station chief himself had to record the air-raid times.

Julie hoped the battle would end soon. If it continued, the library would be bombed sooner or later, or else she would be hit by shrapnel on her way to or from work. As the saying goes, the water jug next to the well will be broken one day.

Did she hope for a surrender or for the Japanese troops to fight their way in?

It's not our war. Is it worth sacrificing one's life for the colony of the British Crown?

Of course, that's just an excuse. It's our war if they're fighting the Japanese.

Nationalism is a common twentieth-century religion. Julie was not a believer.

Nationalism is just a process. We went through it in the Han and T'ang dynasties centuries ago.

That sounds like a cover for weakness. In international relations, talking about three or five thousand years of civilization means nothing—only power and a willingness to fight can win respect.

But what's there to say if you're dead? You have to be alive to achieve anything.

Julie couldn't come to any conclusions, but fortunately her greatest skill was the ability to leave such things unresolved. Perhaps she would have an epiphany in old age. She believed *that* was the only reliable theory, based on her own experience, not parroting what others say.

Just put it to one side. If chaos results, so be it. A theory based on reason may not always be reliable.

That night as she sat in her room in darkness, she suddenly heard Bebe call out to her from the stairs, then emerge with a candle in her hand. Bebe was wearing a gray makeshift nurse uniform. Her hair was casually tucked behind her ears.

"See how nice I am to you! I walked such a long way to see you."

Bebe had been assigned to Wan Chai. *It might be better there. Although it is an impoverished district, at least it's a bustling area with people. It must be safer than holing up in a desolate place outside the city. But would that be where the Japanese army lands?*

"What's it like where you are?"

"Horrible," mumbled Bebe casually.

"How so?"

"Things like wounded people with bones sticking out of their arms."

"Rose is also here."

"Yes, I saw her," said Bebe.

When Bebe asked, "Have you received any rations?" Julie replied with resignation, "Not yet. I haven't eaten anything for two days."

"If I had known earlier I could have brought you something. Food isn't a problem for us. I could bring you dinner."

"No need. I still have three dollars. I can buy some peanuts and biscuits at the store."

"No, don't do that," said Bebe, shaking her head. "It's expensive and they won't be any good. You don't speak Cantonese so the price will be even higher. It's not worth it. If you can really hold out for two more days—I know for sure that they will issue you rations. My source is absolutely reliable."

Bebe was shrewd as always: starving to death mattered little, but being taken advantage of, that was a catastrophe. Actually, Julie didn't really want to go out to buy anything. There were only two general stores nearby on Caine Road. They were carved out of the rock face abutting the road, backing onto the mountain and facing the sea. The dingy run-down general stores resembled nothing more than shady rural trading posts. Just from a glance while sitting on a passing bus, Julie sensed the unwelcoming atmosphere and the likelihood they would cheat strangers.

"What time is it? Do you still want to go back?"

"I'll stay here tonight, then. Do you have a blanket?"

"No, I don't. I'll get some old magazines to cover you with." *Life* magazine was large enough but, being glossy, all too easily slipped off and onto the ground.

Bebe went upstairs to another room from which Julie then heard the sound of laughter and chatting. Soon Bebe returned carrying two military-issue blankets.

Julie didn't ask who provided the blankets to Bebe, and never did learn in which room Rose was staying.

Having no sheets they had to sleep on the bare mattress. After blowing out the candle, they disrobed and got into bed. In the dark, under the coarse blankets, Julie's leg grazed Bebe's thigh. It was cool and firm. Julie was used to her own long legs and was slightly repulsed by Bebe's legs, which reminded Julie, perhaps because she was so hungry, of the stewed frog legs she ate as a child in northern China. She finally felt relieved because ever since Rachel cautioned Julie against a lesbian romance with Bebe, Julie had been harboring a shadow of suspicion, as she indeed was very fond of Bebe's olive-toned round face and those Indian eyes that looked like black suns. "Let me press your nose," Julie would occasionally say to Bebe.

"Why?" Bebe would respond, but move in closer nonetheless.

Julie would press down lightly on Bebe's nose and giggled when she felt an electric current shoot through her arm.

Bebe would often poke down on Julie's calf with a finger and exclaim in Mandarin, "That's the flesh of a corpse," referring to Julie's bloodless, pale skin. Perhaps she, too, possessed something that repulsed Bebe.

Bebe left early the next morning and Julie went to work. At lunchtime, the station chief's wife brought him a meal consisting of several delicacies and a bowl of ham-and-egg fried rice. Julie felt waves of dizziness as she stood beside his feast. The boys on the roof manning the two machine guns took turns coming down, incessantly inquiring about news of the rations. The station chief said he had made numerous telephone calls to pursue the matter and would, of course, inform them as soon as he heard any news.

Right up until the end of the shift there was still no news.

The bathroom in the mission dormitory had just one shallow, gray cement tub. With water restrictions in full force during the siege, it took Julie a long time to fill a jug from the driblets trickling out of the faucet over the tub. She washed one sock at a time. Darkness was falling and soon she would not be able to see.

"Julie!" cried Rose, standing in the bathroom doorway. "Mr. Andrews is dead! He was killed."

Julie's initial response was a sudden paroxysm of possessiveness. *Rose has been here less than six months and is studying medicine. What does she know about Mr. Andrews?* Of course, Julie was startled by the news. She could only faintly utter, "How?"

All the British teachers at the university were reserve soldiers, but Julie had not expected that they had already left for the front lines. She didn't ask Rose the source of her information, assuming it was Rose's brother.

Rose quietly walked off.

Julie continued to wash her socks. All of sudden she began to sob, but like the faucet over the tub, it took an age of shuddering and heaving to produce a paltry flow of pained tears. Now she understood how death ends everything. Julie had hoped to explain to Mr. Andrews one day what had happened to the money. But what was there to say? Now she sensed the chill of a cold draft escaping from behind a slowly closing stone door.

Julie had never ever believed in God, but after days of continuous bombing, she understood why, as they say, "There are no atheists in foxholes." She suddenly raised her head and said silently to the ceiling, "You've really been very kind to me. Halting the final exam was good enough; there was no need to kill the teacher."

Early the next morning, a maid conveyed an invitation from Miss Donaldson. Julie went downstairs and saw all the boarders gathered in the dining room saying "Merry Christmas" to each other. Christmas Day, and she had completely forgotten about it.

Near the ceiling was a small window fitted with an iron grille. Sunlight streamed through the interstices onto the dark green tablecloth. Miss Donaldson was treating the boarders to a breakfast of black tea with condensed milk, along with an assortment of biscuits and sweets. Julie kept a few biscuits in her hand to take with her to work. On the way, she bumped into a classmate who told her that Hong Kong had surrendered. Julie couldn't believe it and went to the Air Raid Defense station anyway. It was completely deserted.

An overseas Chinese doctor who taught in the medical school stepped forward to take charge. Students from other cities who had nowhere to go were moved into a male dormitory where they were fed communally. The day Julie moved in, Bebe had not yet returned from Wan Chai, but now she heard that someone else was looking for her.

Julie went downstairs. The chairs in the large refectory were all stacked to one side. She had not thought it would be her classmate Yen Ming-sheng, who approached her with a smile. He was decked out in a natty Western suit and looked like a junior clerk during peacetime. Yen had once been in competition with Julie, but now that the university had closed, everyone went their own way. *Is he here to say farewell to show he bears no grudges?* She didn't want people to see them together and think he was her boyfriend. Bebe had once been infuriated to hear people say something or other that put her in the same category as Yen Ming-sheng. Like universities in the United States and England, there was a practice of awarding the passing grade of a gentleman's C to a poorly performing student with wealthy parents. Students did not aspire to overachievement.

After some small talk, Julie asked, smiling, "Are you planning to leave?" Julie had her heart set on returning to Shanghai and assumed that others would also want to return to their homes. Yen Ming-sheng's expression was rather ambiguous and Julie didn't know why. At the time, she was unaware that within a day or two of the surrender, Sally had trekked over the hills with a large contingent heading toward the wartime capital of Chungking.

Bebe had also been invited to join a group who said they were willing to take Julie as well. Julie felt a bit insulted when Bebe told her that. Obviously, they thought of her as nothing more than the string tied around a juicy leg of ham.

"The bombing in Chungking is relentless," Julie said to Bebe. "Don't you want to go back with me to Shanghai? Your home is there. It's always better to be at home."

Shanghailanders believed Shanghai, even under occupation, was the best place to be no matter what.

Bebe was indifferent. Chan, the boy who often invited her out, had not left. He had given her a stick of butter he had come across. Bebe gave some to Julie to eat with rice, which was apparently a Persian custom. He also passed her a bottle of chicken-stock soy sauce. Like Bebe, Chan had a baby face but his skin was pale, and he was quite tall and thin. Julie once asked Bebe about Chan. Bebe said he was childish. "He thought he liked me," Bebe concluded.

Bebe probably preferred another overseas Chinese surnamed Kwong, who liked music. Kwong also occasionally asked Bebe out. He took lengthy walks by himself, sometimes all night long, when he was in a bad mood. He had already left with Sally's group so Kwong was probably the one who had invited Bebe to travel together. Later he married Sally on the mainland.

Julie did not look for a spot to sit down with Yen Ming-sheng and stood while continuing to chat. He didn't mention Mr. Andrews dying in battle or anything at all about the war. Julie had not seen any of her classmates when she reported in at Happy Valley. The overseas Chinese students who came from afar to study humanities knew full well that Victoria University was weak in that area, but they had only come to muddle through a degree. Better versed in worldly ways, they would never risk the danger of volunteering at an Air Raid Defense station.

"There's a bonfire outside the registrar's office," said Yen Ming-sheng out of the blue. "They're burning documents."

"Why?"

"They're destroying documents," he muttered, "before the Japanese troops arrive."

"Oh, I see." Somewhat at a loss, Julie stood beside the glass door, her arms wrapped around her, gazing out as though she could see the flames in the distance.

"Do you want to go for a look?" Ming-sheng chuckled. "It's a huge fire. Lots of people are there."

Julie smiled and replied in the negative.

"The fire's enormous," he said. "Don't you want to take a peek? I'll go with you."

"You go, I won't."

"All the documents are being burned, even student records, exam results, everything," he said, then grinned like a cat.

Now Julie finally saw through the purpose of Yen's visit. The university did not issue examination results to students—results were only posted on notice boards behind glass that everyone crowded around to read. Julie had always felt embarrassed to linger in the throng. She usually squeezed her way out after a quick glance, which was enough to make an indelible impression. Now the exam records were being incinerated; it was as if her lifetime of achievements were cast into the wind, irrevocably lost.

Ming-sheng again offered to accompany her to look at the fire. Only with difficulty was she able to send him on his way. She retreated upstairs. Suddenly she recalled a chilling moment in her childhood. Her heartbeat quickened when she realized that the person who had made heavily penciled lines through one of her watercolors was in fact her younger brother.

After Bebe returned, news from the various first-aid stations continued to trickle in. Julie only heard of one incident of harassment that involved a fair-skinned, round-faced female overseas Chinese student. She was short and once had a bob haircut, like a young Japanese student, but now disguised herself as a boy, wearing a boy's shirt and trousers, and a boy's haircut. One day, a Japanese soldier approached her as she was sweeping the courtyard. She escaped indoors, ran upstairs, and stood by a window, indicating she would jump. The soldier didn't pursue her. That could have been a scene straight out of *Ivanhoe*.

Perhaps out of consideration for Hong Kong's international profile, by the time the Japanese entered the Mid-Levels district, military discipline seemed to have improved. On the stage of the auditorium in University Hall, Japanese soldiers often plink-plonked one-handed on the piano. Once, two soldiers wandered into Julie and Bebe's room. They sat on the beds and chatted with one another for a while, then left.

One day, Julie heard there was hot water available in one of the professor's houses to take a bath. All the residents had been packed off to a concentration camp, and she had no idea why hot water still streamed out of a faucet. She quickly grabbed soap and a towel and rushed over to the house, but the bathroom door was shut and someone was already running a bath. She couldn't wander far in case others jumped the queue in front of her, so she went to look around the small library halfway up the stairs.

A vast mess of whiteness covered the library floor, papers scattered everywhere. The house had been ransacked by the poor scavengers who usually gathered firewood around the Mid-Levels neighborhood. In earlier days, on weekends, Julie and Bebe used to chat while sitting on the iron railings by the side of the road, their legs hanging over the side, swinging freely. Fragrance from the small white flowers on the treetops, like little balls of pearl orchids, wafted by in waves. On the slopes below, they would occasionally see bamboo hats with three-inch pleated blue fabric skirts pop out from the mist. Those belonged to the women who gathered firewood. *They ransacked the house.*

Julie's English professor lived here. Looking through his bookcases, she found a copy of Aubrey Beardsley's illustrated edition of *Salomé* and tore out every picture. She was determined to take them back to Shanghai to sustain her connection with Western culture.

Julie waited a long time; the bathroom door was bolted from the inside and no one responded to her knocking. She had no idea if someone was washing clothes or soaking comfortably in a bathtub, asleep. The longer she waited the more she needed to relieve herself. She was afraid that she would end up waiting in vain if she ventured off, giving someone an opportunity to snatch a free slot at the bathroom away from her. Out of desperation, she closed the library door and squatted down. A sound like rain splashing on balls of scrunched up scraps and bundles of loose sheets of paper followed. She remembered when someone once broke into her family home. The burglar had left a pile of excrement behind, which she had heard was a common practice because it was reputed to bring good luck. *As a thief, do I have to be villainous too?*

Miss Hsiang and Mr. Pi came to visit Julie, bringing a packet of dried bean-curd skin for her. She in turn implored them to ask on her behalf for any news of boat tickets.

"We want to leave too," said Miss Hsiang, nodding her head.

Every once in a while, Julie had to trudge a long way to inquire in person because she could not reach them by phone. They no longer resided in the hotel and had moved to a rental property.

Dr. Lee headed the student-relief effort and frequently accompanied Japanese officials on inspection tours. This Dr. Lee was a very short overseas Chinese from Malaya. He had moved into the suite of the former dormitory warden but did not bring his family with him.

A group of students, all from his hometown, became his assistants. Among them was a voluptuous but fierce-looking girl who took a position akin to the wife of a bandit chieftain in a mountain lair.

Every day the students lined up to receive a plate of soybeans mixed with canned beef, ladled out by two boys whose expressions grew angrier and angrier with time, as if they were forced to share their own food with the students. In fact, that was actually the true state of things: late at night a truck pulled up to the gate and took rice and canned goods to sell on the black market—goods that were issued from British government warehouses.

"Audrey and Mr. Lee are going to get married," announced Bebe. "Just a simple civil ceremony, and then they'll move into an allocated room in the dormitory."

Julie knew Bebe felt sorry for Audrey.

Worse, the rubber plantation probably was no more, and Malaya also suffered under Japanese occupation.

Rachel had written from Singapore—of course she didn't mention Lloyd—but now Julie didn't know if her mother was still there.

She went with Bebe to the bank—a white building, recently built. Upon entering the dimly lit lobby a large pile of excrement that Japanese soldiers had deposited on the mosaic tiles greeted them. Behind the brass grille all the tellers were on duty. Someone manned each desk in the banking hall. The Eurasian closest to them furrowed his brow due to the stench in the air. Wide elastic bands around the arms of his shirt held his cuffs higher to facilitate his work—a fashionable look in the West in those days, but Julie felt it was a world away from what was happening around her.

Thirteen dollars remained in Julie's account and she withdrew it all. Bebe offered to lend her money to buy passage on a boat when a ticket opened up.

"Leave two dollars here," said Bebe, "otherwise the account will be closed."

"What do I need a bank account here for?"

Bebe did not share Julie's sense that the Last Judgment was approaching.

A corpse was laid neatly on the footpath. Someone must have straightened out his arms and legs. His Chinese jacket and pants, as well as his shoes, were as clean as could be. He had probably been killed by a stray bullet. The battle had ended days ago and he was still there.

"Don't look!" Bebe quickly shouted. Julie turned her head and looked away.

A journey to the city had to include a little fabric shopping. Julie had only recently discovered Cantonese homespun fabric, with its dazzling green leaves and hot pink flowers highlighted with stippled shadows. You would be more likely to see similar patterns in Japan, but nowhere else in China. Julie thought the pattern probably had once existed in China but the technique was somehow lost.

In the back streets of Central district, steep granite alleys stretched up the hills. After the battle for Hong Kong had run its course, fabric stalls multiplied and people thronged. Hot pink and bright green fabric looked even more dazzling under the bright blue sky. The atmosphere felt like a market day in a remote country town. Bebe helped Julie bargain and the stall owner cried out "*Dai gu!* Big sister!" in protest. Bebe, skeptical about the quality of the dye, moistened the fabric with her saliva and rubbed it to see if the color bled. Julie felt as if a needle pricked her when she saw that, but the stall owner said nothing.

Suddenly they spotted Jenny and Mr. Wei in the crowd. They greeted one another. Mr. Wei stood to one side and didn't say a word. Jenny was very pregnant. It was a warm day and she wasn't wearing an overcoat. Her blue tunic protruded so far it looked like an insect's belly. Julie tried to fix her gaze on Jenny's face and not look down, but the surface area of the tunic was so vast, and no matter how hard she tried to look away the bright blue inundated her eyes and she lost track of the conversation.

"I was sure you two had left," said Julie.

Jenny smiled. A shadow of mystery passed across her face. Julie didn't understand why. She didn't know the word "leave" had taken on the meaning of "go to Chungking," which now wasn't safe to utter in public. Besides, the couple would have to go to Chungking if they ever did leave. They couldn't go to Mr. Wei's hometown because his wife was there. Though even if they wanted to leave, they couldn't secure train or boat tickets anyway.

"Of course, we'd like to leave," Jenny replied ponderously, "but there are complications. His parents are quite advanced in years and need to be taken care of...." At that point, Jenny switched to English and asked Bebe about their accommodations. They chatted a little longer, then nodded and parted ways.

As soon as the couple disappeared, Bebe puffed up her cheeks as if they were full of water. Suppressing their laughter, Bebe and Julie just stared at each other without exchanging a word.

3

JUDY WAS put on leave without pay from the foreign firm soon after the Japanese occupied the foreign concessions in Shanghai, and she had to live frugally. On the day Julie returned to Shanghai, Judy welcomed her with a food-laden table, but the next day she said, "Nowadays, I just eat scallion pancakes." Then explained, slightly embarrassed, "Less trouble."

"I love scallion pancakes," said Julie.

Julie indeed did not tire of scallion pancakes three meals a day because it felt as exciting as playing truant. Since childhood, Rachel had constantly lectured her about nutrition and made Julie feel guilty if for a single day she didn't eat fruits and vegetables, as well as meat and fish.

Every day, Mrs. Ch'in came to wash the clothes and clean the house. Apart from that, all she did was stand over the gas stove and fry scallion pancakes, one by one. Mrs. Ch'in had bound feet and constantly complained that the insufficiency of the beneficial earth element up in the eighth-floor apartment caused her legs to swell.

Rooms were sublet to two German men after Rachel left Shanghai. It was easier to deal with bachelors like them, whereas women tended to be much more troublesome. Judy had only kept one room for herself. Now that Julie had moved in, she contributed half the expenses. Judy asked relatives to find Julie some work tutoring two female middle-school students. Aware her third aunt had only enjoyed a short period of tranquil seclusion, Julie felt deeply guilty for intruding.

Standing by the window one day, Judy caught a pigeon and told Julie to hold on to the bird while she looked for a length of string to tie one of the pigeon's feet to the windowsill. The neck of the large pigeon was covered with iridescent purple and green feathers. The bird twisted and turned, making it difficult to subdue without using excessive force. The women giggled as they grappled with the bird.

"We'll have to wait for Mrs. Ch'in to come tomorrow and kill it," said Judy.

Julie repeatedly went to check on the pigeon; it quietly scampered around in circles outside the window.

"We used to raise a lot of pigeons when we were small," said Judy. "Your grandma said raising pigeons is good for the eyes."

Perhaps the theory is that watching pigeons fly about in the distance prevents nearsightedness. But Judy and her brother are both nearsighted.

Who would have thought that a night of worrying would cause the pigeon to lose half its body weight. It did not, however, turn into a white dove the way the legendary Wu Tzu-hsü's hair turned white overnight when running for his life. The next day it appeared to be an entirely different bird. Mrs. Ch'in slaughtered the pigeon in the rear corridor and stewed the bird over a low flame to make a soup. Julie grieved silently as she ate, as did Judy. Without aniseed and other spices, the pigeon tasted a little gamy, but it was hardly worth spending money to buy spices for a one-off event.

Miss Hsiang and Mr. Pi had returned to Shanghai by train from Shao-kwan, north of Hong Kong, ahead of Julie. Ambassador Pi was advanced in years and didn't go to Chungking. They married. Miss Hsiang would occasionally visit Judy to chat. She had not told Mr. Pi about her son.

"Your second aunt actually helped to bring about this state of affairs with Miss Hsiang," Judy confided to Julie with a chuckle. "Mr. Pi had gone to Hong Kong because of your second aunt, but in his disappointment at unrequited love, he made a deliberate effort to woo Miss Hsiang. Later, he admitted to your second aunt that his little deception turned into reality."

"Second Aunt was furious that Mr. Pi did nothing to help her during the time she was suspected of espionage."

"That was because she broke his heart."

"Why on earth was Second Aunt suspected of being a spy?"

"I'm not sure," Judy replied hesitantly. "Miss Hsiang said Rachel's socializing with the English officer led to suspicions she was collecting intelligence, and he reported her."

It must have been the young man that day at the beach. So he got the credit for being an informant. No wonder Second Aunt was so furious when she left.

And no wonder Mr. Pi was so angry that he did nothing to help.

"Is Lloyd in Singapore?"

All Julie knew was that around the time Singapore fell to the Japanese, Rachel traveled on a refugee boat to India.

"Lloyd is dead. He was killed on the beach in Singapore. We always said his laughing so hard he couldn't finish a sentence or be understood was a bad omen."

In Julie's mind, Lloyd was like William Dobbin and his unrequited love for Amelia Sedley in *Vanity Fair*. He waited many years for one woman, determined to marry her. Julie could never ascertain if he was in Singapore, and after the incident with the eight hundred dollars, she became utterly indifferent toward her mother. She never even thought about her, or gave any thought to why she had gone to Singapore for a year or two without ever marrying and yet did not leave.

It sounded like Rachel had moved in with Lloyd. But now he was dead and Rachel had not remarried, so Julie didn't mention anything about Rachel intimating her intentions to find a husband for herself.

Judy misread the hesitation on Julie's face and mistakenly thought Julie disapproved of her mother's romances. After a short pause Judy said in a low voice, "Your second aunt actually got divorced for Chien-wei, but then he had second thoughts about marrying a divorced woman as it would jeopardize his career—he worked at the Ministry of Foreign Affairs. Back in Nanking, he eventually married a university graduate. Later he came to visit us, and as soon as he and Rachel met again they gazed into each other's eyes for a long time without saying a word."

Of all of Rachel and Judy's friends from the time they had studied in Europe, Ambassador Pi Chien-wei was the only one Julie had not met before moving to Hong Kong for school. *I didn't know she had such a tragic romance. I wonder when that visit was? She divorced for him and then moved out of the family home so the visit must have been to the apartment Rachel and Judy shared. But Rachel only divorced four years after she returned from overseas. If she had planned to get divorced in order to marry him, she wouldn't have waited so long. Anyway, it appears that he had married someone else soon after returning to China, and after he married he visited the Sheng residence to see Rachel. Rachel procrastinated for a very long time then decided to get divorced nonetheless.*

Julie didn't ask Judy about the accuracy of this imagined sequence of events. Curiosity was strictly taboo in this household, which is why Judy only related the faintest outline to her. Judy called Julie's brother, Julian, "sneaky," but the English word "sneaky" doesn't convey the connotation of intelligence in the Chinese word. Actually, Julie knew her brother was entirely ignorant about Rachel and Judy's lives, but his bright feline eyes seemed to be most observant.

Once, during an after-lunch conversation, Rachel casually said to Julie, "Your second uncle opens other people's mail." Judy raised her eyebrows and smiled. Julie would never forget the implication, that only people with a dull life take pleasure in prying into the private affairs of others.

Still, Julie could not help feeling curious about Chien-wei's final appearance at the Sheng household because that was a time when Julie had felt closest to her mother. They were living under the same roof, yet Julie had no idea about Mr. Pi. When visitors came, Rachel would often joke with Judy, "Our little Julie is all right. She calls me Second Aunt, but heaven forbid if little Julian bursts in and blurts out, 'Mommy, Mommy!' That would be something...." Actually, Julian never once referred to Rachel as his mother. He had always envied Julie being asked to call their mother Second Aunt.

Julie, however, devoted little time to revisiting the past and so such thoughts about her family were fleeting. Memories, happy or not, always embodied a doleful note, which, no matter how faint, Julie felt a strong aversion to. She never sought out melancholy, but life unavoidably overflowed with it. Just thinking along these lines made her feel like she was standing in the portal of an ancient edifice, peering through the moonlight and dark shadows that permeated the ruins of a once noble and illustrious household, which was now nothing more than scattered shards of roof tiles and piles of rubble from collapsed walls. That instant of knowing what once existed there.

"Some things you will only understand after you grow up," Rachel said to Julie at the time of the divorce.

"I had an agreement with your second uncle. This time I have come back only to manage his household."

The day Rachel returned to China, Yü-heng, a young male servant who had come to the Sheng household as part of Rachel's dowry, went to the docks to greet her. He was the son of the Pien clan's former steward who accompanied their young children to their classes at the library. For some reason, Yü-heng did not accomplish his mission to meet Rachel, and the maidservants began whispering conspiratorially to each other. Yü-heng again went to the wharf and finally returned in the afternoon, saying that Maternal Uncle's family had picked her up and she would arrive home in the evening.

That night Julie and Julian were already asleep but were woken up to get dressed again. It felt like fleeing from bandits under cover of darkness, something the maidservants often talked about.

The household was an amalgamation of three-bay *shakkumen*, stone-gate town houses. The main hall was square but not spacious. Many large suitcases were stacked up on the floor. Rachel and Judy sat on two wooden chairs separated by a teapoy. The maidservants and Jade Peach, the servant girl who was part of Rachel's dowry, crowded around the doorway, all smiles, though in the dismal light their darkened faces exuded gloom.

Julie didn't recognize them. Both women wore fashionable clay-colored silk one-piece dresses, one darker than the other, with pieces of fabric hanging down from the front and back. It was the only time Rachel ever wore glasses.

"Really!" sneered Rachel. "Those socks are far too tight. Why would you make her wear them?" The thick white socks made in England had become as stiff as stovepipes after many washings.

"Didn't you say they are terribly expensive?" replied Auntie Han obsequiously.

"They can't be worn if they're too small," rebuked Rachel as she pushed back Julie's bangs. "And really, Auntie Han, where are her eyebrows? Her bangs are much too long. They're interfering with the proper growth of her eyebrows. Cut them back a bit right now."

Julie was most unenthusiastic—newly cut bangs, neither long nor short, would make her look stupid.

"I like this handsome young man," said Judy as she pulled Julian toward her.

"Julian, you haven't made your salutations," Rachel prompted.

"He did," said Auntie Han, and then bent down to tell him discreetly to say it again.

"Goodness," said Rachel, "Julian's become aphasic! And why did his maid Auntie Yü leave?"

"Not sure. Said she was old and wanted to go home." Auntie Han, worried that she herself would be suspected of having edged Auntie Yü out, felt a twinge of anxiety.

"Well, Auntie Han certainly shows no signs of aging."

"Madam, but I *am* old!" replied Auntie Han. "Did you like the food overseas?"

"If we couldn't eat it, we cooked for ourselves," said Judy, tossing her head and sniffing haughtily, as was her habit.

"Third Mistress cooked for herself?"

"If not," replied Judy, mimicking Auntie Han's rustic Anhwei patois, "*jeang gao ah*? How'd she eat, eh?"

"Third Mistress is very capable now."

"Just a minute, Auntie Han," said Judy abruptly. "*Jeang shui ah*? How are we going to sleep tonight?" Her tone was jolly but carried a hint of confrontation.

"*Jeang shui*? How are you going to sleep? You can sleep however you want to sleep. Everything is ready."

Hearing that everything was ready seemed to put Judy in a panic again. She was about to say something when she changed her mind. "We have sheets?" she asked.

"Of course."

"Are they clean?"

"Ahhhh!" said Auntie Han. The dialect of Hofei, the capital of Anhwei, has a peculiar way of articulating the word "ah." The sound first rises to the palate, then joins force with the coarse roaring from the throat, before bursting out from a half-open gap of the mouth to imply, with annoyance, "How could you ask such a thing?" Auntie Han continued, "Freshly washed, Third Mistress. How could they not be clean?"

Julie found this all rather strange, the tension in the air. Rachel said nothing, but continued to listen intently.

Julie's father came upstairs and cursorily nodded toward Rachel and Judy as he circumnavigated the room in the dim light of the lamp, his gown fluttering, a cigar in his hand. He perfunctorily asked about their journey, then chatted about her uncle and her father's cousins in Tientsin.

Up to this point, Judy was answering all his questions, but suddenly Rachel spoke. "How can we possibly live here?" She was so angry that her voice had completely changed.

"I knew you wouldn't be amenable unless you could choose your own residence," he replied amiably. "This is just a temporary arrangement."

He spoke some more with Judy before announcing, "Perhaps you should retire now. Early tomorrow morning you'll inspect some houses. I subscribed to a newspaper and have left instructions for it to be brought upstairs as soon as it arrives." He then headed downstairs.

The room fell silent for a moment. The women, who had been crowded at the entrance, had already left. Jade Peach returned and stood leaning in the doorway with her hands tucked into her sleeves.

"Very well, then," said Rachel to Auntie Han, "you may put them to bed now."

Auntie Han quickly assented and led the two children away.

In the new house, Julie's father occupied a room on the second floor, separated from Judy's bedroom by another room. Rachel's room was on the other side of Judy's. The children and their elderly white-bearded tutor who taught them Chinese lived on the fourth floor. The maidservants lived on the third floor to segregate the generations and insulate nocturnal noise.

"You choose for yourselves," said Rachel, "the colors for your bedrooms and the study."

Julie and Julian sat together flipping through the book of color swatches. Julie was ever fearful her brother would slip out of character to weigh in. But as usual, he said nothing.

Julie chose a dark pink for her bedroom and a sea green for the study in the next room. She felt so deliriously happy living for the first time in a world of her own creation that she thought her heart would explode. Even after living there for some time she would go into raptures just from an occasional glance at the painted walls. She also loved the sloping ceiling of the garret on the fourth floor, the narrow windows, the dim light; it was like a fairy-tale cottage in the Black Forest.

At noon, they would go downstairs for lunch. Cigar in hand, her father would pace around the leather-covered square table with copper edges while he waited for Rachel and Judy to descend.

At the dining table, Judy would habitually ask him for news about distant relatives. "How's Yang Chao-lin? How's Ch'ien, the second eldest?"

His answers always seemed sarcastic.

"You people!" she would snigger. "And you had to cozy up to him!"

Rachel rarely spoke at the dinner table, at most offering some advice about nutrition when she served food to the children. Sitting in silence, she would peer downward with the same tender look that Julie later saw reflected in the Repulse Bay Hotel shopwindow when Miss Hsiang straightened Mr. Pi's tie.

Julie's father was always the first to finish eating and the first to leave the table. Then Rachel would embark on postprandial sermons on how important education is, that one should not lie, that one should not cry because only the weak cry. "I always try to reason with you," Rachel would say. "Do you think we had it as easy as you do? Why, when my mother scolded me I'd be red in the face and burst into tears."

Julie found such talk unpleasant. Why should someone have to be so afraid of another person, no matter who that person was?

"Whenever my mother was angered by your uncle Yün-chih, she'd come crying to me, insisting I stand up for her honor."

When Judy finished eating she would practice piano, but occasionally, when she was too lethargic to move, she would sit back and listen to Rachel's sermons. One day when her homily turned to romance, she directed her remarks to Judy with a smile. "As long as you don't have intimate relations, it's truly beautiful when you meet up again. But if you do, then it just feels wrong." By the end of her soliloquy, Rachel was speaking very quietly.

"Little Julian, what do you want to be when you grow up?" Rachel then asked. "Your sister wants to be a pianist. What about you? What do you want to do?"

"I want to learn to drive," mumbled Julian.

"You want to be a chauffeur?"

He remained silent.

"A chauffeur or a train driver?"

"A train driver," he said at last.

"Dear little Julian, will you please lend me your eyelashes?" Judy teased. "I'm going out tomorrow. Lend them to me only for a day and I promise to give them back."

Julian did not respond.

"Will you, please?" She pouted. "What a miser! Won't even lend them to me just for one day."

"One good thing about Ned," blurted Rachel out of the blue, "is that he never questioned Julian's distinctly foreign appearance. Actually, at that time there was an Italian singing teacher. . . ." Her voice lowered and then faded away.

Ned is a pet name for Edward, quainter than Ed or Eddie. Julie had seen her father's calling card and knew he used a different name, though she only ever heard her mother call him Ned behind his back, with a hint of intimacy, which Julie found surprising.

Rachel ordered a maidservant to fetch castor oil, which she then dabbed on Julie's eyebrows with a calligraphy brush to stimulate their growth.

One day, tea was served after everyone finished their fruit. Rachel began talking about their holiday in the Lake District that coincided with a murder case involving a Chinese couple who had arrived around the same time as Rachel and Judy.

"People there knew nothing about China—they'd ask, 'Do you have eggs in China?' It was truly exasperating. And it was in this tiny backwater that a Chinese man murdered his wife—what a disgrace!"

"And he was a doctor of law," Judy chimed in.

"He had studied in America and they were on their honeymoon traveling around the world. The couple met in New York."

Judy tossed her head to one side and sniffed haughtily. "That Miss K'uang was ugly," she said by way of explanation.

"She was older and that Liao Chung-i was quite handsome. The foreigners must have thought it a bit strange, perhaps particular to Chinese tastes. That day he returned to the hotel alone at four or five and took afternoon tea with the proprietress. Judy, what did he tell the old lady?"

"He said his wife had gone into town to do some shopping."

"Yes, that's right. He said she'd gone to buy wool garments because it was colder than they had expected. It was raining when they found her. From behind it looked as if she was sitting under her umbrella on the bank of the lake."

A perfectly normal scene. Especially in China, countless scenic photos looked just like that after the after the May Fourth Movement in the early 1920s. Rachel laughed nervously.

"She was strangled with one of her own silk stockings," Rachel said softly, as if being risqué. "She was barefooted. Both feet were in the water. She must have wanted to be intimate with him and he

couldn't stand it. Really, there is nothing more disgusting than intimacy with someone you don't like." Rachel began to laugh again, that
breathless embarrassed laugh of hers.

"They said he'd withdrawn all the money from her bank accounts."

"It was just absurd," Judy grumbled. "To choose a place like that
where two Chinese people would stand out."

"That's why I say it was an impulsive act," said Rachel. "Of course
afterward he became a bit hysterical. Everyone said he was handsome
and cut quite a figure in the student association. He had a degree and
a brilliant future ahead of him. What a waste."

Julie knew that when her mother said, "There is nothing more
disgusting than intimacy with someone you don't like," she was referring to Ned. And Julie was vaguely aware that Judy compared herself
to that ugly woman, even though Judy would be ashamed to be seen
in her company.

Many years later, Julie read the memoirs of Chief Detective Inspector Wensley of Scotland Yard. He recalled that when he took his wife
on a holiday to the Lake District, he said to her that it was an ideal
location for a murder. He had seen the Chinese couple. But that afternoon, he noticed the man returning across the bridge alone, carrying a camera. That caught his attention.

That evening when he heard that the woman had not returned,
he took a flashlight and went to the bridge to look for her. It was
raining and he found an open umbrella and a body on the ground.
After closer inspection, he concluded she had slid down from a boulder. While she sat on the boulder, someone sitting next to her or close
behind had strangled her. It must have been someone she knew. Her
clothes were unruffled and she had not been indecently assaulted.

When Inspector Wensley accompanied the local police inspector
to visit the husband it was only nine o'clock but he was already asleep.
Upon hearing that his wife had been murdered, he immediately asked,
"Did you catch the robber who killed my wife?" The detective replied,
"I didn't say she was robbed."

The guests in the hotel had observed the wife wearing several
diamond rings, but the corpse by the lake had no jewelry on her. A

search of the husband's luggage yielded her jewelry and bankbooks but no diamond rings.

"According to Chinese law," he said, "what is hers is mine."

His camera was taken away as evidence. When the police developed the film inside it, they only found shots of scenery. Eventually, they discovered the diamond rings in a film canister.

Wensley's memoir didn't mention that the deceased was ugly, perhaps out of concern not to appear racist. Plus, if the deceased wasn't depicted as a seductive beauty, readers would possibly be disappointed. He merely described her as "the shortest woman I've ever seen." Her father was a wealthy Cantonese merchant. Of his dozens of offspring, he trusted her the most and put her in charge of family finances when she was just a teenager. After moving overseas, she also ran an antique business in New York.

While Liao courted her, he deposited two hundred dollars in a bank account, then withdrew most of the funds and deposited them at a different bank. In this manner, he opened many accounts in readiness for her family's due diligence inquiries.

On their marriage day, she wrote in her diary: "I have an appointment with the hairdresser at one thirty; I miss my husband."

Rachel was right when she said that a capable Westernized woman couldn't be fooled as easily as the obedient, old-fashioned women of traditional China.

The diary also recorded the shocking news that her doctor had revealed to her just before they left America: she was barren. The chief inspector believed that Liao killed her because of this. For the lack of progeny is considered the worst of the three unfilial acts. His theory stemmed from the mistaken conviction that he understood Chinese psychology.

Rachel visited West Lake after returning to China. There she took a photograph and wrote on the back of it:

Whenever I recall my visit to the United Kingdom
I wonder about the Llyn Dulyn (Black Lake)
I am sure its roses still wear their tender rosy rouge

As I saw them in the good old days
But the forget-me-nots must have forgotten me
Sadly, I fear I shall never have a chance to revisit them.
My aching, dismantling old frame, how many more times
    can it withstand the chilly autumn wind?
Life is but a dream: Nothing in life is solid, substantial
Even the towers and terraces casting shadows nearby
Could turn into mere phantoms in a second

It would appear that Mr. Pi accompanied Rachel to the Lake District.

Among the many photographs Rachel had brought back with her, Julie noticed one her father had posted overseas to her mother. It was a studio photograph, and on the back he had written a short, classical Chinese seven-syllable verse, though she could only remember part of it:

Just now I heard the cacophony of x x at Tientsin
and then the beating of the drum at the remote frontier
Men of letters x x x x x
To you my love two little words: I'm safe

That made Julie laugh out loud.

One day Judy mentioned that a certain someone had been made a mandarin. Rachel snickered, "How can we still speak of being *made* a mandarin when nowadays they're all supposed to be public servants?" Julie almost laughed aloud, too. She no longer believed anything she read in the newspapers.

At that time Chien-wei was probably still unmarried.

After lunch, Julie followed them upstairs. At the bathroom door, Rachel resumed her dinner-table commentary. A pair of medium-high-heeled shoes made of white snakeskin with black embossing and an ankle strap rested on the bathroom scales. The shoes were as tiny as Cinderella's glass slippers. Rachel's shoes were always custom-made, yet she still had to stuff cotton in the toe area. And no matter how hot the weather was, Rachel wore silk stockings to bed. Julie was not the least bit curious about her mother's bound feet, unlike her fascination when she watched Auntie Yü's tiny feet being washed.

A friend of Ned's treated him to a night out and they engaged a sing-song girl whom he'd met in Tientsin, Miss Seven. She was a former colleague of Ned's paramour Euphoria. Miss Seven began to reminisce about Euphoria. Ned's friend told her to exchange seats with someone so she could sit behind Ned and chat with him more freely. Rachel's brother, Yün-chih, attended the banquet and later mockingly related the incident to Rachel. It was generally agreed in the Sheng household that Euphoria looked quite old, but Miss Seven appeared to be several years her senior. She was thin, with the complexion of an opium smoker and freckles that showed through the pale makeup on her powdered face. But it appeared that Ned's passion was inflamed.

Around that time a maidservant cleaning Ned's room found a silver-gray silk parasol on the steam radiator. She asked Rachel and Judy about it but it was not theirs. Rachel told her to ask Ned, who said he had no idea where it came from. Rachel then instructed the maidservant: "Leave it on the radiator in Second Master's room."

Two days later the parasol was gone. Rachel and Judy amused themselves with this incident for several days.

Afternoon guests were mostly from the Chu family, a gaggle of adult cousins under the wing of Aunt Chu. Sometimes they accompanied Judy and Rachel to tea dances; otherwise they danced at home to phonograph records. If Aunt Chu's sisters-in-law also visited, out came the mah-jongg tiles. When Rachel was in high spirits, she would go down to the kitchen to make wisteria pancakes, deep-fried bamboo-shoot chips, and toffee-coated yams. Ned would occasionally drop by to offer his salutations, then retreat after circling around the room a few times.

Miss Purity and Miss Grace of the Chu family were both in their early twenties. Miss Grace was born to a concubine. One evening, they both wore above-the-knee padded gowns made of fine apple-green light gauze. Each had a light green silk flower sprinkled with silver powder—one was pinned to the lower left corner of the gown, one to the lapel.

Everyone said of Miss Purity that her face was round and thus of a sweet disposition, while Miss Grace had an oval face and, though her eyes were a little small, most resembled a classic beauty.

Julie admired Miss Purity, who had become quite a celebrity after having had her own art exhibition, her picture appearing in the influential English-language *North China Daily News*.

Julie began to sketch caricatures. But the only adult in her drawings always looked like Rachel—skinny women with small chins, drooping eyebrows that appeared to be drawn with a pencil, bright eyes like suns on the horizon, and eyelashes radiating out like beams of light.

"Do you like Miss Purity or Miss Grace?" asked Judy.

"I like them both."

"You can't say you like them both. You must like one more than the other."

"I like Miss Grace." It would be wrong to say she did not like Miss Grace because she wasn't as accomplished as Miss Purity. Miss Purity probably wouldn't care. Everyone liked her.

Just as Rachel and Judy returned, Aunt Chu also posed a question: "Do you like Second Aunt or Third Aunt?"

"I like them both."

"That doesn't count. Which one do you like the most?"

"Let me think about it."

"Very well, you think about it."

Second-Aunt-Third-Aunt was always articulated as one word, as if the two were a single entity. "There was a time when Second Aunt carried you in her belly," Judy would occasionally say. On face value that was a strange thing to say but the reality was even stranger.

"Well, have you thought it through?"

"Not yet."

Julie knew she had a special connection with Second Aunt, but being a little distant from Third Aunt, it would be best to cozy up to her. *It wouldn't matter much if it upset Second Aunt.*

"Well, have you thought it through?"

"Third Aunt."

Judy's face revealed nothing, but Rachel was obviously displeased.

Several years earlier Ned had sat Julie on his knee and fished a gold guinea and a silver dollar out of his pocket. "Do you want the Mexican silver dollar or the gold guinea?" he teased.

The small, golden-bronze biscuit was so lovely, much more fun than the bright, shiny silver dollar. Julie knew that size and value were unrelated and that there was no objective standard for loveliness. As if her thoughts were a millstone, she had difficulty pushing them along. After an agonizingly long moment, she finally replied, "I want the shiny coin."

Ned angrily slid Julie off his lap, gave her the dollar, and walked away.

Aunt Chu was the most frequent visitor. She was plump, wore gold wire-framed spectacles, and her hair was cut short. Rachel gave Chinese nicknames to people using Chinese characters that resembled their physiognomy: Aunt Chu, the principal consort, was 瓜瓜, Gourd Face; the second consort was 豆豆, Bean Face; Rachel herself was 青青, Long Face; and Judy was 四四, Square Face.

"Little Julie is so honest," Aunt Chu would say frequently. "Simple and honest."

"You know the aphorism, 'Simple and honest' is another way of saying useless, don't you?" Rachel said to Julie.

"Who does Julie resemble most?" asked Aunt Chu. "Julian resembles you. Doesn't she look more like her third aunt?"

"She'd be better off not looking like me," retorted Judy.

"There's one thing about her that's not so bad," said Rachel.

In novels, it was always the eyes of heroines that were the central point of beauty. Eyes deep as the ocean, seductive eyes, would be her saving grace. Julie knew that was not her fate, but she lived in constant hope.

"Oh," responded Aunt Chu as expected, "what would that be?"

"Hazard a guess."

Aunt Chu stared long and hard. "Her ears?"

Ears! Who wants ears? My hair completely hides my ears.
"No."

Julie felt a glimmer of hope.

"Well in that case I really don't know. Tell me, now. What is it?"
"Her round head."

Everyone is made the same, as the proverb goes. Who doesn't have a round head?

"Oh, yes," said Aunt Chu as she fondled Julie's cranium. "It is round." She, too, seemed a little disappointed.

Rachel rarely took Julie out shopping by herself. On one occasion, she dragged Julie off to a department store before meeting with Aunt Chu at the Elegance Cake Shop for afternoon tea. The shop assistant heaped piles of merchandise onto the counter as usual and then brought out two chairs. Julie sat there for so long she almost fell asleep—she was only nine at the time. After visiting several departments, they emerged and stood on the curb about to cross the road.

"Walk with me," instructed Rachel, "and be careful. Look both ways to be sure there are no cars." Suddenly there was an opening, but just as they were about to cross the road Rachel hesitated. Perhaps she felt the need to hold Julie's hand. She gnashed her teeth, then seized Julie's hand a little too tightly. Julie was bewildered, as she had not expected her mother's fingers to be so bony. She felt as if a bunch of thin bamboo canes clenched her hand. They hurriedly crossed Nanking Road through a gap in the traffic, and as soon as they reached the footpath on the other side Rachel relinquished her grip. Julie was overwhelmed by the momentary struggle of her mother's emotions. This was the first time she'd had any physical contact with her mother since her return to Shanghai. Obviously Rachel also felt a slight revulsion.

Julie recounted to Miss Purity a translated story that she had read in *The Short Story Magazine*. Next door to a youth lived three sisters. The eldest had black hair, the middle sister blond hair, and the sickly youngest sister silver hair. One day at dusk, the youth saw a girl in his garden. She frantically embraced him and the two madly rolled about on the ground. It was dark; he could only discern that it was one of the three girls but not which one. She said nothing at all. The next day he visited their home. He closely observed their facial expressions and listened intently to their voices but simply could not tell which sister it had been. Was it the demure eldest sister, the lively second sister, or the shy third sister?

Miss Purity listened attentively, stone-faced. She was particularly interested in this story because she empathized with the sisters. None of her own suitors had succeeded, so they pursued her younger sister.

"Then what?"

"I don't remember," replied Julie apologetically.

Miss Purity lost her composure. "Oh come on, think hard," she whined. "How could you forget?"

Julie thought hard for a long time. "I really can't remember."

Julie was young and couldn't possibly understand the story, otherwise Miss Purity would have suspected Julie was too embarrassed to continue and made up the excuse she had forgotten the rest of it.

Julie felt terrible. She pulled out copies of the previous two years of *The Short Story Magazine.* Squatting between two piles of the periodical, flipping the pages, she still could not find the story. Miss Purity grew agitated with anticipation.

Years later after Julie had read this Hungarian short story again, once more for some reason she couldn't remember how it ended, save that it was the third sister, who was named something like Yelina. Yelina was ill and he came to visit, or was it that he was sick and she came to look after him? She probably did not tell him, but Julie could not remember how he found out. Soon after that he had to leave the city and they lost contact.

She forgot the ending twice, probably because her anticipation of the mysteries of romance were intense and the ending of the story was simply too dull for her to remember. Of course, it should have been the third sister. Julie feared she would not live long enough to fall in love and marry.

Now it was too late to finish telling the story to Miss Purity. When Julie first told her the story, she was unaware that Miss Purity was gravely ill. After she died, Julie heard she had suffered from bone tuberculosis. Julie never saw Miss Purity again. At her funeral, Julie kowtowed to the body set out on an austere bed board in the funeral parlor. White cloth covered the body and draped down to the floor. A small square of red cloth was placed on her head, over the white fabric. It all felt unconnected to the Miss Purity Julie remembered. Apart from a slight eeriness, Julie felt nothing.

"She used to be so fond of Miss Purity," Julie overheard Rachel saying to Judy on the way home from the funeral, "but she showed no emotion at all." Rachel was obviously disappointed by Julie's lack of compassion.

Rachel forced Ned into a sanatorium to cure his addiction to morphine. She waited until he was cured, then demanded a divorce.

"The doctor said he injects enough to kill a horse," said Rachel.

"We Shengs," declared Ned initially, "have never divorced." As the appointment to sign the papers at the lawyer's office approached, he went back on his word many times. Rachel said the English lawyer was so angry he was ready to punch Ned. The English lawyers in the foreign concessions of Shanghai had the upper hand, otherwise Ned would have behaved worse and ignored the lawyer's letters altogether.

Rachel and Judy moved into an apartment. One day Julie visited. "I have divorced your second uncle," Rachel announced to the mirror as she did her makeup in the bathroom. "You can't blame your second uncle for this. If he had married someone else, he would have got on just fine. I hope he meets the right person."

"I'm truly happy," said a smiling Julie. She was feeling relieved for her mother, even though she knew her parent's divorce would not be good for her. But she couldn't just think of herself. She also felt smug, knowing that her family had achieved something as thoroughly modern as producing a scientist.

"I'm only telling you to let you know, so you don't misjudge your second uncle," said Rachel, a little annoyed at what she took to be Julie's expression of approval. After all, she was not so much of a Westernized parent that she would seek permission from her children for a divorce.

Ned looked for another place to live but eventually moved onto the same lane where the Pien family lived, hoping against hope to bump into Rachel and that her younger brother could mediate a reconciliation. But as soon as the papers were finalized, Rachel left for Europe. This time Judy did not accompany her, so on the day of her departure Julie and Julian went to see her off, as did all of Yün-chih's family, who surrounded Rachel. With a human shield of relatives, everyone felt more at ease. Julie thought: Did they think we'd cry or something?

Julie and Julian were bored as they nonchalantly wandered about on the fringes of the flock of relatives from their uncle's family. The deck of the ship was festooned with large red-and-white-striped umbrellas. Everyone inspected the cabins and at last sat underneath the umbrellas, ordering orange juice, though there were not enough seats for the children.

At home with Ned life more or less returned to the way it was during those mundane childhood years in the north. Ned was good-tempered and spent his days in his room, pacing around in circles like a caged animal, memorizing and reciting books. The flood of words flowed rapidly, and as he neared an ending he began to chant loudly before concluding with a robust, "Oh!" Anyone who has read a few volumes of string-bound classics will know how much time and effort it involved. Julie felt sorry for her father.

Judy once spoke to Julie about her and Ned's elder brother. "He bawled when he heard the imperial examination system had been abolished," she said, laughing derisively.

Julie, however, felt sorry for him—at least he had passed the examination. Of course, Judy despised him. Judy and Ned were born to his second wife. He was twenty years older than Judy and Ned, and he had been the one who raised the two orphans.

"When your uncle saw kissing in the movies he'd cover his eyes," said Judy of her elder brother. "Around that time the famous female impersonator Mei Lan-fang was performing a new production of the opera *Celestial Beauty Scattering Flowers*. Your eldest uncle heard there was nothing wrong with that opera and granted permission for me to see it. I was so happy that I memorized the entire libretto so I could concentrate on the acting and not have to hold it up during the performance, which would ruin my enjoyment of the opera. Then—who knows why—he withdrew his permission.

"Your uncle constantly lamented that I refused to get married. He cried, demanding to know how he would be able to face our parents in the afterlife. He accused me of being uncooperative, but he barely arranged any meetings with potential candidates through matchmakers.

"Your eldest uncle's wife used to say to me, 'Your second brother just can't be trusted; your elder brother never strays.' She'd then sneer. But she underestimated her husband. Every night, squinting in anticipation, your eldest uncle called out, 'Joy, bring my foot bath.' Who could have thought that over time the foot-bathing ritual would lead to a secret arrangement. Joy was a wily one. At first she demurred, so he agreed to set her up with her own house, knowing his principal wife would not tolerate any such arrangement. He told her that he had married Joy off. The cover story was that Joy now lived as the principal wife of a man with a millinery and shoe store in the Hsia-kwan district of Nanking. The subterfuge was well scripted, and they even gave the husband a name. Joy had been serving your aunt since she was a little girl so your aunt gave Joy a dowry. When Joy had a child, your eldest uncle told his wife, 'Joy gave birth to a son!' That was really wicked."

Following the fracas over their traveling abroad, Rachel and Judy broke off contact with the family of Judy's elder brother. Julie rarely visited and her adoption was no longer mentioned. That year, after the divorce, Ned dispatched Julie and Julian to make New Year salutations to his elder brother, while he arranged to visit separately. The elderly uncle sat alone in the study on the ground floor. He wore a skullcap and spectacles. His short face was adorned with a wispy, white pencil mustache. The two children kowtowed and he politely got up and extended his hand to curtail their obeisances, all the while convivially clucking repeatedly, "Have you eaten? Have you eaten? Have you visited your aunt yet? Have you been upstairs yet? Have you greeted your aunt?" He then gave orders in a low voice to the servants: "Go and fetch the young master. Fetch the young master, right?" Their eldest uncle's first son was in his teens. "Have you been upstairs? Fetch the young master, all right?"

Ned also instructed Auntie Han to take the children to pay their obeisance at their uncle's secret household. Joy was fair-skinned and modest, and indeed resembled the proprietress of a small-town millinery and shoe store. She treated Auntie Han the same as always and did not put on airs, and Auntie Han, for her part, praised the concubine behind the back of the principal wife.

One time Ned neglected to make any preparations for the Lunar New Year, thinking of it just before New Year's Eve. He pulled a ten-dollar note out of his pocket and instructed Julie to take the household automobile to purchase some winter cherry blossoms. Luckily the flower shop was still open. Julie carefully selected two large branches with many blossoms, costing just over a dollar, and returned the change to Ned, who said he liked the flowers. Ordinarily Ned did not hand over money with such alacrity, often leaving Julie standing outside the opium den waiting for an age. Judy commented that he always delayed paying bills. "It gives him pleasure to keep money in his pocket for an extra day or two." Julie knew only too well her father's fears.

"Second Master is most frugal nowadays," said Auntie Lee, the clothes washer, referring to Ned.

Auntie Han laughed. "Oh yes, Second Master now understands what being frugal means. As the saying goes, 'The prodigal son who mends his ways will shine again.'"

Ned was now trading in gold at the metal exchange and was said to be making a lot of money. He suddenly became a rare candidate among the relatives for matrimonial introductions. And there were plenty of unmarried women to choose from.

"Come with me to visit your fourth great aunt," said Ned to Julie one day. "It's time for you to learn something."

They saw a younger female cousin of Ned's, the second in the household of Julie's fourth great aunt. Her younger sister married long ago but for some reason she was not betrothed. She wore no makeup, dressed modestly, and was slightly plump. She was under thirty. Her docile eyes were set on a long broad face, and her hair, with a hint of curls, sat in piles on her shoulders.

Nodding his head with a slightly embarrassed look, Ned greeted her as Second Younger Cousin. He then chatted with her parents while she took Julie by the hand and led her to sit down in an adjoining room.

There were many canopies on the bed in the large shabby room. The two sat on the edge of the bed as she asked Julie all sorts of questions about what she did besides study. "And you also learn to play the piano?" She sounded surprised, obviously impressed.

She held Julie's hand tightly and would not let go.

"Would I want her to be my stepmother?" Julie asked herself. "I don't know."

Julie wanted to tell her that Ned's women were all proverbial beauties and wily characters.

The woman obviously thought Julie's father liked her a lot and would be obedient to her.

Ned enjoyed proffering food to Julie, and always scraped out the duck brains just for her. When Ned paced around the room in circles, he would sometimes gently ruffle Julie's hair and call her "baldy"— *tutzu* in Chinese. Julie didn't like that because she had a lot of hair, unlike her cousin who had boils on her head every summer and had to have her head shaved clean. Years passed before Julie realized Ned was actually calling her *toots*.

It was hard to keep in mind that her parents were products of a transitional era. Although her mother was a modernist, Julie could never understand why it was taboo to say "bump into"; it always had to be I "encountered" so-and-so in the street. The word "delight" was also proscribed. The literary supplement in the *Daily News* called *Forest of Delight* caused her no end of anguish. Why couldn't it have been called *Happiness Forest*? She refused to say "happiness" because that sounded unnatural, so she just used the word "happy." After Julie read the folk novel *The Water Margin*, she realized that "delight" was a sexual term. "Do it" was without question taboo. So, too, on occasion, was the word "broken." And it wasn't just her mother; Judy also felt "broken" to be taboo and forbade any words or phrases that contained it, like "heartbroken" or "nervous breakdown." Looking back as an adult, Julie surmised it had something to do with despoiled maidenhood.

Ned subscribed to *Fortune* magazine. It often had illustrated advertising inserts for automobiles, and he was always acquiring new models. He purchased two items of office furniture made of steel: a desk and a file cabinet. He kept a paper punch on the desk, which he never touched. Julie used it to punch out holes in a piece of paper and then played with her filigree creation. When Ned saw this, he was momentarily startled. "Stop it!" he shouted angrily, snatching the paper punch from Julie, as if her tomfoolery were a personal affront.

A plaster statuette of Napoleon sat on Ned's desk. He spoke English with a stutter and knew a bit of German. He liked Schopenhauer. He purchased a translation of Hitler's *Mein Kampf*, as well as every book available about the situation in Europe. Although he didn't wear a Western-style suit, he did have a vest with a light gray satin back that he wore over his singlet.

Ned also subscribed to *Travel Magazine*. He never traveled—it would interfere with his opium smoking—but he did have a travel clock in a folding leather pocketbook sitting on the teapoy beside his bed.

Julie felt her father's adherence to old-fashioned customs was purely a matter of convenience for himself. For instance, he knew full well that hiring a tutor to teach Julian the classics at home was a professional dead end, but it was cheaper than sending him to a modern school. He said he wanted to wait a few years, with the excuse that a "solid foundation in the classics is essential." Rachel did not put up much of a fight for Julian in this regard, believing that Ned, at the very least, would not deprive his only son of an education.

The last time Rachel returned to China, the family relocated to Shanghai to wait for her, which was one of her conditions for returning. She felt it would be impossible to get divorced in the north, surrounded by the sphere of influence of Ned's cousins. Upon arriving in Shanghai, Ned took Julie to visit Rachel's younger brother. The brothers-in-law were on good terms. Yün-chih, with whom Ned had frequently gone out whoring back in the day, had just woken up and was reclining on the opium bed, satisfying his cravings. Opposite were two single iron-frame beds, upon one of which his wife sat wrapped in a quilt. Ned paced around the room. A cousin of Julie's took her downstairs to play, having dispatched her younger sister to rent some books and buy sweets on the street.

"Bring back thirty cents worth of cured duck gizzards and duck liver," her second elder sister called out from the living room.

"Where's the money?"

"Borrow some from Auntie Liu."

Standing askew in the middle of the living room was an altar table with a red embroidered skirt, dedicated to who knows what deity. The altar table was coated in dust and even the molten wax tears from the candles were dust-laden. The third sister passed by the altar, and hurriedly put her palms together and made a perfunctory nod of obeisance. A bronze chime lay beside the candle stand. Julie wanted to strike the chime for fun and her young cousin hesitantly passed her the clapper. Julie knew that striking the chime was not allowed so she only did it once. An old maidservant heard the chime and appeared immediately. She was blind and extremely short. Her small long face betrayed squinting eyes as she stood unsteadily on her bound feet. It was already the Republican era, but the woman still dressed in the late Ch'ing style—a faded light blue knee-length cotton blouse covered with patches over a pair of tight black trousers. Her bound feet were encased in hand-sewn cotton socks instead of machine-made "foreign" socks.

"I have come to pay obeisance, too," she said as she edged her way along the wall.

"This old maidservant is really wicked," said Julie's second cousin spitefully. "She's always stealing cigarettes!" she continued, as she opened a cigarette tin atop a teapoy to provide proof. "Do you think she really can't see?"

The old maidservant said nothing and continued to feel her way along the wall.

"Oh, all right. I'll guide you."

"Third Mistress is so kind!"

Julie's third cousin led the maidservant to kneel in front of the Alsatian curled up at the foot of the sofa. "She's kowtowing to the dog!" she squealed, jumping up and down, clapping her hands. "She's kowtowing to the dog! She's kowtowing to the dog!"

Yün-chih lived in fear of being kidnapped. He hired a retired detective inspector and kept an Alsatian.

The maidservant stood up and departed grumbling and muttering to herself.

The fourth cousin returned with a complete comic-book edition of the kung fu movie *The Burning of the Red Lotus Temple*, along with the cured duck entrails and cigarette-shaped candies. "The book rental stall said no credit next time."

They stretched out on the beds in the sisters' ground-floor bedroom to snack on their delicacies while they read. Cigarette-shaped candies made almost entirely of white sugar provided an aura of forbidden fruit as they sucked on the sticks they held between their little fingers. The room was freezing cold and they wrapped themselves up in a thick red floral-print cotton quilt. The sweat-laden bedding smelled a little fishy, and mixed with the aroma of cured poultry offal, created a peculiar sensation.

"Play with us a little longer. Stay here, don't go home. Fourth Sister, go upstairs to keep watch. When Uncle is ready to leave, come down and tell us so we have time to hide."

Julie did not want to leave but she couldn't imagine that she would be permitted to stay. When the fourth sister came back down with the news, the third sister grabbed Julie and they bounded upstairs two steps at a time, right up to the third floor where their father's concubine lived in a huge undivided room sparsely furnished with a large pink lacquered bed, a dresser, and a few other items.

"Ma'am, please let our cousin hide here. Uncle is about to leave," she said, dragging Julie behind a white fabric screen before bounding back downstairs.

Julie stood behind the screen for a long time, which in her nervous excitement felt even longer than it was. The concubine was very quiet and Julie could barely hear her clothes rustling. Modestly dressed in a simple lined jacket and trousers, she was scrawny and, apart from her wavy permed hair, looked like an old hag.

Finally someone came upstairs.

The concubine stood at the head of the stairs and called out her greeting: "Esteemed Brother-in-law."

As usual Ned was pacing in circles around the room that was fortunately extremely large. Julie imagined he would appear to be embarrassed to visit the concubine's quarters, but he actually was delighted by the opportunity to tour her love nest.

"Auntie Lee! Serve tea," she ordered the maidservant.

"No need. I'm about to leave. Where's Julie?" He continued to pace the room, smiling while calling "Come out! Come out!" with a hint of impatience.

In the end the concubine probably signaled to Ned with her lips. He went behind the screen and pulled Julie out. She giggled but did not resist.

They took a rickshaw home and Julie sat on Ned's lap. She was eight.

"Uncle's concubine is really unattractive—but his wife is so beautiful," said Julie.

Ned laughed. "Uncle's wife is stupid."

Julie was surprised an adult would say that to a child.

"Your maternal uncle is not stupid, he's just lazy."

From that moment on Julie believed what her father said because he did not have ulterior motives, unlike most adults who were always lecturing children and feared they would carelessly divulge secrets.

Ned read newspapers fastidiously and discussed topics of the day whenever he had visitors. Julie did not understand the conversations but did catch the names of the warlords Yen and Feng. Visitors rarely interrupted Ned, only putting up with his current affairs analyses to savor his opium.

Her father once let Julie give him a manicure. "Not bad. A little rounder would be better."

Julie was quite affected by the discovery that his long thin fingers were identical to her own.

Ned occasionally summoned Auntie Han to do his pedicure. Afterward, she would stand there chatting for a while, mostly about clan dictums of yore.

"In the time of Old Matriarch," she would usually begin.

Sometimes Ned would send Auntie Han down to the kitchen to make some dish the cook did not know how to make, like Hofei deep-fried glutinous rice and pork balls, or flaky pastry with ham-and-radish filling. At the Lunar New Year festival, she would always steam date cakes with crushed walnut filling—the cakes, made of a mixture of glutinous rice flour and date paste, were decorated with an auspicious pattern of clouds and bats and then placed on bamboo leaves.

"Auntie Han was a child bride adopted into the family. She was so timid that the slightest incident would scare her to death," Ned told Julie. Judy had said the same thing. Since childhood they had both loved to make light of Auntie Han being an adopted child bride.

Auntie Han never talked about being a child bride, or her mother-in-law, or her husband. She always spoke of a lone widow, a son, and a daughter, a sorry tale reminiscent of the impoverished widows in the Old Testament following behind the harvesters to scoop up the grains of wheat that had fallen on the ground.

"Nothing to eat at home, *jeang gao*? What to do? I borrow half a bushel of beans from my brother-in-law. Pleaded so hard the tears streamed down my face."

When Julie and Julian were small, Auntie Han would invariably say at mealtimes: "Don't waste your food, those *siatzu*" (she always said *siatzu*, the word for "children" in her Anhwei accent) "in the countryside don't have enough to eat." Otherwise it was: "Them *siatzu* have it rough! They bleated so hard I'd have to ladle out some water and steam up an egg just to calm 'em down."

Auntie Han often told rustic folktales: In the countryside, an autumn monster with white hair and red eyes lived in a tree and ate *siatzu*. Whenever she talked about the autumn monster, Auntie Han cackled like a crone, yet betrayed embarrassment because her own hair was white. Sometimes she'd say, "I'm so old, I've turned into an autumn monster," as if all autumn monsters once were old ladies.

Julie later read about the ancient Japanese and Eskimo custom of abandoning their old. *I wonder whether autumn monsters are old abandoned women. Men, of course, die earlier than women. Perhaps some really did shelter in trees, becoming inhuman monsters that ate children, as they're easier to catch than wild game.*

In her thirties, Auntie Han became a helper, leaving her children behind with her mother. "It was heartbreaking," she'd say, her eyes reddening.

When the male servant Teng Sheng returned from his rent-collecting trips to the countryside, Auntie Han would stand at the gate of the reception room and ask, "Mister Teng, what's going on in the countryside now?"

Teng Sheng and Auntie Han were from the same province and both had served under the late matriarch in the Sheng family. The leased land was also located in their hometown.

"Bandits, lots of bandits in the countryside these days."

"Oh, people are so wicked nowadays," she'd respond, perplexed.

Whenever her son, daughter, and granddaughter took turns coming to the city to find work, they all stayed at the Sheng residence for a while before returning. For a time, her son, Golden Boy, was employed through a recommendation of the Shengs. Back then he was a handsome man in his twenties. He had a glib tongue and played a tricky hand, but everything went wrong, and in the end Auntie Han came to the rescue. From that point on he was unable to get work— one false step brings everlasting grief—but he never gave up. He became terribly emaciated and looked as if the lower half of his face had eroded away. Each time he visited he'd stand with his hands at his side in front of Ned's opium bed listening to Ned explain that no one was doing well these days because of the depression.

"I beseech Second Master to lend a hand."

Julie saw him in the corridor outside the kitchen seated next to Auntie Han, separated by a small table, apparently in discussion, a worn-out middle-aged man pouting like a child.

Auntie Lee from the same district was washing dishes in the kitchen. "Golden Boy knows how to do the rattle-stick dance," she said to Julie. "Tell him to dance for you."

"Golden Boy did the rattle-stick dance for you once when you were small," said Auntie Han. "Do you remember?"

Golden Boy said nothing and did not look up to see who was there. There wasn't the slightest hint of a smile on his face. Julie thought he was jealous of her. She vaguely remembered his movements when performing the rattle-stick dance, vaulting over a bamboo cane instead of a spear sickle. A rattle stick probably represented a sickle with a long handle, Julie thought.

Golden Boy's elder sister had a long face and looked rather dull. Both brother and sister were emaciated and looked like they were made of desiccated meat, a kind of human jerky. Their suntanned skin was a shiny dark red. Where on earth did this red tribe come from?

Auntie Han called her daughter "Miss." The only place where Julie had seen that appellation so applied was in the risqué novel *The Plum in the Golden Vase*. She also called Julie "Miss," and to distinguish the two, her daughter became "our family's Miss." But occasionally, when Julie embraced Auntie Han warmly, she would say, "Indeed, she is my family's Miss."

Once, Auntie Han was about to visit the countryside. "I want to go too," Julie demanded. Julie was quite small at the time and did not persist, but she could see that her request unsettled Auntie Han, who feared she would not be able to be a generous host if Julie really joined her.

Auntie Han returned after two months, sunburnt all red and shiny. She brought back with her the local delicacies of purple-cloud shortbread and pumpkin cakes coated with sesame seeds for Julie to taste.

One day an honored guest visited. The servants whispered to each other in hushed tones: "His Excellency has arrived." Amongst all the relatives, only the Chu branch had one elder uncle who was widely referred to as His Excellency. Once bequeathed a hereditary rank by the former great Ch'ing dynasty, under which he had been an official, he had come out of retirement to take up an important post. Aunt Chu was his wife, but she brought up Brother Hsü in a different household, even though he was not her son. Julie had never met this uncle.

From the balcony that day Julie could hear the loud bombastic discourse coming from her father's sitting room, and surprisingly, they all spoke in the dialect of the Anhwei Province capital, Hofei. It was surprising because every member of the Chu clan, young or old, male or female, spoke perfect Pekinese. She caught a glimpse of His Excellency through the glass doors as he strolled slowly out onto the balcony. He was tall and thin, and was dressed in a much-worn black silk jacket-and-trousers set favored by laborers, rather than a formal gown. A grimy, gray sash was visible underneath his jacket. Perhaps his now pallid complexion was once handsome. His hair, parted in the middle, was fashionable for a time in the early Republican era and was held in place with so much grease that it resembled two large lumps of black medicinal paste stuck to his temples.

Julie later heard that His Excellency was in trouble. By the time she returned from school, the matter had slipped out of the headlines and there were just occasional follow-up stories that did not provide much detail: embezzlement of funds—the figure so astronomically enormous it made her dizzy, and therefore impossible for her to remember—followed by investigation, dismissal, prosecution.

Aunt Chu lived in a tiny Spanish-style house in an alleyway development. The upstairs was furnished with a suite of the white lacquered furniture that was fashionable in the early Republican era. She had many cats.

Brother Hsü, a university graduate who worked in a bank, lived in the small back room facing the landing. Julie always played with the cats whenever she visited. She liked it there because it did not seem like a strict household but rather like two children living in a play house, a little white house in a fairy tale with a big white cat. Julie was not surprised when her third aunt moved in and rented the third floor from them. Judy blocked off the top of the staircase with a screen door, which she latched to deny entry to the cats. Her floor felt like an apartment in itself, with a bathroom, a refrigerator, and a telephone. Judy often sat by the telephone and spent hours talking because, like Ned, she traded commodities and stocks.

Whenever Julie visited, Judy would give her a large pile of old English-language newspapers and let her sit on the carpet to cut out photos of movie stars.

"I am helping your uncle Chu with his court case," Judy said in a hushed voice.

Julie smiled. "Oh, really," she responded. *If you want to help someone, why don't you help Auntie Han's family. That wouldn't take anywhere near as much money.*

"Your grandmother adored that nephew, said he was really talented," Judy retorted defensively. "She said he was the only member of the family who resembled his grandfather."

Julie had overheard Judy and Ned talking about His Excellency. They also said he had "inherited fine traits from his ancestors." His grandfather had a son but also adopted a nephew, so he too adopted a nephew nicknamed Foster Boy who was born to a concubine. Julie also heard that countless people came to him for monthly payments and gifts.

"His Excellency ranks eighth in the Chu clan, right?" Judy asked Ned.

"Yeah."

Foster Boy fawned upon his adoptive father, and consequently grew very much in his favor, becoming more favored than his own son.

"That Foster Boy was thoroughly wicked," said Judy. "Aunt Chu loathed him."

"I read about Uncle Chu in the newspaper," Julie ventured. "What is that all about?"

"He was tricked by Meng Hsiao-yün. Meng was the one who dragged him into it, and when events took a bad turn, Meng piled everything onto Uncle Chu. That's why we say, 'If you have no one in the court to back you, don't become an official.' If you don't have a patron, you only have yourself to blame."

"Where is he now?"

"In a hospital," answered Judy hurriedly, lest she give the impression that he had already been arrested. "He's sick with hepatitis, seriously ill." After a moment of silence, she continued, "He's deep in debt."

She added, "I moved house to help save some money."

Julie ate dinner at Judy's and then went out on the balcony to enjoy the cool evening air. Someone came upstairs and knocked on the screen door. It was Brother Hsü.

The tiny balcony was so narrow that chairs were already pushing up against the iron railings, but another chair was added. They left the light off to avoid attracting mosquitoes.

"Have you eaten?" Judy asked amicably as she wrung out a hot towel for him.

Brother Hsü sighed, as though even this simple question did not have a simple answer. He accepted the towel and wiped down his face before sinking into the chair, apparently exhausted.

Brother Hsü was short. Ever since Julie had shot up a foot she avoided standing next to him so as not to cause embarrassment. But she enjoyed sitting like this in the dark, listening to them talking. They were the most worldly-wise adults in her life. Brother Hsü tittered as he told of the cold reception he had just received. Julie understood nothing of their discussion, which was all about raising funds. They spoke in hushed tones like people who had just set off on a long journey. Julie simply could not imagine how many years it would take to raise that enormous sum.

That afternoon Brother Hsü had also been to the hospital to visit Uncle Chu. As soon as he enunciated the word "father" it acquired a mistiness, yet it also evoked a hint of resentment. Whenever Julie saw Brother Hsü in Judy's apartment he rarely greeted Judy as "Aunt," and when he did, he did not smile. He always spoke with a slightly lower than normal voice, as if he were a little sad. Brother Hsü did not bear any likeness to his father. His long, dark face framed a small protruding nose. The only real connection between the two was that everyone called him Young Master, the suitable appellation for His Excellency's son.

The discussion on the balcony suddenly turned to pondering the question: Does platonic love exist?

"Yes," said Julie, injecting herself into the conversation for the first time.

"And how do you know that?" scoffed Judy.

"Third Aunt and Brother Hsü are an example."

The conversation came to an abrupt halt. Then Judy changed the subject and began to ask him about the day's events.

Julie regretted saying that to their faces and embarrassing them.

"We are suing my elder brother over the inheritance," Judy told Julie one day.

"Wasn't the inheritance settled long ago?"

"We were in a hurry to move so it wasn't divided up fairly. Actually, all the money belonged to your paternal grandmother—it was her dowry."

"Is it still possible to prove it?"

"Yes."

Julie then wondered how Judy could be involved in two court cases at the same time. She couldn't imagine that the second case was related to the first case, as a way to raise funds to rescue Uncle Chu.

"Your second uncle is getting married," Judy told her. "The eleventh daughter of the Keng family—Seventh Aunt's family made the introduction."

Of course, Judy did not reveal that the eleventh daughter of the Keng family once had a love affair with a cousin. They had become intimate, but when her family objected because he was impecunious, the lovers made a suicide pact to take poison together. At the last moment, her cousin backed out and notified the family to take her home from the hotel. After the whole story came out, her father, who had been an important official in the late Ch'ing and early Republican era, wanted to force her to commit suicide. He relented after much persuasion, but from that time on she was tarnished in the eyes of the family and rarely had contact with the outside world. Her father lived into his eighties and for years she smoked opium to relieve her boredom, which of course made it even harder to marry her off.

Ned was introduced to the eleventh daughter. After they had played mah-jongg a few times, Ned said to Judy, "I know about her past, but I don't mind. I myself am not lily-white."

"I have helped a great deal with your second uncle's wedding," said Judy, "purchasing two suites of furniture for him. They were on sale for a very good price. I have to communicate with him about the inheritance." Judy needed to offer an explanation. Otherwise, she would have appeared disloyal to Rachel.

Judy tried hard to curry favor with Jade Flower, calling her "Eleventh Sister." In reciprocation, Jade Flower called Judy "Third Sister." When they chatted they realized they were kith and kin. Ned called Jade Flower "Eleventh Younger Sister" but he found it embarrassing and rarely made *that* salutation in public.

The two female cousins who made the match insisted that Julie and Julian call Jade Flower "mother."

"When you call Ned 'Second Uncle,'" said Judy behind Ned's back to Julie, "it actually makes their marriage sound like a younger brother marrying the elder brother's widow."

In addition to busying herself with two court cases and helping Ned with his wedding, Judy also had to take Julie to see a doctor. While Julie appeared to have no trouble with her father marrying a stepmother, she was in fact very distressed, so much so that she contracted a lung disease and a lump appeared under the skin of her armpit that moved to the touch. Julie took medicine for two years before it fully subsided.

On the wedding day Aunt Chu participated in "teasing the bride." "This bride is too old, she's no fun," Aunt Chu complained to Judy when she came out of the bridal chamber. "So pompous and conceited—she just offered candies and melon seeds. Ned actually was up for some real fun."

The female cousins of the Pien clan waited to see the new bride, and informers kept watch in the lane. Ned complained that Julian had adopted bad habits from the Piens, who were all, in his words, "alleyway surveillance commissioners."

"We saw your mother," the cousins later told Julie. "Nothing much to look at, if you ask me," one of them said. "Really quite old."

The morning after the wedding Julie went downstairs to the living room. Everything seemed the same as it had been when she was small—the vermillion phoenix–motif carpet, the familiar faint trace of dust mixed with the fragrance of flowers. There were two new pots of flowers. In preparation for the guests, four kinds of confectioneries and snacks were arranged on the table. Julie sat down and ate some, though it felt as if she were taking a bribe.

Julian came in and saw the treats in blue cellophane wrappers on the table. He ogled them for a moment, then sat down and began to stuff his face too. Brother and sister did not speak as they devoured an entire plate of chocolate-coated peanut candies. A maidservant, who had accompanied the bride to the groom's household, noticed and without saying anything opened the jar to take out another couple of handfuls of candy, encouraging them to eat. The two smiled and turned to leave.

It was rather awkward for the newlyweds to live near Ned's former in-laws—gossiping and scrutinizing would be inevitable as they walked around the same neighborhood every day. They moved to a large foreign-style bungalow in a depreciated area with cheaper rent. After a meal, Jade Flower went onto the balcony to look out over the neglected tennis court in the garden. Julie followed her, then Ned wandered out slowly. The strong wind blew against Jade Flower's faded silk gown with thin lilac stripes, revealing her dainty waist and bony hips. Her glossy hair was tied back in a bun. In the sunlight, her long rectangular face with a pair of almost rectangular eyes looked particularly pale.

"Goodness, you two are very similar," joked Ned. He sounded a little embarrassed by his comment that seemed to suggest the marriage was fated by heaven, for even his former wife's daughter resembled Jade Flower.

But Jade Flower was not amused. She laughed coldly and responded with only a faint smile and a grunt.

Perhaps we do look a little similar on a first impression. Hard to say for sure.

One of Julie's classmates wrote poetry in classical forms and this year's theme was the mid-autumn moon.

> Beyond the pass three provinces suddenly lost
> The country, like the moon, wanes for all to see

The Chinese-language instructors heartily approved and circulated the poem throughout the school. When Julie went home for the end-of-month break, she jokingly asked her father, "Why hasn't the fighting started?" She felt a little guilty because she had merely overheard people talking.

"Fighting?" said Ned brusquely. "Fight with what?"

Another time, when she came home from school, Julian reported, "Fifth Uncle has gone to Manchukuo to be an official."

This uncle from the Sheng clan was a frequent visitor. The match between Jade Flower and Ned was made by his two younger sisters. He was also an opium smoker, and many people praised his mastery of Chinese painting. A large man with a dark horse-face on which sat a pair of tortoiseshell-framed spectacles, he spoke quietly with a gentle voice. He was fond of Julie and often caressed her bare arms, longingly burbling, "Little darling."

"Fifth Uncle has gone to Manchukuo?" Julie asked her father.

"What else can he do?" Ned spluttered angrily.

Julie did not know that the source of this outburst stemmed from Fifth Uncle always visiting to borrow money. He had been a section chief in the Peiyang warlord government that was established in 1912, but after the Republican government's Northern Expedition put an end to the Peiyang regime in the late 1920s, he relied on his two sisters. He had sent his wife back to the old family home but still maintained a concubine's household and numerous children.

Julie had also observed him caressing Judy's arm, and he borrowed money from her too.

"I don't like Fifth Uncle," Julie said to Judy one day.

"It's strange," replied Judy inattentively, "that you don't like Fifth Uncle. He's very fond of you."

"Fifth Uncle is just a cranky old scholar," Aunt Chu chimed in from the sidelines.

One day Ned was in a good mood and inscribed one of Julie's round silk fans with the words she read as "Meng the Beautiful." Julie already had a rather masculine name, so she was very happy with this feminine-sounding name, completely unaware that it was intended to communicate that her father anticipated more daughters. It also could mean "Dreaming of Daughters." Most people feel that having only one son is cause for apprehension, whereas one daughter is more than enough. Ned, however, was clearly preparing for many more children. Otherwise, why would a family of four live in such a large house.

"Second Uncle gave me the name 'Meng the Beautiful,'" Julie told Judy.

"How utterly common," Judy sneered, frowning bemusedly.

"Oh?"

"Your second aunt has more than one hundred names."

Julie had seen one or two of the names Rachel used in old bank passbooks—Shu-mei, meaning Rime Plum, and Chin-lan, meaning Beguiling Orchid—although she only used one English name and when signing letters, she simply wrote Chel.

"Write a letter to your second aunt," Judy urged with a smile. She constantly pressed Julie, who would finally, under duress, sit at Judy's desk with a guilty smile and pick up her pen. But she could never think of anything to write beyond, "I'm diligently practicing piano" or "It's the winter holidays again." Mentioning anything else would result in a scolding. Rachel's writing style in her letters mirrored her personality. But even in movies "ideology" has to be delivered through pretty actresses. Without the physical attributes present, whatever Rachel's message was, it ended up being nothing more than preaching empty words.

That day, Julie drank tea as she struggled to write a letter to her mother. A drop of tea fell onto the letter and the black ink spread into a blurry splotch.

When Judy saw it she laughed. "Second Aunt will think it's a tear." Julie was mortified. "I'll copy it out again."

Judy took the letter and read it. All the words were clear. "It will do. No need to copy it out again."

Julie smiled sheepishly. "It would be better to copy it out again," she insisted. "I don't mind."

Judy realized her little joke was the root of all this and became annoyed. "It's fine!" she snapped. "No need to rewrite it."

Julie still hesitated, but knowing Judy was in straitened circumstances and could not bring herself to despoil another sheet of fine writing paper, she didn't push it.

During the winter, the only heater lit in the whole house was kept in the living room where Ned and Jade Flower smoked opium. One day at lunchtime, Jade Flower descended the stairs, holding a hot-water bottle with a brocade cover. Ned finished eating first, then, as was his habit, paced around the room. When he came up behind Jade Flower, he suddenly grabbed the hot-water bottle and pressed it on the back of her neck. "I'll scald you to death! I'm going to scald you to death!" he gleefully cried out.

"Stop it," she chortled, turning her head to dodge him.

Another day, in the afternoon, Julie went to their living room to read newspapers and saw Julian reclining on the opium bed, snuggled up close behind Jade Flower. He was still quite small, like a cat. He looked so content, as if he had finally found a safe haven. Julie was stunned. *Since when did Meng Kuang accept Liang Hong's tray?* An allegory from her favorite novel *The Story of the Stone* flashed through her mind. *When did they of all people become such a perfect family? The three of them there on the opium bed are the very picture of a blissful family, as though they were meant to be like that. It's obvious there is no place for me here.*

Judy gave Julie a large doll, as heavy as a real baby, wearing a boy's hat, shorts, and pants of light-blue knitted wool. She also knitted a set of clothes in light green. Julie imagined Judy wanted her own child, one that looked exactly like the doll.

"Lend me your doll so I can put it on display," Jade Flower requested with a smile.

Julie immediately brought the doll to Jade Flower, along with the extra change of clothes. Jade Flower set the doll on the opium bed.

"Your mother surely does want a child of her own," sneered Judy when Julie told her.

Julie never actually liked the doll, but walking past it there on the opium bed with its arms outstretched gave her a creepy feeling. "Go ahead and cast your evil spells," she silently told the doll.

Ned and Judy's litigation with their eldest brother dragged on for a long time and the costs were becoming ruinous. Jade Flower stepped into the fray to mediate. "There are just three of you but I have twenty or thirty brothers and sisters, and we all get along very well." The siblings descended from Jade Flower's mother frequently stayed at the Shengs' house. Her mother, an old concubine, soon brought her two youngest children to stay with her. Julie and Julian called her Good Grannie.

Judy refused to settle out of court and her elder brother stood firm too. "When she dies," he bellowed, slapping his hand on the table, "you can come to me for money to buy her coffin. Otherwise, there won't be a penny for her."

Jade Flower was frugal with the household expenses. She dismissed Auntie Lee, saying Julie was rarely home and Julian was already a big boy, so Auntie Han could keep an eye on him as well as do the laundry. In fact, although Julie was a boarder, Auntie Han still had to deliver snacks to her every week and bring back her dirty clothes to wash.

The pay for maidservants at that time was three Chinese dollars a month, at most five dollars. But the Sheng family had always been paying Auntie Han ten dollars because she was a favorite of the late matriarch. Now her pay was reduced by half to five dollars, but Auntie Han, as ever, tried her best to please her new mistress. Whenever

Auntie Han was called upon while serving at the table she always responded with a heartfelt, felicitous, "Ma'am."

Auntie Han had shrunk with age. Standing short and squat, her wrinkled face widening, she resembled a large crouching dog, obediently looking up to Jade Flower, especially alert because she was hard of hearing and tried to make up for that deficiency with her eyes.

Auntie Han was forever urging Julie to "Go in," referring to the room where her father smoked opium.

Now Auntie Han never uttered her customary opening line: "In the time of Old Matriarch. . . ." That would sound like she was complaining.

Julie returned home from boarding school and saw that Julian had shot up overnight. He swaggered around the house, his lanky frame clothed in a brand-new full-length blue cotton gown, which made him appear bloated. He became extremely volatile, no one knowing when he would next erupt.

"He was fine a minute ago," Good Grannie complained under her breath to a maidservant. "This child. . . . He doesn't come when you call him. Almost as if he has something to hide." Then she added, "It's even embarrassing for us relatives."

Ned liked to call his son using his full name for humorous effect. "Julian Sheng! Fetch that letter for me!" Julian would acknowledge the command, then with great alacrity remove a long Western-style envelope from inside the desk drawer and pass it to his father.

Once, by chance, Julie saw Julian practicing his own signature on a voided check. Jade Flower was sitting on the opium divan and whispered something in Ned's ear. Her big eyes betrayed a mischievous smile. Ned suddenly sprang up and cuffed Julian hard on the ear.

On another occasion Julian was again summoned but refused to go. Auntie Han and two maidservants pushed and shoved but he lay sprawled out on the floor firmly holding on to the doorframe.

"Agh," Auntie Han grunted disapprovingly.

His punishment, known as "brick-and-incense kneeling," was to kneel on two bricks in the garden for the time it took a stick of incense to burn. Julie was by herself on the ground floor but she did not glance once into the garden. She was angry with her brother for having fallen into Jade Flower's trap of making concessions for future gains, and then being such a coward. When he came back inside she ignored him. Suddenly he glared at Julie, and tears welled up in his eyes.

Even the male servant Teng Sheng was disgusted. "He's only got one son and he beats him every day like a slave girl," he railed loudly in the reception room at the gatehouse. Ned did nothing at the time, but after a short interval sent him off indefinitely to the country estate. The old man eventually died in the countryside.

Julie often lay reading in a large gloomy room with just a few rays of sunlight streaking through the angled-slats of the jalousie windows. She fantasized about ways to become rich so she could rescue Julian and Auntie Han. From the laundry room on the other side of the wall, Julie could hear the repetitive sound of Auntie Han pounding the sheets vigorously on the washboard in the concrete tub.

From time to time Judy visited for the sake of maintaining cordial relations with Ned's family. On one such occasion, she wore a beige velvet coat with muskrat-fur trim around the bell-shaped bottom to flaunt her beautiful long legs. "At least your third aunt has good legs," Julie remember Rachel often saying. A little plumper than Marlene Dietrich, not bony, and quite straight. Judy would usually say a few perfunctory words mocking Auntie Han's Hofei dialect, "Ah, Auntie Han. Are you fine? I'm good, oh." Then a customary little snort of indifference followed. And yet one day Judy said to Julie, "It just occurred to me that Auntie Han watched us grow up, too. Why is she so different toward you?"

"Perhaps," replied Julie, unable to think of anything else to say, "old people tend to show more affection toward their grandchildren than toward their children."

Jade Flower brought Julie bundles of hand-me-downs from her family home. Cotton gowns with frayed collars, more gowns than Julie could ever hope to wear, gowns that seemed awfully out of place in her exclusive private girls' school. Julie yearned for a school uniform, but her wish was never fulfilled.

"I'll have some new clothes made for you when you turn eighteen," Judy promised.

To Julie that eighteenth birthday seemed so incredibly remote, an unseeable existence beyond a gigantic, impassable mountain.

"I promised your second aunt I would look after you," said Judy on one occasion. She did not want Julie to feel like she owed her anything.

"We lost the court case," Judy told her in a rather lighthearted tone.

"How did that happen?" asked Julie in a low voice, perplexed.

"They bribed the judge. We bribed the judge, too . . . but they had more money."

Judy did not reveal to Julie that another reason for the defeat was that Ned changed sides and came to a private arrangement with their eldest brother.

"They say my brother has been stealing," Julie told Judy.

"What did he steal?"

"Money."

There was a momentary silence before Judy responded. "When children see small change laying around, it's quite normal for them to take it. But when the Keng clan gets wind of something like that, it then becomes stealing."

The school yearbook planned to publish a photograph of every graduating student the following year. Julie had a photograph taken with her short hair tucked behind her ears. She looked like a little chick. Jade Flower saw that Julie seemed despondent. "You look like that because you haven't permed your hair," Jade Flower said, smiling. "Do you want to get a perm?"

"Mother asked if I want to have a perm," Julie told Judy.

"She just wants to marry you off," chortled Judy.

Julie became wary.

Cousin Lü, an impoverished member of the Keng clan, a distant nephew of Jade Flower's, was a frequent visitor because he accompanied Ned to the stock exchange to learn the ropes. Every classical description of a handsome man applied to Cousin Lü: His "complexion as lustrous as a jade ornament" with "lips like painted vermillion" and "upturned eyebrows as straight as swords above piercing bright eyes," "handsome as a jade tree facing the wind." He wore a dark blue silk gown when he entered Julie's room. After they exchanged greetings, he sat down and didn't say another word as he flipped through a novel on Julie's desk.

To end the awkward silence, Julie asked him if he had read the novel and what films he had seen. Each time she asked a question, he paused, smiled, then shook his head. She ran out of topics; he lowered his head and noisily turned the pages. After lingering for a while, he finally stood up and announced, "Cousin, you are studying, I will not disturb you anymore."

"That Cousin Lü is so annoying!" squawked one of the Keng cousins. "As Sixth Sister tells it, he also goes over to their place, sits down for ages, and doesn't say anything. Sixth Sister says it's maddeningly annoying." The speaker was a member of the wealthy branch of the Keng clan that had two fashionable girls in their twenties. There were so many people in Cousin Lü's branch of the Keng clan and none of them had any money so he never visited *them* and sat quietly.

At first Julie thought the comment made by the cousin from the Keng family was just sour grapes, but when she heard that Cousin Lü had behaved the same toward the two daughters in Sixth Sister's family, Julie felt somewhat at a loss. Soon afterward, Julian told her of Cousin Lü's marriage to a bank manager's daughter. Later, when Julian reported that as soon as Cousin Lü rose from poverty and made a bit of money he acquired a paunch and a taste for dancing girls, Julie felt slightly relieved.

Julian was particularly interested in Cousin Lü's career. Unlike Julie, he was in a big hurry to grow up. One of Jade Flower's younger brothers gave Julian an old shirt and a pair of khaki trousers, which along with a stained necktie that Judy had given him as a child completed the outfit. He looked quite presentable and could often be found lingering in front of the bathroom mirror moistening his hairbrush under a faucet to coax a towering bouffant. Once, when

Julian was twelve, Julie went with him in the family automobile to a movie. It was just the two of them and after the show they went to Welcome Café for ice cream, but Julian ordered beer instead.

"Eldest Uncle died," Julian told Julie when she returned home for the school holidays. "I heard he starved to death."

"He was so rich," said Julie, astonished. "How could he have starved?"

"Because of his illness, his doctors prohibited almost everything he wanted to eat. He was famished and somehow managed to run away to stay with his concubine. She later said, 'I was afraid to feed him because then people would say I did him in,' so he still got nothing to eat. That's why everyone says he starved to death."

Julie was aware that there were strict requirements to avoid certain foods when taking Western medicine, which Chinese people sometimes did not understand, so the relatives assumed he died from starvation. In any event, they all preferred to think that was the true cause of death.

"Someone from Auntie Han's hometown says Golden Boy buried his maternal grandmother alive," Julian continued casually. "Golden Boy was constantly badgering his ninety-year-old grandmother to hurry up and die. One day he lost his temper and stuffed her in her coffin. She clutched the rim of the coffin and he pried her fingers off one by one and pushed them back inside."

Julie was dumbstruck and could not believe it, as if she couldn't hear what Julian had said. "What did Auntie Han say?"

"Of course Auntie Han denied it. She said her mother was indeed very old and had died suddenly without any sign of illness, and that sparked all sorts of rumors."

"Young Master!" a maidservant in Jade Flower's entourage yelled down the staircase. "Old Master is calling for you!"

"Coming," Julian responded loudly. He rarely raised his voice and it sounded unnatural through his tightened vocal cords, yet he calmly and nimbly ascended the stairs.

That day Auntie Han did not raise the matter of her mother's death and Julie did not ask about it.

"I saw an old beggar on the street today," Auntie Han suddenly said to Julie that night. "I gave him twenty cents." Tears welled in her eyes. "Old people are so pitiful," she continued, almost crying. "Auntie Han is going to end up a beggar."

"How is that possible?" said Julie cheerfully. "It *won't* happen." Julie couldn't think of any other words to comfort her. Auntie Han said nothing.

"How could something like that happen?" Julie tried again, painfully aware that her reassurances rang hollow.

Auntie Han sat down under a lamp next to Julie to take a little nap. Julie sketched a pencil portrait. Although Auntie Han's silver hair was thinning to reveal a shining crown, her features still looked delicate as she sat there with her eyes half closed.

"Auntie Han, look at my drawing of you."

Auntie Han examined it for a while, then said, full of mirth, "*So* ugly!"

Julie recalled her childhood attempts to force her cat to look in the mirror. The cat always turned its head in loathing, perhaps because it thought the mirror too cold.

Initially Jade Flower had no idea how much work it took to maintain a tennis court, nor the expense. She had told Julie she could invite her classmates to come over to play tennis. But the court was never repaired, and Julian reverted to hitting tennis balls against a brick wall as before, using an old racket Judy had given him.

Jade Flower read in a newspaper literary supplement that raising geese was a fine domestic venture and decided to try her hand in the sprawling garden. She bought two mature geese but they never managed to produce any goslings. She and Ned often stood by the window watching the geese waddle around the garden, never voicing their suspicions that they had purchased two ganders or possibly two female geese, afraid of the taboo suggestion that in this household even the geese were barren.

"Your second aunt is returning," Judy announced one day to Julie in a subdued voice, without the slightest trace of a smile on her face.

Julie heard this with a heavy heart. She had felt a premonition.

Good Grannie bore no resemblance to her daughter—melon-faced, squat, dressed in a powder-blue Indian silk gown draped over a pro-truding belly. Even Jade Flower frequently vented under her breath like a spoiled child: "That's just the way Mother is!" Embarrassed at hearing that, Good Grannie would then wander out of the living room mumbling to herself.

One day Good Grannie was standing at the top of the stairs. "I'll make some pumpkin cakes," she yelled. "It's time for a jolly!" Only the mother of a village girl like Chang Chin-feng, the heroine in the popular late Ch'ing dynasty novel *The Legend of Heroes and Heroines*, ever used rustic language from the north like that. Good Grannie then went down to the kitchen to fry up a large stack of cakes made of mashed pumpkin and flour. Though not particularly tasty, they were infused with a sentimental flavor.

"When we were little, it was the time of the Boxer Rebellion," she regaled the family. "It certainly scared us to death. We were in Peking then, and we grasped onto the palisades to watch. Oh, how we watched those Boxers." The modest family she was born into relied on cartage fees from their large wagons for income.

She had traveled overseas with Jade Flower's father as the ambas-sadorial consort and had even managed to recite the German alpha-bet: *Ah, bey, czey, dei*. "When guests came to the embassy, the foreign woman all had bare arms and wore strings of pearls and necklaces of precious jewels, and they held each other close and danced. Danced! We crowded around a small window upstairs to watch."

Her daughter- and son-in-law had recently been discussing a new historical novel set in the late Ch'ing dynasty called *Records of a Still Night* in which the courtesan Sai Chin-hwa married into a decent family and became an ambassador's consort. All this talk had clearly triggered the reminiscences about her own experiences.

Julie also read *Records of a Still Night*. She had heard that her grandfather appeared in it but became frustrated when she couldn't figure out which of the historical characters portrayed in the novel represented him. Was it the one who lost his official position because of a flower-boat sing-song girl, or was it another who had a romance with an actor?

"What was Grandfather's name?" she asked Julian. "What were the two characters of his given name?"

Julian wrote them down for her. She had no idea how Julian had come to know their grandfather's name. Ned had never mentioned his father to his two children. Occasionally, when there were guests, he would grandly refer to "our late patriarch," but of course never articulated a name. Judy was even less likely to speak of such matters, as she, like Rachel, considered everything about him to be undemocratic.

Julie raced through the novel and was both astonished and delighted to read this fantastic story about her grandfather. At the time of his greatest misfortune, the patriarch's political adversary, bearing no old grudges, hired him as an adviser and gave him his daughter in marriage.

Ned paced the room as he expounded to Jade Flower, who was reclining on the opium bed, that "our patriarch" could not possibly have encountered a beauty like the daughter of his employer in the magistracy, implying that all the stories in the novel were fabricated. Jade Flower smiled and acknowledged with the occasional "Yes, yes."

"Tell me about my paternal grandmother," said Julie to Auntie Han, aware that her maid had not met her grandfather.

Auntie Han thought for a moment. "Old Matriarch was so very frugal, very frugal. Even frugal with toilet paper."

Julie found that a little jarring, but she could well imagine that, like her own father, her grandmother lived in constant fear: they lived a life of endless expenses but no income.

"Your third aunt wore boy's clothes as a child but Second Master was forced to wear girl's clothes. Even when he was a teenager, he still wore floral shoes with elaborate embroidered binding that no one wanted to wear anymore. When he went out, Second Master would carry a bundle under his arm." Auntie Han tilted her head with one shoulder higher than the other, imitating the way Ned hid the package under his arm. "He'd slip out to furtively change his shoes under the eaves before reaching the second gate. When we saw that from upstairs, we all had a good laugh." Auntie Han giggled as she told her story, nervous that Old Matriarch might hear from the grave.

"When Second Master learned books by rote Old Matriarch would beat him hard. Still, Old Matriarch praised me, said I was meticulous. She'd say 'Old Han is patient.'"

When Julie was small, Auntie Han used to comb her hair and often asked if it hurt. "In the past, Old Matriarch said I was very gentle," Auntie Han would often say.

Auntie Han was a late addition to the ranks of the maidservants, but the old lady ended up trusting her the most.

Julie also asked Third Aunt about her grandmother. Judy did not remember her own father because she was very young when he died.

Judy also read *Records of a Still Night*. "Those poems of your grandmother's are all plagiarized," said Judy. "All those poems she was purported to have written in reply to your grandfather are actually his work. She had only written one poem and it was her favorite:

> By the morrow I'll have passed my fortieth birthday,
> Though I remain ensnared in a cobweb as prey
> Squandered years have ruined my youthful glamour
> While my family has forfeited its prestige and power

"Think about it, in those days forty was already old. Your grandmother was only in her forties when she died, and we're already in our thirties.

"Your grandmother had fair skin and I loved all the red spots on her body. Actually, those little red spots that I liked to touch were burst capillaries.

"Your eldest uncle was terrified of your grandmother. She was always scolding him."

After she died, thought Julie, he embezzled the assets of his two orphaned siblings in revenge.

"Auntie Han said Second Uncle wore floral shoes in his teens. He couldn't possibly wear them to go out, so he carried a pair to change into.

"It's true that they all said your grandmother became cantankerous later in life and refused to meet with people. And she deliberately wanted her son to be shy because she wanted him to be afraid of people since she was concerned they'd teach him bad habits." Judy fell silent, then continued, "Think about it from her point of view. She was married to a man so many years older than herself, even his son was older than her. She probably did not appreciate your grandfather, as much as her father. Of course in the old days people trusted their fathers. . . ."

Julie did not want to think that way. "Wasn't it said they got on extremely well?"

"Of course everyone had to say it was a perfect match of talent and beauty."

Judy found a photograph of her mother at the age of eighteen. It was taken on a summer day. The oval-faced, willowy young girl was covered in loose-fitting light silk and satin. A horizontal V-shape part divided her hair down the middle. Under well-formed brows, her bright eyes betrayed a hint of a suppressed smile. *Was she amused by the foreign photographer, with his head hidden under a black cloth?*

It occurred to Julie that Miss Purity and Miss Grace, who were Old Matriarch's grandnieces, bore a slight resemblance to her. Judy and Rachel both agreed that the two sisters had a "predilection for deriding people." They were quick to look down on others. Julie thought her grandmother probably felt miserable about her marriage. She looked much older than her age in a portrait photo they took together. Her face was plumper, almost unrecognizable, despite the same horizontal V-shape part still dividing her hair down the middle. That was only a few years into their marriage. The time they spent together was just over a decade in total. They lived in a Garden of Eden, the large garden that they had built for themselves.

It seemed to Julie that the relationship between her great-grandfather and his son-in-law was more romantic than his relationship with her great-grandmother—so typically Chinese.

"Your grandfather had liver disease," said Judy. "He drank too much."

His father-in-law, whom he revered as "the Munificent One," did his utmost to make the right introductions, but to no avail. He died in his fifties.

"Why are you so interested in all this?" Judy suddenly asked. "Our generation has turned its back on that stuff, and your generation should be even more forward-looking."

"It's simply because I read about them by chance in a novel," said Julie.

Julie loved her ancestors. They never interfered with her life; they just lay quietly entombed in her blood, and when she died they too would die again.

Rachel read *Records of a Still Night* the moment she returned to China. Julie never once mentioned the book to Rachel. She knew her mother hated her in-laws, especially her mother-in-law, whom she had never met.

After Rachel returned, Julie did not see her mother until the monthly school break, by which time Rachel had already moved into an apartment with Judy. The first time Julie visited, Rachel was in bed and appeared to have just been crying, her voice still hoarse. Julie went again the next day. Rachel was in the bathroom and Judy stood by the bathroom door sobbing as she faced the cabinet opposite the door with one hand pulling on a drawer. She was wearing a check-patterned silk gown that hugged the delicate contours of her stomach as it heaved following a spasm of broken sobs. She saw Julie arrive and walked away.

Jade Peach came, and she too stood in the bathroom doorway weeping. When Rachel was about to leave for her previous trip overseas, Jade Peach was already seventeen or eighteen years old. Her true age was unknown because she had been purchased as a child. To avoid leaving unfinished business behind, Rachel wanted to find Jade Peach a husband before she left. The young male servant Yü-heng did not have a wife. He was older than Jade Peach, but the two of them had grown up together from childhood and both of them were agreeable to the match. Rachel married Jade Peach off to Yü-heng and gave her some money for a dowry. After the marriage the couple operated a small storefront business but it lost money. All of Jade Peach's dowry was lost. To make matters worse, the mother-in-law resented that

Jade Peach was barren and there was much quarreling at home. Yü-heng went off to Chen-kiang to find work and never returned. People said he had someone else there. Jade Peach now worked as a maid in Shanghai and for a while had worked for Judy. She was quite pretty with a round yet clear-featured face and dark skin, though her frame was as large as a wooden door and, being dark-skinned, she looked as intimidating as a burly man.

When Julie arrived, she too leaned on the wall by the bathroom door to report on family affairs. Rachel only had time to talk to Julie while she put on her makeup in the bathroom; it was the middle of the afternoon.

"Didn't you say everything was going just wonderfully?" Rachel sneered sarcastically while brushing her hair. "And you get along well with your third aunt, and you take Julian out all over the place, and you always have a wonderful time."

Julie was surprised that her mother appeared even more beautiful than before, perhaps because popular tastes had changed in recent years. Especially with her hair down, and before applying light pink powder paste from a bottle, her refined face looked like a sculptured brass bust. Rachel always leaned forward as she talked, now pressing up against the washbasin and exposing her dainty back to her inter-locutors as she gazed into the mirror.

When Julie returned home later that day she declared to Ned right in front of Jade Flower, "Third Aunt says she hasn't seen my younger brother for a long time and asked me to bring him along with me tomorrow."

"Hmm," Ned acknowledged.

Of course Ned and his new wife had heard long ago that Rachel had returned.

Rachel prepared tea and cakes, while Judy went out to leave the three of them to chat.

"Julian, what *is* the matter with your teeth?"

He did not answer. Julie also noticed that his teeth were very small, like the ridges on a washboard, and actually looked like saw teeth covered with a green film. Julie thought it was caused by malnutrition, as he always seemed to have a poor appetite at the dinner table.

Once Julie walked into the dining room to see him sitting alone with his head resting on the copper rim of the leather-covered tabletop.

"What's the matter?"

"I feel giddy." He raised his head and scowled. "The smell of opium smoke makes me nauseous."

Julie gave an incredulous gasp, unable to hide her astonishment. *We've been used to smelling that since childhood, and you've even been cozying up like a cat next to them. And now you've suddenly become all shy and delicate.*

Rachel lectured him about nutrition and then, by way of encouragement, pronounced Julian sufficiently tall, that he just needed to fill out. In the end, she told him to have a chest X-ray at a hospital, where he could tell them that Miss Pien had made prior arrangements for the bill to be sent to her. Julie worried that this plan was precarious because the hospital would have no idea what was going on, and her brother would certainly be too embarrassed to explain. And saying that Miss Such-and-such would pay the fees suggested that he was depending on an older girlfriend for his living expenses.

Julian left first, while Julie was to return directly to the school before dinner. Rachel went to wash her face again and Julie stood by the bathroom door wiping her tears. "I want to … to get him to learn horseback riding."

"No hurry." Rachel chuckled. "First get him into school. Who ever heard of such a big boy not yet in school?"

Rachel brushed Julie's bangs into a Charleston-era style parted on one side, but it did not hold for long and collapsed before she arrived at school. Her coiffure was too precious to touch so she just let it sway in front of her eyes, gentle as a breeze.

"Dumb hair, dumb brains," sneered a classmate at the dinner table. All smiles, Julie quickly smoothed her hair back with her fingers.

After Ned's betrayal in the inheritance litigation, Judy had nothing more to do with her brother. Just at this time, Fifth Uncle from the Sheng clan returned, and under his auspices it was suggested to Ned that Julian go to school and Julie be sent overseas. Things had not worked out well in Manchukuo for Fifth Uncle. He had married a sixteen-year-old girl from a traveling theatrical troupe, claiming he pitied her wandering life in Manchuria. So now there were again two households, and his two younger sisters who had been supporting him were extremely displeased.

Another day when no one was in the dining room, Julian came up to Julie. "So you're going to England?" he asked, eyes wide with curiosity.

"I don't know if I'll be able to go," Julie replied.

"I expect that you will not have any problems going," he said. To Julie, her brother sounded like a statesman.

Julie had always believed that one day she would go overseas just like Rachel and Judy, but as she grew older it felt was less certain.

"He promised, it's part of the divorce settlement," said Rachel.

That was when Ned still loved Rachel, thought Julie. It would take another court case to get him to fulfill his already settled obligations. Yet Rachel still had Ned under her spell; every time Julie told him she was going to visit "Third Aunt" he always acquiesced in a soft voice without showing any emotion on his face.

"Your second uncle has plenty of money," said Rachel.

Julie had her doubts; she was keenly aware of Ned's fears.

Ned never said that he didn't have the money to send Julie overseas. Instead he just said, "She can't manage for a day without Auntie Han, let alone traveling overseas by herself when a war is about to start— that's just looking for a way to die!"

"Doesn't little Julie ever want to get married?" Jade Flower chimed in.

When Fifth Uncle related this conversation to Judy, she was both angry and amused. "I can't believe it! Asking a teenager if she wants to get married?!" she ranted.

Auntie Han probably heard something from Julian. With no one else around, she said to Julie, "I can't complain if your mother takes you in." She then mumbled and avoided looking Julie in the eye, "But she won't take you in, she just wants to send you to a faraway place where there is no one to look after you."

"I want to go overseas," declared Julie matter-of-factly. "I want to be like Third Aunt."

Auntie Han yelped at Julie to desist. She had never said anything against Rachel and Judy, except this once.

Julian was again summoned to visit Judy's apartment.

"Little Julian, why are you being so ridiculous?" Rachel asked sternly.

He didn't reply.

Julian had not gone to the hospital to get an X-ray. Julie thought Rachel didn't trust Julian enough to give him the ten dollars for the X-ray fee. Of course, it was also a question of whether or not he would spend it elsewhere if she had given him the cash.

The day Julie returned home after graduating from middle school, the newspaper vendors were selling a special edition. A maidservant went out to buy a copy, which was only one sheet and slightly larger than a flyer. "Why is the paper so small today?" she asked, surprised.

At the bottom of the stairs, Julie read the broadsheet for herself. The paper was covered in large red-and-black characters. The Battle of Shanghai had begun.

Rachel and her brother lived on extra-Settlement roads outside the International Settlement. Yün-chih admitted to cowardice. As soon as the fighting started, he rented a three-room suite in a hotel in the French Concession and took his entire family to seek refuge there. His concubine had long ago been "dismissed." He invited Rachel and Judy to move there too. Rachel probably wanted to fully utilize the exorbitant hotel so she asked Julie to go with her, probably thinking it was also a good opportunity to teach the seemingly hopeless Julie some model behavior by example.

"Third Aunt says we're too close to Chapei here and wants me to stay with her for a few days," Julie told Ned. Jade Flower had gone out, which was a great relief to Julie. She had a tacit understanding with Ned about her mother but always felt uncomfortable using Third Aunt as an excuse to escape when Jade Flower was present.

"Hmm." Ned made his customary grunt without raising his eyes.

The hotel was full of life. A ring of oily scum ran around the lavender-colored bathtub.

"If we must lose our country," declared Yün-chih, "I'd rather be conquered by the British. Those Japanese devils are the worst."

Rachel snorted. "This kind of talk is just infuriating. You think you have a choice over who will conquer your country?"

"Those poor Indian devils," Yün-chih lamented. "Slaves without a country."

"You people never go overseas," said Rachel. "If you did, then you'd know just how humiliating it is to be looked down upon."

"And who ordered you to go overseas?"

Rachel and her brother were the same as Judy and her brother, always jousting whenever they got together. And yet despite the bickering, Rachel and Yün-chih were very close.

"Why don't you bathe?" asked Rachel. "We especially paid for rooms with en suite bathrooms."

"Excessive ablutions are detrimental to the vital element," replied Yün-chih.

Yün-chih and his wife entrusted Rachel to introduce his eldest and second daughters to some students who had recently returned from studying abroad. To make two rooms available for the guests, everyone else had to squeeze into a single room. Rachel and Judy were busy with their Red Cross work: rolling up bandages and knitting socks out of brown wool for the International Volunteers.

"One day at home I heard them playing catch in the living room," said Yün-chih in a low voice. "There was lots of laughter, so of course I was a bit concerned. I walked by the door and caught a revealing glance of a gown that wasn't buttoned down fast. Out of desperation, I called out for Auntie Liu and told her to go in and pretend to get something. I then told her to serve them refreshments, and not just once."

"That's exactly why I say we Chinese know nothing about romance and still never learn," Rachel said in despair. "Who would take a visitor at the gate straight to the inner chamber?"

When the bombing began, everyone said that the hotel staircase was the safest place. Julie sat on a step reading *The Story of a Noble Family*, a popular novel that her cousins had borrowed. She was happy.

The next day there was a huge boom at noon when bombs hit the Great World entertainment center on Avenue Edward VII. From the window Julie saw a convoy of army trucks pass by. A pile of artificial limbs poked out from under the dark-green tarpaulin on one truck as if intended for a department-store window display, except it was a jumble of limbs poking out from a chaotic pile of floral fabrics and gowns and trousers. Glistening rivulets of blood streamed down some of the limbs. She just caught a glimpse of it and would rather believe she had not seen anything.

It now appeared that the French Concession was more dangerous than Ned's house. "Very well, then," said Rachel after lunch. "You may go home."

The tram stop was abuzz with newspaper vendors selling special editions, and hands reached eagerly out of tram windows to buy them. People seemed to be smiling as if everyone was experiencing a new thrill.

It was a hot day and Julie still had to walk a distance from her stop. By the time she arrived home her face was red and puffy from exposure to the sun. She went to wash it before going upstairs to see Ned and his wife. In the bathroom, she could smell the fresh sweat on her body.

After washing her face, Julie bumped into Jade Flower descending the stairs. She immediately interrogated Julie about why she had stayed away from home the previous night without telling her in advance and slapped Julie in the face. She then complained to Ned and accused Julie of slapping her, which provoked Ned into giving Julie a thorough thrashing. The main gate was locked and Julie couldn't leave, so for her own safety, she moved into the two unused rooms downstairs, as far away from Ned and his consort as possible.

As soon as she settled in, Julie felt a little better. The two night-marish storms that had just turned her life upside down were now fading away. If she could be by herself for a while, everything would be fine. This kind of detachment, which Julie had acquired in child-hood, gave her the strength to hold herself together.

Unused furniture Julie had never seen before, even as a child, was piled up in the two rooms, including an out-of-favor teak cabinet with decorative carving on the top. Jade Flower had two brothers studying at university and the rooms were turned into guest rooms when they visited. They slept on the teak-frame bedsteads with stretched woven rattan. Julie only occupied one room so she closed the sliding door between them. Later, when she went next door to look for a book to read, she noticed an inkstone and a brush on the desk, and a piece of paper loosely scrunched up. Julie flattened out the paper. It was a sheet of old-style letter paper, on which were large characters scrawled in her brother's hand:

Esteemed Second Brother,
    Regretfully I did not meet with you when I recently visited. The news of my sister, I believe, is known to you. The disgrace brought to the family is indeed mortifying.

What is this? Julie was not particularly surprised because the score marks Julian once scratched onto one of her paintings had psycho-logically prepared her. Second Brother was a cousin from Tientsin. *Is it an unsent letter or is this the draft? Carelessly leaving something like that on the desk has all the hallmarks of Julian.*

Could he really believe something had happened when I stayed out that night? Jade Flower only accused Julie of disrespect for not inform-ing her that she would sleep away from home for a night, as she knew no one would believe any other accusations. That should be especially true of Julian, who until not so long ago had shared a room with Julie whenever she came back from school, a room with two single beds separated by a small cabinet. Julie had heard Auntie Han say Julian had wet dreams, but when Julie undressed to get into bed he politely looked away and both of them did not think much of it. Julie was busy growing taller and taller, as tall as a bamboo pole. At times she thought it strange that no one arranged for them to live in separate rooms. It was probably because Jade Flower did not want to give people the impression that she coveted the furniture that Judy had brought for the children—on the pretext of Ned's need to set up a new household—so she was reluctant to ask one of the children to move out. It was not until the previous year that Jade Flower had arranged for her own younger sister to move in with Julie.

If he really did not believe I had done something disgraceful, why was he assisting the evildoer by spreading lies like this? Julie didn't follow this line of thinking any further and simply made formalistic arguments angrily to herself. *You read the classics, didn't you? Your rhetorical flourishes show no regard for the seriousness of the consequences.* She crumpled up the letter back to the way it was when she found it and left it on the desk. She never told anyone about it.

After a few days locked up, Auntie Han came in the afternoon and whispered, "Third Mistress has arrived."

Rachel and Judy had caught wind of the incarceration and Judy had come take up the matter with Ned and Jade Flower.

"Under no circumstances can you leave the house," said Auntie Han in a low threatening voice. "If you leave you'll never be able to come back."

Julie nodded and smiled. Of course that was Auntie Han speaking in Julie's best interest. Julie had already written a note for Auntie Han to deliver upstairs:

Second Uncle,
    Mother truly has misunderstood me. I implore Second Uncle to vindicate me. I hope Second Uncle will also forgive me.
                                                                    Julie

Of course, as soon as he saw the note, Ned tore it to shreds. Auntie Han said nothing, and Julie did not ask.

Auntie Han pulled a chair over so she could sit next to Julie. She put on a very stern face to guard Julie but avoided looking at her directly. Julie found it uncomfortable to sit so close, face-to-face. She had sobbed in Auntie Han's arms after Ned beat her, but at that moment she felt Auntie Han was cold. Julie realized she was nothing more than a job for Auntie Han, and Auntie Han loved her job. In the past, Julie had always thought that only Auntie Han truly loved her and she would never be calculating about whether Julie would be a success in the future.

Suddenly Julie heard arguing coming from upstairs. The high-pitched voice didn't sound like Judy's; the shouting continued, words too muffled to be made out clearly.

Third Aunt has only been there for a short time. Perhaps I can seize the chance to dash out and leave along with Third Aunt.

Auntie Han became even more tense.

Julie remained seated, aware she could not overpower Auntie Han, let alone get past the guard at the gate.

A few days later, Auntie Han came to Julie's room at night to tidy up. "I heard they want to move you to the bungalow," she said in a low voice.

"What bungalow?"

"The bungalow at the back. The derelict one."

Julie had never been inside the bungalow, having only peered in once from the corridor. There was a row of wooden rooms built along a wobbly covered corridor with paint peeling off faded dull-green rickety balustrades. The place looked eerie, as if a servant girl had once hung herself there.

Auntie Han's eyes revealed what was on her mind: What furniture would be best to move there to make Julie more comfortable? "Luckily they haven't announced anything yet," continued Auntie Han in a whisper.

Before there was time to lock her up, Julie fell gravely ill. Auntie Han appealed to Jade Flower for medicine and was given a canister of Tiger Balm oil.

At the height of a raging fever Julie dreamed of her father taking her for a drive in the countryside. Outside the city the chauffeur drove very fast. It was all so carefree with the cool breeze of a summer evening. As the streetlights became few and far between, there was more open country on both sides of the road. Julie felt a chill as she was reminded of the case of Yen Rui-sheng and Wang Lien-ying. Yen took a prostitute out for a drive in the countryside, strangled her, and stole her jewelry. Driving with Ned made that murder feel so real.

As soon as she had recovered a little, Julie took advantage of the lowered security since she had fallen ill and slipped away without telling Auntie Han. She made her way to Rachel and Judy's place. A week later, Auntie Han delivered a jewelry box Julie had treasured since childhood. Auntie Han greeted Rachel with the same heartfelt, felicitous "Ma'am."

Rachel acknowledged the salutation as usual, asking if she were well. "Did they say anything after Julie left?" she inquired, smiling.

Auntie Han blinked and smiled back. "Nothing much," she responded in a low voice.

Julie knew that Rachel was short of money at the time, but after Auntie Han left, Rachel said to Julie, "I gave her five dollars. The old dear is so pathetic, having to wash bedding in her seventies. Now she knows what nasty really means. Think about how she treated me in the past! Finally, she can compare and see the difference!"

"What did she do to you?" asked Julie.

"Ha! When we were leaving for Europe—you didn't see the way all those maidservants behaved! Just as we were about to get on the boat, the porters took off with the luggage. Your second uncle pounded his fist on the table and said, 'I'm keeping the luggage.' You didn't see the haughty faces of those people on the sidelines. It was *so* infuriating!"

Judy found work at a foreign trading company and was rarely at home. Rachel worked on making matches for two attractive younger cousins from the Pien branch of the family with students who had just returned from abroad. In the past, Judy's residence also had a disciplined and purposeful atmosphere. It was now transformed from a litigation factory into a marriage factory, and several courtships were simultaneously in progress. An unending stream of Pien relatives came to visit.

"Your third aunt just doesn't like visitors," Rachel groused. "Even one dog is one too many for her."

Nancy was also a frequent visitor.

"Oh dear," Judy said with a sneer, knitting her brow, "that Nancy!"

Julie knew Judy was referring to the inappropriateness of Nancy's makeup and clothing, given her respectable family background.

"You didn't see the sorry state she was in when she first arrived in Paris," said Rachel. "She had just met Charlie and would come running over to us in tears every time they had a fight. In the end, Charlie married her, but his family still look down on her, even now. They're very conservative."

Rachel didn't return from Paris with them. Her Javanese girlfriend insisted she go with her to Java, so Rachel took a trip through Southeast Asia.

"What are the Javanese like?" Julie asked Rachel.

"Flat faces. Nothing much to look at."

Julie was entranced by the two pieces of Egyptian textile art Rachel brought back with her: little orange men leading camels sewn on a base of coarse beige cloth with three faded blue pyramids floating in the distance like the Chinese character 品. Julie had recently discovered in her study of ancient history that the svelte ancient Egyptians had faces and figures that matched Oriental concepts of beauty.

"What about Egyptians?"

Rachel pressed her lips together and furrowed her brow in concentration. "Nothing much to look at. Flat faces."

Julie slept in the same bed as Rachel. Luckily it was a large bed, though the springs and the cotton-padded mattress were ridiculously soft, like a giant powder puff. In the morning, no matter how carefully she moved, the mattress tilted when she tried to get out of bed and she frequently woke Rachel. "The crease in my eyelid doesn't look right when I don't have enough sleep," Rachel constantly whined. She didn't realize that her eyes were revealing signs of aging—the autumn of her life had arrived.

Julie was afraid to ask Rachel for bus fare, preferring to walk halfway across the city from the extra-Settlement roads all the way to the YMCA for her cram classes. Along the way, she passed the racecourse where she saw several goats on the grass, the only milking goats in all of Shanghai. Things are valued in proportion to their scarcity; Rachel ordered a bottle of goat milk every day, complaining that the cost was killing her. At the time it was popularly believed in the West that goat milk was particularly nutritious and would make people younger.

Julie had hidden a five-dollar note inside her shoe when she escaped from Ned's. One day she broke a teapot while washing the dishes. Luckily it was a pure white English teapot that she was able to replace—it cost her three dollars. Rachel said nothing. On Mother's Day, Julie walked past a flower shop and saw an array of common garden peonies in the window. One was flowering beautifully, a long round flower with deep pink double petals and golden yellow stamens—it reminded her of Rachel. Julie walked into the store and pointed at the flower. "I just want to buy one," she said, and then asked timidly, "How much will it cost?"

"Seventy cents," said the old shop boy, as shop assistants were called in Shanghai. His face was yellow, and he wore a white cotton gown. As if he did not mind the small transaction, he was eagerly attentive and cheerfully pulled out the stalk and carefully wrapped it, first in green wax paper and then with white paper, like an infant in swaddling with a single peony as its face.

"My gift to Second Aunt," said Julie as she proffered the flower to Rachel, who removed the white paper and the green wax paper, revealing the whole stem. The peony must have been too heavy, as the stem had broken. A piece of wire braced it.

"Oh no!" cried Julie, an explosion reverberating in her ears, as if the world had just collapsed. She waited for the customary truckloads of abuse to cascade down on her yet again: "I really don't know where this stupidity of yours comes from—even your second uncle is not like this" and "How can you think of venturing out into the world if you keep doing such stupid things?" When Julie recalled the fawning demeanor of the old shop attendant, she felt utterly ashamed.

"No matter," said Rachel in an uncharacteristically gentle voice. "We'll put the flower in water and I'm sure it will last for quite a few days." She filled a large glass mug with water, inserted the flower, and placed the mug on her bedside table. Surprisingly, the peony bloomed for almost two weeks before wilting.

"Young girls don't need to dress up," Rachel often expounded, "and they don't need to perm their hair; just brush it so the hair curls inward and doesn't look so straight." But Julie's hair was not compliant. And when she put on Judy's old blue gown, it was too big for her—she looked like a mouse wearing a lotus leaf. Julie was painfully aware that she did not meet her mother's standards of elegance and beauty.

"You are born with your looks," Rachel lectured, "and there's nothing that can be done about it. Posture and bearing, however, are your own. Your second uncle's actually not bad-looking and was very handsome as a teenager. Next time when you see someone you admire, be sure to observe their *posture*," she said, articulating the last word in English.

Julie was so embarrassed she could not even look at Rachel. The topic was never mentioned again.

Rachel habitually blurted out "Oh là là!" in French whenever she was pleasantly surprised. She also acquired a taste for artichokes, which she cooked by the plateful, piled up like gray-green hedgehogs, and consumed them bract by bract, sucking each one for a brief moment with a melancholy demeanor as if lost in thought.

"Oh, my Philippe is so handsome," Rachel often said to Judy, giggling. He was a law faculty student. Julie saw in Rachel's sketchbook a likeness of his statuesque profile wearing spectacles.

"They're all doing military training now and are scared to death. They hate and fear the Germans. Afraid of fighting a war. He says he'll die for sure."

"Is he waiting for you to go back?" Judy asked casually.

Rachel turned her head and laughed. "In such matters, it's all over when one parts ways."

Nonetheless, Rachel was forever writing on blue airmail letters, with two sheets of paper to hide the upper and lower panels and only revealing the middle, as she asked Julie for help with vocabulary. Julie found all this comical.

"I have two living dictionaries," Rachel often exclaimed, referring to Judy and Julie.

Rachel rarely hosted dinner parties but one day she lamented to Judy, "No choice, owe too many favors and they all want me to cook."

The layout of the small apartment was designed for "tea for two" entertaining, and there wasn't even a formal dining table. A set of glass tables was hobbled together to make do. In the dim yellow lamplight Rachel wore a plain Western-style black velvet blouse with a turndown collar adorned with a carved, oblong turquoise belt buckle.

All the dishes were arranged on the table, the rice placed in a large oval serving bowl with a lid, according to Western etiquette.

"We're still short one chair," said Rachel.

Julie looked for a chair in another room but they had all been moved out. The only prospect was a small armchair. She hesitated at first, then decided there was no other alternative. The chair sat on a small rug and moving it wasn't an easy task. At first it wouldn't budge, and then she almost knocked over a standing lamp. Ever since moving in, Julie had been quick to attend to household tasks to prove her ability to adjust to a new environment. There was a time when she didn't even know how to strike a match. Once, in a chemistry class, she was unable to light a Bunsen burner. The American teacher came over to see what was wrong and, with a look of contempt on her face, struck the match for Julie.

At home, the maidservants had always promptly jumped in to prevent Julie from striking matches, saying, "I'll do it, I'll do it," afraid she'd have an accident and start a fire.

"The ladies of the Pien family go out in the streets alone to buy things!" Auntie Lee used to say in days gone by, as if it were a matter of shame.

Rachel had a set of custom-made rugs with Picasso-painting designs, and these had to be negotiated in order to move the armchair to the living room. Julie could roll up a corner here and there to get by, but sometimes she had to lift the armchair. When the rugs were wrinkled, it was easy to bump into things and break them. After struggling her way past one rug, she encountered another. With great difficulty,

Julie managed to push the sofa into the corridor, and by the time she had made it to the doorway of the living room, she was utterly exhausted. Suddenly her eyes met with Rachel's scowl of disbelief.

"What on earth are you doing? Pig!"

Miss Hsiang, Nancy, and her husband, as well as Mr. Pi were all there. Everyone including Julie pretended not to have heard Rachel's scathing remark, and with a forced smile, Julie pushed the sofa back to its original position. By the time she returned to the dining table, a chair had appeared; Judy must have borrowed it from the next-door neighbors.

Whenever Rachel criticized her, Julie's attempts at an explanation would only elicit angry responses from Rachel: "Well, you always have a reason."

"If I didn't have a reason, why would I do it?" thought Julie, but henceforth she offered no more explanations.

One afternoon while Rachel was brushing her hair in the bathroom she said, out of the blue, "I was thinking: What if you meet a man in England?"

"I won't," said Julie, smiling.

"People have always told me that all girls, whether they go to school or not, end up the same," said Rachel. Then she added that it was best to have a skill to fall back on when married, even if you end up never using it.

Julie knew she had already caused Rachel embarrassment by giving up on piano lessons after so many years.

"It was *her* decision!" said Judy, imitating Jade Flower's tone of voice.

Students had to take piano lessons in school to be permitted to play on the school's pianos, but the teacher's demands conflicted with those of Julie's previous instructor. One wanted her wrists low, the other wanted her wrists to protrude upward. The White Russian instructor shed tears because she was so angry at Julie. With a disdainful smile, the old spinster at the boarding school smacked the back of Julie's hands hard. In the end, Julie decided to learn to draw caricatures instead of continuing with the piano.

"You're already sixteen," said Judy. "Don't change your mind again."

Rachel was constantly bemoaning the lack of opportunities to learn different things during her own childhood. "We missed out because we started too late."

If Julie indulged in a dalliance in England, that would be considered a hard slap in her mother's face. She understood her mother's concerns but also knew that even a written pledge would make no difference to her.

"One always thinks the first love affair is simply marvelous!" said Rachel, seething.

Julie smiled. "I won't get involved with anyone. I want to earn as much money as has been spent on me so I can reimburse Second Aunt." *Packed in a long box and buried beneath a dozen ruby-red roses.*

Rachel appeared not to have heard. "It's so unfair. I've been stuck here since my return—I can't go anywhere. Actually, I could marry you off. There'll always be someone who wants a young woman. Anyway, we Chinese only care about 'virtuous maidens.' The men all want virgins—as long as you're a virgin, even a maid like Jade Peach is worth chasing. Back in the day, Yün-chih used to pester me about letting him have her."

Julie was flabbergasted. *I've had independence drummed into me since childhood and now she thinks she can just marry me off?* Julie found all this talk of maidens and virgins sordid.

"I'm reluctant to introduce boyfriends to you, because as soon as I mention it, you become flustered, and then if I actually found someone, you'd . . . you'd act completely like. . . ." Rachel lowered her voice, and with an intimate yet frightening motion, she flapped her hands in front of her chest to demonstrate the seething restlessness of a girl in emotional turmoil. To Julie this seemed a bit filthy. Despite Rachel's metaphorical allusions, Julie found the constant references to "you" irritating. Julie could not understand why Rachel was saying all this to her. Although Rachel had said "marry you off," which Julie understood to be an old-fashioned forced marriage, she had never imagined that her mother, an accomplished matchmaker, would seriously contemplate making a match for her. Rachel probably assumed Julie was jealous of her cousins. Of course, her cousins were perfect candidates for matchmaking. Unlike traditional girls who grew up in conservative households and would run away at the merest mention of matchmaking, they sat straight up and smiled, listening attentively, and occasionally expressed an opinion. One of her cousins had said, "Marry, and marry rich," which Julie approved of in this case because it felt appropriate for her cousin. But Julie yearned for a romance like those she saw in the movies. She wasn't only hypothetically opposed to matchmaking; if she were put in that position she would become paralyzed with embarrassment. That would never do. Of course, Julie never shared these inner thoughts with anyone. The time for making high-minded statements had passed long ago.

Rachel paused for a moment, and then, dropping in some English, said, "I know that Second Uncle *broke your heart.*"

Julie abruptly turned around and glared at her mother, as if Rachel were a stranger who had intruded upon a private family affair. *She's so sure Second Uncle broke my heart!* "How could he break my heart?" she screamed inside her head. "I never loved him!"

Rachel immediately stopped talking. Julie was unaware that Fifth Uncle's good offices had been recruited to patch things up so Julie could go back home. Rachel naturally assumed that Julie's fury was caused by her discovery of the behind-the-scenes negotiations and did not try her hand at persuasion.

"We Shengs are very cognizant of money matters," Ned said to Fifth Uncle. Then he added, "Ladies living together are bound to quarrel."

"Julie's mother is dropping a brick on her own foot," Jade Flower chimed in.

Julie was convinced Rachel's sour attitude toward her was because of Philippe—she would lose him if she did not return to Europe. *Am I guilty of tearing two lovers apart?* One day Rachel went out and left the key in the lock of the desk drawer. All those blue airmail letters were kept in the top drawer.

"This is unbearable," Julie thought. "I have a right to know exactly what I've done." She steeled her heart, turned the key, opened the drawer, and carefully retrieved the first letter. It was one Rachel had written and hadn't sent yet. Apart from the intimate salutations, it was like any of her other letters, replete with complaints, in this instance of being so busy there was no time to study French, and mentioned she had joined a local art society to learn sculpture. A dozen or so crosses ended the letter which Julie knew represented kisses and were often found in letters written by children in the West.

Even after reading the letter, Julie could not find any clues. She had seen so many endlessly sentimental movies where the central relationship was never consummated. She didn't know these films were edited to evade the censors; film buffs certainly understood the situation. Like many advocates of the ill-fated reforms of 1898, from early childhood on Julie had believed that paranoia was simply a sign of stubbornness and narrow-mindedness.

As usual, Aunt Chu frequently came over to play mah-jongg. But now Rachel said, "The senior consort is no fun anymore."

"She changed after Uncle Chu got into trouble," said Judy.

"I can't stand her swaying when she loses." Rachel chuckled. "The more she sways, the more she loses."

When Aunt Chu became anxious at the mah-jongg table, her upper body swayed from left to right.

Actually, Uncle Chu had already repaid all the money he owed by then and discharged himself from the hospital.

That evening Rachel and Judy took Julie to Aunt Chu's residence for dinner. The young master wasn't at home but the apartment was so small that two extra mouths for dinner necessitated putting the round dining table in the stairwell landing.

"Auntie Vermillion," Aunt Chu called out to the maid from her seat at the dining table, "today the corn dish is delicious. The corn is succulent and the shredded pork is tender. It could use a touch more salt, though—it's a little bland." Aunt Chu was afraid of the maid.

Auntie Vermillion was leaning against the balustrade. "Well, add a little more salt, then," she responded, raising her chin and not hiding her impatience.

After dinner it was announced that His Excellency had arrived.

Aunt Chu, his principal consort, dragged Rachel and Judy downstairs. Julie trailed behind. Uncle Chu paced around the room. There was hardly any furniture in the narrow living room, just a long altar table and a square table for his ritual observances to the ancestors. The lamplight was dim and he had not taken off his coat. He didn't look as filthy as the last time Julie had seen him, perhaps because the hospital had insisted that he bathe. Julie made her salutation: "Uncle Chu."

He nodded acknowledgment and, while sizing Julie up, mumbled to Rachel, "Going to England, eh? She'll be just like you two, with an unlimited future, sure to be outstanding." Rachel muttered something modest in response. "The two of you really are like knight-errant female warriors of yore, genuine heroines. Your lives put all of us to shame."

No one was seated. Aunt Chu stood to one side and emitted an occasional *ahem* to clear her throat.

"Have you been feeling better?" Judy inquired of His Excellency.

"I'm in good spirits but have no hobbies, so I just indulge myself with the planchette in search of revelations from the spirits."

"Is it efficacious?"

"That I do not know. It requires a measure of luck; sometimes its prognostications seem compelling. Would you care to come and watch? It's just upstairs at the Forest of Zen Vegetarian Restaurant. There are two diviners who recite poetry with their acolytes, one of whom is a female celestial being."

"I hear," Judy teased, "that you've been very active there lately."

"No, no," he chuckled, "not at all."

"People say you're coming out of retirement."

"No, no. Definitely not true. That's just people making up rumors because they can't abide the thought of me surviving my ordeal."

"*Ahem.*" Aunt Chu cleared her throat again.

Rachel and Judy had a good laugh about that when they got home. "I can't stand seeing Aunt Chu so tense and stiff in front of His Excellency."

"Some say that the Japanese are negotiating with him to come out of retirement, but I don't know if there's a grain of truth in it."

"He did swear by the heavens and the sun that it wasn't true."

"Of course he'd say that."

Their chats in the bathroom at night and Rachel's genial laughter had become uncommon occurrences. Ever since Julie moved in, she was aware that there was something amiss. Rachel would explode hysterically on occasion, and Judy would meekly yield to her. At first, Julie couldn't fathom why Judy didn't move out. Later she heard Judy say that in order to save money she'd rather live in the small back room facing the landing, which she could still decorate herself. Julie eventually learned that Westerners placed a great deal of emphasis on one's home address, and that it was important for someone working in a foreign company to live at a respectable one. Judy certainly rose quickly in her company.

Rachel entrusted Mr. Pi to apply for Julie's passport, and he turned the responsibility over to someone else. Within a fortnight it arrived by post from Chungking. Rachel reacted with pride. "You'll be in deep trouble if you lose this! You can't stay in a foreign country without a passport, *and* you can't leave—it would be better to die than to lose a passport."

"Be patient," said Judy cheerily into the bathroom one day. "When the time comes, she'll be ready." Julie saw Judy standing by the bathroom door and overheard her side of the conversation. Julie knew that Rachel had been talking about her. In fact, Judy had reservations about sending Julie overseas, and later said quietly to Julie, "I tried to talk her out of it but she wouldn't budge."

Once, when Julie was bathing, she overheard the two of them outside the bathroom door, causing her quite some embarrassment, with Judy bursting into snorts of laughter, saying, "She's so tall and skinny."

"There is a body type like that among preadolescents, you know," said Rachel. "The art society also appreciates that kind of model."

"Oh?" said Judy, who took pride in her own physical attributes and was clearly unconvinced.

That was the first time Julie had ever heard her mother say anything in her defense; it took a lot of effort for her to keep her joy from showing.

Of course, Rachel would never allow Julie to be a model of any sort.

One evening Rachel waited for Judy to help her paint some lampshades. No doubt Judy was working late at the office again; it was after seven o'clock and she still wasn't back yet. Rachel paced the living room agitated. "You know, before I returned to Shanghai," said Rachel out of the blue, "your third aunt was speculating and lost all my money. At the time, she was trying to rescue Uncle Chu, so she speculated larger and larger amounts on margin, borrowing more and more money. Now she has found work that pays a paltry seventy or eighty dollars a month, and is slavishly devoted to her job. That's just ludicrous, isn't it?"

Julie was shocked. "How... is that possible?" she asked weakly. "How could someone else withdraw your own money?"

"To protect the value of my Legal Tender Notes, I entrusted her to do what was needed before I departed because there would be no time to ask me for instructions. Who could have imagined she'd do something like this. Marshal was beside himself when I told him. 'That's theft!' he roared." Rachel stretched her neck out like a pecking kingfisher as she spoke.

Marshal was an English teacher and had visited recently. After he left, Rachel heaved with laughter as she told Judy, "Marshal is as fat as a hog now." She also mentioned that he was married.

"The money was my lifeline, and she severed it just like that," Rachel continued. "Good heavens, I wonder what she'll think of her actions on her deathbed—how will she be able to face herself? Of course, it was all for the young master of the Chu clan. But what did I say to her? Getting on well is one thing, but you don't want to get into bed with him. Now see how marvelously she has done for herself! Her reputation is destroyed and Aunt Chu hates her because of the young master. Their servant told me so."

Julie had noticed that nowadays Aunt Chu was only on good terms with Rachel and was always sarcastic toward Judy, sometimes even outright hostile. Her laugh now seemed derisive and often descended into nasal grunts. But Julie hadn't thought much about it, since Aunt

Chu had completely changed of late. Her hatred of Judy wasn't neces-sarily due to Judy and the young master being so disparate in age. Judy, as the elder of the two, should be the one to blame for seducing him.

"Aunt Chu was also furious that the two of them ignored her, never told her anything, never let her poke her nose into their affairs. Your third aunt flaunted her abilities and the young master just used her. Now everyone thinks of the young master as a capable man. His father was always putting him down, but that's improved a bit. I was thinking that your uncle Yün-chih doesn't know, but if he did, who knows what would pour out of that mouth of his. Come to think of it, it was very hard for me, and it's hard to talk about with anyone—what's there to say?"

Julie was silent throughout, her mind a complete blank. The mo-ment she heard this she "suspended judgment," just as readers of Samuel Taylor Coleridge's *The Rime of the Ancient Mariner* had to "suspend disbelief." Perhaps it was because she felt a bond with Judy, having suffered adversity together.

"And when they were making the match for me," continued Rachel, "goodness knows how they talked up the Sheng family. Initially I was unwilling, but your maternal grandmother wept and wailed at me so many times, saying that your uncle Yün-chih was causing her so much grief and that to make up for it I must win back her honor and respect for her. But by the time I married into the household I real-ized...." Rachel sounded angry, yet also amused by the absurdity.

"At that time your eldest aunt was in charge of the household and she was so frugal that she even economized on soap. Auntie Han was a timid woman. She was scared to death of her mistress and would not dare to ask for a bar of soap, so after laundering, the bedding still reeked of dried saliva. I ended up digging into my own purse to pay for soap, and to pay for food, otherwise the dishes they served weren't edible. Your third aunt was fifteen at the time, and always dropped by and lingered; your second uncle detested her. When the assets were later divided, the will stated that Old Matriarch's jewels should be given to her daughter, so your third aunt took them. There was also a sack of gold leaf and she wanted that too. Your second uncle was never calculating enough. He just said, 'Let her have it.' You could say she was young at the time, but she certainly wasn't too young to be smart."

Rachel talked herself hoarse, pacing back and forth under the dim yellow lamplight. Suddenly she stopped in her tracks. "I'm tied down for a paltry sum of money, stuck here unable to move, yet I still despise money. If I was only after money or status, I'd have no shortage of suitors."

Julie knew she was referring to Ambassador Pi. Judy had teased Rachel about Ambassador Pi's newly widowed status.

"Lloyd was always saying to me, 'You need someone to look after you. You never think of yourself.' All my friends advised against letting you go to school. It's not that I insist on you studying, but you aren't capable of doing anything else. Marshal also said to me, 'Hold on to your money. Don't be foolish.'"

Julie could not help feeling antagonistic toward Marshal. She saw Marshal the last time he visited. He was short with a profile like a Greek statue. When he put on weight he appeared rather chubby. It seemed that all her mother's boyfriends shared the same features, as did her father's women. There was also a French officer. Julie had opened the door for him when he showed up for afternoon tea. He too was handsome, short, and fat, and was dressed in a snow-white uniform, with a floral-rimmed kepi shading his lowered head, which accentuated a double chin. He reminded Julie of the bust of Napoleon on her father's desk.

"Nowadays 'big and strong' is the only thing on their lips," Rachel sniggered, ridiculing the criteria her nieces voiced as the perfect match. "They all want me to choose 'big and strong' for them. In the past that would be considered disgraceful."

Rachel made "big and strong" sound dirty, but at the time Julie didn't grasp the reference to genital size.

On the afternoon of a tea party, Rachel would be in good spirits, chortling quietly to herself as she tidied up the room, arranged flowers, spread tablecloths, and set the crockery.

Rachel was fastidious about her attire, but Julie liked one of her everyday dresses best. It was a dark green knee-length linen dress, which Rachel had made for herself on her sewing machine. There was nothing special about the dress, and it had been the most common style worn around the world for decades—V-neck with narrow sleeves that ended before the elbow—yet it made Rachel look petite and elegant.

When the guests arrived, Julie would take a thick English book to read on the roof of the tall apartment building. The summer sunlight shone down with such intensity at five in the afternoon that she had to sit in the shade of the threshold. From the light pink terrazzo terrace where it was forbidden to hang laundry out to dry, the bleak view was only interrupted by a few chimney stacks and numerous cream-colored concrete bunkers of various sizes. Sometimes Rachel could be extremely pleasant, but that just made her usual behavior even more unbearable. *The money has been spent, so it's too late to say, "I'm not going." And if I don't go overseas, what on earth would I do anyway?* Julie couldn't imagine an alternative and she despised herself.

And that would be so ungrateful.

She wants to help you succeed, and despite her nagging it's all for your own good. She's helping you but you're treating her like an enemy.

Simply because you are relegated to the sidelines you feel disillusioned?

Julie thought about jumping and letting the ground give her an enormous slap in the face. How else could she let Rachel know how guilty she felt about the sacrifices her mother made for her?

Julie overheard Judy on the phone with Brother Hsü. Her voice was hoarse from crying, yet she sounded calm as usual. But now and then, after exchanging a few words, she let her temper fly.

Could that be passion?

Julie took pains to behave toward Judy the same as before so that Judy wouldn't suspect she knew anything.

By now, Judy was probably suspicious of everyone, wondering whether or not they knew about her relationship with Brother Hsü. Julie knew she was the only one whom Judy would not be wary of.

One day Brother Hsü visited. Julie was a little surprised but Rachel acted effusively warm. Ever since her divorce, he dispensed with formal salutations and simply called her Rachel. In general, calling an acquaintance by their given name was considered conceited, but there was no harm in using an English name. They chatted for a while before he mentioned it had become quite inconvenient to bathe at his home. "Might as well have a bath here, then," said Judy somewhat impatiently, conveying the impression that she felt it wasn't worth her while to pretend he had never bathed at her place before.

Rachel entered the bathroom. When she saw that Julie had just taken a bath and hadn't cleaned the tub, she bent over and cleaned it herself. "How can we have someone take a bath when it's like this," she said cheerily in a low voice—the warm and bashful tone of a happy Rachel.

After filling the bathtub with hot water, Rachel came out. Slightly embarrassed, Brother Hsü removed his gown and laid it on the couch. He looked even shorter as he entered the bathroom wearing only a white silk top and matching trousers. Rachel and Julie stared intently at his back, looking him up and down, while Judy teared up, turning her head to the side.

"Auntie Han is leaving," announced Rachel. "You'd better go and see her off."

Auntie Han didn't come say goodbye herself because Rachel would have to give her money again. A message was delivered that Julie would meet her at the Bubbling Well Temple tram stop. She first stopped by the famous old Chinese snack shop called the Old Big House opposite the tram stop to spend the remaining dollar and change she had on two kinds of walnut sweets. Auntie Han didn't say a word when Julie handed the two greasy paper bags to her with a smile. With a blank face and the dexterity of a magician, the two greasy paper bags disappeared beneath her large blue smock in a flash. Julie immediately knew she had made a mistake once again—the gift inadequate. But after all this was just a small token of her appreciation.

"Miss, could you let me have that little box from school?" asked

Auntie Han after she had said her farewells. Julie was momentarily startled but quickly agreed. She was referring to the small tin box the school had stipulated for carrying snacks, inscribed with the student's name. After graduation, Julie had taken the box home, and Auntie Han must have seen it and quietly hidden it with the jewelry box to keep Jade Flower from redistributing these possessions.

Julie had been wearing glasses for only two days and was not yet used to them. They felt like blinders for a donkey about to set off on a long, arduous journey. Auntie Han seemed to treat her like a stranger, just another Judy in her eyes, her dream of living the good life of a maid who accompanies the future bride into a new household shattered. Julie felt she had let Auntie Han down, as if she had deceived her all these years. Standing on the platform, Julie watched her step onto the tramcar. Both of them knew they were parting forever, but neither of them shed a single tear.

Julie passed the university entrance exam and received her passport, but she was still unable to leave Shanghai.

"Let's wait and see," said Rachel. "Everyone says war is about to break out."

Julie never raised the matter, but she was anxious. She didn't especially want to go to England. She had heard Rachel say it was cold and wet every day of the year, with thick pea-soup fogs and a sky that turns dark in the afternoon. "Impoverished students can't go anywhere and don't get to see anything." Even the sun, apparently.

"And all they eat is rock-hard cheese."

"I like to eat cheese," Julie chuckled.

"That stuff is completely indigestible."

All Julie wanted was to go as far away as possible. At the moment, she just wanted to be free.

She was so anxious, yet she didn't want to read the newspaper.

"Someone will surely tell me if anything happens," Julie thought.

Unlike Julie's father, Rachel was not an armchair political analyst.

"It doesn't matter if they start fighting," Rachel continued. "Students will be evacuated to the countryside and given rations. The English are good about things like that."

Julie suspected her mother had forgotten she was no longer a primary-school student. Rachel obviously hoped to take advantage of the opportunity to hand Julie over to the British government's care.

Julie's two cousins were soon to be married. They had swapped their prospective partners and still turned up regularly to complain and cry.

"I return from work half dead of exhaustion," complained Judy, "to find the sisters crying on my bed."

"Wedding nerves," replied Rachel, "can't be helped."

Rachel busied herself buying fabric and helping the sisters with fittings. One afternoon she went to the Pien family residence. Without all the visitors from Rachel's family, the apartment suddenly became quiet, an almost audible silence, the sort of silence that sounds like music. It was a weekend and Judy had nothing planned. "I feel like eating stuffed steamed buns," Judy suddenly declared. "We can make them ourselves."

"We don't have any filling," Julie giggled.

"We have sesame paste." Judy began to knead the dough and admitted, with a laugh, "I've never done this before."

Clouds of moisture pouring from the bamboo steamer fogged up Judy's spectacles. When she took them off to wipe the lenses, Julie asked about the tiny white scar she noticed on Judy's eyelid.

"Your second uncle did that. At the time I had completely fallen out with him. But when you were locked up I had to go find you, and as soon as he saw me, he jumped up and hit me with his opium pipe."

Julie had heard about that but never gave it a second thought.

"I went to the hospital and had three stitches. Luckily, no one can tell," said Judy. Nonetheless, she obviously was not celebrating inside.

Judy removed the sweet sesame buns from the steamer but the dough had not risen and they tasted rubbery. "Not bad," said Judy. Julie chimed in that the filling was quite tasty. Suddenly tears streamed down her face as she ate, but Judy didn't notice.

After the first wedding, Rachel began to plan who to invite over for afternoon tea, but Julie fell ill with a fever that persisted for several days. She moved into the living room, changing places with Judy. And of course the tea party had to be canceled.

Julie was mortified for needing a small washbasin placed next to the couch to vomit into and longed to be able to crawl into a cave rather than defile the exquisite little chocolate house that was straight out of a fairy tale. Rachel burst in. "Oh, you live only to bring disasters!" she exploded. "People like you should just be left alone to die!"

Julie thought that sounded like a curse. She said nothing.

Rachel called a German doctor to examine Julie. He diagnosed typhoid, which would require hospitalization. She was admitted into a small hospital that was recommended by Dr. Feinstein.

She moved into a single-person room. The first night, a girl in the room next to hers whimpered all through the night, not stopping until dawn.

"The girl next door also had typhoid," said the morning-duty nurse, grimly. "She died—and was only seventeen."

The nurse was unaware that Julie was also seventeen. Julie did not look seventeen. She sometimes felt she was thirteen and at other times thirty.

Recalling what Judy once said—"When you are eighteen I'll have some clothes made for you"—that age always seemed so remote to her, so distant. She had already fought off two serious bouts of illness over the past two years and almost didn't make it to eighteen.

Dr. Feinstein visited Julie every day. The overweight, bald man was a famous lung specialist in Shanghai. Every time he leaned over Julie's bed, the smell of antiseptic wafted by, making Julie think of an elephant that had just been hosed down.

He always teased Julie. "How patient you are!" he said, imitating the way Julie clasped her hands under the blanket. She smiled and quickly straightened her fingers.

"Ah, Friday is a good day," the doctor finally said. "You can break your fast." For the first time since checking into the hospital, Julie ate solid food.

Last year Rachel had taken Julie to Dr. Feinstein's clinic, and the doctor also examined Rachel. Julie by chance caught a glimpse of the two of them standing opposite each other, and saw Rachel's scrawny chest in profile. Rachel appeared a little embarrassed and on guard, yet at the same time she also exuded that enamored, intoxicated look of hers.

Rachel and Judy took turns bringing chicken soup to Julie. On every occasion, Rachel tried to engage in small talk with the nurse, taking special pains to praise a nurse called Miss Chen for reading diligently and being conscientious. Rachel was always hoping to get special treatment for Julie.

After Julie was discharged from the hospital, she learned the news of Uncle Chu's assassination. It happened in the doorway of the Forest of Zen Vegetarian Restaurant. Two men wearing white shirts and khaki trousers fired off a few shots and fled. Uncle Chu was sent to the hospital and lingered there for three days before dying. Everyone said they were agents from Chungking. The earlier rumors about him rang true. Brother Hsü resigned from his job at the bank. Aunt Chu was seriously ill, so the relatives were afraid to tell her the news—she had severe diabetes and coronary heart disease.

"People say Uncle Chu's eyes leaked light, an omen of a sudden, violent death," Judy said softly.

"How on earth do eyes leak light?" asked Julie.

Judy had a difficult time explaining it—something about his eyes growing large and the whites of his eyes appearing more prominent.

"Is the rumor about Uncle Chu true?"

"Who knows? Brother Hsü doesn't know, either. Some Japanese guests came to visit, but that wasn't unusual. Some say Foster Boy acted as a go-between, while others say Foster Boy had been swaggering about in the name of Uncle Chu."

Julie had seen Foster Boy at the residence of Aunt Chu. He was small and fat, with a dark oily face and puffy eyes. He looked grumpy that day and did not utter a word. Perhaps he felt he was wronged. Later Julie overheard Aunt Chu tell Judy that the last time he was sent to deliver payment for the monthly expenses, he squandered the money on prostitutes.

Julie felt that Uncle Chu could not shirk responsibility for his own death. He had reached the end of the road. Money had run out and he had to call upon his political capital. At least he must have been trying to maintain his connections and did not want to burn bridges.

Julie was only too aware of her father's fear of running out of money.

Brother Hsü was preparing to head north to find work; there was no place for him in Shanghai and the political atmosphere seemed less tense there. It was agreed that he would manage the clan temple, so at least he would have a place to stay for a time. But for the moment he couldn't leave because Aunt Chu was sick.

Before Julie set off for Hong Kong, Judy and Rachel took her to visit Aunt Chu. The downstairs reception room was full of people, all from Aunt Chu's clan, who were deliberating whether they should inform Aunt Chu about the death of His Excellency. Aunt Chu cursed His Excellency for not visiting her yet during her illness.

The young master of the Chu family—Brother Hsü—was present but didn't say a word out of fear for being blamed if something went wrong. Anyway, Aunt Chu trusted people from her own clan the most.

Rachel and her party of two went upstairs. They did not sit because all the chairs had been moved downstairs. In this mostly empty room, a stick of incense burned on the floor in the corner. Aunt Chu lay on a small brass bed. She wasn't wearing her glasses. Julie barely recognized her—she was so yellow and gaunt, her voice faint and feeble; she obviously wasn't in the mood for chatting. Julie genuinely felt sorry for her and wanted so much to tell her that Uncle Chu had died.

Rachel and Judy accompanied Julie to the ship and at the dock met up with Bebe's family who were seeing Bebe off. The English tutor had suggested they travel together. Rachel was exceedingly perfunctory in her placing of such great trust in Bebe to look after her daughter. The ship was very small and well-wishers were not permitted on board.

"Second Aunt, I'm leaving," Julie managed to say with a wan smile.

"Very well, then. You may leave."

"Third Aunt, I'm leaving."

Judy shook her hand and grinned. Such an English gesture almost caused Julie to burst out laughing.

Aboard the ship, the two young passengers inspected their cabin and found that the luggage had already arrived.

"Let's go out," said Bebe. "They're still there."

"You go, I'll stay. They've already left."

"How do you know? Let's go and see."

"I'll stay. You go."

Bebe went out on deck alone while Julie sobbed in their berth. The ship's horn suddenly made a deafening blare that filled the air. The floor under the bed began to shudder. The Shanghai Julie left behind lay in ruins.

Bebe returned to the cabin and without saying a word began to unpack her luggage. Julie wiped her tears and sat up.

4

JUDY FOUND a job at the German radio station as a Mandarin newsreader. Every night, carrying a small oil lamp, she trudged to work by its dim glow along blacked-out streets. The rose-red frosted-glass chimney of the lamp felt safe in her hands but eventually it slipped from her grip and smashed into pieces. Since the Japanese occupation, roads had not been repaired, and sometimes Judy would step into water-filled potholes she couldn't see in the gloomy light—she had to flounder her way home in the dark. She shook her head and groaned. Over her work gown she wore a navy blue wool coat padded with cotton rather than a proper overcoat. It was her outfit for nocturnal missions, her self-protective attire. Judy tried to learn how to ride a bicycle. She scraped her knees several times and gave up. She had learned how to drive, though not very well. Her Polish chauffeur always sat next to her, ready to trade places.

"I'm useless. Your second aunt can ski with bound feet. But I'm always afraid I'll fall over and break my leg."

T'ang Ku-wu—T'ang the Solitary Mallard—a celebrity writer popular in the 1920s, started a new magazine to which Julie submitted a story. "When your second aunt wanted to elope," Judy chuckled, "she wrote to T'ang Ku-wu."

"Then what happened?" asked Julie, unable to contain herself. "Did they ever meet?"

"No, they never met. I don't know if he ever replied," said Judy. "T'ang Ku-wu was quite handsome, with a cultured look—I saw his photograph once. Later he married and spoiled his wife terribly. He wrote a poem with the line, 'Unless I'm peregrinating, our two heads will stay side by side perpetually.' We almost died laughing."

In those days, it was common for people to write articles pretending to be women. Julie surmised that T'ang Ku-wu didn't reply to Rachel's letter because he assumed it was written by an idle reader impersonating a woman, or perhaps even another writer pulling his leg.

T'ang Ku-wu wrote to Julie that her piece would be published. "When shall we invite him over for tea?" Judy gleefully inquired.

Julie felt there was no need for such courtesies, but seeing how curious Judy was about T'ang Ku-wu, she couldn't oppose it. She dutifully wrote a note. He soon telephoned to arrange a time for tea.

T'ang Ku-wu still looked the way Julie imagined he did as a young man: thin and tall, elegant narrow face. He wore a black robe. However, he was bald and wore a scraggly toupee as stiff as a tortoiseshell.

It became obvious that he felt obliged to attend the tea party, even though he wasn't impressed by Julie's prose. They didn't have much to talk about.

Julie explained that her mother wasn't presently in Shanghai. She gestured with her chin at a large photograph on the wall. "That's my mother."

The picture—mounted in a carved gilt oval frame—showed Rachel's permed hair spilling down over her eyebrows, her stylized bangs a popular look in the early Republican era. T'ang Ku-wu glanced at the photograph, obviously quite impressed. That era was his heyday.

"I see," he replied, "that's your esteemed mother."

Not only did Julie feel it was superfluous to have invited him over but their quarters were barely presentable. The narrow sitting area obviously doubled as a bedroom. Sitting around the crowded table cluttered with tea-making paraphernalia, their knees almost touched. Judy did not mind at all; she was flexible and simply accepted the situation—she was without debt and without stress. She once confessed to Julie, "Back in the day I owed Second Aunt money."

"I know." Julie giggled. "Second Aunt told me."

Judy obviously didn't expect to hear that and was extremely displeased. It was supposed to be a secret between her and Rachel. "I was trying to raise funds for Uncle Chu. I dabbled in stocks and faced a cash-flow problem, so I only intended to use her money temporarily." Her voice went quiet. "I lost it all but I did pay her back later. I still owned all the houses in three laneways—they had all been mortgaged more than once. I repaid your second aunt as soon as I sold them."

"I see. I guessed you repaid her around the time she visited Hong Kong."

Judy went quiet. "When you heard about that, what did you think?"

"I didn't think anything," said Julie calmly.

Judy was unconvinced. "How could you *not* think anything?"

"I thought Third Aunt must have her reasons."

Judy hesitated, clearly not convinced, and thought, "Could it be that Rachel had not told her that it was for Brother Hsü?"

"And remember that time we chatted in the cool night air on the balcony," Julie continued with a smile. "I loved listening to Third Aunt and Brother Hsü talking—the atmosphere among the three of us felt wonderful."

"It did?" Judy couldn't remember the scene but still was delighted at Julie's description. She fell silent for a moment, then continued, "Your second brother deliberately ignored me after hearing about the Brother Hsü affair—I was very *hurt*," she said, saying the word "*hurt*" in English. She fell silent for a moment, then continued. "I had helped him a great deal when he first arrived in Shanghai."

Second Brother was the only nephew from the Sheng clan that Judy liked. She followed Julie in addressing him as Second Brother. After graduating from university, he found a menial job in Shanghai and his wife from Tientsin moved in with him. Despite his family being wealthy, he chose not to depend on them. The family had arranged the marriage; his wife was slightly deaf. Judy once said, "Young people nowadays are the opposite of how we were at that age. They want the family money but don't want the wives the families arrange."

Julie and her brother once visited them together. Julian often went there by himself. His letter about the "stain on the family" was written to this very same Second Brother. The couple lived in two large rooms that occupied an entire floor, a mostly desolate space save for a few pieces of shabby, old furniture. They looked like typical northerners. Second Brother was tall, fair-skinned, and had a long face. Wearing a pair of tortoiseshell spectacles, he could be the protagonist of a Chang Hen-shui novel. His wife also had a long face. She was short though not petite. Overeager to be an attentive host, she moved at a frenetic pace. Julie remembered to speak loudly, but not too loudly. Nonetheless, Second Brother repeatedly had to convey her words again, an obvious embarrassment for him. He appeared rather distant and unwelcoming. Julie felt sorry for them, as their home did not evoke the slightest ripple of a young couple's joy.

Julie read excerpts of the novel *Lu Nan-tsu, an Honest Fellow* by Tseng Hsü-pai, which was serialized in *Truth-Virtue-Beauty* magazine. In it Cloud Phoenix and her nephew fall in love and have carnal relations. Julie only read two installments so it was not clear to her if they were related on the paternal or maternal side of the family.

A clan elder drags him off to the clan temple to thrash him with a birch plank. Cloud Phoenix hires a palanquin and rushes to the rescue. The hero of the novel, Lu Nan-tsu, feared she would also be harmed. The story dated from the early Republican era, but the influence of the traditional patriarchal system remained strong decades later. Even more unfortunate was that, unlike Cloud Phoenix and her nephew, Judy's age wasn't considered compatible with Brother Hsü's. Julie, aware of Third Aunt's sensitivity to this matter, never asked about Brother Hsü's age. He began university studies very late, probably graduating at twenty-six or twenty-seven, maybe even older. He was one of those people whose skinny appearance made his age difficult to discern.

Second Brother probably felt like prey himself. He, too, was at least a generation younger than Judy; she had helped him with such warm enthusiasm that it appeared as if she had other motives. And besides, he had a disabled wife.

Judy fell silent and Julie couldn't think of anything to say to comfort her. "Did Aunt Chu eventually find out about her husband's death?" asked Julie, changing the subject.

"They never told her."

More silence, then Judy continued, "Uncle Chu can't really be blamed for their marriage. Her elder brother forced her onto him. His previous wife had just died and her elder brother badgered him in the study for two days and two nights. They were relatives of long standing. Of course she wasn't as plump in those days. Everyone said she had an auspicious physiognomy. At that time Uncle Chu only had one concubine. When he formally married another woman, he dismissed all the concubines except for Third Concubine, who accompanied him to Peking after he accepted a new position and he formally took her in. Aunt Chu said that when she married Uncle Chu to be his principal wife, 'Third Concubine kowtowed, and I wanted to reciprocate, but the bridesmaids standing beside me stayed stiff as boards and prevented me from bending at the waist.'" Then, imitating Aunt Chu's soft chatty tone of voice, Judy said, "Before the wedding my family had instructed the accompanying servants to watch over me."

She continued on in her own voice, "Third Concubine visited the bridal chamber to keep Aunt Chu company. That house up in northern China had two rows of windows, and the top row could only be held half open with a teak pole. One sweltering day, Aunt Chu called for the windows to be opened, but as there was no one else around, she asked Third Concubine to retrieve the pole. Third Concubine said nothing; but as soon as she left the newlyweds' house, she burst into tears and cried all the way back to her quarters, accusing Aunt Chu of treating her like a maid. Uncle Chu was so furious that from then on that he refused to set foot in the bridal chamber. The dowry maids said their mistress was too forbearing—if he treats his wife like that upon her arrival, then what does the future hold? They instigated the newly married Aunt Chu to make a great fuss. And then who knows what really happened. A rumor spread that the new bride was so strong that she pushed a wall over. Their home was originally a yamen office and so old it was probably on the verge of collapsing anyway."

Julie saw a picture of Third Concubine in Aunt Chu's photo album. A pretty, seductively slender woman with an oval face and dressed in late Ch'ing dynasty couture.

"Uncle Chu kept ignoring his wife. To the point where Third Concubine exhorted him to be nicer to Aunt Chu. They even let her accompany them on outings to restaurants and the opera. Those were Aunt Chu's golden days. One time her elder brother visited Peking. He telephoned and asked to speak to the mistress of the house. Their phone had been installed in Third Concubine's courtyard, and he received the reply, 'Would you like the consort of the east wing or the consort of the west wing?' Aunt Chu's brother was so incensed that he rushed over to slap Uncle Chu in the face.

"After that, Uncle Chu sent Aunt Chu back to Shanghai, though whenever he returned, he never stayed with her, his principal consort, save for on one occasion when he fell ill and his mother worried about him staying at his concubine's residence. He moved into the main residence to convalesce and enable Aunt Chu to attend to him. He lived there for several months. Aunt Chu yearned for a child, but, as she later told others, 'Miss Su lived in the room next to us and her father was far too embarrassed to fulfill my wish for offspring.' It infuriated Miss Su to bear the blame for their lack of progeny."

Miss Su was Uncle Chu's daughter from his previous marriage.

"Brother Hsü's mother was Third Concubine's servant girl," said Judy. "After his birth, Third Concubine sold her off to someone in another city and kept the child for herself. That's why Brother Hsü hates her.

"Aunt Chu now gets on very well with Third Concubine. Third Concubine often visits Shanghai and stays at Aunt Chu's residence whenever she comes. Her hair has thinned so much that she wears a small wig. Uncle Chu rejected her as soon as she turned bald. Brother Hsü complained tearfully to his father. He had been calling Third Concubine 'Mother' because he had thought she was his natural mother. 'Don't be stupid,' Uncle Chu scolded Brother Hsü, 'she didn't give birth to you.' That was how he found out.

"On her occasional trips to Shanghai, Third Concubine never had a chance to see Uncle Chu. It's typical of Aunt Chu that when Third Concubine greeted her with a volley of 'Mistress, mistress,' Aunt Chu felt on the best of terms with her again, and even explained to others, 'She's really suffering now,' completely forgetting that Third Concubine had said such unpleasant things about her to Uncle Chu in front of others. Things like, 'She's *so* fat!'

"Whenever she comes, Third Concubine stays in the small back room facing the landing. Brother Hsü hates it. Aunt Chu bitterly disappointed us when dealing with family matters. She was terrified when we sued your eldest uncle. She felt terribly awkward, always afraid of offending others. 'What a pity,' she said. 'We're all relatives.'"

"She really said that?" asked Julie, surprised.

Judy tossed her head to one side. "That's right! People like her always say, 'We should stay in touch with relatives.' It's important to them. After Uncle Chu fell into difficulties, Aunt Chu went to kowtow to all the relatives, and was angry that Brother Hsü did not accompany her to ask for financial assistance. Who actually helped? That's the sort of person she is."

After returning to Shanghai, Julie thought that the city really was different from Hong Kong. There were virtually no Japanese soldiers to be seen. Everyone said, "Shanghai is still the same."

She wasn't afraid to wear the homespun fabric with red flowers against a willow-green print that she had brought back from Hong Kong and had made into Chinese gowns and simple Western dresses. It was like wearing a famous painting—she felt rapturous and didn't care what others thought.

"There are no movies to see anymore," complained a disappointed Judy with a wry smile. "I loved those comedies with all their witty and playful dialogue."

"Especially Rosalind Russell," Julie thought to herself, knowing the depiction of strong professional women resonated with Judy.

"Those people really do speak like that," said Bebe. Julie agreed. It had become part of a cultural tradition, and almost everyone had a few witty lines ready to fire. Their sophisticated, flirtatious banter differed from what Shanghainese called "eating bean curd," which carried the condescending suggestion of flirting with frivolous, dim-witted girls.

"It's such fun to talk with Jory in the office." Judy chuckled.

Jory—tall, slender, and pale, with full black hair—was a Eurasian who shared an office with Judy. When Julie saw him he looked familiar. Julian as an adult would look the same, thought Julie. He'd also drive his own car, marry early, and be stuck in a job with no future. In most foreign companies, Eurasians had the same status as Judy. Without scientific or technical skills to offer, they had reached the pinnacle of their careers, earning a salary already considered high for a single woman.

"I was on bad terms with Brother Hsü at the time, and often stayed late at the office, flirting with Jory. But then I became scared...." Her smile disappeared and her voice lowered to a muffle as she faded out. It was clear she was referring obliquely to rape.

Julie could picture the empty offices after work, the desolate commercial buildings at night, but she couldn't imagine that a handsome young colleague would rape Judy. It seemed so unbelievable that she almost laughed, but at the same time Julie felt profoundly sad.

Judy fell silent, then continued, "For Brother Hsü to have an affair with Brother Wei's wife, that made me so angry."

"He had an *affair* with Brother Wei's wife?" a stunned Julie feebly asked. Brother Wei's wife was a real beauty from the second branch of the Chu family, who actually made a perfect match for Brother Wei and had given birth to many children. She had a pointy chin and a pretty face. The red-orange rouge on her cheeks made her almond-shaped eyes look even brighter. Her slightly short stature was coupled with a matchbox-like figure. She usually wore a large, light pink silk flower à la Carmen Miranda, which made her appear even more glamorous and radiant. As a child, Julie was enthralled with Miss Purity and Miss Grace from the Chu family, who were nowhere near as pretty as Brother Wei's wife, yet back then Julie didn't really like her, perhaps because she found her Ch'ang-shu Mandarin extremely irritating. She referred to her mother-in-law as *niang*, pronouncing it with a falling tone instead of the elegant Peking-dialect rising tone, which made her sound insincere.

You couldn't see that in Brother Hsü, so it's true you can't judge a man by appearances. Julie was disgusted; she felt he had let Third Aunt down. Judy had given him confidence, and yet, with the courage of a philanderer, the world was his oyster. All the other members of the younger generation of the Chu clan married late as was the custom of the times. Only Brother Wei married early. Because he had been fooling around with dancing girls as a teenager, it was decided to find him a pretty young wife to curb his carnal instincts. His family chose a beauty from the Yang-tze River delta, a distant relative, whose family was conservative but poor, believing she would be a responsible wife.

The Chu clan's assets had almost completely dissipated before the generation of Brother Wei and Brother Hsü, who had 絲, the character for silk, incorporated in their generational name. The many members of the second branch of the family in particular put a substantial strain on their finances. And marrying did not rein in Brother Wei from his pleasure seeking. His wife sought revenge and Brother Hsü, a cousin of her husband, was the most logical candidate. Being in-laws in the Chu family provided ample opportunities to meet clandestinely; plus, his ordinary looks didn't attract attention. Moreover, they had known each other for many years and she knew his cautious ways, how he guarded his mouth like a closed bottle. For a woman in her position, maintaining secrecy was naturally paramount. And for his part, he had probably admired her for a long time. He didn't display the haughty temper of a scion of the family like Brother Wei, so she probably felt more important from all the attention she received.

Julie now recalled that Brother Hsü enunciated "sister-in-law" with a gentility that resembled the way he spoke of his father. Of course he had spoken like that in front of Judy, but strangely his voice didn't reveal the slightest indication of a guilty conscience. *Was it because at that time nothing had happened yet, or was it that Judy had not found out? Or did she already know, and he remained calm about it?*

Julie surmised Brother Hsü used his dalliance with Brother Wei's wife as a reason to break away from Judy. The pretty wife clearly knew all about Brother Hsü's affair with Judy, addressing her as "aunt" in a particularly unpleasant voice that oozed with enmity.

"Before Brother Hsü departed, I opened my heart to him. We were still very close friends. If I hadn't spoken frankly, I would have felt terrible."

Julie felt sad; she realized that, though their affair had later turned ugly, Judy wanted to end it on a beautiful note, just as it had begun, or else the memories would be unbearable.

"He's married now," said Judy sounding cheerful, "to the third daughter of a distant relative." Judy was also a third daughter and her tone of voice seemed to suggest she thought this coincidence was fated. "She's dainty, petite, and a finicky type, completely spoiled; she expects him to look after her with every breath. He's working in Tientsin now, living with his mother-in-law, who spoils *him* terribly."

Judy paused before saying in a low voice, as if it were a passing afterthought, "He likes you."

Julie was shocked. *What could he have liked about me? Did he admire my height? Or was it just sympathy because we had both grown up in the shadow of our parents?* No one had ever liked her before and she wanted to know all the details of him sharing this information with Judy. But her third aunt had must have endured enough pain for delving so much into the past, and so Julie didn't press her. She only affected a startled smile.

Julie didn't like Brother Hsü, and it was not just because of his affair with Brother Wei's wife. Being devoid of maternal instincts, Julie couldn't appreciate his poor-little-street-urchin demeanor. Perhaps they were too much alike, and Julie couldn't stand anyone too similar to her, especially men.

When Julie was in middle school, memento books were all the rage. Everyone had one and everyone was asked to write something in it. If you didn't want to write a personal message, you could always jot down a moral homily, such as "Studying is like boating against the current: if you don't exert yourself you will fall behind." Julie asked Brother Hsü to paint something in her book. He had learned Chinese brush painting from Fifth Uncle, but Julie said, "Paint anything except a Chinese painting." As a child, Julie took painting lessons from an old teacher who taught her to paint "with only two pigments: ocher and cyanine." *That's like being half blind!* Julie gave up after just two days. She had always craved brilliant colors.

Julie could only remember speaking to Brother Hsü on that one occasion; he had certainly never initiated a conversation with her. He smiled as he took the memento book and returned it after painting a blond dancer in the Art Nouveau style that was popular at the end of the nineteenth century. The figure had a sharply curved goose-egg-shaped face and smooth hair parted in the middle and pulled back tightly—she seemed to resemble his enemy, his father's third concubine.

After Third Aunt found employment and Julie began to receive payments for her writing, one of the two German tenants moved out, freeing up a room. They no longer lived on scallion pancakes and the housekeeper, Mrs. Ch'in, retired. Judy could, in fact, cook and had even attended a culinary school while overseas. But if she cooked "one meal out of friendship, the second would set precedent," and she dreaded slipping into the role of housekeeper. Now, however, Judy gladly cooked a few simple dishes. Julie's only culinary skill was to cook the rice and shop for groceries. One night she went out to buy some crab-shaped pastries wearing a short, tight purple cotton gown with a floral pattern. She strolled, tall and willowy, her hair long and wavy. The wheat-cake vendor from Shantung gave her a curious look, unable to discern her class. Walking home in the moonlight, Julie felt a wave of emptiness. *I'm twenty-two and writing love stories without ever having fallen in love—no one can know that.*

One afternoon Bebe visited. The recently recovered living room stretched out spaciously in an L shape and included a red brick fireplace. The weak November sunlight streaming through the glass doors didn't reach far but hazily filled the room, motes like willow catkins floating in the air.

"Someone wrote a positive review of my book for a magazine—a government official who works under Wang Ching-wei. Yesterday my editor sent me another letter saying the reviewer has been thrown into prison," Julie told Bebe, amused, as if she were describing the absurdity of the times.

Wendy, an editor at the magazine, sent Julie the galley proof of the book review. The style closely resembled the acerbic wit of the famous left-wing writer Lu Hsün. The thin, snow-white paper with the editorial corrections in bright red made the galley proof look like a page from an antique string-bound volume. Julie was tempted to keep it. After receiving the proofs back, Wendy sent another letter in which she said, "Mr. Shao has now lost his freedom. He is unyielding and won't be bought off."

Julie worried that the review wouldn't be published. Wendy, however, didn't bring it up with her, and so she felt a little assured. She fantasized about rescuing Shao Chih-yung. But she also despised youthful fantasies.

In the end, it was Araki, a Japanese military adviser, who marched into the detention center armed with a pistol and got him out. Later, when Mr. Shao visited Shanghai, he asked Wendy for Julie's address so he could call on her. That day he wore an old black overcoat, and she thought he looked very handsome. He spoke Mandarin with what sounded like a slight Hunan accent, in the manner of a professional activist.

The first time Judy met him, she asked politely, "Did your wife accompany you?"

Instantly, Julie smiled. Every Chinese man of a certain age had a wife, so a reminder from Third Aunt was hardly necessary. Nothing could be more obvious.

Chih-yung also smiled as he answered.

"At least his eyes are very bright," commented Judy after he left.

"You seem so young and innocent around your aunt," remarked Chih-yung, "but when you're not with her you seem quite worldly."

He visited every day. Judy and Julie did not, as a custom, keep all the doors open in their home as many Chinese families did. Because of the tenants, all the doors in the corridor remained shut, which made Chih-yung feel like he was in a hotel, though if the doors had been open, he'd feel as if he had intruded into someone's home. Once seated in the living room behind a closed door, he stayed for a long time, making Julie feel terribly awkward. With a furrowed brow, Judy grumbled in a low voice, half smiling, "He comes every day, yes indeed!"

Julie would forever see his profile in silhouette as he sat backlit on the sofa opposite her—his cheeks gaunt, his sunken eyes wan and sallow, his arched, Cupid's-bow lips. When the room fell silent, he twirled a loose thread from the sofa around his fingers, smiled vaguely, and looked down at the ground, as if he held a full glass of water and was trying not to spill any of it.

"Your face has the radiance of a goddess," he exclaimed softly with amazement.

"I have oily skin," Julie explained with a giggle.

"Really? Is your entire face oily?" He also laughed.

Chih-yung arranged to visit Hsiang Ching with Julie because, he said, Hsiang Ching wanted to meet her. Hsiang was known as a writer before the Japanese invasion and now was of some repute in the occupied zone. After dinner, Chih-yung rode his son's bicycle to meet up with her and then hired a trishaw for Julie. It was a chilly winter evening and the journey was quite far. Hsiang Ching lived in a Western-style garden cottage. People crowded into the large ebony-paneled parlor room, but it was a cocktail party without any cocktails. Julie wore spectacles with pale yellow frames, and her face, free of cosmetics other than peach lipstick, looked as translucent as a freshly peeled lychee. Her slightly wavy hair, as fine as gossamer, neither black nor glossy, fell in a shapeless pile on her shoulders. She wore a peacock-blue padded gown of Nanking brocade with bell-shaped sleeves. The whole ensemble looked strange and she felt awkward; indeed, only a few guests engaged her in conversation.

"I'm actually a distant uncle of yours," Hsiang Ching told Julie.

Julie's family had a large number of relatives. When Second Aunt and Third Aunt lived overseas, they constantly said, "Don't look over there—that person might be a relative of ours."

Hsiang Ching had returned to China after studying abroad. Soon after his return he donned a traditional long scholar's gown and partook of the opium pipe, but was still quite a handsome man with a Grecian profile. His wife, the same woman his family had chosen for him before he had left, wasn't at the party. It had been a long time since he had written a word, and now he had even more reason to conceal his genius.

Julie wanted to leave and searched around for Chih-yung. She found him sitting on a sofa in conversation with two others. For the first time Julie saw a look of disdain in his eyes. She was stunned.

Julie worshipped Chih-yung, and yet why couldn't she tell him so? It was just like giving a bunch of flowers to someone passing by, as hopeless as love in medieval Europe, the love between a knight and a king's wife being so formal that even the king didn't bother to intervene. She had always felt that only love without motives could be true love. Of course she never spoke to Chih-yung about the Middle Ages, but he did later write in a letter about "searching for the Holy Grail."

After every one of his visits, Julie retrieved all his cigarette butts from the ashtray and saved them in an old envelope.

She showed him two photographs of herself that she felt displayed her true visage free of eyeglasses. One was a portrait Wendy had taken for the magazine. She had arranged a sitting with the German photographer Sieber, whose studio was located across the street from her. It cost so much that she only paid for one print. Her face was all that emerged through the shadows, her hair not visible, as if it were a Rembrandt painting. The photograph looked too dark and washed out in the magazine, and so the lone print was truly unique. He said he liked it so she gave it to him.

"This is just one side of you," he said of the other photograph. "This one reveals the whole person."

Despite the picture being unclear in the magazine, Chih-yung said, "When I saw it in the detention center, I could tell you were very tall."

As he was about to leave she casually opened the desk drawer and showed him the envelope full of cigarette butts. He laughed.

Whenever he asked, "Am I interfering with your writing?" she always shook her head and smiled.

He noticed that she ate, slept, and worked in the same room. "You're still living the student life," he chuckled. She just smiled.

"I don't think poverty is normal," she later said to him. "With poor families, even eating a piece of fruit can be a moral dilemma."

"You're like me when I was young. I worked in the post office then. Someone once posted a rubbing of a calligraphic inscription. I really liked it, so I kept it."

He once loved the fourth daughter of a family in his hometown. She planned to study in Japan; they could have gone together. "I needed four hundred dollars that I didn't have," he recalled with a smile.

"I saw a recent photograph of her. She hasn't changed much, still wears men's shirts and long pants."

He didn't say if she was married and Julie didn't have the heart to ask. Julie imagined she must have married long ago.

Apart from telling a few anecdotes from his life, Chih-yung had many theories to expound on. Julie, however, felt theories without evidence were mostly "wishful thinking"—the blind use of induction to force facts into a preexisting framework. His views were somewhat leftist, but he "didn't like" the dismal and chilling atmosphere of the Communist Party, and couldn't bear to obey their rules and regulations. In her mind the concept of communism wasn't that impressive; contemporary values held that everyone deserved to have enough food anyway, and things like education should meet individual needs. Implementation, of course, was another matter. And as for obedience, once you hand over all your freedom, it would be impossible to get it back.

When expounding on the Wang Ching-wei government's Peace Movement, Chih-yung couldn't be particularly realistic, so he resorted to grandiloquence. His idealization of Chinese village life seemed to Julie to be nothing more than nostalgia, and she paid scant attention to it. But every night after he left, Julie quivered with exhaustion and felt completely drained as she sat in Judy's room, bending over the small electric heater, embracing herself as she stared at the glowing red element. Judy didn't speak much, as though she sensed an imminent disaster, and when she did speak, it was always in a low voice, as if a gravely ill person lived in the house.

Julie never invited people over for meals because that would mean asking Judy to cook. It became embarrassing when he stayed to chat until seven or eight and they never invited him for dinner. Julie also felt guilty for troubling Judy. Eventually she couldn't endure the pressure of being placed in such a dilemma and wanted to break out of the vicious cycle by secretly going on a trip. Julie had a classmate who apparently had almost been slapped by a Japanese soldier at the station en route to a teaching position in Changchow; she never mentioned her idea. It wasn't a good time to travel, and besides, she didn't have any spare money.

One evening, as Chih-yung was about to leave and Julie had already stood up to see him out, he extinguished his cigarette, put both hands on her shoulders, and said with a smile, "Take off your glasses, will you?"

She removed her glasses and he kissed her. A violent spasm radiated down from his arms. She could feel his strong muscles though his clothes.

"This man really loves me," thought Julie. But the unyielding tip of his tongue felt as dry as a cork when it ventured between her lips—he had talked too much and no saliva remained in his mouth. He instantly sensed her revulsion and withdrew his hands with a faint smile.

Two days later, he stopped by after attending someone's dinner party. When Julie served him tea, she could smell alcohol on his breath. After chatting for a while he sat beside her.

"Let's be together forever, all right?"

Julie was sitting on the sofa in the dim lamplight. She turned her head and looked at him with a smile. "You're drunk."

"When I'm drunk, I feel good things are even better and bad things are even worse." He took her hand, turned it over to study the lines on her palm, and then examined the other one. "This is ridiculous." He laughed. "It looks like I'm reading your palm." Then he repeated his earlier entreaty: "Let's be together forever, all right?"

"And your wife?"

Did he hesitate?

"I can get a divorce."

And what would that cost?

"I don't want to get married right now. I'll come find you in a few years." She couldn't tell Chih-yung that would happen after the war—after a long and arduous journey, she would find him in the small town he had fled to, their reunion taking place also by the dim light of an oil lamp.

He smiled and said nothing.

Then he began to tell her about asking a guard in the detention center to buy him a copy of the magazine where he read her newest work. "I recommended your writing to the guard and he became very friendly to me."

He continued, "Your name sounded so feminine, and yet it didn't seem to be a nom de plume. I thought it might even be a man hiding behind the name. But even if it had been a man, I still would have sought him out. Any relationship that can be forged must be forged."

He stopped her in the doorway on his way out. With one hand on the door he gazed at her intently for a long time. His face appeared quite broad from straight on, a little feminine, with the aggressiveness of a boorish woman. She didn't look at him but smiled vaguely off into the distance over thousands of miles of rivers and mountains, where, in a few years, they would meet again under dim lamplight in a remote small town.

He finally spoke: "Your eyebrows are so high."

After he left, Julie smiled as she told Judy. "Shao Chih-yung said, 'Let's be together forever, all right?' and that he could get a divorce." There had to be a good explanation for the many hours they had spent together. Julie didn't like telling people anything unless she felt a real need to. She told Bebe nothing at all. There was a time when Julie and Bebe could talk about anything; while still in Hong Kong, Julie even wrote long letters to Judy. But ever since she started to publish her writing, she felt she would be understood no matter what she wrote, and if not understood, she felt confident that at least *someone* would understand. Once you've fallen in love with someone, no one else can compare. Now she felt even less capable of expressing her true feelings in conversations so she spoke to no one about how she felt. Each time she tried, she felt no comfort, only regret.

When Judy heard the news, she laughed. "I've always wanted to know what people really say when they propose. Once Brother Hsü said, 'Why haven't you married?' I was lying in bed and didn't hear clearly. I thought he said, 'Why haven't you married me?' I replied, 'You never asked me.'" She lightheartedly told this story in English, just like a bit of witty repartee in a Hollywood movie, though what came next had to be an anticlimax. "He said, 'No, I mean why haven't *you* married?'"

Julie was extremely embarrassed for them, but Judy didn't seem to mind, and Brother Hsü, apparently, survived the awkward moment too.

"Of course you realize," Judy continued after their pleasant exchange, "concerning marriage, your situation is different from his."

"I know."

Chih-yung didn't show up the next day. A few weeks later, Judy commented out of the blue, "Shao Chih-yung hasn't visited for quite a while."

"Yes," replied Julie, forcing a smile.

The leaves on the French plane trees lining both sides of the road were just beginning to bud, each tree lifting up a bowl made of light green spots. The spring chill felt slightly damp. Julie appeared to be carefree, spirits high, as she walked along the road. Something had come to a perfect conclusion, she hoped, but at the same time she still felt something was missing.

5

JUST WHEN she thought her torment was over, he reappeared. She didn't ask him why he had not come to see her for so many days. Later he confessed, "At the time I thought if it really couldn't work out then I should just forget about it." She smiled, a little dazed.

On another occasion he said, "I thought if you turned out to be a fool, we wouldn't have a future."

Before that he had said more than once, "I think it will be hard for you." Which was to say it would be difficult for Julie to find someone who'd love her.

"I know." Julie smiled. Actually, she wanted him to leave.

In Hong Kong she had once said to Bebe, "I'm afraid of the future." She didn't say what she feared, but Bebe knew. "Life has to be lived," Bebe said with a sad smile.

"I can't stop myself telling people about you," said Chih-yung cheerfully. "I asked Hsü Heng, 'Do you think Miss Sheng's beautiful?'" Hsü Heng was a painter she had met at Hsiang Ching's place. "And he said, 'Her disposition is quite good.' I was furious."

Julie kept smiling. The searchlight on the other side of the harbor found her. Inside the niche at the temporary shrine she felt the blue mist freeze her from head to toe.

He gave her several albums of Japanese woodblock prints and sat beside her as they looked through them together. When they finished, he once again held her hand and examined it. She suddenly noticed her very thin wrist inside her peacock-blue bell-shaped sleeve. She realized that he was also looking at her wrist and couldn't help saying in her own defense, "Actually, I'm not usually this thin."

He paused. "Is it because of me?"

She flushed and lowered her head. All the clichés in old novels flashed through her mind, like "She was unable to raise her head. It felt as heavy as a thousand pounds." Now she couldn't raise her own head. Was this really the case, she thought to herself, or was she acting?

He gazed at her for a long moment then kissed her. The peacock-blue sleeves timidly climbed up his shoulders and wrapped around his neck.

"You seem to be very experienced."

"I saw it in a movie." She giggled.

This time, and repeatedly, again just like in the movies, he only kissed her on the lips.

He embraced her as she sat on his knees, cheek to cheek. His eyes, so close to her cheek, sparkled like diamond pendants.

"You have piercing eyes."

"They say I have 'droopy eyes.'"

Who could have said that to him? She thought it must have been a classmate or a colleague when he was a teacher.

In the silence she could make out a popular love song playing over the radio some distance away. To hear a folksy love song at that moment made them both burst out laughing. It was not the sort of music one usually heard in the upper floors of an apartment building—it belonged in the streets. Yet at that moment, even the hackneyed lyrics sounded profound. Every so often they could clearly make out a line or two.

"Hey, these songs are actually quite good." He was listening, too.

Although Julie couldn't be sure, she thought it resembled an English song Second Aunt and Third Aunt used to sing:

> Down the river of Golden Dreams
> Drifting along
> Humming a song of love

Julie had never felt this safe since childhood. Time became drawn out, boundless, and infinite, a golden desert, majestically devoid of everything except vibrant music, and the palace doors to the past and the future flung wide open—surely this is what immortality must be like. She had never experienced time like this in her whole life, the moment totally unrelated to anything else in her life. She would merely accompany him a short distance—in a rowboat on the river of golden dreams. She could disembark and go ashore at any time.

He gazed at her. "You *are* beautiful," he said. "Why do you say you are not?" And then added, "Your smile wasn't quite right, but now it's perfect."

"Simply because the smile is unaffected," she thought.

He was thirty-nine. "When people reach my age, they all become apathetic." He chuckled.

From his tone of voice she could tell he feared adversity. But of course he meant he was unlike other people, that he had the determination to start a new life. She also vaguely knew that without the aura of enduring love, her golden eternal life would never be as she envisaged.

He calculated the age difference between the writer Lu Hsün and his wife, Hsü Kuang-ping. "They were only together for nine years. Too short, really.

But Hsü Kuang-ping was his student," he continued. "Lu Hsün always saw her as a young woman worthy of being cherished."

Chih-yung constantly analyzed their relationship. He also talked about Wang Ching-wei and Ch'en Pi-chün. When they were comrades in the Nationalist Party, Ch'en Pi-chün went to see Wang on official business. She stood in the rain the entire night, then the next morning he opened the gate and invited her in.

Julie had seen a photograph of Ch'en Pi-chün. She was short and fat, wore glasses, and was quite ugly. People said Wang Ching-wei was very handsome.

"We like each other equally, so there's no issue of who is pursuing whom." When he saw Julie laugh without responding, he added, "I've probably gone six steps and you have gone four steps," as if he were bargaining, which made her laugh even more.

On another occasion he said, "Women with too much initiative tend to scare away most men."

It is because I simply want to express my feelings for you. We'll never have a future together. This relationship won't go anywhere. But at the time she couldn't think of how to respond. And even if she were able to defend herself to him, it felt like the wrong time to bring it up. Later he would understand—not much later. How much more time would there be?

She ran her fingertips around his eyes, his nose, his mouth, to sketch the same profile of him in silhouette she had seen before when sitting across the room, smiling vaguely and looking down. But there was a trace of desolation in his smile.

"I'm always wild with joy," she said, "while you seem mournful."

He smiled. "I'm like a child who has cried a long time for an apple, but continues to sob after he's received it."

She knew he was saying that he had always wanted to meet someone like her.

"You look like a Six Dynasties Buddhist statue," she once said to Chih-yung.

"Yes, I love those Buddhist statues with their willowy, thin waists. I don't know when it began, all those big-bellied Buddhas."

Those stone statues were specifically from the northern dynasties. He claimed his ancestors were descendants of ancient nomadic Chiang tribesmen.

"Hsiu-nan says she's never seen me like this."

Hsiu-nan was his niece. "My niece has always been with me; she looks after my household affairs and is very good to me. She realized my life will always be unsettled, and to help with my daily expenses, she married a lumber merchant, a Mr. Wen. He's also from my hometown. A good man."

Julie had met Hsiu-nan once when she visited Chih-yung's residence in Shanghai. A pretty, fair-skinned, angular face. Long wavy hair draped down her back; blue cotton overcoat. She appeared to be in her twenties at the most. Mr. Wen was there, too. He bowed awkwardly to Julie. He wore a suit and appeared to be in his thirties. His face was pockmarked—hardly a good match for Hsiu-nan.

"She loves her uncle," Julie thought to herself.

Chih-yung told Julie he had written in letter to a friend. "Miss Julie Sheng and I, *are in love*." There was a slight emphasis on the last three words.

Julie didn't say anything but she was delighted. She itched to share the news. And this letter was publicity.

Her legs weren't particularly skinny. A band of skin, smooth and white, remained exposed above her socks.

He caressed that part of her leg. "Such a wonderful person to allow me such intimacy."

A gentle breeze caressed the palm fronds. The tide rose on the sands as the meandering white line stretched to the horizon, imperceptibly ascended and then retreated, yet seemingly motionless. She wanted this feeling to last forever, or at least to let her luxuriate a little more in this golden immortality.

One day she found herself sitting on him again, when suddenly something below began to lash her. She couldn't believe what she saw—a fly whisk fashioned out of what looked like a lion's or tiger's tail connected to a police truncheon wrapped in fabric. She hadn't seen such an object in the two erotic albums she had perused, and for a moment couldn't understand what she was seeing. She ought to have jumped up and giggled, acted like she didn't care. But before she could execute this strategy the whipping ceased. She didn't immediately slide off his knees. That would have been too obvious.

Later that day she told him, "Hsiang Ching wrote some disapproving things about you in a letter to me. He warned me to be wary of you." She let out a small laugh.

"Hsiang Ching is a good person who really understands me. He said it wasn't easy for a person as poor as me to have accomplished as much as I have. He said he couldn't do that."

He doesn't trust me! She couldn't believe it. *Why would I want to say bad things about Hsiang Ching to him? Maybe he thought I was trying to show that someone else cares for me in order to sound important.*

Julie was confused, but sensed Chih-yung had a lot of faith in his own ability to influence people and simply couldn't believe anyone would betray him. He was very possessive about his friends and didn't want to lose a single one.

She kept the letter in her desk drawer. First Hsiang Ching praised her short "masterpiece" then went on to warn her to be careful of "the demons in this society who eat people alive." Of course he didn't mention any names, but even Wendy by this time observed, "Everyone's saying that you and Shao Chih-yung are extremely close."

Julie didn't retrieve the letter to show Chih-yung. She was always afraid of embarrassing people, and him even more so, though she shouldn't have been. Perhaps she was unwilling to face the fact that he was rather unquenchable when it came to romance.

In the end, she asked Judy to help her write a polite yet obscure reply to Hsiang Ching.

Chih-yung returned to Nanking. He wrote to say he was meeting with friends as usual, playing chess, and taking walks on Mount Ch'ingliang, "But everything feels wrong. Life is like a fish writhing in my hands—I want to grab hold of it but I'm repulsed by the fishy smell."

She wasn't fond of this metaphor—for some reason the tiger-tail fly whisk flashed into her mind.

But his long letter seemed respectable; she showed it to Judy to prevent her from suspecting that something inappropriate had taken place.

"It's about time—you deserve a love letter," Judy observed with a wry smile.

"I love traffic lights," said Julie to Bebe as they crossed a road.

"So wear one in your hair," retorted Bebe.

The next time Chih-yung came to Shanghai she said to him, "I love Shanghai, even the curbstones are so clean that you can sit anywhere you like."

"Um," responded Chih-yung smiling, "that's not really true."

Why not? He's the one who said, "Tall buildings sometimes feel intimidating." Isn't that just as subjective?

"You don't actually make people feel inferior," he once said to her.

Chih-yung rang the doorbell and Julie opened the door. "Every time I visit I feel like there's someone actually in the door," he said. His tone of voice seemed to suggest that a female spirit resided behind the door and even the door was beguiled. She didn't like the idea of that.

"You two have decorated this place very well," he said. "I've been to many chic homes but none of them can compare with this one."

"It's all the work of my mother and Third Aunt," she said, smiling. "Nothing to do with me."

"How would *you* decorate it?" he asked, appearing somewhat surprised.

A deep purple cave, she thought. She loved all vivid colors, but she had never seen a deep purple wall, except in a dance hall. She wanted a color that wouldn't invoke any memories, memories inevitably leading to sorrow.

"Different from any other place," she replied softly, still smiling.

He looked worried and didn't pursue his line of questioning.

His nervousness made her feel slightly resentful. *Is he already thinking about finding us a new place?*

He said he still dearly cherished the memory of his first wife who had died while living in the countryside. The marriage had been arranged, and they only saw each other once before the wedding.

"I don't like courtship, I like marriage." With his face buried in her shoulder, he then said, "I want to settle down with you."

She couldn't understand him. How could they marry if he didn't divorce his current wife? She didn't want to raise the matter of divorce with him and, in any event, without money it was simply impossible. At the same time his words sounded a little jarring, maybe because she sensed that what he called marriage was something else entirely.

He repeated himself twice but she didn't respond. Then one day Chih-yung said, "Let's just let things follow their own course, all right?"

"Oh." She knew this relationship could end at any time. He would leave and never come back.

They embraced on the sofa. A carved wooden bird perched above the doorframe. The tawny double doors were open flat against the wall. What was the foot-high bird perched on? Even though she had her back to the doors, she knew the bird was three-dimensional, not simply painted on the wall, and that there wasn't an eave or shelf above the threshold. It looked like a primitive sculpture. Was it an idol of sacrifice in ancient times? The bird watched her. She was ready to stand up at any moment and walk away.

Over a decade later in New York, she made an exception to her usual practice and bathed in the afternoon. Bathing while waiting for the abortionist to come was like those housewives in the West tidying up the house before the maid arrived.

It's a desperate situation. Four months already. She had read in novels that it was too dangerous to have an abortion after three months. It was so difficult to find someone willing to do it.

Her breasts became fuller while she was pregnant, but now as she lay in the bathtub they flattened out. She already looked like a female cadaver, drained of blood, pale, bobbing up and down in the water.

Every woman's destined to risk her life.

She wore a black, sleeveless pullover vest and light-brown twill pants that tapered at the bottom. Rudy preferred her to wear long trousers or casual skirts. She could no longer fasten the skirt, despite having moved the button, though Bebe assured her no one would notice.

"A little Sheng would be nice," Rudy initially said, though his voice faltered as he spoke.

"I don't want one," she replied. "Even in the best circumstances— enough money and a reliable nanny—I still wouldn't want a child."

The doorbell rang and Julie went to open the door. They were living in a large apartment they had rented for the summer, the owner gone on vacation. A tidy-looking pudgy man in his thirties stood at the door. Pale complexion, dark brown hair, neatly dressed and carrying a briefcase, like an insurance broker. He looked fully alert as he entered.

"There's no one else here," she said. That was one of his conditions. Rudy had left.

She led him into the bedroom and he examined her on the bed. He took off his jacket, revealing the short-sleeve shirt he wore beneath it. He retrieved an array of vessels, then sterilized his hands.

So it'd be the suppository method. "Old woman Wong's suppository string" was mentioned in the Republican-era novel *Tides of the Hwang-poo*. Living in a foreign land while being killed by a suppository at the hands of a midwife in early Republican-era Shanghai—the overlap of time and place in her mind veered into the absurd.

"What if it doesn't come out," she asked anxiously.

"You want me to cut you open?"

She didn't respond. She thought a curette involved a minor surgical procedure. He made it sound like the ancient Chinese punishment of death by dismemberment, which she took as a veiled threat, though she had no solid knowledge of such things.

As he was about to leave she reiterated her concerns: "I'm just afraid it won't come out and will get stuck inside there. I'm already at four months."

"That won't happen." But he paused for a moment to ponder the situation again. "If you're still worried you can call this number."

He gave her the telephone number for a Marsha, who worked in the largest department store in town, if she encountered any problems. Julie thought Marsha probably wasn't her real name and she wouldn't necessarily be waiting at home for telephone calls.

He left.

Not long after, Rudy came back. He opened a cabinet and returned a kindling ax to its original location. The fireplace in the apartment was only used to create a cozy atmosphere, as the building had central heating in the winter.

"I didn't really leave," he said. "I was just waiting in the stairwell. I heard the elevator come and watched him get in. Earlier I had looked around for a weapon and found this tomahawk. Just in case something happened to you, and I could kill the son of a bitch."

Julie wasn't surprised. Judging from Rudy's big build this was believable. Maybe their relationship was somehow connected to her addiction to movies as a teenager and his drifting around Hollywood for many years.

"I've always been cheap," said Rudy.

Well, he's never saved any money. He'd buy a house after winning a poker game and then sell it later for no good reason. He often mocked himself, saying, "What a joke, everyone says, 'Rudy's good with money.'" At script-writing sessions he was always asked to handle scenes about money.

"I'm a coward," he said. People like him felt an affinity for old westerns and would start a fight at the drop of a hat.

"We have the damnedest thing for each other," he said, bewildered, with an embarrassed smile.

She never felt any regrets for having met him so late in life. He was old, but if they had met several years earlier he would not necessarily have liked her and their relationship would not have lasted long.

"I always hit and run," he said.

She could feel the string of the suppository hanging down and brushing against her thigh like the fuse of a bomb. After several hours nothing had happened. They called Marsha. The saleswoman sounded like a chubby thirtysomething Jewish woman. Obviously her job was only to offer comforting words. "Hold her hand," she advised Rudy. Julie did not call her again.

For dinner Rudy bought a chicken at the rotisserie across the road. Deep pains churned in her belly but he still encouraged her to eat while he himself devoured the food with gusto. She felt a bit resentful. Did she really need him to hold her hand?

That night, under the bathroom light, she saw a male fetus in the toilet bowl. In her terrified eyes it was at least ten inches long, leaning upright against the white porcelain, partly submerged in the water. The thin smear of bloody liquid on its skin was the light orange color of newly planed wood. Fresh blood accumulated in its hollows and outlined its form distinctly. A pair of disproportionately large eyes protruded and its arms looked like the retracted wings of the wooden bird that used to perch above the door in Shanghai so long ago.

In that moment of horror, Julie flushed the toilet. At first she worried the fetus would not flush away, but it soon disappeared into the billowing vortex.

"So did anything come out?" asked Bebe about the abortion. But when Julie told her, Bebe was incredulous and suspected that Julie had simply imagined it all and wasted four hundred dollars.

"We walked into this with our eyes wide open; we were never irrational," said Chih-yung.

Perhaps he too felt something perched above his head, observing them.

"I have some business to attend to tomorrow," he said. "I won't be coming."

That weekend, Julie went to visit Bebe. Bebe had transferred to the same university as her younger sister. The two sisters were very amiable, but the prejudice against Indians was much greater in Shanghai than in Hong Kong because Shanghai lacked the British connection that existed in Hong Kong.

Most Indians in Shanghai belonged to different religions and did not intermarry. Believers invariably preferred to return to their hometowns in India to find a bride, suspecting the Indian girls in Shanghai of having picked up bad habits and not being sufficiently conservative. The British and Americans were all interned in concentration camps. In the living room of Bebe's home hung large portraits of two Muslim monarchs. After the Shah of Iran divorced Princess Fawzia, the royal daughter of Sultan Fuad I of Egypt, because of a lack of a male heir, Bebe's family added his portrait to the wall, as if they considered the Shah a suitable candidate for a prospective husband. Bebe explained to Julie that by her family's standards King Farouk was not fat—of course that was before he became truly rotund.

Farouk later married a commoner, Narriman Sadek, the daughter of a Cairo shopkeeper. They lived in a world far less isolated than wartime Shanghai. Julie found them strange, but the Muslim world had always been mysterious to her. A goat tethered in the small courtyard by the rear gate of Bebe's house was waiting to be slaughtered for a religious festival; its throat would be cut open. The goat, as large as a pony with dirty wool that curled like a fur coat, stretched its neck though a kitchen window to eat vegetables stored in a basket.

That day they didn't have anywhere to go—it was a torment in Shanghai without any good movies to watch. Then Julie remembered that Hsü Heng, the artist, had given her his address and told her to visit any time to look at his paintings. She asked Bebe if she wanted to go, and together they set off for Hsü Heng's home to view his paintings.

The Hsü household wasn't far, located in a typical alleyway house. They entered from the rear kitchen door into a spacious, dark living room with a dozen or so unframed oil paintings hanging on the wall or on the floor leaning against the wall. Hsü Heng gave them a tour but didn't say much; he seemed both servile and overly polite. He was only in his thirties but around the house wore a faded dark green suit of the kind the aesthetic-movement types used to wear—in places it had faded to a paler light green.

Suddenly Chih-yung walked in. Julie knew he was close with Hsü Heng but never expected that he would be there. Chih-yung had once met Bebe at Julie's home so everyone began nodding their greetings. In the darkened room, she caught a glimpse of his broadly smiling face that betrayed a hint of unease. Bebe's Chinese wasn't good enough to discuss art in any depth, so she switched to English. Julie thought Chih-yung felt awkward because of the language issue. Conscious of Chih-yung's and Hsü Heng's pride, she bravely filled in the gaps by talking nonstop. Julie didn't like Hsü Heng's paintings at all, which made her even more reluctant to leave after a cursory view, so she made two full circuits.

Then Hsü Heng brought in two more paintings from another room. The family seemed to occupy only two rooms on the ground floor. After viewing the paintings, Julie and Bebe announced their departure. While the host and Chih-yung escorted them out through the kitchen, they passed some people playing mah-jongg at a table set up in a small passageway leading to the kitchen. Julie didn't get a chance to look closely, but it appeared that all the players were women.

The next day Chih-yung visited and Julie learned that one of the mah-jongg players was his wife.

"You had a lot to say," he chortled, "babbling on endlessly like that."

"So terrible," she confessed, giggling. Then she recalled a woman seated at the table who appeared to be fuming. Julie had passed by quickly and only remembered she seemed tall and young.

"She said to me," reported Chih-yung, "'Surely you don't think I can't compete with her?'"

He once said to Julie, "Everyone says my wife is beautiful." Julie had seen a small photograph of her taken outdoors. She was beautiful by any standard. Long, angular face. Tall and curvaceous. She appeared to possess a strong personality. In the photo she stood frowning in front of a banana tree, her eyebrows plucked into parabolic lines. She used to be a sing-song girl from the Ch'in-huai River entertainment district of Nanking. Chih-yung had promised himself, "This time I'm going to marry a beautiful woman." When he took her as his wife she was only fifteen, but it wasn't until several months after their nuptials that their affections for each other blossomed and the marriage was consummated.

"I loved her even more when I got out of jail, but she, however, she became cold toward me." Then he chuckled. "It was as though she wanted to negotiate terms with me! I was very annoyed."

He didn't mention, of course, that his wife had slapped him in the face in front of everyone at the Hsü residence, saying to Julie only, "If it were someone else, our relationship could have grown stronger after such a fuss. But nothing's changed between us."

Julie had inadvertently worn an especially garish outfit that day—a claret-colored long vest over a peacock-blue cotton gown. The vest was fashioned out of a large old scarf from the early Republican era, with its original fringe swaying from the hem of the vest. She must have left a very bad impression, Julie thought. And worse, she caused him embarrassment. She felt disheartened. They should have ended their relationship long ago. But of course they shouldn't let that happen simply because his wife had caused a scene—that would be laughable. Julie wasn't plagued with guilt, nor did she harbor any bad feelings toward Chih-yung's wife; she felt she had nothing to apologize for. She hadn't stolen anything from his wife because her relationship with Chih-yung was different.

Chih-yung again stayed until late in the evening. The next day he returned. Julie served him tea, then planted herself on the carpet beside his armchair.

"You're actually very attentive," he said, somewhat surprised, "like a Japanese woman. Your innate allure must have sublimated into a purer form."

She laughed, as if long accustomed to such flattery.

"Yesterday, when I left, the doorman was annoyed at having to open the gate for me at such a late hour. He swore at me. I became angry and hit him." With a look of contempt in his eyes, he raised his head and inhaled on a cigarette. "Oh, I hit him hard, yes I did! He tumbled and fell right across the pathway. A big guy, and completely useless. I've practiced tai chi, you know. Actually, I often give the doormen tips, especially the one who operates the elevator."

The apartment building's two doormen were both burly men from Shantung Province who had retired from some sort of militia. They wore khaki uniforms, switching in the summer months to English-style short pants. They reclined on cane lounge chairs, blocking the way with their yellow knees exposed.

"That gentleman isn't tall," the elevator operator told Judy, "but he's very strong. He hit the doorman so hard the man's got a big bruise on his face and has been too embarrassed to show up for work the past couple of days."

For some reason, Julie felt differently about Chih-yung after he hit the doorman. She no longer needed to fantasize about their romance.

"I've fallen in love with Mr. Shao and he's looking for a way to get divorced," Julie eventually told Bebe in a breezy tone while they were clinging to the rubber hoops hanging from the ceiling of the bus. She had chosen that moment to break the news, to avoid giving Bebe the opportunity to explode.

Bebe smiled back. But it was that terrified smile of hers. "The first person to break through your defenses!" Bebe later scolded. "You're completely devoid of feminine guile." And then she chuckled. "If only I were a man, I would have saved you a lot of trouble."

Bebe met Chih-yung at Julie's. She of course treated him with friendly chatter and laughter. Chih-yung found Bebe extremely charming.

"Julie has split ends which can be pulled out into two strands," he suddenly told Bebe.

Julie was mortified. She knew Chih-yung was showing off just how intimate he was with her. Bebe's expression changed, obviously considering it very ungentlemanly to say something like that, but then she simply changed the topic of conversation. That evening he departed with Bebe.

One day, Julie and Chih-yung were discussing Julie's reputation as a money-grubber, and that she bickered over trivial amounts of her remuneration as a writer. "I need to earn more money," Julie told him, "in order to repay what I owe my mother." She had told Chih-yung that her mother used to complain about the large sums she had spent on her. But this time she felt dreadfully embarrassed as soon as those words came out of her mouth—Chih-yung must have paid off the "debts" of his sing-song girl to buy back her freedom. It must have sounded all too familiar to him, a prostitute in a Shanghai brothel trying to extort more money just like in a Republican-era novel. But that was then, and she was fully aware of his present impecuniousness; she simply wanted him to understand her attitude toward money.

Chih-yung's expression changed slightly, too, but he quickly smiled in acknowledgment.

Chih-yung returned to Nanking again. Julie assumed he had come directly from the train station to her house when he arrived in Shanghai that day in the early summer, carrying a medium-size suitcase.

Perhaps he couldn't mention it in a letter, but he told her after he arrived that he would be moving to central China to set up a newspaper. Then he smiled as he picked up the cheap leather-trimmed tweed suitcase. He set the suitcase down and opened it. It was full of banknotes. Knowing it must be part of the funds to finance the newspaper, she didn't look closely. She casually shut the case and left it standing in a corner.

Julie waited until he left to reopen the suitcase. Unlike the eight hundred Hong Kong dollars Mr. Andrews had given her, there were no small-denomination notes. Julie couldn't keep up with Hong Kong dollars let alone Chinese paper currency, especially after the innumerable changes to the monetary system. Then factor in inflation. She couldn't tell the value of the money but knew, even taking inflation into account, it surely must be a very large sum.

Julie showed the suitcase to Judy. "Shao Chih-yung brought me this to repay Second Aunt," said Julie, grinning. Actually, he didn't say that, but at the moment it didn't occur to her to say otherwise.

"Well he certainly knows how to acquire funds," Judy commented.

Now Julie had an excuse and didn't feel awkward asking him to stay for dinner. But the next night, after eating a simple evening meal at her place, she nonetheless felt terribly embarrassed. As soon as she passed him a hot towel, she left the table, and turned her head to smile at him.

Chih-yung stared at her, apparently enchanted. When she returned to the living room, he laughed, saying, "This towel is too dry and too hot. How can I possibly wipe my face?"

Square hand towels folded into triangles were usually placed, cold and moist, onto dinner plates; they could easily be mistaken for two small sandwiches. Julie assumed he preferred a more comforting hot towel, which opened up the pores, so she had gone out of her way to prepare one specially for him. This involved walking over to Judy's bathroom at the other end of the corridor. Worried that the small towel would cool down while she carried it back over such a great a distance, she had held the towel under running hot water and then wrung it out forcefully, scalding her hands in the process.

"I'll get another one."

When she returned, he said, "Shall we go out on the balcony?"

The large balcony was empty of any furniture. High, bulky concrete balusters enclosed the rectangular space with its complex geometric design. There was hardly a night view of the city to speak of during the wartime blackout. Only the dusty purple sky glittered like agate above the darkened balcony. A faint smell of rust filled the air. And suspended in the heavens, a half-moon radiated pure light with a glowing halo.

> Brightness, bright as the moon
> When can I pluck it from the sky?

"Here and now," he said, and striking a pose he grabbed hold of Julie. Both of them burst out laughing. He had forgotten he still held a cigarette in his hand. When he realized he had burnt the back of her arm, he burbled like an anxious parent.

He kissed her. Like the flame of a candle she bent away from the wind. But the hot wind persisted and he pressed his face to hers.

"Is this real?" she asked.

"It is, for both of us."

His daily visits resumed. One afternoon Hsiu-nan came to look for Chih-yung. After exchanging greetings, Julie took her leave to allow them to talk. She returned with a pot of tea, but Hsiu-nan left without drinking any. Julie and Chih-yung watched from the balcony on the top floor as Hsiu-nan left the building, turned, and waved at them.

"Hsiu-nan said to me, 'You two seemed to be in heaven,'" Chih-yung reported to Julie the next day.

"That's because she loves him," thought Julie, feeling a little sad.

During the temple fair at the time of the Festival of Bathing the Buddha, the nearby streets were full of stalls. The buzz from the street, clearly audible from the height of her apartment, instilled an early-summer ambience. Julie went down to buy two slipper uppers embroidered with gold thread. But nothing in the market possessed the rustic charm of the homespun fabric she had seen in Hong Kong.

"Your clothes are like a country child's," said Chih-yung.

Snuggling up to Chih-yung, Julie fondly recalled his profile when sitting across the room. "I seem to only like you from a certain angle," she said out of the blue.

Chih-yung's expression suddenly changed at the thought that her enthusiasm for him occasionally waned. But then his eyes displayed contempt as he bent over to stub out his cigarette. "You love me, of which I am deeply aware," he said with a smile and, like the hulking shadow of a mountain that blacks out the sky, turned to kiss her. A lock of hair fell across his forehead.

After chatting for a while he casually turned to kiss her again, a small animal peering around on the bank of a stream and intermittently lowering its head to drink.

The brick-red curtains, like red sails, blew against the gold-painted iron security bars running horizontally across the windows. The large round mirror on the wall resembled a moon gate. The setting sun reflected in the mirror formed two small rainbows. They gazed at the rainbows in silence, almost with a kind of horror.

"No one else lives like us, together all day," he chuckled.

He recited lines from "Sitting Alone by Ching-t'ing Mountain" by the T'ang dynasty poet Li Po:

> Never tiring of watching each other
> Mount Ching-t'ing, there is no other

"If only we could sleep embracing, always embracing," he said. "In the countryside you can find a muntjac, a kind of large deer with a small head. I once caught one. It was very strong and it almost got away. I was exhausted and fell asleep embracing it. When I woke up the deer was gone."

The rainbow vanished. They lay next to each other on the sofa. In the fading light of dusk he stared into her eyes for a long time. "All of a sudden I feel you are like a fox seductress in *Strange Tales from a Chinese Studio*."

Chih-yung told Julie that his first wife missed him so much, she became enchanted by a fox spirit and dreamed about him every day. Eventually she caught tuberculosis and died.

He really believes in fox spirits! Julie suddenly felt that the entire vast central plains of China separated them, a chasm so enormous that her heart began to palpitate.

The carved wooden bird perched above the doorway as always.

Chih-yung returned to Nanking.

"I am truly happy you are with your wife in Nanking," Julie wrote in a letter to him.

Julie then recalled what Bebe had said about men visiting prostitutes after being with their girlfriends. Julie didn't feel she was insulting anyone—in any case, Chih-yung and Crimson Cloud remained husband and wife as before. She knew that he would never let Crimson Cloud leave him without giving her a large alimony payment.

Julie didn't feel Chih-yung had anything to apologize to Crimson Cloud for. *So beautiful, and just over twenty—she's bound to land on her feet isn't she?*

Julie felt no envy toward people in his past, or people who would soon be in his past.

"I am still concerned about our future together," she wrote in the same letter.

"As to our marriage," he wrote in reply, "it is indeed a quandary. But let me carry the burden of all the unpleasantness. Last night she suddenly went to the dining room to open a cabinet and find some alcohol to drink. I snatched it out of her hands and she laughed maniacally. 'Father, pity me!' she wailed."

Julie's flesh crept when she read that, but she never asked what Crimson Cloud meant. Julie assumed that from the age of fifteen, Crimson Cloud had replaced her late father with Chih-yung in her eyes, and now she bares her soul to her late father.

"Now everyone knows that Julie Sheng is Shao Chih-yung's woman," he wrote in his letter.

Julian must have caught wind of it, too, and dropped by for a visit. His eyes looked wider and rounder than ever, but the household seemed completely normal to him and he couldn't discern anything.

After Fifth Uncle put in a good word to Ned on his behalf, Julian was able to attend a high school attached to a university. Two years later, he was admitted to the university, but after staying two years, he decided not to continue and wanted to work instead. Since Julian had no interest in his studies, Julie saw no point in him continuing; but she was unable to help him find work and was even less willing to ask Chih-yung to help.

"You can't always rely on others for help," Judy said in Julian's presence.

Julie felt slightly offended. She thought a born loser like Julian would need a helping hand, at least at the beginning of his career. Otherwise, how would he survive?

Once when Julian was sick as a child, Judy cared for him day and night, preparing droplets of medicine every two hours. Julie had heard this from Judy's own mouth, but Judy had hardened her heart in recent years in self-defense, afraid the whole clan would take advantage of her.

Julie wrote to Chih-yung about a dream. She dreamed that she told her old maidservant everything about him. She saw Chih-yung smiling in the bright sunlight, but for some reason his face was dark red and covered with one-inch swastikas cut in relief that cast distinct shadows. She thought it strange that she had never noticed this before and ran her fingertips gently over his face, wondering if his wounds still hurt.

In his reply, he said he didn't know what the swastikas carved into his face meant. She knew that exiled prisoners were branded and that the swastika represented the Axis Powers.

She wrote a vernacular poem:

> Never have I occupied any places
> In his life's bygone phases
> As his years of solitude streamed past
> He incarcerated himself in a silent courtyard
> The empty rooms filled with sunshine
> A sunshine left behind from ancient times

I have a good mind to crash into the compound
And shout: "Here I am! Look, here I am!"

He never admitted it, but he clearly didn't like the poem. His past had been colorful, not empty, just waiting for her to crash in.

6

CHIH-YUNG went to central China in the summer. When he returned to Shanghai the following October, he told Julie, "I've brought a sum of money for Crimson Cloud to resolve the matter with her."

Julie had never raised the issue of his divorce, except once in a letter saying she was concerned about their future together. But now that he had brought it up, she smiled and said softly, "There's also your second wife."

Chih-yung had married her while teaching in the interior. Apart from his eldest son, whose mother had died, his other children were hers. She suffered from a mental illness and lived with the children in Shanghai, under the care of Hsiu-nan.

"Legally, she *is* your wife."

"Everyone recognizes Crimson Cloud as my sole wife."

"But when you married Crimson Cloud you had not divorced *her*."

"I can't simply drive her out!"

She smiled. "It's just a legal procedure." Then she walked away.

Finally the day arrived when he showed her two newspapers printed with the same two advertisements side by side: "Announcing the divorce of Shao Chih-yung and Crimson Cloud Chang" and "Announcing the divorce of Shao Chih-yung and Jade Phoenix Ch'en." It looked quite absurd. He tossed the newspapers onto a low, lacquer teapoy and sank into the sofa. Behind his grin a disconsolate expression peeked out.

Julie knew he felt sad because of Crimson Cloud. She sat on the arm of the sofa and caressed his hair. He flinched, as if she had touched a sore spot. She only smiled in reply and returned to her seat.

"I bought a truck for Crimson Cloud. She wants it for business."

"Oh."

They chatted some more, then fell silent. "I'm truly happy," Julie suddenly blurted out.

"I knew you wouldn't be able to contain yourself."

"Shao Chih-yung feels terrible for his wives," Julie later told Judy.

Judy furrowed her brow and smiled. "Really! That's just like the saying, 'In your mouth it's just flavorless bone, but if it falls on the ground it turns into juicy meat in your mind.'"

She added, "Of course, that's a good sign—he'll do the same for you some day."

As soon as the announcements were published, the newspapers naturally deduced their plan to marry.

"All the major papers and tabloids are reporting it," sniggered Judy, with a triumphant smile. "But I am very annoyed that they say you don't want to get married so soon after moving in with me. Isn't that ridiculous?"

The relatives had been gossiping with tales of Judy infecting Julie with her celibacy. Of course, that was before the news of Chih-yung spread. Judy had not told Julie about this.

"So when will you get married?" Judy asked.

"Chih-yung mentioned the same thing but, given the current circumstances, it'd be better not to—at least for me."

He actually put it this way, suggesting with bravado, "An announcement would be fine. And we could invite friends over for drinks. That would be fine too."

He's trying to make amends. Julie felt sad.

Chih-yung, observing Julie's unresponsiveness and seeming uninterest in his proposal, retracted the offer.

Judy nodded and grunted in acknowledgment when Julie mentioned "current circumstance," but then she frowned and asked, "What will happen if you have a child?"

Under normal circumstances Julie would just giggle in surprise at a comment like that, but today aunt and niece were behaving out of character. "He said if we have a child he'd ask Hsiu-nan to raise it," replied Julie, smiling.

"Pay no attention to him," Judy scoffed. "The whole process can be very painful. Maybe like me you'll be infertile. Heaven knows how many abortions your second aunt had."

"Second Aunt had abortions?" Julie parroted in shock.

Judy snorted, grinned, and then, apparently regretting her slip of the tongue, looked at Julie and added sotto voce, "I thought you knew."

Julie's indifference toward Judy's relationship with Herr Schütte could have contributed to Judy's misconception. In Hong Kong, Rachel had said, "Your third aunt has an ability to find friends as soon as I leave." When Julie returned to Shanghai, she guessed her mother had been referring to Herr Schütte, the principal at the German school whom Judy got to know during her German studies. Julie had met him. He was thin, of medium build, with blond hair, and he wore spectacles. He was rather handsome, but he always seemed to speak in a sarcastic tone of voice. Julie went to Bebe's for meals whenever he visited Judy.

"I truly never knew," Julie tittered. "Second Aunt always seemed so fiercely opposed to sexual entanglements."

Judy shook her head wearily and sighed. "One time she had an abortion because of Chien-wei." She snorted in exasperation. *Was it because they were strangers in a strange land that had made it even harder to find a doctor?* "I didn't know much about anything in those days. At the time, she thought that if she really couldn't get a divorce then I could marry Chien-wei as cover, which I agreed to." She paused before continuing. "When your second aunt moved in I was only fifteen years old. I thought I was in love with her."

Judy didn't come out and say she loved Chien-wei, but of course she loved him too. Julie was so shocked at hearing this revelation that her ears throbbed. Although tragic, she saw nothing wrong with this ménage à trois in which one willingly beat the other who was in turn willingly beaten.

"Why didn't you go through with it?" asked Julie.

"Then there was the Northern Expedition, right? Divorce was prohibited during the era of the Peiyang government."

No wonder the inscription on the photograph Chien-wei gave to Judy oozed with regrets. "To Judy, forever my little sister." The long face in the photograph conveyed a sentimental expression, with big black oval eyes, thick eyebrows, a widow's peak—a handsome visage indeed.

Of course, the three of them traveled together to the Lake District that time. Rachel had written in her poem: *I am sure its roses still wear their tender rosy rouge.* Red roses bloom in the cool summers of northern England, where Lake Poets like William Wordsworth lived long ago and where, more recently, that overseas student killed his wife when they were there. Perhaps Judy's morbid fear of people coveting her assets was triggered by that murder, and so she preferred the cocoon of her warm little coterie, willingly sharing a man with her sister-in-law; she in the open, Rachel secretly.

"There was also Marshal," Judy said with a chuckle, "as well as Honest Nephew. Your second aunt had many stories in this vein."

"I don't remember Honest Nephew."

"How could you forget?" Judy became agitated as if her credibility was being questioned. "Honest Nephew! The one with TB."

"I only remember Fat Nephew and Pigtail Nephew." One was fat and the other had a long queue running down his back as a child. "And that Colonel Boudinet."

Judy obviously didn't consider the French military officer who once came for tea worth mentioning and thus couldn't be counted. "Your second aunt was not as beguiling the last time she returned from Europe!" Judy said, shaking her head.

Julie had always thought Rachel looked most ravishing in those days.

Judy noticed Julie's shocked expression and abruptly stopped. Feeling numb about her own mother was one thing—she felt offended listening to someone else criticize her.

"But Dr. Feinstein was because of you," Judy chuckled.

Julie was dumbfounded. So the German doctor treated her typhoid for free! That freshly hosed-down elephant who bent over her bed and assailed her nose with the smell of antiseptic. Rachel standing opposite the doctor in his clinic. A clinic in an old ornate, Western-style residential building. The two silhouetted against a stained-glass window as he lowered his head to listen to her dainty chest with his stethoscope; Rachel's guarded expression on her blushing face.

No wonder Rachel cursed Julie at her bedside, saying, "Oh, you just live to bring disasters! People like you should just be left alone to die!"

Perhaps the doctor even paid the hospital bill.

Sometimes in life we learn things too late, as if all the principal players had already died. Julie felt numb. She knew she shouldn't, but she couldn't help it—she felt nothing. This revelation changed nothing: her affection exhausted, no emotions remained.

Perhaps Rachel had so many lovers that one more made little difference. But one can't really say that because she had loved all of them. They were the ones who chose not to make long-term plans with Rachel, so to whom could she be loyal?

The more Julie thought about it, the more she felt that she had known all along. After the afternoon-tea guests left and Julie returned from the roof, she had noticed the steaminess in the bedroom and the carelessly made bed—the sheets and comforter were ruffled and everything about the room seemed a little messy. Of course, it had been a momentary impression that quickly got pushed aside.

But how could she have no memory of Honest Nephew? He must have felt guilty and receded to the background. After Rachel and Judy moved, he never visited, unlike his siblings.

Julie felt somewhat resentful toward him alone, though not because of her mother's association with him as a married woman. It would be absurd to talk of legalities now. Perhaps Rachel was taking her revenge; that was around the time Ned had set up a separate household for his concubine. Julie resented Rachel's relationship with Honest Nephew simply because she treasured her childhood. She felt that period of her life was somehow exclusively hers. Many years later she encountered a family in the New England countryside. A young boy led a burro along the path. It was adorable, though its face wasn't as long as the ones she had seen before. After they had been walking together for a while, Julie stretched out her hand to pet the burro's neck. The boy instantly looked upset. Julie understood because she still remembered how possessive she had been as a child.

One year they invited the nephews over to celebrate New Year's Eve. Judy still kept a small photograph of the occasion. Ned was there—the only one not wearing a golden paper crown on his head. Julie didn't sit at the table but still remembered the red crepe paper that Rachel and Judy had used to wrap the flower pots before the banquet. Crepe-paper crackers were placed on the table; the suspended lanterns and colorful banners were made of crepe paper, too. It was the first time she had ever seen such decorations and she loved it, but she still couldn't remember Honest Nephew. Nor was he in Judy's photograph.

After Rachel and Judy traveled overseas, Auntie Han would take Julie and Julian by rickshaw to Honest Nephew's house for New Year visitations. It was a long journey through a district of low whitewashed houses, all with flat roofs since the dry northern climate made roof tiles moot. The desolate row of oblong white buildings was similar to the Middle East. A small, ancient, spruce wood gate, blackened with age, opened in a wall to many gloomy courtyards housing family members and some distant relatives.

The children were led down a winding corridor to a tiny dark room where a tall old man wearing a gray gown sat on a rattan recliner. He was a nephew of Julie's paternal grandfather, whom she greeted as Second Uncle.

"And how many Chinese characters do you know?" he asked Julie, as was his custom when he encountered children. "Do we have any snacks for them?"

His fourth daughter-in-law, a petite old woman with bound feet, appeared in the doorway. After a brief discussion with the old man, she went to prepare the snacks. None of Julie's cousins were anywhere to be seen—they were busy eating.

"Recite a poem for me," the old man said to Julie.

Standing on the tiled floor a young Julie swayed from side to side, transferring her weight from one foot to the other as she chanted a T'ang dynasty poem from memory, without knowing the meaning: "The Shang songstress knew not the torment of a vanquished state." She watched him wipe tears from his eyes.

Julie learned from the male servants at home that when the Taiping rebels breached the defenses of Nanking, this same Second Uncle had been the provincial governor. From high atop the city wall, he was lowered down in a basket and escaped.

The only close relatives who lived in the vicinity were two paternal uncles and their families. The other branch of the paternal family was wealthier, and the servants referred to them as belonging to the "New House." This residence was their newly built Western-style mansion painted inside and out in a cream color with all the furniture lacquered white. In each room tassels adorned with emerald-green glass beads hung from the lampshades. This branch of the Sheng clan closely observed the clan traditions. Not only were the two brothers in the family addressed by their seniority rankings as Eleventh Master and Thirteenth Master but even their concubines were ranked by seniority. Madam One belonged to Eleventh Master, Madam Two and Madam Three belonged to Thirteenth Master. The numbering went up to Madam Nine and Madam Perfect—the perfect number ten. It made one's head spin.

Eleventh Master was a cabinet minister in the Peiyang government. Whenever Auntie Han took Julie and her brother to visit, they were made to wait by themselves in a large reception room on the second floor. Auntie Han stood behind their chairs as they waited, usually for at least a full two hours. Every once in a while, Auntie Han would twist a piece off of an oblong strip of a cherry-blossom jelly confection for the siblings to snack on, from a tall-footed glass tray on the table.

A seventeen-year-old concubine from Chefoo that an acquaintance had recently bestowed to the head of the family stood languidly by the fireplace, arms folded. She appeared even daintier in her tight, full-length, deep purple gown when standing in front of the green tiles of the mantel. Her hair was braided into two buns that sat on each side of her head, with sparse bangs in the front; her small round cheeks were rouged a rustic red.

"How many years have you been in service, eh?" she asked Auntie Han icily. "Where are you from, eh?" She had been left out in the cold, too, and wanted to strike up a conversation to fill the awkward silence. Auntie Han deferentially greeted her with a respectful "miss," but avoided engagement.

After a long time, even the new concubine had left, but the three of them were still kept waiting. Finally, Seventh Mistress summoned them—even the old women of the family were ranked by seniority. Seventh Mistress sat on the edge of her bed while she made detailed inquiries into the family's well-being. "What do you eat? Your mother prohibits so many different foods I'm afraid to give you anything. Surely you can eat crucian carp with steamed eggs? What else?" After ascertaining each acceptable dish, she sent orders to the kitchen. It was only then that she lowered her voice and asked, "Is Sixteenth Master well? Are there any letters from Sixteenth Mistress and Nineteenth Sister?" It was natural for her to use the seniority ranking to refer to Ned, Rachel, and Judy. "Goodness, how could anyone abandon these two children? It makes one feel so sorry for them. Thank goodness for you senior retainers."

"You mean besides the letter mentioned last time? We underlings do not know of such things, madam."

"These two are so civil. Not like our lot."

"They do get on well with each other, no fighting."

"How has Sixteenth Master been of late?" she asked again in a lowered voice, indicating that this time she was questioning in earnest. She then whispered something else.

Auntie Han blinked momentarily before replying in a quiet voice. "We do not know, madam, because we are all upstairs. These days it's just two opium-pipe preparers downstairs."

When the interview concluded, Seventh Mistress said to the children, "Go outside and play. If you want anything just ask. If we don't have what you want, you can tell them to go and buy it for you. Make yourselves at home, no need to behave like guests."

There was no one to play with them so Auntie Han took them up to a huge open room on the fourth floor that served as a workshop. Madam One cut fabric and pieced together quilts on a long table. She was making a curtain, working the treadle of a sewing machine that whirred away. Large bolts of woven silk velvet stood in the corner of the room. She no longer applied makeup to her sallow face. Jet-black hair, forever-frowning eyebrows, small black eyes like tadpoles—she never smiled.

"Oh, Auntie Han, sit. Have you seen Old Matriarch yet?"

"Yes, we paid our respects to the elder mistress, we did. Madam One is busy."

Madam One emitted a breathless laugh. "Indeed, I am—well, I never have any spare time. Old Wang, serve tea!"

"Madam One is so capable!"

Old Matriarch made good use of the discarded: out-of-favor concubines were assigned tasks. Madam Two, big-eyed and as thin as a matchstick, looked even more aged than Madam One. Skilled at social niceties, she was put in charge of entertaining female guests and remained Old Matriarch's favorite.

Madam One had a six- or seven-year-old son who closely resembled her. He was about the same age as Julie and Julian but refused to play with them. He ran upstairs and tugged on his mother's clothes, pestering her and mumbling to himself.

Madam One was embarrassed by her son's performance in front of the guests. "What is it?" she scolded, then fished some money out of her pocket. "Very well, then," she said dismissively. "Now go." He stomped loudly down the stairs.

"Lunch is served." A maidservant appeared and led them downstairs to eat.

Old Matriarch guided several grandsons and granddaughters along with Julie and Julian to sit around a large, round, white-lacquered table. A few of the same dishes they ate at home every day were placed in front of Julie and Julian. Auntie Han stood behind them, picking out bits from various dishes to place in their bowls.

After lunch Old Matriarch asked Second Brother to take them to the Commercial Press Bookshop and buy something for them. Second Brother was in middle school. He looked plump beneath his blue gown and more layers of clothes. He was so cold his long oval face had broken out in red-and-white blotches. He paced back and forth for a long time in front of a row of glass display cabinets filled with all kinds of fountain pens, mechanical pencils, elaborate pencil cases, glass paperweights, and instruments with mysterious functions. Julie was too shy to look closely, afraid she might be mistaken for a customer wanting to buy something.

A shop clerk rushed over with excessive attentiveness, perhaps because he recognized the car outside the door and knew the boy as the scion of the cabinet minister's family. All of a sudden Second Brother raised his eyebrows angrily, and in the end bought nothing.

That evening Julie and Julian were driven home in the car. They took great delight in competing with each other to call out the characters they could read on street signs.

A former male servant in the New House had been recommended to employment as a steward on an ocean liner. Julie remembered how his bulky build filled out his dark serge jacket and trousers; his face glistened like a large waxed red apple.

"They can 'carry merchandise' and make a lot of money," Julie overheard the servants say. The others were all envious.

He gave them a basket full of cherry apples from Chefoo. The basket was almost as tall as a man. The maidservants sneered as they chomped the fruit, almost embarrassed. They became sick of cherry apples well before completely devouring the hoard.

On moonlit nights, the maidservants brought benches outside to sit and enjoy the cool breeze in the rear courtyard.

"Auntie Yü, how big is the moon tonight?"

"Well, what do you say?"

Auntie Han turned to Julie. "How big do your little eyes make out the moon to be? Is it as big as a silver coin? A ten-cent coin, or a twenty?"

The tiny moon, high in the sky, glowed faintly through the haze. *Where should I hold the silver coin? If I hold it close it will be big; if I hold it farther away, it will be smaller. If I hang it high up in the sky, how small would it become?* Julie was in a state of confusion.

"A ten-cent coin," said Jade Peach. "Auntie Han, what do you think?"

"I'm too old," an embarrassed Auntie Han said with a chuckle. "My eyes are no good. It looks like a wicker basket to me."

"I'd say it's no bigger than a twenty-cent coin," said Auntie Lee. "You're young."

"Young? I'm old." Auntie Lee sighed. "None of us has any choice but to work for others," she continued. "Auntie Yü's family has farmland and a house, yet she still stays in the city to work for a family despite her advanced years."

Auntie Yü said nothing and Auntie Han didn't respond, either. Jade Peach and Auntie Yü both came from the Pien family as part of Rachel's dowry.

People whispered behind her back that Auntie Yü had quarreled with her son and daughter-in-law and left home for this position in a fit of pique. Her son still wrote to her quite often.

"Hairy Boy, don't squat on the ground," said Auntie Yü, calling Julian by his infant name. "The mole crickets will bite you. Why don't you sit on the stool?"

In the north, mole crickets look like little lumps of earth three or four inches long, or like caricatures of fat little dogs without ears, a neck, or a tail. They have smooth, light-brown bodies and two black dots for eyes. When they crawl on the ground you can barely see them, and they disappear in a flash. That you can only catch sight of them for an instant makes them truly scary.

"Hairy Girl, burn my name into my fan for me," said Auntie Lee. Everyone owned a big banana-leaf fan that looked the same. To avoid confusion, a lit mosquito coil was used to scorch dots on the fan into a surname, but care had to be taken to avoid burning holes.

Teng Sheng extinguished the lamp in the gatehouse and moved a chair into the doorway.

"Uncle Teng, why don't you come out here to cool off?" said Auntie Han. "It's hot inside there."

Teng Sheng put a white top over his singlet before moving the chair out.

"Uncle Teng is so prim and proper, that he feels obliged to wear a top before coming into our presence," Jade Peach said with a sneer.

Teng Sheng was thin, with a shaven head. He first entered the Sheng household as a page boy. The Shengs eventually found him a wife, but she died.

"This is how Uncle Teng presents his master's visiting card." The houseboy and Teng Sheng were from the same town. Sometimes for fun, the boy would imitate the way in which formal visits were announced in the manner of the previous dynasty's custom: several rapid steps in front of his master's carriage followed by a large exaggerated stride and a Manchu salute on one bent knee while holding the card high with the other hand.

Teng Sheng's face didn't betray the slightest hint of a smile.

Julie wanted to say, "Uncle Teng, show me how you present a visiting card," but she didn't, knowing she'd be ignored.

A few years earlier he had taken her out into the street on his shoulders to watch a puppet show, then treated her to hawthorn-fruit rock candy and a visit to Talutian amusement park in Tientsin.

Once, Julie overheard the maidservants disparaging Teng Sheng for going to a brothel with two of the male servants from the New House.

"What's a brothel?"

"Shush!" hissed Auntie Han in a low voice, though she was smiling.

Julie was very fond of playing in the gatehouse. Inside, there was a crudely made old-style desk scarred with cigarette burns, a yellow rattan teapot cozy, and light-orange warm tea that poured out of the teapot. She had permission to use the inkstone and to fill the account book and sheets of writing paper with her doodles. They even let her keep an unused account book. Once, when she had a bloody nose, she was carried inside the gatehouse and someone used a calligraphy brush to apply some black ink inside her nostril. The cold, moist brush licked her once; the stench of ink exploded in her nose for a moment. It seemed to work—the bleeding stopped.

"When I grow up I'll buy Uncle Teng a fur-lined gown," Julie announced.

"Miss is a good girl," he said. Julian was silent as he scrambled over Teng Sheng's wood board bed, prying the pillow up to look at all the copper coins beneath it.

"What about me?" teased Auntie Han, standing in the doorway. "Nothing for me?"

"I'll buy Auntie Han a fox-lined jacket," replied Julie.

Auntie Han winked at Teng Sheng. "Such a good girl," she said softly.

Mah-jongg was always being played in the gatehouse.

"Who will win today?" the servants asked Julie.

The maids upstairs primed Julie to answer: "Everyone. The table and chairs lose."

One of the two male opium servants was tall and skinny. He had a triangular face with pale cheeks. He was so thin his shoulders seemed frozen in a permanent shrug like *anitya*, the ghost who whisks the soul away after death. He was introduced to the household as one who knew how to inject morphine. Originally, only the midget who resembled a monkey prepared the opium. He had cut off his own ring finger to overcome a gambling addiction—a cause of great mirth at the mah-jongg table. Julie grabbed hold of his hand and saw the finger still retained one segment, the end as white and smooth as a dice. A bitter smile erupted on his orange-peel face.

"Tall and Skinny bad-mouthed the midget behind his back. The midget was furious, really furious. Said he'd skewer him." Auntie Lee also washed clothes for members of the household who lived downstairs and had reliable sources for information.

Whenever they heard thunderclaps, the maidservants would say, "The good ol' god of thunder is dragging his mah-jongg table across the sky."

When the sky cleared after it rained, they said, "It won't rain again. The sky is blue enough to make a pair of trousers."

The servants from farming families always watched the weather. Upon rising from bed one autumn or winter morning, they would cry out "Frost!" and hold Julie up to the window to see the frost on the red roof tiles across the lane. The frost began to melt in the morning sun. The ridges of the tiles glistened with moisture, while the troughs stayed white. The vast expanse of red tiles and the dazzling white of the frost looked magnificent to Julie.

"Wind!"

When gales blew in and the sky turned yellow, a layer of yellow dust settled on the tables despite all the windows being closed tightly, the dust reappearing soon after being wiped away. The maidservants laughed as they wiped the dust.

Auntie Han slept in the same bed as Julie and licked her eyelids as soon as she woke, like a cow tending to her calf. Julie didn't like it but she knew Auntie Han believed that, first thing in the morning, her tongue possessed pure *chi*, which was good for the eyes. Of course she never said as much, and never licked her when Rachel was in the house.

Auntie Han diligently followed Rachel's instructions to take the children to the park every day with Auntie Yü. Even in winter a part of Julie's legs remained exposed, her wool socks not long enough to cover her knees. As soon as she entered the park gate, Julie would squeal with delight at the sight of the undulating expanse of yellowing grass and run madly straight ahead, cutting the vista neatly in half. She vaguely heard Julian shrieking as he ran behind her.

"Hairy Boy! Stop running this instant! You'll fall flat on your face!" Auntie Yü squawked like a parrot as she struggled precariously on her bound feet. Nearly two years earlier, Julian had suffered from a calcium deficiency and would often fall over when he walked. A wide, red strap tied around his chest restrained him in the park. Auntie Yü held both ends of the strap as if she were walking a dog, which was quite a spectacle. Her bound feet were too slow for Julian, and he leaned forward and struggled with all his might, looking as if he'd burst into tears.

As Auntie Yü belonged to Rachel's dowry, she was put in charge of raising the boy. All the military officers who had fought with the Taiping rebels settled in Nanking, so the Pien clan servants were, without exception, Nanking natives.

"Your surname is Bump," Auntie Yü teased Julie. "Whichever household you bump into will be your family."

"My surname is Sheng! Sheng! Sheng! Sheng!"

"Hairy Boy is surnamed Sheng. In the future, he'll wed a young lady, not a sharp-tongued nun like you."

Before Rachel left China, she frequently admonished: "Those customs don't apply now. Boys and girls are equal—they're all the same."

Auntie Yü responded with a hostile, "Oh?" The bags under her eyes on her delicate, chubby face suddenly darkened. Her hair, though thinning, was still jet-black. Womenfolk south of the Yang-tze did not sow the fields, and following tradition, their feet were bound. Auntie Han and the others had natural feet.

"We didn't need to work in the fields," Auntie Yü announced, with a hint of pride.

Whenever she saw Julie turn a fish over with her chopsticks after having eaten one side, Auntie Yü invariably said, "The gentleman does not eat overturned fish."

"Why?"

"Because a gentleman just doesn't."

Julie could never understand why; she just assumed it was because a gentleman would leave the other side of the fish for the servants. Half a century later she read in a newspaper that Taiwanese fishermen believed eating an overturned fish was bad luck and would cause their boat to capsize. There were no boats in the parched lands of northern Anhwei, and Auntie Han and her fellow provincials did not have sayings about overturned fish, but Auntie Yü from Nanking with all its rivers and lakes also seemed unaware of the origins of this taboo.

Auntie Yü recounted an ancient tale: "Long, long ago a great flood covered the land. Fate decreed that all the people drown save a sister and her brother. The little brother wanted to marry his elder sister to continue the ancestral line. The sister was unwilling. 'If you can catch me,' she said, 'I'll marry you.' The brother agreed. The sister ran off and the brother set out in pursuit but couldn't catch her.

"Who would have known that a tortoise would trip the sister, causing her to fall to the ground and enabling the little brother to catch her. She had to keep her promise and marry her brother. But she hated the tortoise so much that she smashed its shell with a rock, splitting it into thirteen pieces. That's why, today, tortoiseshells have thirteen segments."

Julie felt extremely embarrassed when she heard that story and didn't look at Julian. Julian, naturally, didn't look at her, either.

There was no running hot water in the house. To bathe, kettles of hot water were carried upstairs and poured into a Western-style bathtub. To save time and effort, the children bathed together, two maidservants washing them, one at each end of the tub, Julie and Julian never once raising their eyes.

In the summer, the children spent all day in the rear courtyard with the servants. The cook squatted next to the drain scaling fish while the maidservants washed clothes under the faucet, except for Jade Peach who, being unmarried, rarely went outside. Julie brought out a three-legged stool with a red leather cover to sit in the shade below the dazzling blue of the northern sky. Auntie Yü squatted to one side as she held Julian up to urinate.

"Don't let the mole crickets bite his little dicky bird," the cook said.

One day Auntie Han said, "The cook hasn't been able to buy any duck for several days."

"If there is no duck," said Julie, "we can eat cock."

"Shush!" bellowed Auntie Han.

"I only said if there's no duck we can eat a little cock."

"Stop it!"

In the winter a jar of malt sugar was placed on the stovetop with a pair of bamboo chopsticks inserted into the jar. Frozen malt sugar took ages to melt, and Julie found the wait excruciating. When it was finally ready, Auntie Han twirled a lump around the chopsticks. Julie raised her head and opened her mouth, eagerly waiting the brown rubbery mass that glistened in the sunlight like a writhing golden snake, descending ever so slowly.

The maidservants saved the black ceramic malt containers to use as moxibustion suction cups. No matter what the ailment, they scrunched up newspaper to burn inside the containers, and then placed them on the naked skin of their freckled backs.

In winter Julian wore a sleeveless left-over-right-closure waistcoat made of golden brown satin over a peacock-blue padded silk gown embroidered with orange butterflies. "Little brother is so cute," said Julie as she planted many kisses on his delicate face, which owing to its thinness felt like kissing soft silk. Julian looked down with a squint, pretending not to notice anything.

The maidservants were cheered by this scene, and even Auntie Yü silently looked delighted.

"Look," exclaimed Jade Peach, "aren't those two adorable."

Auntie Yü could read, which was unusual for a maidservant. She was also the only maidservant who didn't have to send money home and saved a little more than the others. One day she bought a storybook at a secondhand books stall. After dinner, she read from it for everyone to hear. Under the dim electric lights, a row of glistening oily faces froze, mesmerized; some only understood a little, some didn't understand anything, but all were riveted. Especially hearing the line, "Today we take off our shoes and socks, for who knows if upon the morn we shall wear them again." Auntie Yü recited this line over and over, and several older members of her audience were deeply moved, too.

Sometimes Auntie Yü talked about the Buddhist netherworld. To Julie it seemed like a huge cellar with gray cement walls, just like the staircase at the Talutian amusement complex, except that it went downward, leading to the different departments of hell: Dark Mountain, Sword Mountain, Flaming Mountain. Then there was the Wicked Demon's sin-revealing Mirror of Retribution at the Platform for Viewing Home One Last Time, and the Great Wheel of Reincarnation that towered high up in the sky. Of course Julie would just go for a quick tour and not suffer the torments of hell. Why would she want to do anything bad? But she didn't want to be too good, either, and break free from the cycle of reincarnation to be personally received by the Jade Emperor, who would descend the steps of his throne to greet her. Julie wanted eternal reincarnation; she wanted to experience all kinds of existences, and from time to time enjoy a luxurious and beautiful life.

No matter how hard she tried to believe those karmic stories, Julie never could—they sounded too good to be true, simply fabricated to fulfill people's every desire. Unlike the stories she heard after she entered the mission school. Their heaven, high in the clouds, involved eternal harp plucking and hymn singing—as if there hadn't been enough church attendance on earth. Every morning the students had to attend a religious service for half an hour. In the evenings, a classmate would always be twisting your arm to go and listen to another student sermon in exchange for attending class for you. The services on Sunday lasted three hours with the only relief being the American pastor's stilted Soochow dialect that brought silent tears of mirth to the students' eyes, silent because in every other row a female teacher kept close watch on everyone. Julie gazed at the blue sky beyond the small, narrow windows of the chapel—so much like the windows of a medieval watchtower—and thought it a crime to be shut indoors. On occasion a certain bishop would preside over the service. He used to be a missionary in Shantung where he had picked up a heavy accented Shantungese, which the students also found hysterically funny.

But the Bible is a great work: the Old Testament a historical epic poem; the New Testament a biographical novel, with divine inspiration, as when, for example Jesus tells Judas, "Before the rooster crows today, three times will you deny that you know me." When Julie read this passage in school she immediately recalled an incident that occurred when she was six or seven years old. After her mother left, Euphoria moved in. Formerly the third mistress of the House of Lunar Euphoria, the tall and slender Euphoria had a pale heart-shaped face, a fashionable horizontal S-shaped bun resting on the nape of her neck, and bangs that covered her eyebrows. Her eyes transformed into narrow slits when she laughed. When her seamstress visited, she ordered a set of clothes for herself and another set exactly the same for Julie. A waist-hugging lilac velvet top with no slits, no edging on the high cylindrical stand-up collar, and tight elbow-length sleeves.

With a pleated, full-length skirt the fashionable outfit resembled a simplified version of Western women's attire.

Euphoria had the figure of an haute-couture model—thin, but not so thin that her ribs showed. Clothes hung on her frame more elegantly than on anyone else.

In a large, gloomy room, a full-length mirror with a carved-teak frame tilted forward. Julie stood in front of the mirror. She was so chubby the seamstress pinched about her midriff in an unsuccessful search for her waist. Euphoria, standing beside them, impatiently joined the search and grappled for it. "A bit higher would be better. Raise the waist a bit to show some shape."

After the seamstress left, Euphoria cuddled Julie and sat her on her lap. "Second Aunt just refitted old clothes for you. These will be made with brand-new material. So who do you like better, Second Aunt or me?"

"I like you." Julie thought that to say otherwise would be far too impolite, but it felt like a chimney popped up on the top of her head, pointing straight into the predawn sky. The faint sound of a rooster crowing could be heard in the distance.

The clothes were delivered. That night, Euphoria took Julie out in a rickshaw. It was late in the year, and the wind picked up strength; the rickshaw driver unraveled a tarpaulin to protect the cabin from the gusts.

"Are you cold?" asked Euphoria, wrapping Julie in her cloak.

Euphoria smelled fragrant in the darkness, but seemed fragile. Wisps of the sweet aroma of opium mingled with her pungent perfume.

They turned down a long lane, dismounted the rickshaw, and stood in front of a red double-door entrance, above which hung a lamp with the character 王, the proprietor's surname, in red. The lamplight dazzled her eyes; the northwest wind howled, clearing off every speck of dust. Euphoria rang the doorbell. She turned up the collar of her black velvet cloak, exposing the crimson-purple velvet lining—it looked as if her delicate head rested on a velveteen flower. She then took out a messy bundle of banknotes as large as a brick from her black rhinestone-studded purse.

"A bandit would grab that," thought Julie. The hair on the back of her neck stood on end. She looked back and saw the rickshaw man had already gone. Neatly attired with Venetian fabric shoes and snow-white socks, he only served a few old customers. At that moment, in Julie's eyes he was a savior, an armed guard who would protect the houses of the wealthy; but at the same time, she also thought that if he saw the cash he might be tempted to snatch it.

The door opened before Euphoria had finished counting, perhaps a deliberate move to show off her wealth. The large room they entered was newly painted but quite unrefined. A staircase dominated the corridor, which bustled with people coming and going. Others sat around tables, each one illuminated by a large overhead lamp that cast a bluish-white light on their faces. As soon as Euphoria removed her cloak, the identical mother and daughter outfits became the center of attention—a mysterious lady and a chubby little girl both dressed exactly the same.

A former colleague from her days in the brothel came over to greet Euphoria. She threw a curious glance at Julie, with an air of hostility.

"Second Master's child," Euphoria hastily explained, and then turned to Julie to say, "Now you sit here, all right? But don't wander off or I won't be able to find you."

The two women walked away, but soon the other woman returned with a handful of sweets for Julie before quickly leaving again.

Julie watched people gambling, though she couldn't make out what they were playing or where Euphoria was sitting. A couple who looked like movie stars walked by the miniature potted palm. The woman wore a short skirt with a white, three-foot-long silk scarf fluttering behind her. The man's hair looked as shiny as lacquered leather. Their conversation was inaudible: a modern-day silent movie. Julie sat for a very long time just as she did in the New House, waiting for hours, bored to the bone. By the time Euphoria returned, she had fallen asleep.

After that occasion, Euphoria never took Julie out again but always went out with Ned instead.

"They say...lost a fortune," the maidservants furtively whispered among themselves, horror on their faces, "went every day during the New Year. Never gambled such high stakes at the club ... said ... by a cheat ... and this time in a friend's home ... had a falling out with Fourth Master Liu...."

"After the New Year we'll engage a private tutor." Julie had heard the threat often enough, but this time a tutor really did appear in the new year.

"Is the paddle open for business today?" the servants, including the cook, cheerfully inquired at regular intervals, though Julie couldn't fathom why.

The paddle was positioned on the desk next to the brass foot rule. Julie never looked at it closely, assuming an attitude of disdain. Teng Sheng, who had once served as a page boy in the study, retrieved the entire set of tutoring paraphernalia previously allocated to the school-room of Second Master, Julie's father. The paddle was the size of a spectacle case, though slightly thinner. Blackened with age, the paddle had split in one section where a small piece was missing, re-vealing the uneven wood grain. Despite being worn smooth, Julie worried there might be splinters.

The tutor began with historical anecdotes from *The Outline and Mirror*.

"The Konghe Regency of 841 BC was jointly ruled by two dukes, just like Auntie Han and Auntie Yü managing the household," thought Julie.

When the tutor expounded upon Po Yi and Shu Ch'i, who out of loyalty to the previous ruler were dying of starvation on Mount Shou-yang, refusing to eat the grain that grew under the new ruler, Julie imagined herself and her younger brother scavenging for wild vegetables in the withered grasses, refusing to eat any Chou dynasty provisions while the people in the plains below carried on as usual. She suddenly burst out weeping. The tutor, shocked that his exposi-tion had moved Julie to tears, felt a little embarrassed. The more she cried, the more devastated she felt, to the point that the tutor suspected it was a ploy to boycott class. Consequently, he put on a stern face and, ignoring her distress, continued his lecture while at the same time explicating the classical text. Julian, head lowered, pursed his thin lips. Julie knew he was thinking, "She's putting on a performance again!" As she was sitting right next to the tutor, her wailing drowned him out. Only when she realized that, did she gradually quietened down.

Around this time Ned rarely entertained guests, spending more time supervising the education of his children. After two random inspections, he thought they weren't reciting the classical texts with proper fluency. He ordered them to study at night. Upon finishing dinner, he made his children sit opposite each other at the dining table and review what they had learned during the day. When they finished memorizing a passage, they were ordered to stand in front of him and recite it from memory. When the tutor heard about this arrangement he said nothing, though he obviously felt humiliated.

The sliding doors between the two rooms opposite the reception room and dining room usually remained open, making one large room with a vaulted door in the middle. The dim lighting and the clouds of blue opium smoke made it feel like a cave. Ned and Euphoria reclined facing each other on the opium bed with only one lamp on the teapoy. Euphoria wore a seductive dark wrought-iron-patterned stiff gauze jacket with red lining over matching bell-bottom trousers. A line of embroidered black spiders on her fashionable white silk stockings marched from her heels to her delicate ankles. Nowadays, Euphoria ignored Julie, and Julie never greeted her. Ned didn't want his children to make salutations to her. But reciting texts in the presence of Euphoria didn't feel comfortable.

Tall and Skinny sat on a stool preparing the opium. He wore a white top with short sleeves that stuck out. Occasionally he quietly mumbled a few words obsequiously to the couple on the couch, but they never said anything.

Ned took the textbook handed to him and sat up. He wore a singlet and his eyelids were puffy. He had the irascible look of someone half intoxicated. Julie stood in front of him, swaying as she recited. She stumbled in the middle.

"Take the book and read it again!"

The second time, too, she couldn't get through to the end. Ned threw the book to the ground.

The more Julie feared disgracing herself in front of Euphoria, the more trouble she had reciting from memory. On the third attempt Ned jumped up, grabbed her arm, and dragged her back to the school room where he hit her on the palm of her hand a dozen times with the paddle.

Julie began to bawl. Auntie Han observed furtively from the corridor, but didn't enter until she saw Ned leave. At that point she quickly ushered Julie upstairs.

"Shush! Stop crying!" She made a face as she rubbed Julie's palm.

After that the servants no longer asked in jest, "Is the paddle open for business?"

Every night, Julian sat opposite Julie reciting the texts in a low, wretched voice. Julie couldn't bear the sound of Julian's recitation but nothing ever happened to him.

Euphoria's father moved into the house with her. He was a burly man with a large, yellow-tinted face, probably in his fifties. He floated in and out of Euphoria's room like an apparition.

"He's afraid of Second Master," the maidservants whispered.

"They say he's not even her father."

He often stood by the chest of drawers in the corridor downstairs scraping opium dregs from used pipes for his own consumption.

Euphoria continued to abide by the traditions of the bordello in avoiding eating at the same table as the menfolk. She usually ate alone two hours after the others, sitting at a slant as she wearily poked at the rice in her bowl, only nibbling at a few pickled and pot-stewed dishes.

At Euphoria's welcoming banquet, her "sisters" were invited and all sat at the same table with the male guests. The host directed male guests to the dining room and Euphoria directed the female guests. Julie was only four at the time. She hid behind the velvet curtain by the sliding doors. As the female guests walked by in light-colored short jackets and unremarkable dark gray pleated skirts with triple wide-band braiding, they all seemed so ordinary, no different from the wives of the other relatives. After all the guests made it into the room, the sliding doors were closed and all Julie could hear was the sound of her father talking, sometimes loud, sometimes quiet, as if he were grumpy. Only two round-faced pubescent sing-song girls remained in the anteroom, sitting side by side on a sofa. They wore identical pale turquoise jackets with dogtooth embroidery and rhinestones, along with matching trousers. Julie thought they looked delightful, and slowly wrapped the curtain around herself in the hope that they would see and talk to her. But they didn't appear to notice and only exchanged an occasional few quiet words with each other.

Beyond the deep pink carpet with a vermillion phoenix motif, a fire raged in the fireplace. The sound of chopsticks clinking on bowls and boisterous chatter drifted in from the other room.

Only a tiny corner of the velvet curtain now curled around Julie, but the two sing-song girls still didn't see her. Julie concluded that they were ignoring her.

Auntie Lee helped serve the food, passing dishes to junior maidservants to carry into the dining room. "I don't know why," she said in a low voice, "but those two are not allowed to eat and are not permitted to leave. Heard they're sisters." When she peeked into the living room, Auntie Lee caught sight of Julie. She clicked her tongue impatiently and furrowed her brow, smiling to herself as she led Julie away from the festivities and delivered her back upstairs.

"He is now injecting himself," Auntie Lee confided to Auntie Han in hushed tones. "He chases her around the room insisting on injecting her too." They giggled uncomfortably.

Yü-heng regularly wrote letters to Rachel overseas, giving her updates. Rachel hid one such letter among some small photographs after she returned to China, which Julie chanced upon:

Madam,

Please be graciously informed hereby: I believe you have already received our previous dispatch. Recently, Thirteenth Master summoned your humble servant to inquire about the matter of injections. Your humble servant advised that Euphoria is now also receiving injections and is severely addicted. At this stage the best solution is to lure the tiger out of the mountain and let Thirteenth Master find an excuse to take Sixteenth Master to stay with him for a while. Then, at the same time, find a way to force the woman out. Sixteenth Master should postpone traveling to Shanghai because Euphoria is a southerner who would possibly shadow him there. Sixteenth Master is easily swayed by others and is incapable of exercising control. Yesterday, your humble servant surreptitiously entered Sixteenth Master's quarters to acquire a packet of the drug which he passed on to Thirteenth Master for chemical analysis. . . .

Yü-heng worshipped the New House and followed their custom of calling Ned Sixteenth Master. He felt proud of himself for his "covert operations," like those in the drama *Chiang Kan Steals a Letter*, and for establishing a connection with Thirteenth Master. However, this didn't win him any rewards. After Rachel and Judy returned to China he asked them to make introductions for employment, but Rachel replied, "The government has moved the capital to Nanking and we have no more connections."

One day, when Euphoria sauntered up to the third floor to rummage for something in a trunk, she passed by Julian's door. Julian was very ill at the time but she didn't drop in on him.

"She didn't even turn her head," grumbled Auntie Lee.

Auntie Yü said nothing.

"Yep, and she didn't even ask after him," said Auntie Han.

Even if she asked, thought Julie, it would be insincere. Euphoria didn't have any children of her own so she could never bring herself to accept him as Ned's son. Julie couldn't understand why Auntie Han and Auntie Lee made such a fuss about it.

For a long time, Julie wasn't summoned into the room to recite her classical passages from memory. Julie passed Ned and Euphoria's door and saw a single brass bed in the passage by the door blocking the way. Ned sat on the edge of the bed facing the door, with a gauze bandage wrapped around his head. He looked very strange, but his slightly irritable expression was still the same as when he listened to her recite. He looked downward bitterly, both hands resting on the bed, his short-sleeved undergarment revealing surprisingly plump arms.

"Thumped him with the spittoon, she did," the maidservants whispered. "No idea what started it."

A car sent from the New House collected Ned, unbeknownst to Julie. In the afternoon, she heard a commotion downstairs.

"Thirteenth Master has arrived," announced the maidservants excitedly.

Auntie Lee and Jade Peach went over to the staircase to listen, while a stone-faced Auntie Han sat silently, cradling Julie in her arms to prevent her running downstairs. Julie heard Thirteenth Master pounding a table with his fist, cursing, and a woman wailing and shouting in spurts of loud, repulsive Yang-tze-delta Mandarin, followed by silence. *Was that Euphoria?* Julie was petrified.

Thirteenth Master left with Ned in the car. A frenzy of packing broke out downstairs. The male servants were all helping. Before the sky turned dark, several flatbed trishaws were piled high with baggage and filed out of the front gate. Upstairs everyone crowded around the windows to catch a glimpse.

"Wonderful!" blurted Jade Peach. Auntie Yü stood silently to one side.

Then another trishaw left. And another.

Yet another left. Jade Peach and Auntie Lee sniggered contemptuously. "How could there be so many things for her to move?" whispered Jade Peach.

Everyone looked concerned, as if the rooms beneath their feet were being hollowed out.

"They're letting her take all her possessions on the condition that she doesn't set up shop in Tientsin or Peking," said Auntie Lee.

"She's going to Tungchow because that's where she's from," Jade Peach chimed in.

"Is that the Tungchow in the south or the northern Tungchow?" asked Auntie Lee.

No one seemed to know the answer.

Did Euphoria return to the north after the Peiyang warlord government collapsed? If she had returned, would she have been able to set up shop again? Wouldn't she be a bit too old? And besides, she was a morphine addict. Julie never mulled over such matters, but whenever Euphoria's name was mentioned, Julie would always defend her: "Well I still thought she was very attractive."

Julie forgot about all the things she couldn't understand at the time: Ned in hot pursuit in the cavernous bedroom, him capturing his companion and administering morphine injections, the gloomy scene of ecstasy. Ned, though, had no respect for Euphoria and so instructed Auntie Han to prevent the children from greeting her by name. This contempt excited him, along with being bashed on the head with a spittoon. Ultimately, that provided the family in the New House sufficient reason to intervene and they then severed the ties between the proverbial loving pair of Mandarin ducks. Not only that, Euphoria didn't receive any compensation for her termination—her future prospects were probably quite grim.

Julian recovered and Euphoria was gone, but for some reason Auntie Yü lost heart and resigned, saying she wanted to go home. The Sheng family was about to return to the south, and if she went with them she could save on travel expenses, but anxious to return home as soon as possible, she just couldn't wait.

Jade Peach tried to fill an awkward silence, saying, "Auntie Yü is leaving, but she'll come back when Hairy Boy gets married." She immediately realized she didn't sound convincing and appeared a little uncertain of herself. No one responded.

A white leather suitcase, a basket, and her bedding formed a pile in the middle of the room. Julie burst into tears—it suddenly hit her that everything comes to an end.

"Hairy Girl is such a good child," said Jade Peach. "Wasn't even raised by her, yet she still cries like that."

Auntie Yü said nothing as she busied herself packing her things. Julian silently stood to one side.

Word came from the ground floor that the rickshaw had arrived.

Just as she was about to leave, Auntie Yü spoke: "Hairy Girl, I'm leaving now. Hairy Boy is younger than you, so take care of him. Hairy Boy, I'm leaving. From now on Auntie Han will look after you. Be good and take care."

Julian said nothing and didn't look at her. The houseboy went upstairs to help with the luggage. Auntie Han and Jade Peach went with her downstairs to see her off in a flurry of farewells.

Since then, Julie always thought Auntie Yü had entrusted Julian to her and the other maids. She felt she had let Auntie Yü down. Auntie Han perhaps felt the same.

Now it was their turn to move.

"We're going to Shanghai! We're going to Shanghai!" Jade Peach jabbered.

The furnishings had been dispatched by sea and all that remained was a small iron-frame bed. Julie squatted in front of the bed eating a pomegranate sent over from the New House. It was the first time she'd ever seen a pomegranate.

The seeds looked like little red crystal dice. After eating the pomegranate, she used the kernels to make an array of soldiers ready for battle. She then placed the peach-pink paper band wrapped around the lid of the fruit basket under her bed to represent the muddy waters of the Ch'in-huai River that runs through Nanking for her army to cross.

Then the iron-frame bed went and Julie slept on the floor with Julian, between Auntie Han and Auntie Lee. Dismantling an entire household fulfilled childhood fantasies of destruction. The lamp high above their heads seemed especially distant and dim as the children faced each other with their heads on the same pillow, giggling. Looking into Julian's large oval eyes, Julie thought he appeared as fragile as a soda biscuit. She couldn't resist the urge to hug him tightly through the bedding and crush him.

Julie's earliest memory of just the two of them was of sitting side by side on the bed, not too close in case one of them pushed the other off. They resembled two unstable clay dolls. The people crowding into the room were from other worlds while only Julie and Julian were of the same kind, mindful of each other. A lacquer bowl placed in front of Julie contained "objects of prognostication." All manner of virtuous objects, like calligraphy brushes and inkstones, were deliberately placed right in front of Julie, while wicked things such as dice and dominoes were set farther away, well out of reach. Auntie Han and Jade Peach recalled Julie took hold of the calligraphy brush and the cotton-rouge applicator, but after much shilly-shallying, she put them down again. No one remembered what Julian went for.

Perhaps there was an earlier memory, of a time before Julian was born, when Julie squirmed in her gilded vermillion lacquered standing-barrel crib to avoid the white copper soup spoon that fed her. *Where is the porcelain spoon? The white porcelain spoon with the little crimson flower. I don't like the metallic taste of this thing.*

"*Aiyee,*" Auntie Han moaned each time a spoonful of congee spilled.

Infants are unable to focus their eyes. Auntie Han's face loomed huge and blurred.

Suddenly Julie caught hold of the spoon and threw it far away, so far she couldn't see where it went; she heard the clatter as it hit the ground.

"Grumpy today for some reason," grumbled Auntie Han.

Julie was too small to speak but could understand words. She became annoyed when they picked up the spoon, sent it out of the room, and replaced it with another copper spoon.

Other people came and went but Julie couldn't make out their faces.

Suddenly she heard a loud drumming sound and her legs felt warm. The barrel crib consisted of two sections, and it amplified sound like the famous ancient Sound Corridor in Soochow. She knew she had done something wrong and had turned victory into defeat. Auntie Han muttered to herself as she picked Julie up to change her clothes and wipe the base of the crib.

One day, as Julie stood next to Rachel's dressing table, which she now equaled in height, Rachel lost her temper and slapped Jade Peach.

"Get on your knees!"

Jade Peach knelt down but still appeared unusually tall, her upper body disproportionately long. Julie stared for a while then began to wail.

"What a horrible racket!" barked Rachel, frowning. "Auntie Han! What are you waiting for? Take her away."

Another day Rachel was packing her suitcase while Julie watched from the side as maidservants passed a steady stream of lovely objects to Rachel, one at a time.

"All right, you may look but not touch." That day Rachel's voice felt particularly soft. But after packing her suitcase for a while, Rachel suddenly became agitated and turned to Julie, saying impatiently, "Very well then, you may go now."

A constant stream of female visitors flowed from the New House and back, all of them dispatched by Seventh Mistress to exhort Rachel to stay.

The night before Rachel's departure a burglar stole many pieces of her of jewelry.

"He even dropped a big turd on the floor," tittered the maidservants in revulsion.

Rachel posted toys to them from overseas: foreign dolls, army forts, a miniature spirit stove that really worked, a large fur ball with blue-and-white-striped ripples. No one knew what the ball was for. Julie called it a "tiger egg." Pretending the upturned table and chairs were a truck, she drove with Julian into the desert to conquer the barbarians and, along the way, they stopped to make lunch, cooking the tiger egg.

"Do you remember Second Aunt and Third Aunt?" asked Jade Peach in her customary shrill voice.

"And who is this?" asked Jade Peach, showing Julie a large picture of Rachel that she had colored herself.

"It's Second Aunt," replied Julie casually, after a quick glance at the picture.

"And where have Second Aunt and Third Aunt gone?"

"Overseas."

The questions and answers were like a catechism.

Jade Peach put the picture away. "They're all right," she said softly to Auntie Han, "they're not pining for their mother."

"They're still young," said Auntie Han, blinking her eyes.

Julie knew it was out of the ordinary for Second Aunt and Third Aunt to travel overseas, but the more the adults around her made it sound mysterious, the less interested she was in asking about it.

While Auntie Han stooped over the bathtub to wash clothes one day, Julie undid the ribbon of her blue apron, which slipped off and fell into the water.

"*Aiya!*" exclaimed Auntie Han crossly.

Auntie Han tied the ribbon and Julie untied it again and it slipped back into the water a second time. Julie laughed, though felt it was a boring prank.

Sometimes Julie wondered if everything about her life was a dream, that one day she would wake up to find herself an entirely different person, perhaps a foreign child playing with a toy sailboat at the edge of a pond in a park. Of course, some days seemed endless, but dreams could be just as long.

Many years later, on a secluded street in Washington, D.C., Julie came across a little girl with light brown hair cut in the same short bob she once sported herself. The girl was alone, climbing up and down an iron gate, holding on to a horizontal bar with both hands. Up one step, then down one step, again and again, repeating the same action yet never seeming bored. It suddenly occurred to Julie that she was looking at herself. She always felt like a foreigner—even in China—because of her isolation.

She was like a tree, inching toward Chih-yung's window, indistinctly blossoming tiny flowers in the lamplight coming through the window. Yet she was only able to peek at his world through the glass pane.

7

BROTHER Hsü visited Shanghai after the war ended. He had gone to Taiwan to look for work but couldn't adapt to the place. He was only passing through on his way back to northern China.

"What is Taiwan like?" asked Julie.

"Phew! It was hot!" He shook his head and heaved a sigh of relief, as if he had just returned to Judy's balcony with a hand towel to wipe his sweat away after an exhausting day running about. Now it felt to Julie as though nothing had changed—Brother Hsü, Judy, and herself all chatting away on that same dark balcony. "The sun in Taiwan is scorching. Brand-new roads everywhere, wide and long. It takes forever to go to from one place to another, even by rickshaw," Brother Hsü continued.

Julie imagined it was the same as the blinding sunlight at noon on hot summer days at the Sun Yat-sen Mausoleum nearby in Nanking.

"And the food was awful," Judy added with a hint of a smile. "He was miserable. And he was homesick."

What a spoiled man, thought Julie. He had not lived the high life before. His new mother-in-law spoiled him. Mother and daughter finally found a man to front the household, and in return, Brother Hsü found a marital shrine in which he took shelter.

Of course, he would have heard about her romance with Chih-yung. "Judy must have told him," Julie said to herself. There was always a bond of understanding between Brother Hsü and Julie. Despite not seeing him for years, Brother Hsü sometimes popped into her mind when Julie thought about certain things. Then she would remind herself: *So what? Understanding won't change anything.*

Logically, Julie shouldn't have forgotten that he had liked her, since so few people ever took an interest in her. Yet, as if she had an excess of romance to discard, she forgot everything that had happened between them. Remembering would only have made the reunion awkward.

Judy must have told Brother Hsü that Julie liked to listen to them, and he spared no effort in holding forth. He shared a string of stories about relatives in the north. These people reminded Julie of her father and younger brother. Brother Hsü also mentioned her father:

"I heard Second Uncle is enthusiastically helping to arrange funerals. He likes to give advice on rituals, quoting the classics."

Judy went straight into mocking Brother Hsü for being homesick. She declared that she wouldn't mind bringing up his wife. But Julie didn't mention "Sister Hsü," nor did she think to ask him if he had any children. It was as if nothing had changed. The three of them once again chatted away the summer night on the same dark balcony.

Jade Peach dropped by. Now in her thirties, she had become somewhat attractive, and even her big-boned figure seemed less offensive. She was wearing a long gown instead of her maid's outfit, yet she retained her modesty. Short hair with her bangs swept to one side.

"Hairy Girl has found a suitor?" asked Jade Peach, using Julie's infant sobriquet.

She must have heard it from the Pien family.

Julie smiled awkwardly. "No. He was married and is now divorced. But he had to leave because of his previous ties to the Nanking government," she explained.

Jade Peach listened with a blank expression at first. "Oh dear!" she suddenly blurted out. "I hope you weren't taken advantage of!"

"No, no, not at all," said Julie defensively.

Jade Peach didn't press the issue.

Julie then found an excuse and retreated. After Jade Peach left, Judy told Julie about her latest news. "She said she's taking care of someone's household, even the finances, and her employer trusts her," said Judy. "It sounds like she's now with him."

Miss Su had recently moved to Shanghai. Miss Su and Brother Hsü were consanguineous siblings. The daughter of Uncle Chu's first wife, she was about the same age as Judy. They had been close friends since childhood. Judy kept little contact with most relatives except the few she got along well with. Another female cousin, also from the Chu family, was fond of Miss Su, too.

Once, when Herr Schütte, the principal of the German-language school, came up in conversation, Judy remarked, "Luckily, no one outside knows anything about what your second aunt and I got up to." She sounded relieved but also a little disappointed—people usually thought of her as a classic wallflower. But then she added, "Is it true that people with secrets are likely to suspect others, and people without secrets won't suspect others?"

"Don't know," Julie responded. "Maybe."

But Julie rarely suspected others, not even after she had discovered her mother's secrets. She didn't see anything outrageous when Judy suspected Jade Peach had become her employer's mistress. She thought Jade Peach had never been happy working in her family, though she hadn't been mistreated, either. Visitors from Nanking liked to bring their local delicacy, preserved duck, with them. Julie remembered other maids in the household used to laugh at Jade Peach for taking pleasure in devouring the "pope's nose" of a duck. Jade Peach had always remained silent. From her stony face, Julie could sense that she simply wanted to eat what others didn't want to eat.

Jade Peach had been the youngest maid in the household and was married off, but her husband deserted her. Having gone through so many ups and downs in life, Jade Peach felt content once she found a good employer. Although he had taken an interest in her, nothing likely happened. This was China after all.

When she lived in northern China, Jade Peach was a part of Julie's childhood. That was a particularly tranquil time when they were shielded, as if by a supernatural force, from the traumas of life, from illnesses or deaths. This surely influenced their mind-set. Julie once mocked Jade Peach for being naive without realizing that she herself was hopelessly naive. She had always assumed Chih-yung wasn't romantically involved with Miss K'ang and Opportune Jade while on the run.

In the first letter Chih-yung sent to Julie after fleeing to central China, he already mentioned Miss K'ang. He said he stayed in a hospital compound while working on his newspaper because the hospital was clean. He said everyone spoke well of a very nice nurse named Miss K'ang, who was only sixteen years old. He said he liked to joke with her.

In her reply to Chih-yung's letter, Julie asked him to pass on her regards to Miss K'ang, followed by a casual remark: "I'm a very jealous woman, but of course I'm pleased to learn that you're not living in solitude over there."

Perhaps Chih-yung wouldn't believe her: Julie had never been jealous of Crimson Cloud, his wife, nor Wendy, the editor. Julie thought Chih-yung's relationship with Wendy was merely an aberrant reaction after being released from prison, when he certainly must have felt he had narrowly escaped death. Wendy followed the style of foreign female writers who didn't seem to pay much attention to their appearance. She had a rather sharply featured long face and a stout figure. Over her traditional gown she wore a bulky brown cardigan knitted with a bunch-of-grapes pattern. For the carefree Wendy, the one-off intimacy with Chih-yung wouldn't have meant much.

"Do you have any venereal diseases?" Wendy asks bluntly.

"No." He smiles. "What about you? Do you have any?"

A classic exchange under these circumstances.

Chih-yung shared many romantic anecdotes from his past that Julie always chalked up to him not having found the right person yet.

"I like women," he once admitted, with a slightly embarrassed smile. "But I don't like older women," he added as a redundant aside.

Julie chuckled.

She had thought "like" meant nothing more than "have an appreciation for." She knew that was true for shy men—because of the distance from the object of their admiration, they often idolized the other party though they rarely acknowledged such behavior. An occasional slip of the tongue usually came across as rather angry.

Chih-yung brought his Japanese friend Araki to meet Julie. Araki was a tall man with a long angular face. The only Japanese features about him were his clean-shaven head and a pair of dainty, black-framed round spectacles.

Araki had been to Mongolia, which Julie found fascinating. On their next visit, Chih-yung brought his gramophone and a record of Mongolian singing. Instead of following a melody, the singing sounded more like chanting from a great distance, though different from, say, Alpine yodeling, which involved repeated changes in pitch. Julie thought Japan's Noh chanting also was limited in melodic phrasing, but its muffled ghostly vocalizations reminded her of a murder victim's spirit trapped in an urn. These types of singing possessed strong local characteristics, so strong that they verged on the comical. But to Julie, the Mongolian chanting sounded different—a youth's bland voice; a distant, primitive voice. Julie played the record several times before she insisted on returning both to their owner.

Araki had lived in Peking for a long time and could speak better Mandarin than Julie. Chih-yung told Julie that Araki's neighbor in Peking had a mischievous daughter. Araki used to joke with her over the wall in the courtyard and eventually the two fell in love. Of course the relationship didn't receive the blessing of the girl's family, and she subsequently was married off to someone else. Araki then became engaged to a student in Japan of his own volition. During the war, his fiancée lived with him for a time, but on her way back to her family the train was bombed and she died. Araki later married a maid who worked for his family, the ceremony held in a Shinto shrine.

The Peking girl's husband was a typical loser. The couple had many children. For years Araki not only helped her financially but also referred jobs to her. One time she couldn't bear the marriage any longer and decided to leave. Her husband knelt down and begged her to stay. Her children also dropped to their knees. She slowly combed her hair while holding a mirror. Then she sighed and let the mirror drop, telling them to get up.

Julie had seen her only once. A lean, bony woman whose shockingly weakened appearance must have been caused by the vicissitudes of destitution and emotional despair, though she wasn't ill, per se, and not old. Her hair was permed. Her delicate pale face, with a round forehead like a toddler's, still revealed a faint trace of innocence. Her tall, thin figure was loosely wrapped in a long-sleeve northern-style brocade gown with embroidered borders, the collar much too big for her. She sounded relaxed when she chatted with Araki, their conversation exchanged in an intimate tone of voice.

"She treats Araki like a younger brother. Sometimes she scolds him," Chih-yung later told Julie.

Julie believed Chih-yung could achieve this ancient Eastern state of mind. However, he was too generous with his love for women, and too ready to fantasize and idealize. He felt compelled to scatter his love. A life of solitude while on the run must have been pure misery, and this kind of romantic excitement even more necessary to him.

"I actually quite enjoyed life as a high-school teacher," Chih-yung once commented.

Julie imagined life in a dormitory for newspaper staff most likely similar to that in a dormitory for teachers. *He must have liked to teach because of all the students who worshipped him and the pretty female colleagues he could share jokes with. But teachers are often restrained by many factors. His interaction with Miss K'ang must have been limited to sharing jokes. What could possibly happen with a respectable sixteen-year-old girl?*

Chih-yung's exhaustion was genuine. In addition to running a newspaper, he also started a literary monthly. But apart from reprinting a few articles here and there, he was the only contributor, writing under different pseudonyms.

In her letters to Chih-yung, Julie often asked him to pass on her regards to Miss K'ang; in his letters to Julie, he frequently mentioned Miss K'ang. He quoted her like a proud parent sharing his child's ingenious remarks.

Gradually, Julie sensed the importance of such romantic excitement to Chih-yung. *That's him. What can you do? If you truly love someone, how can you sever a part of him like chopping off a branch of a tree?*

She dreamed of resting her hand against a leaning palm tree, the light gray striped tree trunk firm and long. Then her gaze moved from the tree trunk to the horizon, where the sea and the sky merged into one. She could barely keep her eyes open under the blazing sun.

It was clearly a Freudian type of dream, which Julie didn't realize also revealed a glimmer of hope: palm trees only have one trunk and no stray branches.

That autumn Chih-yung returned to Shanghai and telephoned Julie. "Hello, I'm back," he said. His voice triggered a wave of dizziness. After recovering, she felt a sudden sense of relief, as if falling backward and being caught by a wall to lean against, but in fact she didn't move.

It was two days after the Mid-Autumn Festival, traditionally an occasion for family reunions.

"Shao Chih-yung is back," Julie informed Judy.

"After celebrating the festival with his wife," Judy commented sarcastically.

Julie just smiled but didn't respond. She didn't know if Chih-yung had first gone to Nanking before returning to Shanghai, though it didn't matter as she never bothered to celebrate the festival anyway. Besides, her birthday was the next day. As a child, she had always confused her birthday with the Mid-Autumn Festival.

Chih-yung brought a lot of money for her again, but this time Julie felt a little awkward accepting it. Obviously he didn't believe what Julie had said about repaying her mother.

He must have thought it was just an excuse to ask for money. With the previous bundle I bought gold to preserve its value. Who knows whether or not it will be enough to make the repayment one day. The currency system is bound to change again when the government changes hands, and today's money will be worth nothing after a few rounds of conversion—a trick any government can use. It's wiser to save a bit more.

Julie had always wanted to ask Third Aunt to help her calculate exactly how much money Rachel had spent on her so she could have a clear sense of what she owed. *But what's the point of calculating in advance when the currency value fluctuates so much? I can't ask Third*

Aunt to calculate again and again. Constantly blabbing about compensation is distasteful.

Julie didn't bother to mention repaying Rachel to Chih-yung again—he wouldn't believe her anyway.

"Let me look after you financially, all right?" he asked.

Julie smiled but didn't say anything. The money she earned from writing wasn't enough. She wasn't writing enough. Only the first editions of her books sold well. She had been more productive at the beginning of her career but couldn't sustain the momentum; she had always been afraid of being forced to churn out rubbish. *A little extra money would be helpful. Isn't he also supporting the painter Hsü Heng, as well as a poet? At least I'm more promising than them.*

"I started the newspaper for money, of course, but I also believe it will benefit the country and the people. I wouldn't have done it otherwise," proclaimed Chih-yung.

As they snuggled up to each other, Chih-yung said apologetically, "I feel like I'm driving with one hand while embracing a lover with the other. My mind is wandering."

Julie could feel a chill in the air.

He started to talk about Miss K'ang: nothing but trivial matters. Their interaction sounded like constant bickering. There were also playful fights—one snatched things from the other then ran. The other gave chase while calling out, "You're terrible!"

So that's what it's all about, Julie thought. This kind of folksy flirting wasn't acceptable to aristocratic families and therefore only existed among ordinary people in the form of affectionate bickering. It wasn't that Julie would flirt in a more respectable manner—she just couldn't help feeling contempt.

"What does Miss K'ang look like?" Julie politely asked.

His voice lowered, almost completely muted. He sounded cautious, talking in circles, and didn't reveal anything significant except, "Even an ordinary blue cotton gown looks refreshing on her."

"Is her hair permed?"

"No. It just curls inward a bit." He struggled to draw a likeness in the air.

That sounded exactly like what Rachel had said a young girl should look like.

Their relationship was changing. Perhaps because of the emotional distance between them, or perhaps because of the hidden worry she harbored. To compensate, Julie intuitively retreated in her mind to the time when they had just met, when she wholeheartedly worshipped Chih-yung. At least she was the only one truly capable of that.

Julie became infatuated with the new essays he churned out with astonishing speed and quantity. He had been going to her place to write. To Julie, the man sitting at her desk looked like an exquisitely detailed statue made of dark silver.

"You look like the small silver god on my desk."

After dinner, Julie washed the dishes and returned to the living room. Chih-yung walked up to Julie and kissed her. She slithered down and knelt in front of him, embracing his leg, her face nestled against his thigh. With an embarrassed smile, he pulled her up with both hands and raised her up in the air. "I worship my wife!"

Chih-yung brought Yü K'o-ch'ien from northern China to help at the newspaper. Yü was the principal disciple of the most famous writer in China at the time. Chih-yung took him to meet Julie. Yü K'o-ch'ien had the demeanor of a scholar, but Julie noticed him spying on her from behind his spectacles. "He's a devious one," she immediately concluded. After he left, Julie said nothing about the visitor to Chih-yung. From her experience with Hsiang Ching, she knew Chih-yung would not be willing to listen to anything negative about his friends.

"Araki complained about Crimson Cloud, saying, 'I've been to your house many times but I've never once seen you eat a dish you like,'" said Chih-yung.

Julie said nothing when she heard this. Actually, she was the same. Whenever Chih-yung came, all she did was simply go to the Old Big House nearby to buy cold cuts of beef stewed in soy sauce and some minced meat wrapped in bean-curd skin, known locally as "quilt rolls"—all things he didn't particularly like to eat. She knew Chih-yung favored more refined fare, but Third Aunt would mock her mercilessly if she started to learn how to cook. As for ordering food from restaurants, Julie was mindful that she had to avoid appearing to be a presumptuous houseguest. The names on the apartment deed were Judy's and Rachel's. Although she was allowed to live there and paid her half of the living expenses, she knew she should adapt to the modest house protocol. After all, Judy was a very tolerant host.

Judy had a hobby: apartment hunting. Sometimes, for no specific reason, she studied classified advertisements in the papers and inspected rental apartments. For her, it was like window-shopping. Once she found an elegant studio apartment. The space wasn't big. To maximize the living area, a foldable ironing board had been cleverly installed on the back of the wardrobe door. Judy fancied she could live in a place like that. Julie constantly reminded herself that she must be considerate because she knew how much Judy yearned to have a place of her own.

There are similarities between the desire for food and for sex. Just as she couldn't prepare refined dishes, Julie wasn't prepared for intimacy. Each time it happened like an unexpected event, and she felt too embarrassed to make any preparations. Apart from the underwear she wore that was eventually removed during their encounters, she never prepared in any other way. When she washed her underwear the next morning, she could smell an odor that reminded her of the warm congee she was given as a child whenever she became sick.

"We'll live with your third aunt in the future," Chih-yung once said to Julie. She later mentioned it to Judy. "Just you is already more than I can cope with. How am I going to bear it if there's also a Shao Chih-yung here?" Judy teased.

One day while they were eating, Julie mentioned an incident that occurred a few days earlier. That day she went to the home of Hsün Hwa, the magazine editor. The office was a long way from where she lived, but Mr. Hsün resided in a nearby alley so she always delivered her manuscripts to his home.

The Hsüns lived in a small room at the back of the house on the second floor. Just as she started to walk up the stairs, several Japanese gendarmes came in from the back gate and followed her. Julie had nowhere else to go so she kept walking up the stairs. The editor's door was wide open. She peeked inside but no one was home. A Japanese gendarme followed her as she walked down the stairs and stopped her to jot down in pencil her name and address in a notebook. On her way back out to the alley, a woman approached from behind. It was Miss Chu, Mr. Hsün's mistress. Julie had bumped into her there previously.

"Hsün Hwa was arrested and taken away by the Japanese gendarmes," said Miss Chu. "Mrs. Hsün just left to inquire about him so I came to look after their home. When I saw Japanese gendarmes had come to investigate, I hid next door and then slipped away."

Chih-yung appeared preoccupied. After hearing Julie's account, he said, "It's not acceptable for the gendarmes to run wild like this. Hsün Hwa seems like a good person. All right, I'll write a letter for the family to submit to the gendarmes."

Julie thought Chih-yung was only asking for trouble. They didn't know Mr. Hsün well. *Who knows what really was going on?* Of course she had heard Wendy praise Mr. Hsün before.

After the meal, Chih-yung wrote a letter to the commander of the military police unit. It totaled eight lines. Julie was slightly amused to see one of the lines that read, "Mr. Hsün Hwa is considered honorable in general...." She recalled the incident when she bumped into Miss Chu a different time while delivering her pages to the Hsün residence. No one was home that day, either. Just as she was leaving, the same Miss Chu called out from behind and told her that Mrs. Hsün had gone out and she was there to look after their children. Julie initially thought Miss Chu was Mrs. Hsün's friend, but then Miss Chu mumbled that she actually worked in a publishing house and already had three children with Mr. Hsün. She also told Julie that he and Mrs. Hsün weren't officially married, either—the real wife resided in the countryside—but this Mrs. Hsün, a primary-school teacher, was a ferocious one.

Miss Chu, a tall, big-boned woman with large docile eyes set on a long, broad face, reminded Julie of the distant aunt who had failed to become her stepmother. Similar to this distant aunt who used to hold her hand tight and not let go, Miss Chu also clasped the sleeve of Julie's peacock-blue padded cotton gown and did not let go. Julie thought Miss Chu needed someone to listen to her vent her despair, but she didn't want to bring her home for fear of annoying Judy and of entertaining a guest who might be difficult to get rid of. She stood in the alleyway to accompany Miss Chu without knowing that Miss Chu had mistaken her for Mr. Hsün's new girlfriend and was trying to warn her off.

In the Nanking dialect such situations are called "a mixed-up mess like a pot of congee," which Julie never felt applied to her own romantic situation. She thought that the bond between herself and Chih-yung was unique and no one could truly empathize with her, and that, in fact, even a casual glance her way would risk misunderstanding her.

Julie immediately delivered Chih-yung's letter to Mr. Hsün's residence. Mrs. Hsün was home this time.

"The last time I came I heard Mr. Hsün had been arrested. Mr. Shao happened to overhear when I mentioned it today. He was outraged and offered to write a letter to see if it would help," Julie explained.

Mrs. Hsün was shorter than Miss Chu. The outer corners of her eyes bent upward, the high cheekbones on her square face were dusted with yellowish patches of powder—a ferocious visage indeed. And yet she repeatedly thanked Julie. The next day, Mrs. Hsün and Miss Chu went to Julie's home to express their gratitude some more. Fortunately, Chih-yung had left Shanghai by then.

"Hsün Hwa's principal wife and secondary wife came hand in hand, thanking you," Judy remarked after the women had left.

A few weeks later, Hsün Hwa was released, perhaps because of the letter, or perhaps not. He went to Julie's home to thank her in person. Hsün Hwa, who always dressed nicely, looked even more immaculate that day in a well-pressed suit. His narrow triangular face beamed.

"They suspect me of being connected to the Communist Party," Mr. Hsün explained. His face was all smiles.

Julie smiled back. "Are you?" she asked. Judy smiled, too.

"Of course not," Mr. Hsün answered, still smiling.

Then he turned the conversation to the tiger bench, a method of torture that targets the kneecaps. Julie was curious but for some reason her mind resisted digesting the information, as if the cries of pain couldn't pierce a thick stone door to reach her. It was probably the same door that slammed shut when she heard the news of Mr. Andrews's death.

After Mr. Hsün left, Judy commented, "Who knows if he really is a member of the Communist Party or not."

Julie wasn't sure. *In Pa Chin's novels, all Communist Party members live in small back rooms like Mr. Hsün's, so they could be vacated in the blink of an eye if something happened.* But unlike other small rented rooms commonly cluttered with bric-a-brac, the Hsüns' kept theirs very tidy. An iron-frame double bed with a pink-striped sheet. Mr. Hsün had five children, maybe six. The eldest daughter was already twelve or thirteen. *There must be another residence. Three wives and two households overflowing with children—what a mess. Are they his cover?*

"He wrote me a letter before, trying to persuade me to go to Chungking," Julie told Judy. "Of course that's not enough to prove he's not connected to the Communist Party, but I was grateful to him for being willing to ask me. It's dangerous to express things like that in writing, especially for a 'man of letters.'"

Julie could not recall when she received Hsün Hwa's letter but vividly remembered one sentence: "Only words written on paper can be counted upon"—which suggested everything else is false. He seemed to be subtly referring to Chih-yung. This meant her close association with Chih-yung was no longer a secret. Was Hsün Hwa the second person to warn her about Chih-yung? Or the first, before Hsiang Ching? What he said was too ambiguous and polite, and at the time she didn't understand. Only now did Julie vaguely see the connection.

But in the end it was Chih-yung who saved Hsün Hwa's life, if his letter had indeed been effective. A few days later, Hsün Hwa stopped by again. Judy didn't come out to see him this time.

After Hsün Hwa's third visit, Judy asked Julie, mixing in English,

"Should this be considered *courting*?" She smiled, but Julie could read the anxiety in her eyes and felt humiliated.

Thanks to Judy's remark, however, Julie realized that Hsün Hwa had mistaken her intention to help. He probably thought she was a real-life protagonist from the Chinese movie *A Lovelorn Actress*, which she had seen as a child, in which a warlord's concubine rescues a falsely accused man of letters from jail.

Hsün Hwa had previously adapted a literary work to the stage to much acclaim, but his real talent involved acting as a go-between among members of the prewar literary circles. During his visits, he liked to tell anecdotes about literary figures that put him in difficult situations. He would always conclude with his pet phrase: "Awkward, very awkward!"

Most of his stories went right over Julie's head as she had never read the books by those writers in his anecdotes, nor was she familiar with their names.

Hsün Hwa acted with extreme tact. He would smile and mumble, his words barely audible. Then he'd end with a few deep cackles, and conclude: "Awkward, very awkward!"

Though it turned out that the man wasn't a complete fool after all. He stopped coming after three visits.

Chih-yung brought money to Julie on each of his return visits. Once he said, "You should also have some," and then added in a lower voice, "some money in your place."

The words "in your place" sounded irritating.

Julie felt uneasy every time he handed her money and Chih-yung immediately sensed it. For some reason, Julie felt her heart shiver. Not a good sign.

One day Chih-yung mentioned central China. "Do you want to visit me?"

"How can I? I couldn't even board the plane," Julie protested. He had come on a military aircraft.

"Yes you can. Just say you're a member of my family."

Even Julie could tell that "member of my family" was merely a euphemism for "concubine."

She smiled but didn't respond. Chih-yung changed his mind, saying with a smile, "Perhaps it'd be best if you stayed here after all."

The implication being, Julie gathered, that she'd give people a bad impression if she went with him. She felt the same way, having turned into a lone fox spirit haunting the two-room apartment.

One day, in the middle of a conversation with Julie, Judy made a remark, dropping in an English word: "You're an *expensive* woman."

For a moment Julie was taken aback. She certainly could be considered a big spender, though in an invisible way. She was constantly consulting doctors and dentists, partly as a result of the chronic maladies from the two severe illnesses she had at the age of seventeen—her annual medical expenses were huge. Also, unlike Judy, who was anxious about putting on weight and could endure meager meals, Julie wasn't frugal about food. Moreover, she could never resist the eccentric outfits Bebe designed for her.

Judy found that unfair. "It's infuriating that Bebe doesn't dress *herself* in such a quirky way," she once declared.

Julie smiled but didn't defend her friend. Bebe was ill-suited to wear eccentric clothing because of her short stature and was always on the verge of being overweight ever since childhood. Of course Bebe would never admit to her own slight imperfections. She often said that Julie was "too pale and shy, and therefore needs help to attract people's attention."

Julie didn't mind feeling as if she were being molded by Bebe. But these days they shared little in common—there were no more Hollywood movies playing, she hadn't read a book in English for a long time, and her personal life had become secretive.

Judy once said of Bebe, "It's like you love her."

Bebe's bold creations met with Julie's enthusiasm for archaically fashioned outfits, resulting in a wardrobe without one single piece of "normal" attire.

Years later, Julie stood in a line on a footpath, waiting to register her paperwork. She wore a modest light blue flare-sleeved shirt made of rationed fabric and a pair of lilac-blue cotton trousers. She had stopped wearing glasses long ago. The official in charge, who sat behind a desk on the footpath, saw a bumpkinish woman approach and asked, "Can you read?"

"Yes," answered Julie softly. She was pleased. Finally she was seen as a member of the masses.

"Your hairstyle is always the same," said Chih-yung.

"Right." She smiled, as if she couldn't sense his disapproval.

Chih-yung returned on Julie's next birthday. At the time, U.S. warplanes had been raiding central China. In his letters, Chih-yung told Julie that many people died during the air raids. Some people's clothing, and even their skin, had been scorched away, the victims looking like those red arhat deities found in Buddhist temples. The stories weren't as dramatic when retold face-to-face. He didn't continue, obviously feeling a little disappointed.

They went out to the moonlit balcony. She couldn't wait until they returned to the room so she could show Chih-yung her latest portrait. In the photograph she was smiling, and a thin gold necklace Bebe had loaned her hung below her exposed collarbone. The purple gemstone pendant dangling from the necklace looked like a nipple.

Chih-yung glanced at the photo under the moonlight. "You look rather ambitious in this picture!" he exclaimed with sudden exuberance.

Julie smiled but didn't respond. Bebe had assumed the role of artistic director during the shoot. "Think about your hero!" Bebe suggested. As she imagined Chih-yung in a faraway place, Julie gazed out into the distance. It reminded her of an image in a famous nineteenth-century poem:

> Roll up the blinds for morning ablutions
> Gaze out at the tempestuous Yellow River

That night Yü K'o-ch'ien came up in conversation. "That Yü K'o-ch'ien isn't trustworthy," complained Chih-yung. "He's already left. What a devious . . . ! He wanted to court Miss K'ang so he gossiped about me behind my back, telling her, 'He has a wife.'"

"Who?" thought Julie. "Me?" At the time, Chih-yung had not divorced Crimson Cloud yet.

So the editor and his deputy became love rivals over Miss K'ang and the deputy resigned? But Chih-yung condemned Yü K'o-ch'ien for being "devious," most likely not because Yü had revealed that "he has a wife" but because Chih-yung blamed Yü for degrading his innocent relationship with Miss K'ang—at least Julie preferred to believe that.

"When he first arrived in Shanghai, he told me that he missed his family very much. He talked a lot about his wife and how unique their relationship was," Chih-yung sneered.

His tone changed when the topic of their conversation switched to Miss K'ang.

"During the bombing raids," he said on a more serious note, "when we were all in the air-raid shelter, Miss K'ang behaved as if she were there to protect me."

Apart from this detail, all Chih-yung had to report was his usual playful banter with Miss K'ang.

The possibility that Julie had always thought "can't be true" gradually became a reality. "Know thyself and know thine enemy," Julie thought to herself. "If I still want to hold on to him, I'll have to hear him out, no matter how hard it is for me." But as she listened with a frozen smile, she felt as if a storm of invisible cleavers hacked away at her heart, until the image in front of her disappeared.

The next day Bebe visited in the afternoon. Chih-yung placed two chairs in the middle of the room. Bebe smiled apprehensively as she watched him arrange the furniture. Chih-yung nudged her into one chair then sat directly opposite her, very near. Sitting like a Japanese man with both hands on his lap, he earnestly told her how terrifying the air raids had been.

Bebe reacted like Julie, responding with the English custom of smiling somewhat uncomfortably while listening. The two women had both experienced bombing attacks without even the protection of air-raid shelters. On the sidelines Julie felt embarrassed and walked away, listlessly pretending to look for something or other on the desk.

Bebe and Chih-yung went onto the balcony.

Julie sat in front of the desk by the window that looked out onto the balcony. She overheard Chih-yung ask Bebe, "Can someone love two people at the same time?" Suddenly the sky outside the window appeared to darken, and she didn't hear Bebe's reply. Bebe probably didn't answer seriously, thinking Chih-yung was just flirting. She never mentioned this conversation to Julie.

After Bebe left, Julie smiled at Chih-yung. "When you asked if someone could love two people at the same time, I felt the sky suddenly darken."

Chih-yung smiled weakly and flinched, as if she had pressed a sore spot on him, then nestled his face into her shoulder.

"Such a wonderful girl...I simply must help her continue her education," he said at last. "Must nurture her...."

Julie immediately recalled what Judy said of her days with Rachel when they lived overseas: "They all thought we were the concubines of some warlord or other"—following the usual practice of dispatching out-of-favor concubines overseas. *Just spent all that money to divorce one and now you want to take up the burdens of yet another five-year plan?*

"But she's so beautiful!" he moaned again in agony. "Even the clothes she washes are always exceptionally clean."

Disdain flowed from the deepest recesses of Julie's heart. She also washed her own clothes with exceptional meticulousness. She was sure she'd also wash his clothes if she had to.

Rachel often claimed Chinese men didn't understand romance, "Which is why people say that if one has loved a foreigner, one will never love a Chinese man again." Of course it's impossible to generalize in such matters, but practice makes perfect, and in the past Chinese people lived under so many restrictions that they simply lacked experience. One shouldn't stop with a single individual in matters of love but love one at a time, in succession, while keeping past loves in the heart—only a Western mind-set could facilitate this kind of compartmentalization, enabling isolation. But isolation requires money. Otherwise it would become like the case of Mrs. Hsün and Miss Chu, who were bound to join together to defend against external aggressors. It demanded discipline, too—something Chih-yung couldn't cultivate.

This is one of life's ironies. Rachel had trained Julie from a young age not to be the least bit curious about people close to her. Julie always reserved her curiosity for outsiders. The closer a person was to her, the more space Julie reserved for that person. It was like following the principles of Chinese painting—sufficient breathing space is essential—or like arranging layers of cotton padding to protect precious jewelry. If a letter wasn't addressed to her, she wouldn't even look at the envelope. Yet Chih-yung felt compelled to tell her about his romantic adventures. Of course, realization meant acceptance. But for him, sharing stories was a matter of pride.

Julie once accompanied Third Aunt to visit Herr Schütte's home. His wife, a former student, was very young and quite pretty. Pale skin, brown hair, slightly neurotic. Under Nazi rule, German women were discouraged from wearing makeup. She gave birth to a son in China, and the couple called him "the Chinaman." Even if she regarded Judy somewhat suspiciously, she certainly wasn't aware of what really occurred—foreign women do not possess that much self-restraint. Herr Schütte loved to make sarcastic remarks about the most trivial matters in an attempt at humor, but it made him difficult to fathom. He must have been a Nazi Party member, otherwise he would never have been made the school principal.

"They really treat Jews terribly," said Judy in a hushed voice. "Whenever they enter a shop owned by Jews, they complain that the stench is unbearable."

"One good thing about Herr Schütte," said Judy on another occasion, "he had my teeth fixed. Thanks to him, even the shape of my mouth changed."

Herr Schütte had introduced a young attractive female German dentist to Judy, and put up the money. After her teeth were straightened, her mouth gradually grew smaller, her lips thinned a little, and the shape of her face became daintier, making Judy's countenance much more attractive. Unfortunately, it was a little too late, though as the adage goes, "Better late than never."

The next time Chih-yung returned to Shanghai was for a lecture he was invited to give, which Julie attended. It took place at a secluded garden villa, most likely expropriated. At the gate, they bumped into Chih-yung's son wheeling his bicycle along.

Perhaps few people were interested in the lecture, or perhaps it was just intended to be an informal talk to a small number of people, as only a dozen or so audience members showed up and sat around a long dining table. A few youths asked questions like seasoned reporters—Julie couldn't tell if they were students or journalists. By this time the Axis Powers were in a hopeless situation and there really wasn't much that could be said, but Chih-yung spoke eloquently. She felt he did a fine job, regardless of the venue, much more interesting than the articles he wrote. A young woman with glasses who spoke Mandarin with a heavy Cantonese accent asked several overbearing questions, but Chih-yung parried them leisurely, one by one.

"I brought my wife *and* my son," chuckled Chih-yung when it was over.

He was supposed to leave very early the next morning, but that night, out of the blue, he said, "Come to my place, all right?"

It was almost midnight and Julie didn't inform Judy when the two of them snuck out. The autumn night was pleasantly cool. Under the dim streetlights there were no pedestrians or cars as he led her by the hand down the middle of the road. The wide asphalt road looked like it had been poured out from the heavens as they walked on the dark-blue sky sprinkled with stardust.

He brought her to a rather large alleyway house. A maidservant opened the door, looking obviously surprised. The members of the household were probably all asleep. They sat in the living room for a while and tea was served. Hsiu-nan appeared, greeting Julie with a smile. Like a reunion after a long separation, everyone looked a little uneasy under the dim yellow lamplight. Chih-yung walked over to Hsiu-nan and spoke a few words to her, whereupon she retreated.

Chih-yung returned, smiling. "I don't have a place to sleep in the family home anymore."

After they sat for a while longer, he took her to a messy room on the third floor, latched the door, and left. The lamplight was even dimmer here. Julie stood as she looked around, placing her overcoat and purse on a chest of drawers. Suddenly the door opened. A tall woman poked her head in, looked about, then silently closed the door. Julie just caught a glimpse of a long jaundiced face with bright eyes and refined eyebrows, a wave of hair across the middle of her brow. Julie assumed it was Chih-yung's mentally deranged second wife, which, reminding her of Jane Eyre's story, sent shivers down her spine.

"She's very tall," Chih-yung once told Julie, "but her features are a little severe."

He had revealed snippets of information to her about his second wife from time to time.

"A friend introduced her to me." They went home after the wedding, "And immediately I carried her into the boudoir."

Perhaps the Western tradition of bearing the bride across the threshold has a similar origin.

"It's a rather mute marital relationship," he had written in a letter. He was probably referring to his second wife.

After he joined the Peace Movement, Chih-yung ran the newspaper and was often so exhausted rushing out editorials that he shook with fatigue, unable to pick up the cigarette on his desk. When he finally returned home late at night, his second wife would have psychotic episodes, raging at him with blind suspicions.

She didn't appear to be mentally ill just now, but of course sometimes such things aren't evident.

She certainly chose the right time to go mad—or was it Crimson Cloud who triggered her madness? Julie was never sure.

Soon afterward Chih-yung returned. Julie made no mention of the intruder. Chih-yung brought two books of Egyptian fairy tales for her to read.

The wood-frame bed wasn't large. The grayish-white muslin canopy smelled of dust. The sheets appeared to be fresh. Julie was a little afraid, feeling like she was a prisoner of war. He too seemed slightly embarrassed as he disrobed and got into bed.

Nonetheless, this time it didn't hurt. Normally Julie usually asked him not to turn off the lights, "I want to see your face—otherwise how could I know who you are." His flushed face peered down upon her. To Julie, his face was a golden lotus flower floating in an abyss of misery.

"Why doesn't it hurt today?" he said. "Is it because today's your birthday?"

His eyes sparkled with excitement and he wriggled inside her like the undulations of a fish tail, flashing a smile at Julie.

Suddenly he withdrew and crawled toward her feet.

"Hey! What are you doing?" she asked, terrified. His hair brushed against her thigh—the head of a wild beast.

The beast sips at the eternal springs of a dark cavern in the netherworld, slurping with his curled tongue. She is a bat hanging upside down at the mouth of the cave. Like a hermit hidden within the bowels of the mountain being explored, encroached upon, she felt helpless and hopeless. Now the small beast sips at her innermost core, small mouthfuls one at a time. The terror of exposing herself mingled with a burning desire: She wants him back, now! Back to her arms, back to where she can see him.

She was about to fall asleep but the autumn mosquitoes viciously attacked her, despite the mosquito net.

"How can there still be mosquitoes!" he said, using his fingertip to smear saliva on the bites, which reminded Julie of the time Bebe used saliva to determine if a fabric color would run.

When Julie awoke the next morning, she couldn't wait to flip through the book of Egyptian fairy tales that was on her pillow. Chih-yung told her that a heartless girl just like Bebe appeared in one of the stories. Julie knew he must be referring to Bebe's reaction to the bombing.

He couldn't really say Julie was heartless.

On that cold morning, Julie brought the two books of fairy tales home with her, and the only thing on her mind as she unlocked the door was to not wake up Third Aunt.

8

FROM THAT morning until the end of the Second World War, for some six months, Julie lived in a state of emotional chaos. White wax sealed the chaos inside her—on the surface, she appeared calm and secure. During this period, everything seemed to have occurred in the previous year or in the following year, unless outside evidence proved otherwise. Julie remembered nothing from that year, which could be designated a lost year.

One day in that time of emptiness, while Chih-yung read the newspaper and the afternoon light streamed in, Julie sketched him reading reports about the Potsdam Conference.

"The war's ending," he said calmly as he raised his head from the paper.

"Oh no," Julie moaned, smiling, then adding blithely, "I hope it goes on forever."

His face darkened. "So many people have died and you want it to go on forever?"

"I said that only because I want to be with you," she explained in a gentle voice, still smiling.

His stern expression softened a little.

Julie didn't feel guilty. Up to now, she had lived her entire adult life in the shadow of the Second World War. War, though brutal, seemed permanent to her, always on the horizon of her life. People fear momentous change, so it was natural for her to want it to continue. But whatever her wishes happened to be, would they change anything? Before, she was so worried fighting would break out, but didn't the war start anyway? If she had elected those who caused the war, then as the saying goes, "Everyone has a duty to their country" and she ought to feel a sense of responsibility.

One day after a snowstorm, in the spring before Germany surrendered, Herr Schütte bought a bottle of whiskey and slipped on the icy steps to his home. The bottle smashed on the ground, and he sat on the steps and cried.

Judy helped him sell off his clothes and loaned him money to return home. One item, a midnight-blue overcoat made of an expensive fabric one couldn't get anymore, had not been worn many times. Julie bought it for Chih-yung, though she didn't know when he'd have a chance to wear it. Ever since Julie met Chih-yung she knew he'd have to go into hiding after the war, but now that the moment had arrived, she became confused. Also, in her lost year she had lost her way.

"Dressing Shao Chih-yung up, are you?" mocked Judy.

One night, Julie was woken up by the sound of fireworks and cheering. She heard Judy say Japan had surrendered, then rolled over and fell back to sleep.

In the penultimate issue of his newspaper, which Chih-yung mailed to Julie, he wrote in an article, "The person I yearn for is like a lotus flower: rootless, leafless, a bright light floating in the darkness. . . ."

Early in the morning two weeks later, she dreamed she heard a telephone ringing, a U-shaped sound, faint on both ends but deafening in the middle. Amplified in her grogginess, the sound turned into a stream of green garlands flying through the crisp cool air.

Julie finally woke up and ran to answer the phone.

"Hello. This is Araki. Um, he's back. I'll take you to see him. Right now okay?"

I had to perm my hair two days ago. It's at its worst now, short and uncooperative. Nothing I can do about it.

Araki arrived half an hour later. To avoid traveling in the same rickshaw, he ordered one for each of them. It was a long journey and excruciatingly slow. Along the way she saw two men wrestling with all their strength, somewhat akin to Mongolian wrestling but different. There were few cars on the road, though occasionally a convoy of trucks transporting Japanese soldiers passed by. Two men with clean-shaven heads, save for a few tufts tied like ponytails pointing upward, wrestled like bulls among the rickshaws, flatbed tricycles, and bicycles, horns locked as they did battle. They only wore singlets and khaki pants, and were very thin, unlike those enormous sumo wrestlers. Julie thought it was some kind of Japanese performance— Japanese residents of the city and Japanese soldiers facing what felt like the end of days would probably be more susceptible to spending money on things that induced homesickness.

A man following behind the wrestlers shook a section of bamboo filled with beans to beat time. The two men followed the cues and changed their stance, always with heads bowed. At the next traffic light, the two rickshaws stopped next to each other. Julie wanted to ask Araki about the situation but she remained silent. All of a sudden it felt like everything seemed inappropriate to say.

By the time the rickshaws reached Hongkew it was already around half past ten. They stopped at a row of houses in a lane. After ringing the doorbell, they were met by an unassuming Japanese lady who opened the door. She was short and wore a floral-patterned dress, her small oval face powdered and pink with blush. Araki spoke a few words with her, then led Julie into the house. She followed them up the stairs. This wasn't a Japanese-style house. They entered a room and Chih-yung sat up in the bed. He had smuggled his way onto a Japanese military ship, disguising himself as a soldier, his head shaven. Feeling embarrassed, Chih-yung put on a boat-shaped khaki hat. He had fallen ill on the ship and had lost a lot of weight.

Araki sat for a while, then left.

Chih-yung rose from the bed and moved to Araki's chair. "Initially, I thought the situation there would allow me start all over again and survive for a while," he said quietly with a smile, "but then things changed and I couldn't hold out any longer."

Julie also smiled. Whenever she encountered situations like this she tried even harder to appear normal.

After chatting for a while, Chih-yung blurted out with a small laugh, "Still my love, not wife."

Julie pretended to take that as a compliment and laughed, too.

Chih-yung then said in a low voice, "Now, after the surrender, it seems that none of the high-ranking Japanese military officers can speak frankly with me."

Julie was in a daze. There were no windows in the room, only two shutter doors that led out to the balcony, making the room very dark. Suddenly she felt she was sitting in the pitch-black room of a one-story Chinese house, the shadows cast by a window grille falling on rice-paper panes like silhouetted cutouts.

"There was a huge steerage cabin on the troop carrier where many people constantly threw up."

Such a dark image chilled Julie to the bone.

"Can you make it to Japan?" she asked softly.

He shook his head faintly. "There is a fellow provincial whose family once provided me with financial assistance to attend middle school. Over the past few years when they needed help I gave them a lot of money. I can live with them in the countryside."

Perhaps this is the safest solution. In his hometown he won't be a stranger who would attract attention. The Americans are occupying Japan. How could he go there? It would be like turning himself in. Foolish of me even to think that was a possibility.

"How long do you think you will need to hide?" Julie asked in a low voice.

Chih-yung thought for a moment. "Four years."

Julie felt transported again into a tiny dark room with cloud patterns silhouetted from a window grille onto rice-paper panes. *Is this déjà vu, or is the mysterious future linked to the past?*

"You'll be fine," he said, with that slightly contemptuous look of his.

She thought of asking him if he needed money but didn't say anything. Her mother would return as soon as transportation links were reestablished and then Julie would have to repay her. When the postal service resumed, a letter arrived urging Julie to return to Hong Kong to complete her studies. The university administration had tentatively agreed to send her to Oxford University for graduate studies, as long as she continued to achieve good marks. But now that she was a few years older, she feared she wouldn't be able to knuckle down and take up that long and arduous journey again. Besides, it was too late to apply for the same scholarship she had before because the school year was about to begin. Plus she didn't have sufficient funds to travel overseas. And yet, if she couldn't earn enough money writing in Shanghai, perhaps it would be best to just go regardless and worry about money later. At least she had taken that path before, having studied in Hong Kong for a while before winning the scholarship.

If she were to tell Chih-yung he would definitely think she was leaving him. Maybe being so accustomed from her childhood years to her mother's comings and goings, Julie didn't give it much thought. It was simply a question of money.

As far as the living expenses at Chih-yung's household were concerned, Hsiu-nan's Mr. Wen could handle them. Hadn't Hsiu-nan always sacrificed for Chih-yung?

It was almost noon and Julie had no idea when this Japanese family ate lunch. She didn't want to trouble the host.

"I'm leaving. I'll come back tomorrow." She stood and picked up her purse.

"All right."

The next afternoon, Julie bought a large cream cake for the Japanese family. She took the tram, but halfway there she noticed Hsün Hwa was also on board. He warmly waved to her, edged his way through the crowd, and stood in front of her, one hand hanging on to a rattan handle.

After exchanging pleasantries, Hsün Hwa said, "Do you now understand the line I wrote in my letter, 'Only words written on paper can be counted upon'?"

"Really?" she thought. "Not sure about that." Julie just smiled in reply.

No wonder he was so happy to see her—he had a chance to say, "Didn't I tell you so?"

The tram was very crowded. The cake, purchased at a famous bakery and topped with cream, would soon be crushed into a soggy mess.

Hsün Hwa took advantage of the crowd to suddenly squeeze her thighs between his knees.

Julie had always been opposed to women slapping men in the face, especially close acquaintances, because it attracted attention with its ostentatious display. She had to wait a short while before turning in her seat and easing herself away as if nothing happened. But in that instant she shuddered—his knees had made her go through the agony of the tiger-bench torture.

Julie feared that he would disembark at the same tram stop and she wouldn't be able to get rid of him. She didn't know the way well herself, nor did she want him to know the address.

Fortunately he smiled and nodded but didn't get off the tram with her. It was almost nothing really, but the incident served as a reminder that, as the wife of a traitor, all and sundry could harass her.

This time Julie came alone and when the Japanese lady opened the door, she looked obviously displeased. Julie perceived that Japanese women bowed and scraped when meeting a man though weren't particularly polite to women, especially Chinese women, but she intuitively felt a hint of jealousy from this lady. She didn't even smile when Julie gave her the cake.

Julie saw Chih-yung and mentioned her encounter with Hsün Hwa. She told him how anxious she was about him getting off at the same stop, but didn't say a word about Hsün Hwa's act of ingratitude.

How did Chih-yung and Miss K'ang part? Of course that question had crossed her mind the previous day, but she was afraid to hear the answer. Luckily, Chih-yung never raised the issue. While they chatted, however, his face suddenly clouded over for a quiet moment. Julie knew it was because she had not asked him about Miss K'ang.

Ever since Chih-yung's confession of simultaneously loving two people, Julie never asked him to give her regards to Miss K'ang again. She simply couldn't act in a way that exceeded the boundaries of her conscience. Chih-yung had agreed to leave Miss K'ang of his own accord, and Julie had never reminded him of this, the same way she had left his two divorces entirely up to him.

Now there is no time to save funds to pay for Miss K'ang's university education. However, he wouldn't simply leave it at that. He must already have given all his extra cash to her. He had plans to settle in a safe place to achieve something big, which meant he must have had some cash in hand.

Secretly, Julie hoped Miss K'ang would be more calculating. *After all, didn't she like him because he was a big fish in a small pond? But it must be difficult to be calculating when the man generously gifted funds before running for his life. Even if there were signs of devious calculations, he would have convinced himself otherwise.*

Julie pretended she did not notice Chih-yung's displeasure.

"How's Bebe?" he finally asked, smiling wistfully.

"Celebrating the opening of communications to the West," replied Julie cheerfully.

Chih-yung smiled. "Oh, I see," he said.

The day after the Japanese surrender, Bebe dragged Julie out to celebrate. They sat opposite each other in a European bakery by the large bright windows, but in fact Julie was both anxious and joyful.

Chih-yung spoke about his old colleagues—obviously, he had heard some news via Araki. "Such unthinkable fools," he sneered. "One after another they sit at home waiting to be arrested."

Then he smiled. "Yesterday the Japanese lady here showed me a huge cabinet, suggesting I could hide in it if there was ever an inspection. I can't hide in there. It would be much too embarrassing for me to be found inside a cabinet."

"That's him," thought Julie. *What he fears most is an assault on his pride.* In the morning, before leaving the apartment, Julie would always tell him to carry his shoes in his hands and put them on outside.

Chih-yung would pause for a moment, then say, "I better put them on now. Otherwise it would be too embarrassing if Third Aunt suddenly opened the door."

Chih-yung stomped noisily down the corridor in his leather shoes. As she lay in bed her heart shuddered with each step he took.

"Third Aunt knows for sure," he frequently speculated.

Julie knew that her aunt knew, and her heart sank at the thought, but she always replied with a worried smile, "No, she doesn't."

Julie saw Chih-yung out the back door. It was a shorter distance and wouldn't be as noisy as shutting the front door, which Judy would certainly hear. The kitchen door opened onto the rear terrace. Beyond the iron balustrade of the long and narrow terrace, the vast expanse of Shanghai opened out in the distance. Wisps of clouds buffeted in the gentle breeze; the horizon appeared so high at the edge of the world. At the end of the terrace, the flimsy back entrance with wooden horizontal slats resembled a humble cottage door. In the gentle morning breeze Julie only wore a long dark green singlet that covered her briefs, her bare legs exposed, her thighs as slim as her waist.

After he left, Julie latched the wooden door, returned to her room, and emptied the cigarette butts from the mosquito coil tray next to the bed.

As it wasn't possible to use an alarm clock, Chih-yung would focus his mind before going to sleep and wake up at the right time, then kiss Julie once and nudge one leg aside, leaving her other leg bent with her foot still on the bed.

"Again?" she'd say hazily.

Julie didn't want to wake up, preferring to just lie beneath the canopy of the mosquito net. As the ship lurched from side to side, she drifted off to sleep, as if being rocked in a cradle.

"They have a huge green mosquito net, as big as a whole room," he joked when they were back in the Japanese family's house. "They hang it up at night."

"Just like in an Ukiyo-e woodblock print," Julie replied. She didn't mention that she found the mistress of the household quite attractive, unlike the chubby long-faced women who hung mosquito nets in Japanese woodblock prints, women with faces that looked a little like half-full sacks of flour.

He went to close a slatted door. She stood up and followed him. "Don't . . . haven't you only just recovered?"

"Don't worry. I'm fine now."

She still thought it inappropriate to be intimate in someone else's house during a time of danger—especially in an atmosphere of hostility.

Chih-yung closed the other slatted door. Julie stood watching the silhouette of him slipping on his cotton shoes.

The large wooden bed wasn't as comfortable as her own narrow couch. Perhaps because their encounter this time was rather listless, she felt the need to demonstrate her affection. She curled up in his embrace and suddenly murmured, "I want to go with you."

She was so close to him she could feel a twinge of fear pass through Chih-yung, but he calmly replied, "Wouldn't that be both of us surrendering."

"Right now I have no way out anyway."

"That's only temporary."

In her mind's eye the countryside was a barren land stretching for a thousand miles, like a bird's-eye-view photograph in which, for some reason, light and shade, protrusions and depressions were reversed to make paths between the fields look like trenches as deep as a person's height, in which people rushed back and forth. But in this infertile land of crimson mud, there was no place to hide the smallest item, even the metal container Auntie Han brought with her, unless one buried it in a cavern.

Chih-yung and Hsiu-nan probably had connections and solutions, unlike Julie who knew nothing of such matters. *Perhaps it'd be all right if he went. But just hand him over to them like this?*

"Could you go to England or America?" she asked. Her voice was barely audible, but as soon as the words left her lips she felt another strong wave of fear pulse through Chih-yung. To be a coolie? Illegal entry by a war criminal. She would have no way of supporting herself without a degree, so why drag him along? It was all because of her mother that, like a seaman's daughter who always faced the sea, Julie would think about escaping to a foreign land whenever danger loomed, despite being aware of the hardships of living far away from home. Rachel had stressed again and again how difficult the average student's life really was abroad, fearing Julie wanted to go just for fun.

Chih-yung opened the slatted door. The Japanese lady's young daughter had come to invite Julie over for tea to thank her because she had presented a gift, as well as to pray for everyone's safety.

She must have already come by and, seeing the door closed, went back to report to her parents. Julie furrowed her brow.

The living room was fitted with a traditional tatami straw-mat floor and rice-paper screen doors, though the host sat on a chair. The stout man, a typical Japanese military officer, nodded in greeting.

The little girl, who had a pageboy hairstyle, slid open the screen door, carried the tea tray in, and knelt down to place the tray on the tatami mat. The hostess poured the tea and served it. Offerings had been placed on the table in front of the altar dedicated to Buddha, along with a bronze chime and wooden fish, but the scene didn't look right to Julie. Then the host struck the chime and recited some scriptures while the hostess chanted in a manner that seemed discordant with the way Chinese monks chanted sutras.

The windows and the weathered latticework, a faded green, all faced west, making the room very hot. The chanting and reciting dragged on past sunset, though Julie didn't understand a single word. The exotic atmosphere, the almost tropical heat, for some reason reminded Julie of a scene in a novel written about a black youth who lived in the West Indies, which described his returning home during the high-school summer break. The small wooden house with a tin roof faced the sea, its back to the hills, making it as hot as an oven. His mother toiled a whole day under the eaves, cooking a local dish called green parrotfish curry, with piles of red and yellow curry powders at the ready.

The ritual finally ended and Julie returned to Chih-yung's room. It was about time for her to leave.

"They chant sutras from morning to night," Chih-yung grumbled.

Julie again felt she should ask Chih-yung if he needed money but held back.

"Maybe you shouldn't come tomorrow."

"Yes," she conceded with a detached smile. "Wouldn't want to bump into anyone on the way here again."

When the tramcar reached the Bund it encountered a victory parade and couldn't continue. Everyone had to disembark and Julie found herself in the middle of a writhing crowd. She squeezed her way past the Shanghai Race Club. The entire length of Nanking Road was a sea of thousands of bobbing heads. The usually flat winding road became three-dimensional, standing up in the dusk as if covered with insects, wriggling and squirming. Through a series of ceremonial arches set up in the middle of the road, a convoy of jeeps and military trucks slowly passed by, but everything seemed insignificant compared to the vast hordes of people everywhere. Even the bursting of firecrackers could barely be heard, the occasional pop and bang and loud echoing explosions all muffled.

An American air force officer sat high on the hood of a vehicle. A group of men walked along next to the jeep, stretching their arms out to touch his leg. The young Jewish man was obviously a little overwhelmed by the enthusiasm of the crowd. His eyes sparkled with joy under his boat-shaped cap, and he was smiling so hard it exaggerated his hooked nose, though his smile also betrayed embarrassment. Although homosexuality seemed quite common in America, especially in the military, he obviously felt a little awkward with many Asian men caressing his thigh. Julie only saw that one face out of all the hundreds of thousands of faces in the crowd, though he never saw her, something she found unfathomable.

Julie did her best to walk slowly against the tide of humanity, but she knew she had feet of clay and going against the tide of the times was doomed to failure. She moved at a glacial pace, thinking to herself: *It takes three hours to hit upon one metaphor, and still the fear I won't understand? So extremely tedious.*

The throngs of people were jubilant. Women strolled leisurely about but apparently no one took advantage of them—even the pickpockets had taken the day off.

By the time she finally arrived home Julie was exhausted. She shook her head, groaned, and collapsed onto her bed.

Two days later, Hsiu-nan showed up at night with Chih-yung and

arranged to pick him up the next morning. After seeing Hsiu-nan
off, Julie dropped into Judy's room to inform her, "Shao Chih-yung
is here."

Judy came out into the living room to meet him. She beamed with
warmth when she greeted Chih-yung, acting friendlier than usual.

Chih-yung had exchanged his shabby army uniform for a Western
suit, but he still looked as thin as he did when he had just recovered
from his illness. He leaned against the steam heater. "My little rebellion didn't get off the ground," he said in a self-mocking tone. Then
he spoke of the chaotic events in central China after the cease-fire.

While Julie helped prepare dinner, Judy chuckled. "Shao Chih-
yung is behaving like he wants to be emperor."

Julie also laughed. She returned to the living room and asked, "Do
you want to bathe? It might not be as convenient in the countryside."

She searched unsuccessfully for a clean bath towel, and handed
him a face towel first before finally finding a large towel, which she
brought to the bathroom. Julie couldn't resist running the tips of her
fingers down his golden spine. His back was tight and supple, as if
water would roll off his skin and dry without the need of a towel.

This was the first time he openly spent the night at the apartment.
After dinner, Judy immediately retreated to her room. All the doors
along the corridor were closed tight like an impregnable wall, as if
the doors all knew the two of them would embark on a night of ca-
rousing. Julie felt uncomfortable.

At the Japanese family's house Julie had once said to Chih-yung,
"If it's no trouble, please give me the letters I wrote to you. I'd like to
write about us."

Hsiu-nan must have brought the letters with her. After Hsiu-nan
departed, Chih-yung handed over a large bundle to Julie. "Here are
all your letters." His eyes betrayed a hint of contempt.

Why? Did he think it was an excuse to get all those steamy letters back?

She couldn't help thinking of the marriage certificate buried in
the trunk.

That day he probably had a function to attend in the evening because he came back early, around two o'clock, and said, "Let's take a nap." The nap lasted for two hours. "Not done yet?" she asked in amazement every so often.

"Ow, ow! I'm going to be in pain *again*."

Getting out of bed felt like leaving a morning movie screening. The sun was still high and she didn't know what to do with the rest of the day, making her feel empty.

Chih-yung probably felt the same way. He asked if she had an inkstone, then said, "Buy a blank marriage certificate, all right?"

Julie didn't like secret marriage ceremonies, believing them to be nothing more than a self-deception. But she recalled seeing large marriage certificates with red dragon and phoenix designs in the shopwindows where Bebe took her to buy velvet flowers at the embroidered goods stores on Fourth Avenue. She loved the atmosphere of that street and set off alone, taking the tram to Fourth Avenue. She chose a gold-colored blank certificate with the most classical design, which also happened to be the largest.

"Just one?" asked Chih-yung when he saw it.

Julie stared at him with a startled expression. "I didn't know we needed two."

It hadn't occurred to Julie that each party should retain a certificate. The shop clerk hadn't mentioned it, either. She didn't want to imagine what had gone through the shop clerk's mind—naturally, he would assume it was for an unofficial union and the certificate for the bride was proof of said union. Most old-school merchants like him are kindhearted and wouldn't disabuse Julie. She wondered what had become of the other certificate.

The shop was too far away to go back and buy a matching certificate. She felt depleted and drained.

Chih-yung smiled as he prepared the ink stick and wrote, "Shao Chih-yung and Julie Sheng hereby contract to live forever as husband and wife, in harmony and tranquility, serenity and blissfulness." He then said, "I know you don't like stringed instruments so I didn't use them as convention dictated, 'As harmonious as the *chin* and the *sze*.'"

He smiled again. "In this case I'll have to put my name in front of yours."

The two of them signed. Julie took possession of the one copy for safekeeping. But as it was so big she couldn't find a good place to store it, nor did she have a strip of silk to tie it if she rolled it up. She ended up hiding it at the bottom of a trunk and never showed it to anyone.

"Araki wants to go to Yen-an," Chih-yung told Julie on their last night together. "Quite a few Japanese officers have thrown in their lot with the Communist Party in order to be able to keep fighting. When you see him tell him it would be better for him to return to Japan. There is still hope for the future of his country."

Now at last he talked about Miss K'ang.

"When I was getting ready to leave she cried nonstop. She's just as beautiful when she cries. The hospital compound was chaotic with people coming and going and rushing about, but she just lay in bed crying. 'He's a married man,' she lamented. 'What can I do?'"

So he only came after he and Miss K'ang parted like lovers, saying their final farewell.

"Lay in bed crying." Where was that bed? In the nursing staff's dormitory? Was he allowed in there? In the hinterlands perhaps a person of influence can go anywhere he likes. In the West, in the days before sofas, wasn't it common for people to receive guests at their bedside?

Once again, Julie attempted to excuse and justify what she had just heard because she couldn't face reality. *Of course it was his bed. He was about to leave so of course it was his bedroom. She lay on his bed crying.*

Chih-yung had never said whether or not they had sexual relations, but what he insinuated already headed down that path.

Now Julie was convinced that Miss K'ang was a manipulative girl who, despite being only seventeen or eighteen, had matured early and already must have had a few years of experience in the real world under her belt. But hinterlands were notoriously conservative places. Miss K'ang wouldn't dare share intimacies, and so Chih-yung must have idolized Miss K'ang even more. Julie felt this to be a sore point that she couldn't broach with him. He still felt insecure about Miss K'ang, and to him that really was their final farewell.

During the day, Julie's single-bed couch in the corner of the L-shaped room was covered with a bronze-colored brocade bedspread and a pile of colorful cushions.

It had never felt particularly cramped before when the two of them shared that bed, though it did feel like they each possessed an extra arm, which she wished she could have amputated. Now it felt very crowded, as if two trees had fallen on top of each other, branches entangled, each getting in the way with the other.

That summer the heat made it unbearable to lay against each other, as if suffocating on smoke, but soon after peeling apart, they'd roll into each other again. Like busy little ants scampering up an endless range of volcanoes, only to tumble down before clambering up again. Suddenly lavender lightning flashed several times, illuminating the room then throwing it into darkness again. After a brief duration, deafening peals of thunder rolled past, slow then fast, hurtling down to the earth from every angle of the sky.

A heavy rain fell for a long time, a cacophony of splatters and splashes, while in the darkness glassy sprouts seemed to grow out of the ground, luxuriant white weeds, followed by trees and a forest of rain.

"I'm so glad I have no reason to go outdoors." Julie laughed.

Chih-yung paused. "Hey," he responded, "perhaps you could try not to be quite so self-centered."

"And you're not in any danger going back home? Does anyone follow you?" it suddenly occurred to Julie to ask.

Chih-yung smiled. "The secret police have long known I come here every day."

Julie said nothing but looked obviously shaken. Her vanity solidified in Chih-yung's mind. He used to fear that Julie would suddenly fall in love with someone else, like Natasha in *War and Peace*. Later, when he realized she had no second thoughts, he stopped worrying about her loyalty and became less restrained. What other choice did she have?

Actually, Julie didn't harbor any thoughts of leaving him; she simply couldn't help reminiscing now that the bed seemed too small and narrow for them.

There were so many memories crammed into the corners of this small room—it felt suffocating without recollecting any of them. The wall light illuminated the brick-red curtain, casting a red glow.

Finally the day came when the two of them became entangled to the breaking point. Chih-yung, annoyed, sat up to smoke a cigarette. "This is a matter of trust."

Julie always felt instant antipathy toward people who put her down with hyperbolic accusations. Chih-yung's words sounded all too familiar. *Do fickle men in love stories always say things like that?* Julie slid behind him and off the bed without saying a word.

Concerned, he studied her face.

"Let's go up to the roof, all right?" Chih-yung proposed.

Might as well get some fresh air, it's suffocating in here.

No one ever went up to the roof. With the wartime blackouts no neon light from the city was reflected from the night sky. It was as if they strolled through a huge public square, but where was the public square? Nothing in any direction as far as the eye could see, just the sky above.

On the roof, she still felt like she was suffocating, but couldn't imagine that she once had contemplated jumping off this same roof.

The view of the giant fortresslike chimney stacks and machine rooms looked the same.

Chih-yung and Julie didn't say much, and what they did say the breeze dissipated and muffled for the most part.

They stood beside the cement balustrade for a while.

"Let's go down," he said.

Julie gingerly opened the apartment door with her key, aware that Judy knew they had gone out and returned.

Back in the room they sat down, but the suffocating atmosphere hadn't changed and they just exchanged a few irrelevant words.

He stood up after sitting for a while, forcing a smile while taking her hand to lead her to bed, their arms stretched out horizontally in a line. In the dim light, she suddenly saw five or six women whose heads were wrapped in Islamic shawls or perhaps ancient Greek attire. They were dark silhouettes, one following another, walking before their eyes. Julie knew they were women from his past, but in the midst of her horror something made Julie feel calm, as if she had joined the ranks of the shadowy group.

Both Aldous Huxley and the eighteenth-century writer and politician Lord Chesterfield said of sex, "its position . . . ridiculous"—and they were right. Julie began to laugh hysterically. She laughed so hard that he felt deflated.

He smiled, sat up, and lit a cigarette.

"We really have to get this right today."

He kissed her incessantly, trying to make her feel at ease.

But it became even more hilarious—it felt like rhythmic pounding on an earthenware urn.

"Ow, it's no good, I can't do it," she almost blurted out, but she knew it would have been in vain.

The mechanical pounding of the earthenware urn felt endless. She felt she was tied to an instrument of torture pulling her in two directions to rend her asunder. She could sense the torturers' patient determination.

More pounding, more pulling, no end in sight. Suddenly she felt she was suffocating and almost vomited.

He looked intently at her face, as if checking to see if she had stopped breathing.

"Just now you had tears in your eyes," he said in a soft voice. "I don't know why, but I don't feel guilty."

He fell asleep. She gazed at his face in the dim light, a frontal view she didn't like.

She felt lost, as if setting sail at dusk on unfamiliar waters, on a distant journey.

It was the night before he planned to flee. He slept with his back to her.

The meat cleaver in the kitchen is too heavy. The watermelon knife

with the long blade is easier to handle. Just one stab into his well-tanned
back. He's a fugitive now. Just drag the corpse downstairs and toss it in
the gutter. What could Hsiu-nan do about it?

But Julie knew from her reading of detective novels that all the
best-laid plans of criminals inevitably have defects and fall apart when
someone stumbles upon them by chance.

"Would you be willing to die for someone who doesn't love you?"
she asked herself.

She could visualize a team of plainclothes detectives handcuffing
her and then frog-marching her away along a wall.

The abject shame of going to jail for him would not be worth it.

He seemed to sense something and instantly rolled over but didn't
appear to wake up. Not wanting to sleep facing him, she rolled over
too. They were like sardines in a can, lined up in one direction.

Hsiu-nan came early the next morning to collect him. They needed
a bedsheet to tie up a bundle of his possessions but Julie couldn't find
a clean one. Soon after they left she rushed downstairs with a sheet
and ran to the gate, but they had already gone. She stood there frozen
and dumb for a while. A piebald puppy sat on the step in front of her,
its little ears pointed forward. In silhouette the puppy appeared happy
with everything he surveyed—the street, the clear autumn morning.
Julie felt the same: it seemed that everyone was gone, and her world
had become pleasantly uncluttered.

Julie turned around and went back inside. A little girl, the daughter of a Jewish neighbor, sat on a step singing: "Hello! Hello! Goodbye! Goodbye! Hello! Hello! Goodbye! Goodbye!"

In the countryside, Chih-yung stayed with the Yü family. Once,
when Mr. Yü had business in Shanghai, he brought Julie a long letter.
"I was ready to eat it if they searched me," Mr. Yü told her.

"You'd suffer from indigestion if you ate such a long letter." Julie
chuckled.

Mr. Yü didn't seem to have the haughty mannerisms of a scion of
a provincial family. Precocious in appearance and proper in speech,
though he still couldn't resist laughing as he told Julie, "Hsiu-nan
teased Chih-yung for not being able to keep himself from falling

asleep on the train when she took him back to the countryside—he was exhausted from working so hard the previous night."

Julie could only smile. "Our bed was so narrow," she thought, "and he was probably a bit jumpy that night, so he didn't sleep well."

The night Chih-yung stayed with Julie he observed one of Judy's handbags, an adorable, shiny American bag made of little squares of soft plastic, newly arrived postwar merchandise. "I want to buy one for my wife," he wrote in a letter.

"Even I can't get used to life in the countryside now," he wrote.

Julie constantly pleaded with Chih-yung not to write excessively long letters, particularly if sent by post, due to the dangers involved, but he ignored her, turning out voluminous screeds. He craved an audience.

"Shao Chih-yung is so bored in the countryside he's about to go completely mad," Julie said to Judy, giggling.

"Is it that bad?" Judy frowned.

Mr. Yü stopped by another time to tell Judy that in the countryside, even one unfamiliar face would raise suspicion. Out of security concerns he had moved Chih-yung to another town to live with his relatives.

Rachel finally left India but didn't seem to be in any great hurry to return to Shanghai. She traveled to Malaya and settled down there. Julie didn't return to Hong Kong to resume her studies, telling her mother that she wanted to continue writing. Rachel scolded her in a letter for having the limited horizons of "a frog at the bottom of a well."

Judy, however, was not enthusiastic for Julie to pursue her degree. "Going out into the world and working is another measure of success," Judy often intoned. Left unspoken was Judy's belief that it wasn't worth spending any more money on Julie's education because she wasn't suited to academe—she might as well try her luck at her chosen occupation.

Although Julie said nothing, she had always thought of overseas study as last resort. However, she was aware that life in postwar Britain was extremely arduous; residents there could barely look after themselves. She had even less confidence in her ability to survive in America.

"Americans are unpredictable," Judy frequently commented.

To play it safe all she could do was stay at home and send manuscripts overseas, but that never yielded any results.

Chih-yung used a pseudonym to write a letter to a famous scholar to discuss Buddhism. Julie forwarded the letter and transmitted the answer back to Chih-yung once she received it. She thought the author's tone was amiable, though he said Chih-yung's letter was a bit long and that he "could not fully comprehend" it. In his next letter to Julie, Chih-yung blamed himself "for bringing disgrace on his own head" and apologized for letting her down.

Why is he so fragile? A famous person hardly ever responds to a reader. He didn't know who you are. And even if he did know he might have ignored the letter altogether. Chih-yung simply can't bear to be out of the limelight. He's falling apart.

Julie suddenly felt the overpowering urge to see someone from Chih-yung's family. At that moment she felt she had no other family.

Julie went to see Hsiu-nan. The house looked the same, most likely because Mr. Wen was now helping out. After her marriage to Mr. Wen, Hsiu-nan continued living with Chih-yung's family to manage the household. Julie had not even congratulated Hsiu-nan and Mr. Wen on their marriage.

Hsiu-nan greeted Julie with a cordial smile but was obviously surprised at her visit.

"He sounded extremely anxious in his letters, no patience at all," sobbed Julie, tears streaming down her cheeks. She didn't know why she had never cried in Chih-yung's presence.

Hsiu-nan was quiet for a moment, then said, "When he's impatient he's extremely impatient, but when he wants to be patient he can be incredibly patient."

Now Julie didn't say anything. Perhaps only a woman like Hsiu-nan could truly understand the man she loves. *That film star Errol Flynn famously said, "A man and a woman should never speak the same language." Perhaps he was right.*

Julie sat briefly, then left. Upon returning home she reported to Judy, "I visited Shao Chih-yung's home." Julie saw Judy's expression change, not knowing the reason was that Judy thought Julie could no longer cope with separation and wanted to follow Chih-yung.

Almost two years had passed. After the war, the value of gold dropped. If her mother didn't return soon, Julie wouldn't have enough money to repay her, no matter how frugally Julie lived. All thoughts of studying overseas had long ago flown out the window. Aside from the frustration of not being able to pave the way for the future, Julie mostly stayed at home, reluctant to socialize and yet quite at ease.

"You're surprisingly calm," Judy commented more than once.

Mr. Yü returned to Shanghai. When talking to him about Chih-yung, the tears unexpectedly flowed down her face again.

"If you miss him so much," said Mr. Yü softly, "you can pay him a visit."

Julie smiled faintly and shook her head.

The conversation moved on to other topics but when it returned to Chih-yung, Mr. Yü casually said out of the blue, "From his conversation I'd say he thinks more about Miss K'ang."

"Oh," Julie acknowledged politely, not saying anything more.

She never asked for any news of Miss K'ang.

But she did want to ask Chih-yung face-to-face what his plans were. Suddenly the uncertainty was no longer bearable. Writing letters seemed pointless, his words now seeming invariably vague.

Judy did not approve of Julie visiting Chih-yung but of course didn't prevent her going, either. Her only advice for Julie was to have a blue, extra-thick padded cotton overcoat made, just like the self-protective attire Judy had worn when she stumbled her way in the dark to get to her job at the radio station. Of course Julie selected the most eye-catching peacock-blue fabric.

Mr. Yü would be returning home at the end of the year and they planned for him to take her with him. After the Lunar New Year, he would take her to the township where Chih-yung lived in hiding.

"If you are sold down the river, I'll have no way of knowing," said Judy on the day of Julie's departure.

"I'll send you a postcard as soon as I arrive," Julie replied with a smile.

9

OPERAS were performed during Chinese New Year in the country-side. A small elegant stage was set up in the courtyard of the clan temple. The stage canopy abutted the ceiling of the hall and a shaft of light streamed down through the gap onto the side of an actress's face like a real theatrical spotlight. She sat on a chair in a corner, ruminating and singing to herself. The percussionist loudly beat the hardwood clapper. Wisps of blue smoke wafted through the angled shafts of sunlight. Even the sun in this ancient story was covered in dust.

The actress's puffy cheeks, adorned with thick white powder, were slightly too plump and her back protruded like a camel's hump. She wore a long lemon-yellow jacket buttoned down the front and festooned with embroidered red flowers and green leaves over a white silk skirt. Wooden signboards hung on a pair of black lacquered columns entwined with gilt dragons at the side of the stage read LOUD NOISE PROHIBITED! and SILENCE! A large chiming clock showing half past two contrasted incongruously with the ancient sunlight.

"Why is every one of them so ugly?" someone jeered. The hecklers in the audience were mostly women.

"This year the troupe has good costumes but the actors are just ordinary," said a man in the back row, espousing the voice of reason.

"We could never afford a truly good troupe anyway, could we?"

The front row consisted of wooden horseshoe-back armchairs. Mrs. Yü brought Julie in, sat briefly, then bundled up her child and left. She was short, and the five- or six-year-old child she carried in her arms was almost as tall as she was; she had trudged for quite a long journey along the paths between the fields. Her attire was rather girlish; her bangs touched her eyebrows and her hair hung down to her shoulders. Under her peacock-blue overcoat she wore a white silk gown with a red floral pattern and a bright red trim. Her footwear consisted of homemade fabric shoes with fastening straps. She first met Mr. Yü in the county seat when both of them were running for shelter during an air raid. It was quite romantic.

When they arrived at the theater, the young male protagonist had already taken his leave from his parents and was at his aunt's house to study in solitude. He went inside to change into a fresh white gown with embroidered emerald-blue flowers. The scrawny young girl who played the role of the young male student was just in her teens and had very thick red makeup unevenly plastered on her narrow face.

"Why is every single one of them so ugly?" heckled another voice in the audience.

"This year the troupe has good costumes. . . ." It was probably the manager, who sat in the back row, pointing out how frequently the actress changed costumes.

On the stage, the young male made an obeisance to his aunt and greeted his female cousin before taking his seat. As he sat down the stagehand swept up the back of his gown and set it over the back of the chair, clearly revealing the gray singlet that covered his waist.

The *tan*—the student's female cousin—sat alone singing, then wrote a poem and gave it to the young maid to pass on to her cousin in the study. The slave girl's face looked like a horse saddle; she wore matching slate-blue silk jacket and pants, and swayed her way out of the room to deliver the poem. On the way to the study, she placed a hand on her waist and sang out her troubled thoughts.

"Why is every single one so ugly?"

The young lady sat embroidering in candlelight as the young male furtively approached and gingerly touched her hair with his fingertips again and again, holding his fingers to his nose to savor the aroma. She suddenly discovered his presence and jumped in fright, her chubby shoulders vaulting up in the air in the same way as the ferocious General Tsao Tsao would in a Peking opera. Her face was made up white like the general's, though not quite as white.

Another wave of jeering. "Why is this one so ugly?"

When the *tan* settled down again, she invited her male cousin to sit and chat as if the nocturnal visit were nothing out of the ordinary. Gradually she broke into song, swaying from one side to the other and shrugging her shoulders to represent her rising ardor.

"Why is this one so ugly?" A peal of laughter resonated.

Two stagehands, one on each side of the stage, held up a doorway curtain—or rather, just the overhanging fringe of a curtain—and, uncertain when they'd be needed, fussed about in the wings, sporadically rushing forward only to fold back the curtain and retreat. After a while they swaggered forward again. The two performers concentrated on singing a duet, the curtain a Freudian symbol hovering behind them.

The stagehands finally got the timing right, hurried forward, and stood in place to let the two performers fly hand in hand through the symbolic opening.

The old *tan*—the mother—held up the candle to inspect the room and called out for her daughter. From behind the curtain the daughter cried out in a quavering voice, "Maaaamaaaa...."

"What is this Maaaamaaaa, are you planning to murder me?"

The mother lifted the curtain; the young man somersaulted out and then kneeled down in respect, but the back of his gown flopped over his head.

"Goodness me, who is this giving me such a fright?"

The daughter appeared and also kneeled next to her mother.

After a stern rebuke, the mother encouraged the young man to take the imperial examination, and only then, after being admitted to imperial ranks, would she give him her blessing to marry her daughter.

On his journey to take the examination the young scholar encountered a beauty, a young girl from another family.

"This is a good one!" came the approving comments from below the stage. "This one is quite pretty."

The actress, obviously aware of her own beauty, carried herself with exquisite care, moving so gracefully that her dress didn't even sway as she floated across the stage. She wore less makeup than the others and her costume was less garish, just a simple, elegant long turquoise jacket embroidered with pink flowers. She entered the temple to burn incense and the young man knelt beside her.

"This one's really good-looking," came a shout from a new admirer.

Mrs. Yü had already been waiting for quite a while, standing in the back row holding her tall child. Julie couldn't linger any longer. She stood up and jostled her way to the back of the theater, deeply regretting not being able to witness the unveiling of the lovers' secret pledge to marry without parental permission, the scholar returning a licentiate and marrying both girls, the joyful reunion with the two beauties (or maybe even three).

A swarthy thin woman with sunken eyes stood in a passageway handing out sugarcane to some children. She easily could've been mistaken for an Indian woman. A pair of metal-framed spectacles perched high on her nose. She had an old-fashioned coiffure. Over her padded cotton gown, she wore a black cotton overcoat. Obviously, in the eyes of people around her, there wasn't anything particularly special about her. She was simply so-and-so's wife.

The people around Julie were all merely geometric points with fixed positions, but each possessing no length or breadth. Only Julie, wearing her thick, bulky blue cotton overcoat had length, breadth, and height, but possessed no position. Inside this picture comprised of a myriad of dots, Julie stood out as a mass of peacock blue. She clumsily struggled to squeeze her way through the rows of chairs toward the exit.

10

AFTER the Chinese New Year, heavy snows blocked all the roads. Finally the roads were cleared, and early one morning Julie and Mr. Yü set out on palanquins. Behind the snowdrifts on the hillside the blue sky looked so blue that Julie felt she could stretch out her arms and scoop up a handful.

Mr. Yü chose a route along the back roads, like a fugitive from justice, possibly out of fear someone would recognize Julie. As soon as they were out of Shanghai, they clambered onto a truck. All the passengers sat on their luggage. The truck was open at the rear, and the tailwind blew into the passengers' faces the whole journey and turned Julie's hair into a matted, dust-encrusted mess. She tried to comb it into some semblance of order but was unable to pull her fingers through the tangles. The weather, however, was perfect, and the rural scenery south of the Yang-tze River was beautiful: sparse, graceful winter foliage and emerald-green vegetable patches wedged between bright blue ponds. The truck rumbled along, the scenery constantly changing outside the square opening at the back, like a landscape painting rapidly unscrolling.

At an out-of-the-way station an army officer boarded. First a cane recliner appeared for him to sit on, followed by a young woman who arranged a traveling rug on his lap and then squatted at his feet, poking at the ashes in his foot warmer. She was a hefty woman, wearing a peacock-blue overcoat with tight sleeves. She was fair-skinned and quite pretty with a rather childlike brow. Her hair was long and permed with bouffant bulges near the temples. He had probably purchased her from who knows where but they seemed a good match.

The army officer was in his thirties, with a scrawny face, vacant jaundiced eyes, and a weary smile. She occasionally spoke but he never responded.

Julie and Mr. Yü took a cargo boat and stopped at a small town where they stayed the night in the local Nationalist Party branch office. Julie really couldn't understand how travelers could stay in a party office as if it were a temple. And staying in the Nationalist Party facility while on the way to visit a wanted war criminal was rather ironic. Mr. Yü must have had his reasons, though Julie didn't ask what they were. A small paper replica of the Republic of China's flag, commonly called Blue Sky, White Sun, and a Wholly Red Earth, was pasted prominently on the wall opposite the door of the main hall. But in the paper replica, the red earth was a dazzling pink, as bright as roses. *Is this New Year's wrapping paper the only red paper they have here?*

Travelers must find lodgings before dusk. From a window Julie watched a shaft of sunlight slant into the courtyard of the gatehouse as a bean-curd vendor entered with his cart. A young clerk in a long gown came out carrying a balancing scale. He pulled back the fabric cover on top of the bean curd and weighed out a portion like a frugal housewife.

This distant land, his native land, was also an alien land.

The farther they traveled, the warmer it grew. The next night they stayed with a family. The living quarters consisted of a large room some three stories high with a dome made of bamboo poles covered with a woven reed mat. It looked like a large bird coop. Looking up so high made Julie dizzy and she couldn't tell if its construction materials included wood. *Is this China or Africa? At the very least it's Borneo.* In the brown semidarkness, the room appeared boundless. Someone sleeping on bed planks set against the far wall coughed.

Mr. Yü and Julie switched to wheelbarrows to continue their journey. Julie's wheelbarrow led the way. For an entire day in the backcountry it was her against the sun, together, face-to-face against a hot brass plate. Skin burnt to a crisp, tailbone worn down to the marrow. The wheelbarrows headed up a hill and along a narrow path next to a stream. The purple boulders on the mountain side of the road resembled the backdrop of a folk opera that continued on and on interminably for days and days.

Mr. Yü's uncle lived in one of the best houses in the small town, complete with a rock garden and a goldfish pond in the courtyard. The outside wall was painted a dark pink with a section plastered in a black-and-white pattern intended to imitate marble, the whole effect evoking a faux-Italian style. On the upper reaches of the fake marble wall, a bell-shaped opening embellished with wave motifs rising up from the lip of the bell stood out for its comic vulgarity. China can always surprise, sometimes treating the rare and exquisite with indifference.

Julie and Chih-yung strolled around the town. While walking below the bamboo poles on which clothes had been hung out to dry, she saw a tattered quilt cover printed with a blue roundel motif that featured a depiction of Jesus and the Twelve Apostles. In the elegant style of a Chinese painting, the images were enclosed in an ornamental border just like those employed on a potbellied vase from the K'ang-hsi period.

Julie pondered the influence of Catholic missionaries in the seventeenth century during the early years of the Ch'ing dynasty, when blue-and-white porcelain was popular. She was tempted to ask the price of the holy relic, a tourist's habit she had acquired from her long association with Bebe.

Even the square-toed thong sandals made of fine woven straw provided in the guesthouse were charmingly anachronistic.

In a corner of the stairwell outside the door of their room, two sticks of incense stood at attention in the small wooden shrine that included a space for a deity's spirit tablets.

Outside on the street, a small cavity in a large banyan tree housed a similar shrine.

One day, just before they were about to go out for a stroll, Chih-yung stood at Julie's side while she prepared to apply peach-colored lipstick. Suddenly he said, "Don't put that on, all right?" He didn't say he was worried the lipstick would attract attention, and he still took her to the bookshop. They spoke in hushed tones while flipping through pages, even though she was constantly on guard.

On another occasion, he was talking loudly in the hotel room when suddenly a curious voice drifted through the wooden partition from the next room: "Who's that next door?"

"Accent sounds foreign...." The voice conveyed a touch of mystery as it trailed off.

Julie immediately became tense. Chih-yung didn't say another word.

After they had parted in Shanghai, Julie received no income whatsoever, though she now knew that if she had gone on the run with Chih-yung she would have courted catastrophe. Julie always wanted to maintain her composure and he would never want to show any fear. When they were together he simply couldn't resist expounding his opinions. It would never have worked, even if Opportune Jade Hsin had not been in the picture.

Naturally, Mr. Yü had told Julie about his father's concubine, who turned out to be quite entrepreneurial after his father died, running a sericulture training school. People respectfully addressed her as Master Hsin.

As Master Hsin was from this town, she was tasked to accompany Chih-yung on the journey—a man and a local woman traveling together were unlikely to attract attention on the road.

Julie's heart fluttered when she heard that account. "Here we go again," she thought, though she didn't believe it could be true.

When Julie first arrived, she followed Mr. Yü into a large gloomy room in his uncle's home. There were many people, but she quickly noticed a fair-skinned pretty face next to a female relative quietly observing her. The womenfolk of the family sat around her. She was of medium build and wore a dark sweater over a simple gown. Her hair wasn't permed. She must have been in her thirties but looked much younger. As soon as she saw her, Julie immediately guessed her to be Opportune Jade, and now the situation became crystal clear in Julie's mind. Chih-yung walked up and greeted everyone, then turned around and walked out. He was supposed to know Julie as a Mrs. Wang.

Julie heard the animated voice of Chih-yung laughing in the next room. She knew her bulky blue-padded coat and her badly sunburnt nose made him lose face in front of Opportune Jade.

Julie didn't allow her thoughts to dwell on that, though when she first heard the irritating laughter she shivered and felt a wave of disgust wash over her. She then suppressed her disgust and tried to push it back into the dark recesses of her mind.

"I truly appreciate you coming to see me," Chih-yung solemnly declared when they could finally be alone. Then he smiled and continued, "This time Master Hsin indeed delivered me in the manner of the opera *Emperor Tai-tzu Escorts the Maiden Ching-niang on a One-Thousand-Li Journey.* It was very cold, especially during the long rickshaw ride. She placed a basket with a brazier inside it under my feet. Incidentally, I burned a hole in her clothes. I was mortified but she cheerfully brushed it off as unimportant."

"Sometimes when you burn a hole that way," Julie said and giggled, "it can turn out as pretty as the halo of the moon." She had burnt a hole in the pant leg of her navy-blue brocade. Indistinct concentric rays of moonlight with a patch of yellow in the middle, which disintegrated when touched, revealed a white silk floss lining that looked like the moon.

Chih-yung was mesmerized by the account. "And a flower could be embroidered over the hole," he added.

He obviously thinks I am able to appreciate this story and can accept how things stand. Is he suggesting that this is what a writer should expect, the same way a coal miner should expect to get black lung disease?

Julie had never blamed Chih-yung for grabbing what he could in times of adversity, but he acted the same way during good times too, if not more so. She didn't want to follow this line of thought to its logical conclusion because she felt her heart sinking, but at the same time it all struck her as comical.

There was only one guesthouse in the town and it would not have rooms available until the next day. Julie didn't want to bother Mr. Yü's relatives. "You can stay the night at Master Hsin's mother's home," said Mr. Yü.

When Opportune Jade was a child, her mother sold her to the Yü family as a servant girl. Her mother lived in a small room with a tiled roof in a large courtyard compound. Many rooms in the compound were unoccupied and so it felt uncannily quiet. Chih-yung guided Julie along the twists and turns through the numerous courtyards, empty of people but crowded with trees. The tidy room was long and narrow; a mosquito net covered a small wooden bed in one corner. To one side was a desk with two drawers. The floor, covered in small gray tiles, had become aged and uneven. A brick had been placed under one leg of the desk to compensate for the uneven flooring. A whitewashed mud stove sat at the other end of the room.

"This will do fine," said Julie. *I can breathe more freely here.* Mr. Yü's uncle put on the airs of an official. He was a short, skinny man with a pencil mustache. And polite, though occasionally his eyes revealed a piercing stare.

"How has Chih-yung been able to live in their house for so long without a good reason?" Julie later asked Mr. Yü.

"It's all right," replied Mr. Yü impassively, turning away to avert her gaze.

Opportune Jade's mother was a jolly little old lady without a chin. She broke some eggs onto a plate, which she placed on a rack inside a concave rice pot, covering it with the wood lid of a wok. By the time the rice was ready, the eggs were an overcooked mess and firmly adhered to the plate. The whites tasted like rubber.

The next day when Chih-yung came to pick her up, she told him about the eggs. "I've told her not to cook them like that many times but she keeps doing it. She says it's the way things are done here."

Chinese cuisine is famous, and this place no remote backwater, and yet some people here don't know about fried eggs, scrambled eggs, or poached eggs.

Julie found it incredible.

She didn't know why, but Julie believed Opportune Jade and Chih-yung were actually at the very most simply fond of each other. "They must have had plenty of opportunities on the road," she imagined hazily.

Julie should have known that both the man on the run and the woman who was no longer young needed to seize the moment. In this town, they could have assignations in Opportune Jade's mother's place, on the same bed where Julie slept. When she first saw the small room she felt momentarily ill at ease but gave it no further thought. She was in denial. Things had become too much of "a mixed-up mess like a pot of congee."

And now Chih-yung told Julie that when he stayed with the Japanese family he had an affair with the housewife. Julie knew that Japanese women were more open compared to Chinese housewives. Moreover, Japanese people naturally had a fresh, overpowering sense of the apocalypse, though in this case Chih-yung was actually in much more danger than the Japanese lady. Julie actually didn't mind that sort of fleeting affair, and she even felt that Chih-yung must have expanded her own horizons. He probably felt the same way, though she never asked him, and didn't encourage him to tell her.

Chih-yung once brought Opportune Jade to the guesthouse. Julie treated her as she would any other visitor, with customary excessive courtesies. When she really couldn't think of anything else to say, she smiled and exclaimed, "She's too beautiful! Let me sketch her." She then fetched a pencil and a sheet of paper. Chih-yung was delighted, but from beginning to end Opportune Jade didn't say one word.

After sketching for a long while, Julie only managed to render one crescent-shaped eye, its double eyelid shaded by eyelashes, from the whole of her perpetually-smiling face. Chih-yung took one look at the work in progress and appeared baffled, only managing to mumble some respectful praise.

While Julie was examining her work, she suddenly said to Chih-yung, "Don't know why but the eye looks a bit like yours." Although Chih-yung's eyes were smaller than Opportune Jade's, without the rest of the facial features in the sketch there was no way to ascertain the relative size.

Chih-yung's face darkened. He put the sketch down without another glance. Julie abandoned her sketching.

Opportune Jade sat for a little while then left.

After she departed, the conversation turned to Yü K'o-ch'ien. "His character is flawed," Chih-yung proclaimed. "His writing is very polished, making it difficult to discern his true nature." Then he added, "If you have a bad conscience, the writing will be bad, too."

Julie thought he was saying she was miserly, so she pretended not to understand. *Pointing at the mulberry to abuse the locust; making oblique accusations like a cursing farmer's wife. The gossiping, boorish woman side of him has finally emerged into full view.*

But what he said did not worry her. Ever since her "lost year" she had written very little, all of it terrible. For the past two years, she mostly had been translating her own earlier writings.

The room became suffocating, and they went out for a walk. She wore a dark plum-colored cotton coat with narrow sleeves. Each cuff was decorated with a large bluish-green knotted button.

Chih-yung said it looked like a sword dancer's costume. It was very eye-catching, but she didn't have any clothes tailored for the journey other than the peacock-blue padded jacket that she used instead of a winter coat, which was not only ugly but now the weather was too warm for it.

"What will people think when they see us?" Chih-yung said while they strolled along. "What a fashionable woman; the man, though, doesn't look the part." He laughed bitterly. "I'll even have to change the way I walk and alter my accent."

Julie knew how difficult it was to lie low, and that it must be even harder for Chih-yung, who had nurtured his public persona with such exactness. But Julie didn't feel his appearance had changed much—the goatskin coat he wore seemed quite appropriate.

"Once, while on the road, I tried to carry a heavy load with a shoulder pole," he said with a hint of embarrassment. "That was not easy. For those who have never done it before it's actually quite difficult."

Julie had also noticed the small steps porters took, each step of their trot executed at exactly the right moment.

The rapeseed plants outside the town were in bloom, their bright yellow flowers stretching out to the horizon. The land was so flat Julie could not see very far, just a band of yellow up to the horizon.

It was a clear day; the sky appeared a pale light blue in contrast with the yellow. This vista satisfied Julie's general love of colors; it was even more magnificent, more dazzling, than the azalea-covered hills of Hong Kong blooming against the emerald-blue ocean. Even the occasional stench of manure wafting by didn't seem malodorous— otherwise it all would surely have been an illusion.

Walking and looking at the scenery, Julie marveled at everything she saw. Finally, she spoke. "What have you decided? If you can't give up Miss K'ang, I can leave."

Opportune Jade had been Chih-yung's camouflage, and now his sole comfort, so Julie didn't mention her.

Chih-yung was obviously taken aback. He paused a moment. "Why must a good tooth be extracted? Having to make a choice like this isn't ideal. . . ."

Why is having to make a choice not ideal? Julie was perplexed. She didn't see that as sophistry but rather as the logic of a madman.

The next day he brought a copy of an ancient classic, Tso Chiu-ming's commentary *Spring and Autumn Annals*, for them to read together. "When Duke Huan of Ch'i was still a prince, he encountered misfortune and had to flee," recounted Chih-yung, smiling. "He ordered his fiancée to wait twenty-five years for him. But she said, 'I'll be old if I wait twenty-five years. Why not just say wait forever?'"

He seemed to be waiting for her to say something.

Julie smiled and said nothing. To wait or not to wait was not for her to decide.

Chih-yung had mentioned "four years." Half of the four years had already passed. A certainty has now, however, become elusive.

Life in a small town was like living inside a clock that ticks very loudly. Time passed but being so close to it she didn't know what time it was.

On the day of her departure, he didn't wait for her to speak. "Please don't ask me again," he pleaded, smiling weakly.

Julie smiled back and questioned him no further.

She didn't realize at the time that he had already answered her. A few weeks after she returned to Shanghai Julie had an epiphany.

Perhaps he was waiting for the day when he could show his face in public again and have a reunion with his three beauties.

It was only then that she understood the English phrase "iron in the soul." She had never experienced its meaning, never knew what it referred to. Perhaps it would be better to phrase it as "iron entered into the soul," meaning the soul was made stronger.

And then the phrase "the dark night of the soul" suddenly jolted Julie's heart.

Pain, like the low, dull rumble of a train running all day and night without end, plagued her heart. She'd wake up and realize the rumble was in fact the relentless ticking of her wristwatch right next to her pillow.

By chance, while walking along the street, she heard Peking opera music drifting out of a shop. The voice of the male performer singing the part of an elderly male character who wears an artificial beard resembled Chih-yung's central Chinese accent, and tears welled up in her eyes instantly.

While sitting at the dinner table Julie thought about how Chih-yung depended on the charity of others, the way he sat with the host family at the round dining table. She ate vegetables as if they were wet rags and crunchy foods as if they were paper, unable to swallow.

She dreamed of herself standing in front of the small red-lacquered cabinet in the stairwell of her previous home in the north. A large crack ran along the top of the cabinet. Old and dilapidated, it had been left behind when they moved to Shanghai. In her dream Julie spread jam onto a slice of bread that she would bring to Chih-yung. He was hiding in an empty room next door.

Julie never cried in front of Judy, but of course Judy knew she was suffering. One day Judy saw her hurriedly putting away a bowl and a pair of chopsticks to prevent Judy noticing she hadn't eaten. "'Eating little during a time of trouble cannot be sustained,'" Judy gently prodded.

Julie put her dinnerware into the cabinet, returned, and sat down. "Shao Chih-yung fell in love with Miss K'ang, and now he has this Master Hsin and I didn't get a chance to ask him if he needs money."

Is it worth agonizing like this over a paltry sum of money?

"Pay him back then!" responded Judy.

"Second Aunt will soon return. I want to repay Second Aunt."

"You don't necessarily have to repay right away."

Julie fell silent. She *needed* to repay her mother immediately.

She couldn't say this out loud—that would appear indignant. *But if I don't say it Judy will think I want to repay Second Aunt while I still have the money in hand.... Hopeless! As if the money could never be earned again.* But Julie's childhood years were more difficult than Judy's, which is why Julie tended to view everything as difficult.

After a long silence, Judy laughed softly. "He's really a bit too generous with his ardor."

Judy once retold some old family stories. "We Shengs are descended from impoverished scholars from the northern countryside, unsophisticated and stubborn. But the Piens are the family of a high-ranking military officer. When the old man retired, he continued to behave as if he were leading troops, rising at the crack of dawn. He'd kick on the door of anyone not up and curse. He even treated your grandmother like that when she was his daughter-in-law." Judy paused as if thinking, then said, "The whole Chu family is depraved."

Julie knew Judy was referring in particular to Uncle Chu and his son, Brother Hsü. And those were men she loved. She helped Uncle Chu out of affection for his son, though she also had feelings for him.

"You're wicked," Judy once said to Julie.

It was nothing like the great sage Confucius saying, "While he may sound disappointed, he was secretly pleased," as she once harbored a sense of admiration for Julie. Judy herself had experienced heartache, but now as she observed Julie's suffering, she couldn't help feeling disappointed—after all, Julie was just an ordinary woman.

"No man is worth it," she said coldly in a soft voice.

"I don't know why," Julie once casually admitted to Judy, "but when I begin to like someone I feel pure rapture, but when I'm low I don't feel anything, just numbness." Judy laughed at her, thinking her words bizarre.

Julie was by no means prone to melancholia. On the contrary, she was quite resilient. And in truth only her mother and Chih-yung contributed to her suffering. Back then she had wanted to kill herself to make a statement to her mother: "*Now* do you know how I feel?" As for her psychological state during her relationship with Chih-yung, suicidal thoughts lingered but she didn't let them surface, knowing how foolish an act would be. Chih-yung could talk himself into believing anything. If she killed herself he would come to a perfect explanation: "That, too, is ideal," he'd say, and everything would be just as wonderful as ever.

But she continued to write long letters to Chih-yung as before, telling him of her torment. Now it was his turn to ignore reality, not comprehending Julie's feelings, or perhaps feigning incomprehension. He replied with long letters, too, full of explanations and supplications. His letters were thick bundles, as if he were oblivious to attracting attention at the post office.

Julie lived on large cans of American grapefruit juice, which she found milder and not overly sweet compared to orange juice. One day while walking on the street after a couple of months on her grapefruit-juice diet, Julie gave herself a fright when she saw a haggard, scrawny woman coming toward her, reflected in a shopwindow. Years later she read reports of women in mainland China no longer menstruating during the famine years. Julie hadn't had her period for several months.

Mr. Yü arrived.

There was a nasty fright in the small town, he explained perfunctorily—*Was it because he received an unending stream of long letters?*—so Chih-yung decided to move back to the countryside.

After chatting a while he knitted his brow. "He wants to be with Miss K'ang. How will that work? Her accent isn't local and will certainly attract too much attention in the village, but he insists that I go and get her."

Mr. Yü sounded desperate. He was having trouble shouldering the extra burden and wanted Julie to help out. He knew that mentioning Miss K'ang would rile her up.

Julie just smiled as he spoke. *Will she go? Hard to imagine. It's not time yet for a reunion. That's asking her to live a life underground.*

"He's not very practical when it comes to women," Julie blurted out. She had always believed that had Chih-yung really been intimate with Miss K'ang he would not have idealized her so much.

Mr. Yü was momentarily lost for words. "He's very practical! He is!"

Now it was Julie's turn to be lost for words. The two of them didn't speak any further.

At least they had parted intimately. Of course they had. The ritual for the reunion of the three beauties required a memento—otherwise pledges of eternal love would mean nothing.

Julie didn't blame even herself for being so naïve and not foreseeing this outcome. All she felt was that it was over, that she had come to the end of a very long road, because she now realized that Miss K'ang was waiting for him.

While she wasn't committed to monogamy, she also knew she wouldn't be able to bear the situation. She was fluent in the language of suffering, it being her first language.

Opportune Jade was passing through Shanghai and Hsiu-nan accompanied her to Julie's home. Julie didn't ask how many days she'd be staying and obviously had no intention of hosting Opportune Jade. Hsiu-nan said she would return in a little while to pick her up.

Now it was obvious to Julie that while "escorting the maiden Ching-niang on a One-Thousand-Li Journey," Opportune Jade and Chih-yung had consummated their relationship. But when Julie came face-to-face with Opportune Jade, she didn't think about such matters and simply served her guest a cup of tea, then quickly returned to the kitchen to assist Judy.

"Should I make a few more dishes?" Judy asked softly.

"No, otherwise she'll think we're living too comfortably."

While Julie observed Opportune Jade at the dinner table, and how she seemed to have lost her appetite, a revulsion rose up from deep within her viscera.

Judy engaged in chitchat but Julie only managed to an insert an occasional word or two. She didn't ask about Chih-yung, nor why Opportune Jade and him had to live apart for the moment. No doubt he had returned to Mr. Yü's family home, but they were more or less living together openly.

Soon after they finished eating, Hsiu-nan returned to pick up Opportune Jade.

"She looks like quite a good match for Chih-yung," Judy said softly with a smirk.

Julie smiled in acknowledgment—she didn't mind at all.

Julie no longer wrote long letters, simply sending off short businesslike notes to Chih-yung from time to time. Chih-yung assumed she had gotten over her misery. In a letter he wrote: "Yesterday Opportune Jade came by after her noon nap; her face exhibits signs of youth departing, yet I love her more than ever. One night, while asleep together, she woke up to discover that the fasteners on the front of her chest were undone and said to me, 'If we can spend five years together I'll die happy.' My problem is I'm perpetually self-satisfied, and I want to share every little thing that happens in my life with you. I think she's equally wonderful and you ought to be a bit jealous of her. But if you became genuinely jealous, well, I wouldn't be able to take that, either."

Julie felt as if she had received a love letter sent to the wrong address. It made her both angry and amused.

11

HER MOTHER returned.

Julie went to the docks with Judy to meet her when the vessel arrived. As usual, the entire family of Julie's maternal uncle went to the dock, this time with the addition of several sons-in-law who were all the product of introductions made by their aunt Rachel.

Ever since she wrote that scathing account of her relatives in the Pien clan, Julie had not seen any them. At the dock, they greeted Judy warmly as always; toward Julie they acted quite normally though with a smug look on their faces. Now, at last, they could point their accusatory fingers at her. Naturally they had filed a full report long ago concerning Julie's relations with Chih-yung.

"I saw your second uncle on the street wearing a blue cotton gown," a cousin gleefully reported. "He's a bit chubbier now."

All her cousins were now fashionable wives with children, which they didn't bring along.

Julie stood at the back of the crowded cabin. As always her uncle's family acted as a human shield. Finally it was her turn to step forward, smile, and formally greet Second Aunt.

Rachel grunted her acknowledgment, and simply threw a stern sidelong glance at Julie.

The relatives crowded into the narrow cabin chatting and laughing boisterously, though the atmosphere felt slightly subdued because Rachel had aged.

A few wrinkles as one ages matter little, but for major facial features to erode away, changing the relative position of the eyes and mouth—

it's as if she had transformed into another person. A few years in the tropics also deeply tanned her skin, making her look even skinnier.

After disembarking, everyone headed together to the Pien residence. The living room was still decorated the way Rachel had designed it, the walls painted a "bean-paste shade" of dusty brown, neither dark nor light, which didn't conform with the fashions of the time. Rachel's brother Yün-chih had disapproved of it because it looked too understated, with which Julie agreed, thinking the color created a cold and bare effect like a theater backdrop for a slum.

Brother and sister had always been close. "You've become an old lady!" joked Yün-chih. "And I see your false teeth weren't correctly molded."

He was the only person who could say things like that. A slight titter passed through the room, but a hint of a smile was the most everyone present could display.

Rachel didn't smile. Instead, she responded unaffectedly, "You have no idea how much time the dentist spent on the measurements. He proudly confirmed that he had put in an enormous amount of effort and that this was his best work."

"That is to say," thought Julie, "the dentist admired her."

Julie sat on a sofa with a female cousin, who told her, "When cousin Julian visited last, he said he was looking for work. Other avenues had not proved fortuitous and in the end we found him a position in our bank. The job wasn't perfect but now he has been transferred to Hangchow and the remuneration is much better. Cousin Julian is a good person without any vices, besides being too fond of eating out…." She dragged out the last sentence as if she was undecided if she should continue or not. Most likely she was about to recount how she had admonished Julian to save a little money so she could introduce a girlfriend of hers for marriage. But to her it seemed inappropriate to discuss such matters with Julian's infamous sister.

Of course, Julie had heard that her cousin had arranged a job for Julian, as Julian himself had mentioned it. This cousin was obliged to help Julian because Rachel had introduced her to her husband. Telling all this to Julie was a way of saying Julie was ungrateful, whereas her uncle's family didn't hold a grudge and on the contrary helped her brother. It demonstrated the contrast with her own indifference as Julian's elder sister.

Rachel chatted with her relatives until late in the night. Judy and Julie left first. Rachel's seventeen suitcases had arrived before her. The husband of one of the cousins arranged for retainers to accompany the luggage to the house. Everyone marveled at the ludicrous amount of luggage.

She had more than a dozen pieces of luggage when she passed through Hong Kong the last time. But then it seemed normal and no one laughed at her.

"It would appear that your second aunt has returned well-prepared to play the part of a matriarch," Judy tittered behind Rachel's back.

Perhaps Judy was referring to Rachel's stern demeanor.

On another occasion Judy was unable to restrain herself from whispering to Julie, "Locking drawers like that when she goes out. As if she's moved into a den of thieves."

The last German tenant had moved out long ago. Rachel moved into his room, which had an en suite bathroom, her accommodations very private, indeed.

"Best not to come to my room so often," Judy warned Julie.

"Yes," Julie responded with a knowing smile.

Out of fear Rachel would encounter Julie and Judy talking about her behind her back, Julie not only hid from Rachel but also avoided being seen alone with Judy. Julie felt as if she had ceased to exist.

At the dinner table Rachel revealed some of her experiences abroad. In India, she had worked as the personal assistant to Jawaharlal Nehru's two sisters. "Goodness! Unbelievably arrogant. Like princesses."

While in India she would have paid more attention to her attire than she did now, back in Shanghai. She often wore a floral-print dress and either a pair of black leather riding boots or short white bobby socks and mid-height heels, which looked quite incongruous.

"Why are you wearing short socks?" asked Judy.

"Everyone does in Malaya."

Julie wondered if wearing short socks prevented the English from contracting fungal infections in the tropics and the riding boots protected against snakebites.

In Pune Rachel had lived for a while in a leprosarium. "It was the most hygienic place in the whole of India."

Later Julie heard Judy say that one of Rachel's lovers was an English doctor. He probably worked at the leprosarium and was with her the whole time she lived in Malaya.

"The English in India have incredible status."

"Is it still like that?" asked Julie, not directly referring to Indian independence.

"Yes, even now."

One day Julie heard Rachel grumbling to Judy, "When a woman gets a bit older, men are only interested in her for *sex*." She emphasized the last word in English.

Rachel noticed Julie's reticence and began to soften toward her. One day after lunch, with no one else around, Rachel leisurely asked, "Are you still waiting for that Shao Chih-yung?"

"He's gone," said Julie, smiling. "He's gone, so of course it's over."

All of Chih-yung's letters were posted to Bebe's house for Julie to collect.

Rachel nodded, apparently believing Julie. Maybe she had seen Yen Shan visit once or twice and also overheard Julie telephoning him, though Julie never spoke more than a few words before hanging up.

Having just returned to Shanghai, Rachel had not seen any of Yen Shan's films yet and did not know him. He was difficult to miss, though, with his tall slender stature, fair-skinned squarish face, handsome features, bright eyes, and widow's peak.

Julie met him during her grapefruit-juice-diet days. A movie studio was considering an adaptation of one of her novels and the studio boss sent a chauffeur to pick her up for negotiations. It was the first social gathering Julie had attended since the end of the war. She was skinny though it was less obvious when she put on a cheerful face. After all, she was still young and quite small-framed. That day Julie wore a bell-sleeved top made from an antique quilt cover that used to be

Judy's, the rare ivory-colored silk printed with a black phoenix pattern. The bird's feathers were mixed with dark purple elements. She pinned a large purple velvet butterfly with white stripes in her shoulder-length hair. It was meant for traditional-style chignons but dangled from Julie's hair like a purple flower about to drop to the ground.

Many people milled about in the reception room of the mogul's home and Julie didn't know a single soul, though a few faces looked familiar. The mogul introduced some people to her, Yen Shan being one of them. Later on, Yen Shan saw Julie sitting off to the side and went to sit beside her with a smile. His gestures seemed a little exaggerated. Julie couldn't help being reminded of Hsün Hwa on the tram and she felt he harbored bad intentions, that he was "happy to take advantage" of her, so she smiled politely and looked the other way. He sensed it too and sat quietly hugging himself. That day he wore a pale, fluffy check-pattern Irish pullover, which he seemed unaccustomed to wearing, and appeared surprisingly innocent.

Julie had written some theater reviews when she first returned to Shanghai. One time she went backstage during a production of the play *Chin Pi-hsia*, which starred Yen Shan. Julie saw him descend the stairs with his head lowered and arms held tightly against his body as he rushed past in a long gown. Wearing no makeup and looking on guard, he slunk by Julie and disappeared. It immediately reminded her of an encounter she experienced on the boat returning to Shanghai. That was just after Pearl Harbor, on a tiny Japanese vessel.

A group of people pressed against the handrails of the narrow walkway. A middle-aged man surrounded by a cluster of lesser luminaries walked toward Julie. He was tall, with a square pale face and a pencil mustache. His suit fit snugly, though it had the appearance of being borrowed, making him look like a man in disguise, as if he were fleeing for his life, shunning contact with people, fearful of being taken advantage of, despite being surrounded by a phalanx of escorts that included Japanese officials and officers in uniforms, even the ship's captain. Julie couldn't help casting a few more curious glances at him. Later she heard that the Peking Opera star Mei Lanfang was also a passenger on the ship. If it had not been for that fleeting memory, Julie would have told Yen Shan, "I saw you backstage at the performance of *Chin Pi-hsia*. You even stayed in character offstage, it was *so* convincing." But of course she didn't. Yen Shan remained quiet in the mogul's home the whole time. Then the famous director arrived and they ushered Julie over to meet him.

"If one doesn't have a good script," thought Julie, "it's best to keep one's mouth shut."

However, his silence shook Julie out of her slumber.

After that occasion, Julie didn't see Yen Shan again until three months later when he came with a friend who was visiting her. By then she felt much better—in fact, she didn't need him to make a personal appearance. She just needed a fantasy romance to caress her face and remind her that she still dwelled among the living.

Rachel hired a seamstress to make her a Chinese gown. She rarely wore Chinese gowns.

The seamstress arrived and took Rachel's measurements in front of a mirror. Julie noticed her mother's incensed expression but didn't know the reason behind it. Who would have thought Rachel was angry at Julie for not introducing Yen Shan? Rachel assumed that Julie thought her own mother was inappropriately dressed and therefore unpresentable.

One day while Yen Shan was visiting, the living-room door suddenly swung open violently and then banged shut. Julie sat far away from Yen Shan with her back to the door. She turned her head around in time to catch a glimpse of Rachel slamming the door behind her.

"Looks like a Malay," whispered Yen Shan in a frightened voice.

On another occasion, when Julie was taking a bath, the bathroom door suddenly opened violently. Rachel stormed in, glared at Julie, opened the cabinet behind the mirror, grabbed something from the cabinet, and slammed the door shut, leaving a startled and infuriated Julie standing in the bathtub, naked. She finished bathing and stood in the tub, head lowered as she looked herself over. "Did you have a good look?" she fumed to herself. "What's there to see?"

Julie's figure hadn't changed in the nine years since she and Rachel lived together in the apartment. But the day she went to the dock to greet Rachel she appeared a little different. That day she wore a coat fashioned out of a wool blanket. The foreign tailor had cut the thick material at an angle, creating something out of nothing with outstanding workmanship, for whenever Julie neglected to pull the coat forcefully downward, her bosom bulged out. When Julie saw Rachel's eye briefly scan over her, she was certain Rachel had observed this embarrassing phenomenon.

Since Rachel felt the need to ogle me in the bath, it's obvious Judy has not disclosed details about my relationship with Chih-yung. She could have told the truth: "Julie makes her own decisions and won't listen to anyone else's advice—it's pointless to try." Otherwise, how could Judy explain anything? If she tried to pretend she didn't know, Rachel would snap at her: "Did you drop dead? Of course you know." Or maybe she could just say, "Ask her yourself." Hard to imagine she would do that.

But Julie never asked Judy.

After the physical examination in the bathtub and random, cursory investigations into Julie's relationship with Yen Shan, Rachel began to doubt the rumors flying around and calmed down somewhat, changing to a policy of conciliation. She gave Julie a brooch of a white enamel greyhound, the sort a primary-school student would wear.

"I don't wear brooches," said Julie apologetically. "The pinholes damage my clothes. Where did Second Aunt buy it? May I go there to exchange it for something else?"

"Fine, then. You go and exchange it." Rachel gave the receipt to Julie.

Julie exchanged the brooch for a pair of red copper rose-shaped pendant earrings. She showed them to Rachel.

"Hmm. Not bad."

One Night Stand finally screened.

The movie studio initially planned to adapt the story, then dropped it. Three months later, they picked it up again because Yen Shan couldn't find the right project for him to direct, as well as write the screenplay for and star in. They completed the filming before Rachel returned to Shanghai. Julie and Judy attended a preview screening at a theater. The adaptation simplified the story, while making it very disjointed. As soon as the last shot went black, Julie said softly, "Let's go." She was repulsed by the thought of everybody congratulating her as soon as the lights came on.

They had not sat with Yen Shan but he caught up with them at the staircase. "Why are you leaving?" he chuckled. "Couldn't bear to stay to the very end?"

Julie frowned. "We'll talk later," she said with a smile, and continued down the staircase.

Yen Shan blocked her path. "I didn't ruin your story!" he protested. He was anxious. Instead of his usually cautious demeanor, he became so carried away that in a lapse of etiquette his trouser cuffs brushed over the instep of her bare, open-sandaled feet. Standing beside Julie, even Judy cringed with embarrassment.

Voices from the projectionist booth signaled the screening had finished. Fearing others would come out and see them, he let her go.

At the official opening, Judy and Julie accompanied Rachel to the screening, which Rachel, to Julie's surprise, genuinely liked.

"She's become just like any other mother," Julie marveled, "easily satisfied with her daughter's achievements."

Rachel expressed only one criticism of Julie's novel: "You have no real life experience. You can't just rely on imagination." And added her oft-repeated quip, "People say it would be wonderful if *I* were to write a book."

One afternoon, while boiling water in the kitchen to make a cup of Sanatogen, Rachel bumped into Julie. "Come to my room for refreshments," said Rachel. She made another cup for Julie and retrieved a box of small cakes from the refrigerator, arranging some on a dish.

"Oh. I'll get some napkins."

"Hmm." Rachel approved.

Julie returned to the living room, opened her drawer, and placed two taels of gold inside a napkin. Before Rachel's return, Julie had asked Judy, "How much money has Second Aunt spent on me?" Judy did some mental calculations, then answered, "Now it would be the equivalent of about two taels of gold."

Her travel expenses to visit Chih-yung cost her one tael. She gradually exchanged what remained for daily expenses, her savings slowly dwindling. Now she had just over two taels left. Her old dream of presenting her mother with a long box packed with banknotes buried beneath a dozen ruby-red roses now was in danger of slipping through her fingers like two little croaker fish, to be lost forever.

Rachel engaged in small talk as they nibbled on the cakes at the little round table. Then she said to Julie, "I don't think you look so grotesque. I just want you to promise me one thing: Don't lock yourself up."

Then Rachel began to mumble to herself. "In those days there was no shortage of candidates; now there's not a single one."

It sounded like Rachel intended to introduce more boyfriends to her. Ever since watching *One Night Stand* and learning that Yen Shan was just a movie star, there was no possibility for him as far as Rachel was concerned.

"Surely," Julie thought, "she must have been aware that almost all of my cousins' husbands were secretly fond of her. Consequently, she harbored some fantasies of her own about young men." Now there was definitely no more danger of Rachel attempting to be her matchmaker, so Julie felt no need to explain her distaste for matchmaking to her, at least as far as Julie herself was concerned.

"We were rarely together," continued Rachel, "so when I was with you I always scolded you. Who would have known that we would live in the same house for so long—it just didn't work out. At the time, we were not sure if the war would break out in Europe. Otherwise, you could have gone there ages ago."

Julie seized the moment to pass the gold taels to Rachel. "That was when Second Aunt spent so much money on me, which I've always felt terrible about. I now repay Second Aunt," said Julie obsequiously.

"I don't want it," retorted Rachel firmly.

"In the past I said I wanted to repay her," thought Julie, "but she never said she didn't want it. Of course I was just making empty promises then, and she, naturally, paid no heed."

Tears streamed down Rachel's cheeks. "Even if I was just a stranger who once treated you nicely, you don't have to act like this toward me. 'A ferocious tiger does not devour its cubs!'"

Julie was astonished that when Rachel quoted a proverb from Nanking, it was reminiscent of something Auntie Yü or Jade Peach would say.

The room fell silent. Head lowered, Rachel wiped her tears, dejected.

Julie had caught glimpses of her mother crying before, but Rachel had never cried in front of her. *Should I feel sad?* Trying as hard as she could, Julie felt nothing at all.

"Those affairs," wailed Rachel, "I had no choice, they forced me." She choked and stopped talking.

Because there were a lot of them—now, isn't that a little comical?

"She's completely mistaken," thought Julie. "I never judge anyone," she screamed to herself, "how can I judge Second Aunt?" *But how do I tell her that?* When she was around sixteen, Julie read the preface to the complete dramatic works of George Bernard Shaw. She later felt him laughably juvenile at times, but at least, due to his influence, there were no sacred cows in her life.

Julie knew that as soon as she opened her mouth Rachel would fire back: "Fine! You just don't care."

If she were to speak, Julie would turn victory into defeat. She always adhered to the wisdom of keeping one's own counsel.

Time passed minute by minute, second by second. Those remembrances of things past slowly fossilized, trapping both of them within its solid matrix. Julie could feel the tendons of the grayish-white fossil and smell its dusty scent.

Julie gradually saw the light. *Perhaps it's better this way. Just let Rachel assume she's paying the price for her love affairs. Heartbreak isn't so bad for a miserable, sinful woman.* Wicked thoughts crawled along the edge of Julie's consciousness for a long time before creeping in.

Maybe that time Rachel took Julie down to the Repulse Bay beach was meant to give her a hint of what was going on, so that later it wouldn't be too traumatic if she suddenly discovered it by chance.

Julie had never imagined that Rachel would take the repayment as her wanting to sever relations forever. As the stalemate continued, Julie came to feel that Rachel was trying to preserve some of the affection they once had for each other by not accepting the money.

"Don't take it, then," thought Julie, "I have nothing else to give...."

In any case, as long as Julie simply listened submissively, no one could accuse her of being impolite. Julie glimpsed her face in the mirror. In that moment, she felt completely content with her dreamy eyes, delicate nose, diamond-shaped pink lips, and oval face. She hadn't scrutinized her own countenance for nine years, and now she felt gratified for still being the same person she was nine years earlier.

Rachel appeared to stop weeping. The silence continued to the point where the conversation could be considered over. Julie quietly stood up and walked out.

Back in her room she realized dusk had already fallen. Julie suddenly felt the room to be terribly gloomy and quickly switched on the lamp.

Time was on her side—it wasn't a fair battle.

"In any event, you won't meet with a good end," she said to herself.

Later she told Judy, "I tried to repay Second Aunt but she flatly refused to accept anything."

"How could she not want it?" asked Judy, perplexed.

"Second Aunt cried." Julie then continued in English, "She made a scene. It was awful." But she didn't tell Judy what Rachel said so she wouldn't be too disillusioned.

Judy didn't ask. She paused in silence, then said, "You still have to pay her back."

"She definitely won't accept any money, and I don't know what to do." *Do I have to force it into her hand?* Actually, Julie had thought of that, but didn't want to reenact the charade of forcing a gratuity on a maid. If she touched her mother's hand.... She had forgotten the time her mother had held her hand on that occasion crossing the road when she was a child, and the way, for some reason, she was so afraid of touching her mother's fingers, so scrawny that they felt like a bunch of thin bamboo canes clenching her own hand.

At the dining table Julie always appeared distant and aloof, affecting cinematic "fade-outs." This usually happened during lunch because Rachel almost never ate dinner at home.

One day Julie was vaguely aware that Rachel was telling the story about finding a snake in her riding boot. She noticed Julie obviously wasn't paying attention despite the fact she had been directing her tale to Judy. She became agitated and abruptly stopped. "You're not interested in anything I tell you," she snapped.

But on another occasion, she recounted the previous night's dream. Judy had once jokingly complained to Julie, "Your second aunt just has to tell people all about the films she's seen and the next morning she always has to tell people about her dreams."

"Little Julie always seemed stiff." Julie was astonished to hear that sentence from her mother's mouth. How on earth did she find her way into her mother's dream? It felt like she had strayed into forbidden territory.

The more she listened, the less she could take in. Rachel went on about how strange the dream was, how everything was so bizarre.

And why did she use my baby name? Was it because calling me "Julie" would mean treating me like an adult and therefore considered a politer appellation?

On another occasion after watching a movie, Rachel expounded at the table about Joan Crawford playing a waitress in *Mildred Pierce*. Struggling to support her children she opened her own restaurant, but in the end her unfilial daughter turned on her, even stealing her mother's lover. "I cried my heart out when I watched that film. Really it was too much," she lamented, her voice a little hoarse.

When Julie herself reached her thirties, she cried too, almost wailing while watching *Fear Strikes Out*, the biographical film about the baseball player Jimmy Piersall. Anthony Perkins played Jimmy, whose father groomed him from a young age to be a baseball player. He experienced enormous pressure, and no matter how hard he tried he couldn't earn his father's esteem. Finally he achieved success, but then went mad.

After hitting a home run, he ran around the field and climbed up the stadium fence shouting, "How was that? How was it? Was it good enough? I showed 'em."

Her mother wrote to Julie from her deathbed in Europe: "My only wish is to see your face one more time." Julie didn't go. After her demise, a world-famous auction house sold off Rachel's effects to settle her debts. When Julie received the detailed inventory, only a pair of jade vases had any value. They were among the antiques Rachel always took with her when she traveled overseas—she waited for the right price to sell things but she never actually sold anything.

On the occasions when mother and daughter were together, it seemed as though Rachel was forever packing—being a seasoned world traveler, more often than not she had to be ready to set off at a moment's notice. From the age of four Julie stood by her side watching her pack, and when she grew a little older she helped pass things back and forth. The only skill her mother taught her was how to pack a suitcase: every item assembled in flawless order, so that the soft things wouldn't be wrinkled and the hard things wouldn't be broken or crushed. Clothes never needed to be ironed after they were taken out of the suitcase. Once, when Julie traveled to a small town overseas, there were no porters to be found so she hired two university students to carry her suitcase. It was very heavy and they lost their grip, sending the case, which was as solid as a marble slab, tumbling down the stairs, though not the slightest noise emerged from within. One of the students looked on admiringly. "That case was well packed," he marveled—at last, someone who truly appreciated something about Julie.

However, Julie had never seen the jade vases. When she examined the inventory from the auction house, the edge of her lips curled into a bitter smile. "Never afforded me an opportunity to broaden my horizons," thought Julie. "As the saying goes, 'One must not reveal valuables to strangers.' The older generation really treated us as if they needed to guard against thieves."

When Rachel returned after the war, she didn't punish Julie to exact revenge for Rachel's brother, Uncle Yün-chih. That disappointed the Pien family, who were now no longer as warm toward Rachel as before.

The cousins used to worship Rachel as some kind of fairy godmother, but when they saw how much she had changed, they lost interest in her, only performing their welcoming duties perfunctorily.

"My Rick was really good to me," said Rachel to Judy out of the blue. They were sitting at the dining table. "He stuffed two hundred dollars into my suitcase. He always said I needed someone to look after me."

Julie felt numb, save for a slight twinge of desolation. Being pressed hard from all sides, Rachel needed some warm memories. She treasured them as dearly as her own life.

Dollars. Rachel must have met up with him that time when she made a side trip to Java on her way home from Paris. Rick had gone to Southeast Asia for a vacation. He was the "awful" pathology teaching assistant the female students complained about—a squat, pasty young man.

Julie did her best to numb herself. Perhaps she was too thorough because she didn't just behave this way toward her mother. She went into hibernation. She didn't notice that the copper bed warmer had burnt her leg until she woke up the next morning and found a blister the size of a chicken egg above her ankle. Winter was so cold she couldn't manage without socks, so she simply cut a hole in her sock. But the blister refused to recede. It became infected, its color changing to a yellow-green.

"Let me take a look," said Rachel.

Nancy was also there. She *tsk-tsked* upon seeing Julie's wound. Nancy and her husband had been back in Shanghai for a while.

"Ought to be lanced." Rachel always had an extensive first-aid kit on hand. She sterilized a small pair of scissors and stabbed the pustule. Julie felt a momentary coldness, then pus spurted out, emptying completely. Rachel gently cut back the broken skin.

Julie was quite accomplished at anesthetizing herself. She sensed her mother's pleasantly cool fingers, but she suppressed her emotions and remained unmoved.

"Goodness," chuckled Nancy from the sidelines, "Rachel's hands are trembling."

Rachel continued on, holding back a smile, as she cut away Julie's dead skin without saying a word.

Julie felt extremely embarrassed. In the old days, she would have died of shame.

After antiseptic was applied the wound stubbornly refused to heal. Finally, Nancy said, "Get Charlie to come and take a look." Dr. Yang was a renowned surgeon who lectured at a university medical school outside the city. Asking him to treat a blister was like wielding a slaughterhouse poleax to kill a chicken, but the ointment he applied didn't work, either. Every day he brought a freshly picked leaf of Chinese honey locust from the university botanical garden to place over the wound, which he then wrapped with gauze. The dressing was changed daily and after several months the wound finally healed. By that time Rachel was about to leave for Malaya.

"She's really like a wandering Jew," joked Judy in a low voice behind Rachel's back. *Condemned to wander forever, just like in the myth.*

Julie stayed silent. There was no way of knowing if Rachel planned to settle down this time, but she knew without a doubt that she was the cause of her mother leaving in a fit of pique. Rachel couldn't really stay in Shanghai anyway—it wouldn't be appropriate for her to set up another household in the city.

There was a brief time when Rachel spoke of moving to West Lake to join Second Master in her religious practice. This Second Master, an old spinster of the Pien clan, had entered a nunnery on the banks of the lake.

When the departure date was set, Rachel couldn't wait and moved out early, taking up residence in the luxurious Park Hotel, apparently to make a statement.

Rachel had always harped on and on in the same vein: "When I return I must have a place to call home." But this time Judy returned half of the key money to Rachel; she probably didn't plan to go back to China again.

While Rachel was packing, she became attracted to a turquoise biscuit tin that belonged to Judy.

"Take it," said Judy. "You can keep bits and bobs inside it."

"You keep it. I can buy a tin of biscuits for myself."

"Take it. I really have no use for it."

"Second Aunt and Third Aunt, friends until death, indulging in such courtesies over a tin can," thought Julie. She felt disconcerted.

Before leaving Rachel took out a pair of jade earrings and placed them beside a small pile of jewels, loose red and blue sapphires, and asked Julie to choose. She picked the earrings.

"Give the rest to your brother. When he gets married have them set so his bride can wear them."

Jade Peach stopped by. She had visited when Rachel returned, but when she came again this time, Rachel had already left Shanghai.

Judy and Jade Peach chatted, and inevitably the conversation turned to the change in Rachel's temperament. "She's a terror when it comes to settling accounts." Judy chuckled. They always believed the adage "Even siblings keep careful accounts," because otherwise people always feel they've been taken advantage of. It was human nature. However, whenever Judy settled accounts with Julie, her niece, she'd habitually say, "Repay me six dollars and fifty cents and there'll be no hint of discontent." That day when she talked about Rachel, Judy laughed it off. "She always shortchanges me and then becomes offended if I say anything."

"Acts like an idiot when receiving money but becomes very smart when asked to give money," snorted Jade Peach, in the Nanking dialect.

Julie was surprised to hear that. "Why are people so snobbish?" she thought. "As soon as she grows old, kith and kin betray her."

Yen Shan visited.

At dusk, they sat snuggled up to each other. She told him about her mother and their mother-daughter relationship. Because she had not introduced him, she needed to explain everything to him.

No romantic talk ensued.

"If anyone overheard me, they would think I was completely heartless and ungrateful," she said at last.

"Of course I believe you've done nothing wrong," he said.

Not that she didn't believe him—she just felt a wave of gloom fill her heart.

Julian visited.

Like Jade Peach, he had also come earlier. That was right when his cousin, the wife of his superior, summoned him from Hangchow. Julie wasn't present for the meeting between mother and son.

No doubt he had heard from his cousin that Rachel had left, but he nonetheless asked, "Second Aunt is gone?" Suddenly, a strange sarcastic smile appeared on his face.

His smile implied Rachel had changed.

Julie served tea. "Will you be staying at the family home while in Shanghai?" she asked politely.

"I'm staying in the bank dormitory with a friend." He sipped his tea. "I went home once and brought two sacks of rice with me. Stayed one night. A friend gave me some money to look after for him but at some point Second Uncle found it and took it all. He said to me, 'What's this money for? Why are you carrying all this money? Leave it here with me and when you need to use it come to me.' I said, 'This is not my money, it's a friend's, and I have to hand it over to him immediately.'"

Julie was shocked. Her first reaction was to blame her brother for being careless. *How could he bring money with him when he went there? Of course it was his own savings. A friend gave him a pile of money for safekeeping? What nonsense—as if he's reliable.* He didn't mention Jade Flower. Maybe she was the instigator.

"Second Uncle wrote a letter to Brother Hsü asking for a loan," Julian continued. "He asked me to post it for him. I may have a chance to go up north to reconnect with Brother Hsü. It's not a good time to borrow money from him, so I didn't post the letter."

This shocked Julie even more.

"How can Second Uncle be so hard up? Didn't both of them stop smoking opium?"

"Second Uncle's just like that now," Julian said, frowning. "He's nearly insane. When the mortgage is due he just tosses the bill in a drawer. Mother told me. She's furious."

"Mother is probably angry he doesn't put everything in her name."

"No," Julian retorted. "You don't know, Mother is good. It's Second Uncle who doesn't care and has let everything fall apart. Mother, however, is cool-headed."

"He loves Jade Flower," thought Julie.

Julie, of course, understood that in all human relationships, there's room for distortion, making it easy to deceive oneself. Not at all like Rachel doggedly locking him out of her life.

Julie once asked Julian which female film stars he liked. He said Bette Davis—an older woman also with large empty eyes, though Jade Flower's face was a little longer. She often played a villainous woman, sometimes a teacher who protected young students, or an older woman who sacrificed herself for her illegitimate child.

"Why do you like her?" Julie asked at the time.

"Because her English pronunciation is very clear." Then he began to stutter. "Some actors you can't hear very clearly," he added, fearing she would think his English was no good at all.

Julie could imagine that after finding an excuse to send Ned away, Jade Flower would exchange some private words with her stepson, complaining how insane his father had become and giving Ned the opportunity to rummage through his son's luggage.

Julie stood up, opened a cabinet drawer, and retrieved the pouch of jewels. She opened the small paper packet. The cluster of small precious stones was hardly impressive, especially after he had just lost all that money.

"This is from Second Aunt. She said to wait until you married and have them set for your bride."

Julian suddenly beamed ecstatically, probably because no one had ever mentioned the subject of his marriage to him before. Julie couldn't stop the waves of sadness from sweeping over her heart.

"It's not that I don't take an interest in your younger brother's affairs," Rachel had always maintained. "He's the only son and I expected they would let him have an education no matter what."

Even if they didn't provide him a proper education, they would find him a wife. After all, the greatest offense against filial piety is to have no heirs.

When Ned remarried, he wanted more children. So why is he now so unconcerned about becoming heirless? Of course, having his own child and his son having a child was a distinction of self and other. Julie always knew that her father's adherence to tradition was simply self-serving.

Or was it that Jade Flower now depended on Julian, so she didn't want him to marry?

Because Julie felt sad and also embarrassed for him, she couldn't bear the silence. She anxiously searched for something to say. "Second Aunt asked me to choose between two groups of jewelry," said Julie, smiling awkwardly. "I chose a pair of jade earrings."

"Oh." He smiled, grunting an acknowledgment, obviously expecting her to show him the earrings. They were in the same drawer in the cabinet but she remained seated. He couldn't hide his astonishment, staring with his large round eyes. He sat for a while longer then left, scooping up the pouch of jewels with a smile and slipping it into his pocket.

Julie related to Judy what her brother had told her. "From the sound of it," Judy fumed, "he's saying your second uncle is old and mad and unable to think straight, and he himself should be in charge of everything."

"Now she's defending the brother who betrayed her?" pondered Julie. "For some people only blood relatives can criticize and the criticism of outsiders only provokes resentment."

No. Judy is merely being loyal to her own generation, resenting the new always taking the place of the old like "future waves on the Yang-tze River pushing up against the previous waves."

The flat hoop-shaped, deep green jade earrings were less than an inch in diameter and each hung from a short gold chain. Julie's ears weren't pierced so she could only wear them if she asked a jeweler to add screw buttons. She held them up to her ears. Her hair was long, and the dark green hoops were barely visible through her bouffant curls.

A year later Julie still hadn't worn the earrings. She finally decided to sell them. She didn't actually need the money at the time but the earrings reminded her of her mother and brother, causing her too much pain.

Judy accompanied Julie to an old-fashioned jewelry store to help negotiate the sale.

"You got a good price," said Judy.

"Because they knew," thought Julie, "that I didn't really want to sell."

Of course they always know.

12

"Hey," Yen Shan said, smiling. "Tell me, are you a good person or a bad person?"

Julie laughed. "That's like when we watched movies as children. As soon as a new character appeared we'd immediately ask, 'Is that one a goodie or a baddie?'"

Of course she knew he was really asking about her relationship with Chih-yung. He had heard rumors, though after getting to know her, she didn't fit the picture in his mind.

He embraced Julie and mumbled softly, "You're like a cat. A very big cat." And continued, "You have an attractive face.

"But tell me," he said, still smiling, "are you a good person or a bad person?"

"Of course I think I'm a good person," Julie replied genially. When she saw his eyes suddenly sparkle with hope, she frowned.

"I don't go to the movies anymore," she had said when she first became acquainted with Yen Shan. "Just a matter of habit. For a few years during the war there were no American movies to see and my craving evaporated."

Yen Shan appeared to be awed by Julie's attitude, probably thinking that it was also a form of patriotism. Actually, Julie was simply trying to be frugal. But she did feel a sense of detachment when she saw the advertisements for postwar American movies. They didn't appeal to her, perhaps because of the slight resentment she harbored against the victor.

After a while he said, "I think not watching movies is your own loss."

Julie went with him twice to the cinema. As soon as the lights dimmed, gazing at his profile deep in concentration, she too felt awed by him, observing his expert eyes staring at the screen. Julie felt deep admiration, as she did for the tradesmen who install light fixtures, because that was something she could not do. *Since ancient times, men of letters tend to despise each other.*

Likewise, Yen Shan initially found Julie unfathomable. Once, after listening to her speak for a long time, he smiled and said, "Hey! What *are* you rattling on about?"

Yen Shan rarely wore dark glasses. Most of the time he wore somber black-framed or tortoiseshell spectacles that completely altered his appearance, giving him a low-key profile that didn't attract attention the way dark glasses would. They never patronized fashionable restaurants—sometimes they dashed all the way to the city center to eat local dishes or to frequent a dreary, frigid, traditional northerner restaurant where they would be the only patrons present on an entire floor.

On one occasion the two of them stood on a small pier. A large wooden ship was moored nearby. The vessel was unpainted and glowed with the natural yellow brightness of new lumber. It looked more than two stories high, probably a cargo transport. The bulky ship with creaking masts was unlike any of the traditional Chinese ships depicted in illustrations.

"It's headed for Poo-tung," he said.

Just a suburb across the Hwang-poo River, so near yet so far away. In the misty sunset, she wondered from what dynasty the ship had set sail. She couldn't imagine any circumstances in which she'd be able to board such a vessel.

"Your hair is red."

That was because golden sunlight slanted across her hair.

Yen Shan's Mandarin wasn't particularly fluent. He was a rarity in Shanghai: locally born. One day he got into an animated conversation with Judy about the fate of various edifices in Shanghai—such-and-such building originally belonged to this company or that foreign firm—the two of them constantly cutting each other off. While

Julie liked Shanghai, she lacked their appreciation of the city's history. Julie was delighted that Yen Shan and Judy had much in common. She felt like she was on that same tiny dark balcony when she had listened to Judy discussing fund-raising with Brother Hsü—high finance was a topic she knew nothing about. This time, however, she felt a tinge of jealousy. Dusk arrived and the room began to darken, but she restrained herself from standing up and turning on a lamp because she didn't want them to think she was bored sitting on the sidelines and only turned on a light to interrupt their conversation. And yet they sensed something in the air and self-consciously ended their discussion.

Julie felt she was compensating for the first love she never had, with the young man she never met. Yen Shan was a few years older than her but looked younger.

Soon after her mother left, Chih-yung passed through Shanghai.

Hsiu-nan telephoned; Julie waited by the elevator with the door unlatched so the visitor wouldn't be forced to stand momentarily outside the door after ringing the bell and then possibly be observed by someone in the corridor. It was cold. Julie pushed her hands deep into the pockets of her heavy overcoat. She had initially kept the wool fringe along the hem of the long coat because it otherwise looked too short, but when Yen Shan said, "Those frayed edges look a bit strange," she cut them off.

Chih-yung stepped out of the elevator. Hsiu-nan nodded and smiled before the doors closed and the elevator descended.

"You look beautiful," Chih-yung said hesitantly.

She smiled as though she had not heard, turned, and led him through the doorway. She sensed Chih-yung had noticed her lack of response to his comment.

They sat in the living room; the telephone rang just as Julie served the tea. She went to answer it but absentmindedly didn't close the door behind her.

"Hello?"

"Hey." It was Yen Shan's voice.

A rumbling instantly resonated next to her ears like the roar of two heavenly bodies brushing past her. Her two worlds were about to collide.

"Hey, how are you?...I'm fine. Have you been busy lately?" She bantered politely, but kept it very brief while she waited for him to say what he wanted.

Yen Shan, sounding a bit annoyed, said it was nothing in particular and he'd call again another day; he hung up.

She returned to the living room and found Chih-yung anxiously pacing in circles.

"Your Shanghainese sounds very alluring," he said. Obviously he had eavesdropped on her telephone conversation.

"I didn't learn to speak Shanghainese until I moved to Hong Kong," she explained. "There were some students from Shanghai in the dormitory." There was no way to explain how someone who grew up in Shanghai couldn't speak the language.

She didn't say who had called and he didn't ask.

Judy came in and chatted for a while but didn't stay long.

Mr. Yü arrived.

When the conversation turned to Bebe, Chih-yung asked, "Have you met her?" Mr. Yü answered that he had. "Do you think she's pretty?"

"Yes, she's pretty," Mr. Yü replied, chuckling softly.

"Well then you should pursue her," said Chih-yung, grinning.

"Um," said Mr. Yü, turning serious, "that wouldn't be appropriate."

This exchange grated on Julie's nerves. "You think casual conversation and sharing a few laughs means she is easy prey," Julie thought. "That's what a country bumpkin thinks." She also found it vulgar. It was a distasteful act of flattery to "present the Buddha with borrowed flowers."

Mr. Yü often modestly bragged, "I have no accomplishments, other than a reasonably good marriage."

They chatted until dusk, and Mr. Yü left. Julie saw him to the door. When she returned, Chih-yung grumbled to her, "Mr. Yü has really been...doesn't such kindness to me merit a dinner invitation to this house?"

This was the first time they had ever quarreled. Julie said nothing. He should have known better. Julie and Judy rarely had people over for meals, and not being able to invite Chih-yung for dinner in the past had been excruciating for Julie. Mr. Yü certainly knew better. He had once worked in Shanghai as a dental assistant and probably stayed with Chih-yung at the time. He frequently visited, bringing along a thick dentistry textbook that he asked Julie to translate for him. She actually couldn't translate such specialized material but the dentist didn't appear to notice. He was pleased to have picked up a bargain in hiring this assistant who could translate for him and help garner him accolades. Whenever Mr. Yü visited in those days, Julie would go to the refrigerator and ladle out a small bowl of stewed black dates with grated lemon rind for him. The delicacy was supposed to help digestion, and Mr. Yü loved it. "I bought this with my own money," Julie told him, to prevent him from declining out of politeness.

Julie went out to the kitchen. "Shao Chih-yung is angry," she reported to Judy, "because I didn't invite Mr. Yü to stay for dinner."

Judy's face instantly darkened. Of course she knew Mr. Yü wasn't asked to stay because of her. In the past she had instructed Julie, "Just blame me." Now Judy simply grumbled, "Cruel," in English.

"I think you're treating him differently now," Judy said quietly as she prepared the evening meal.

Julie acknowledged her third aunt with a faint smile, thinking it was superfluous of her to have said that.

As usual, Judy retired to her room after the evening meal. Julie let Chih-yung stay in her bedroom with easier access to the bathroom, while Julie herself could use Judy's bathroom.

She brought an ashtray to the bedroom. Chih-yung smoked a cigarette as he recounted how prior to their arrest, some Wang Ching-wei government officials "went to stay with their women." He then concluded, "Women are like cans of peanuts—men can't stop eating them as long as they're around."

Julie assumed that by "women" he was referring to mistresses.

"Do you have anything to drink?" he suddenly asked, agitated.

Peanut canapés to aid imbibing liquor? Or do you need alcohol to liven things up? "At this time of night," she replied coldly without smiling, "I wouldn't know where to go to buy alcohol."

"Oh," he said quietly, obviously struggling to control his temper.

After dispensing with news about mutual acquaintances, Julie gave a faint smile and asked, "Were you ever intimate with that Miss K'ang?"

"Um," he acknowledged, "only once, when I was about to leave." His voice lowered. "In the end I forced myself upon her... perhaps that is always inevitable—but of course you were different."

Julie said nothing.

He was silent for a while before speaking again. "Hsiu-nan defends you by asking, 'Isn't that Miss Sheng good enough for you?'"

Julie immediately felt deeply offended. "Fine," she thought, "now I need someone to speak up for me."

Chih-yung took a small photograph out of his pocket and genially proffered it to Julie. "This is Miss K'ang."

The creased, glossy photograph displayed a full-length portrait of Miss K'ang standing on a lawn. She had chubby cheeks and crescent-shaped cheerful eyes that pointed upward at the corners. She wore a thin cotton gown, probably sky blue though it looked as white as snow in the photo, revealing her ample bosom. Her medium-length hair curled slightly inward. She was a little plumper than Rachel's ideal body type for a young girl.

Julie had just begun to examine the photograph in her hand when she raised her head to catch Chih-yung's terrified expression. *You really think I'm like the wives of our friends you talk about and that I would tear it up?* She sneered and immediately passed the photo back.

He stuffed the picture in his pocket and changed the topic.

As the conversation progressed, seeing that Julie didn't display any sign of anger, Chih-yung placed the ashtray on the bed and even leaned toward her. "Why don't you come and sit here?"

She sat closer, smiling with her head lowered, not looking at him.

"I almost died from torment." Julie had to sit up close to Chih-yung to be able to say something like that. She couldn't clearly explain her suffering in a letter; she needed to say it to his face, to explain her feelings that evening.

She could feel him watching her intensely, yet there wasn't the slightest trace of tears in her own eyes, which made her words less convincing, even to herself.

He obviously was waiting for her to continue, to tell him why she now felt better.

"He doesn't care at all if I live or die," she thought, "he's only concerned with his own possessions."

But she didn't go on. Then Chih-yung spoke. "To experience suffering like that is also ideal."

That is to say, it was good for her to experience passionate affection. His old routine of "ideal" or "not ideal" was enough to make her laugh out loud and scream in disgust.

In the past he had said, "Formal marriage can end in divorce, but informal arrangements can never be severed." At the time she thought, "I certainly don't believe that."

But she also grew curious. Is it really true that "habit is second nature"? After all, man is a "creature of habit," so *that* behavior of his could be more animal instinct than habit.

"Take this off, all right?" she heard him suggest.

While they were sitting face-to-face Julie had already perceived the strange desolation of the room, as if something were missing—the electricity that once filled the air, the streamers of affection. Without those streamers she felt the two of them were somehow impoverished. Sitting on the bed felt even stranger, as though they were living inside some kind of humble hut built in a vacuum, a structure less tall than an average person that enclosed them from above, and in that vacuum, no movement felt right.

But then she found herself wriggling out of her black plum-colored narrow-sleeved cotton gown, the one he said looked like a sword dancer's costume. He sat so close and yet felt strangely distant; she couldn't tell if he was deliberately avoiding physical contact as she struggled to pull herself out of the narrow sleeves, feeling totally alone with no one else around.

She laughed at herself and sighed. "We really are fulfilling the proverb, 'The lamp is out, the fuel is spent.' This isn't an unnatural death—there will be no disembodied spirits." She smiled as she put her arms back inside the sleeves—underneath she only wore a silk singlet with straps—and saw Chih-yung's aggrieved glare following her every move.

Again, her thick overcoat became the cause of resentment. He must have thought she had another lover because her bosom had changed.

She quickly fastened the buttons of her gown, smiling as she rushed out, pretending to retrieve some trifle she had left behind.

Returning to the living room, she pulled off the bedspread, disrobed, and plunged under the duvet—the fresh bedding on this cold night as frigid as an icy cave. She quickly fell asleep.

Early the next morning, Chih-yung shook her awake. Julie opened her eyes. Suddenly she wrapped her arms around his neck. "Chih-yung," she whispered. Their past, like the Great Wall, undulated on the horizon. But in the modern age the Great Wall served no purpose.

She saw his mortified smile—it was the same smile that she saw him give at the artist's home when she encountered his wife.

"He's embarrassed because he doesn't love me anymore," she thought as she quickly pulled her arms away, sat up straight, and pulled the gown over her head. This time he didn't even look at her.

He returned to the bedroom; she prepared some breakfast on a tray and delivered it to him, dismayed to discover that her desk drawer was in complete disarray.

Fine, have a good look and see what you can find.

After the war ended she had started to work on a full-length novel. The manuscript was piled in a stack on her desk.

"Hardly anything about me in here!" exclaimed Chih-yung, wide-eyed. He sounded angry, yet grinned. Then of course he tried to patch things up, adding, "But you write about yourself extremely well."

Whenever she wrote about him it was either in profile or in silhouette.

She remained silent. She had never believed in anything, really, except him.

Before they had a chance to finish eating breakfast, Hsiu-nan arrived. Julie produced the two *taels* of gold she had prepared in advance to give him and handed them over to Hsiu-nan with a smile.

Chih-yung watched from the sidelines but said nothing.

He returned to the small township. Upon arriving, he seemed to finally realize how wrong things had become. Letters followed: "*Meeting with no words, only tears....* I was disconsolate you did not kiss me. I never imagined that two people needed to make an oath to carry on well together, but now I say to you, 'I love you forever.'"

"He thinks I'm afraid he'll abandon me," Julie thought. "Actually, he has never let go of anyone, including his male friends. People are essential resources for all his activities. I told him I could walk away if he wouldn't give up Miss K'ang, but he didn't believe me."

Julie's replies to Chih-yung's letters were brief and never mentioned anything about their relationship. She sold a film script and remitted some more money to him.

He wrote again saying that he would soon have an opportunity to work, obviously afraid she would think of him as a burden. She replied: "Do not be too anxious to find work before your health is restored."

Julie went to visit Bebe. An American sailor loafed about their house that day. He was young and blond, making him the ideal page boy to the immortals in the movies. When he saw Julie walk in wearing a peacock-blue satin jacket with peach-pink floral brocade over a pair of wide-leg black silk pants, his eyes flashed momentarily, as if to say, "Now that's more like it." Apart from the palatial gasoline filling stations, nothing in Shanghai had an Oriental flavor.

The three of them sat around a stove. He took out a pack of cigarettes. "Smoke?" he asked Julie.

"Thanks, I don't smoke."

"Don't know why but I thought you smoked and she doesn't."

Julie smiled. She knew by that he meant Bebe appeared more innocent.

That day, Bebe put on her "girl next door" demeanor. She never had the courage to flirt with a sailor, but if it were a man with a shy personality, she'd occasionally slip in a few racy or even sexually explicit remarks, which sounded rather shocking to Julie's ears. In this way Bebe feinted an attack to mislead the enemy, stimulating his curiosity so he'd have to chase for a long time before her victim realized he had been duped.

Julie asked him if he had fought in any battles. He called it "combat," his face turning pale as soon as he uttered the word. Julie thought combat involved mounted knights of the Middle Ages, or perhaps two individuals engaging each other on the battlefield. This was the first time she had heard it used to mean going to the firing line. It sounded archaic and comical. The combat zone really is another world.

Julie didn't stay long as the couple seemed to have plans.

"These Americans are truly an unsophisticated bunch," Bebe said later and sneered. "Some of the conscripts had never even worn shoes before joining the army."

Bebe said, "While they'd be quite happy to marry you, they'd be just as happy to divorce you. It's nothing for them, really."

Bebe angrily blurted out, "They all say you had lived with Mr. Shao."

Stories about the romance of Julie and Chih-yung had spread far and wide. Even someone like Bebe who didn't read the Chinese press had heard all about it.

Julie could only smile weakly as she said, "Only when he was about to leave."

Why did she borrow Chih-yung's answer about his affair with Miss K'ang, or at least borrow half of it? She didn't borrow the part about rape. Julie herself felt it was too painful to look deeper, but she thought her explanation was the most Bebe would be able to withstand.

"That certainly wasn't worth it," said Bebe.

That is to say, Julie didn't have an opportunity to savor the joy of sex. Bebe had read in a book: "Unmarried people should not have sexual relations. As soon as they do, a need is established and that will actually cause misery." Bebe believed in chastity before marriage, but she needed to formulate the theoretical underpinnings for her decision. Otherwise, it would appear she merely surrendered to the reality of Chinese and Indian men not marrying women who weren't virgins.

Julie told Yen Shan, too.

He was a little startled. "Isn't that sacrificing one's body?" he asked softly.

Julie's heart convulsed in abhorrence, but she fought off the feeling to avoid letting it show.

"He seems to have the ability to dominate you," Yen Shan said, smiling.

"Last time I saw him he was entirely different. We didn't even shake hands."

To be precise, they had never actually shaken hands.

"Don't let him touch a single hair on your body," Yen Shan said in a sudden loud outburst.

Julie suppressed her mirth, though she also felt moved by his words.

After a long silence, Yen Shan said, "You probably like older men."

At least they've lived more life. Julie had always been fascinated by the complexity of life.

After Yen Shan left that day, Julie wrote a short letter to Chih-yung. She had delayed writing the letter because she thought it would appear heartless to break it off while he was in trouble. Paying him back the money, of course, slightly assuaged her conscience.

When Yen Shan visited again, she smiled and passed him the letter. "I'm just letting you take a look. It has nothing to do with you; I had been wanting to write it for a long time," she said, not wanting him to think he was the cause of the letter.

Nevertheless, it wasn't possible to avoid Yen Shan's influence after all. The previous day when she told him the reason for her split with Chih-yung, Yen Shan coldly scoffed, "So it was because of jealousy." For that reason she had written, "It isn't because of all those women of yours, it's because I have come to realize that I will never be happy being with you." Originally, she also had intended to add: "Even without them, there would have been others, and I cannot be enemies with half of mankind."

But then she thought that would sound too much like venting her spleen, or at least wouldn't appear sufficiently earnest. *Forget it—that's just the way it is. What's the point of agonizing over the wording, again and again.*

Before she sent the letter, she received two letters from Chih-yung. It was like receiving letters from someone already dead. She felt terrible.

After that Chih-yung wrote two long letters to Bebe: "She used to love me with her entire being, yet she now asks me never to write her again."

Bebe was in a quandary. "What am I supposed to do?"

"Give the letters to me and you will have no further responsibility."

Later Julie heard through the grapevine that the Shao family was so rattled by this new situation that they moved and Chih-yung left the small town. This time he probably didn't dare return to the countryside, even though he had been moving back and forth between the two places.

"As if I would turn you in," she sniffed to herself.

Brother Hsü wrote a letter to Judy in which he mentioned Ned and Jade Flower: "I heard that Second Uncle's wife went to your elder brother's house to say to your nephew: 'If your second uncle had not sided with your family during litigation, you wouldn't necessarily have won. He is now in difficulty, so you should make space for him and take him in. You surely can't deny him this, can you?' His nephew then gave them a room and they've already moved in."

Julie was shocked her father had become so impoverished. In the past, Judy frequently spoke in hushed tones: "His opium expenditure is exorbitant." Inflation soared and the price of opium soared ever higher. The money they spent on the drug grew to an astronomical sum, as both of them smoked. But later they made good on their pledge to abstain.

"Your second uncle is loaded," Rachel intoned incessantly.

But the last time Rachel returned to Shanghai she had absolutely no contact with Ned before the divorce, though she did have two huge fights with him over domestic expenses. Yü-heng had sent her reports while she lived overseas, but he was merely a servant, not a close confidant.

Julie recalled the look of dread on the maidservants' faces when they talked about her father and his paramour Euphoria losing at the tables for days in a row on their gambling sprees.

Julie's father never actually admitted that he didn't have any money. He never would. That would be the same thing as someone else saying, "I'm really quite uneducated" or "I lack morals." Who would give credence to that?

He never told Julie about having insufficient funds for her overseas schooling, preferring instead to thrash her and lock her up. If he had said anything about his finances, people would've gossiped—Jade Flower especially could never know. Otherwise, they wouldn't have been such an affectionate couple, taking turns cajoling each other.

A young female cousin from the Pien clan posted Julie a wedding invitation. Julie attended the ceremony but did not want to be present at the dinner reception. In the wedding hall on her way out she bumped into Nancy.

"Julie," Nancy gushed, "the beads are *so* pretty."

"A gift from Second Aunt," replied Julie, removing the purple imitation-agate bead necklace as she spoke, "which I now present to my auntie Nancy." Julie also felt in debt to Nancy and her husband, though Dr. Yang's daily visits to treat her over the course of two months were principally because he was doing Rachel a favor. The necklace wasn't worth much but was nonetheless a rarity.

"No, no, no," Nancy protested, "Rachel gave it to you. How could you think of giving it away?"

"Second Aunt would be thrilled to know I passed it on to Auntie Nancy."

After further exhortations, Nancy finally accepted the gift.

Julian wasn't in Shanghai at the time and didn't attend the wedding. He talked about the newlywed cousin on his next visit. The lowly ranked cousin was never coddled nor doted upon. Self-defensive from a young age, she was rather shrewish. Only Rachel liked her, and gave her the sobriquet Roundy.

"That Roundy is so ferocious," chuckled Julian. "Even as a child she was really fierce when we roller-skated around the alleyways."

Julie recalled the time when she and her brother lived in the same alleyway as Uncle Yün-chih. The older female cousins loved to tease the handsome little boy: "Roundy is betrothed to our little cousin Julian. You didn't know?" They also liked to say, "Aunt Rachel adores Roundy. Roundy's going to be her daughter-in-law." As soon as they saw Julian they'd shout: "Roundy, your husband is here!" That was when Roundy was just seven or eight years old, though she was so small she looked no more than five or six. No matter what was going through her head she always put on a fierce expression of permanent condescension. Julian was three or four years older than Roundy, and Julie could see that he enjoyed listening to the mocking remarks of their cousins. From the tone of his voice it was now clear to Julie that Roundy was his first love, with all his fond memories of skating through the alleyways. Julie didn't know how to skate. The male cousins in the Pien clan were always calling on Julian to join them to play outside. Ned referred to them as the "alleyway surveillance commissioners."

"Do you have a girlfriend?" Julie asked casually.

"No," Julian stammered, "I think it'd be best to find one who has a job."

"Of course that would be ideal," Julie agreed.

Julian didn't mention their father seeking refuge with his nephew, probably out of shame.

Julie first began to apply cosmetics at the age of twenty-eight. It was all because Yen Shan once queried, "You never use makeup?"

"A bit more here," he suggested as he sized her up, hesitantly pointing to a small spot on her brow between her eyes.

She had intended to retain some luster in the depression between her eyes, but now she applied more powder.

"It's like covering my face with a quilt," she gasped gleefully, "it can't breathe."

Yen Shan felt a little embarrassed.

He set his head upon her thigh while she caressed his face. She didn't know where the sadness came from but felt as if she were "cupping her hands to hold the water's reflection of the moon," the water slowly slipping through her fingers.

His eyes were impenetrably deep. But then it occurred to her that when you love someone, your lover will always seem deeply mysterious.

Julie had always been suspicious of handsome men. In her mind beautiful women can maintain their composure much better when facing their admirers because beauty is practically a duty for women and not being beautiful is unnatural. Handsome men, however, don't maintain their composure as well as women and inevitably all kinds of twisted characteristics manifest themselves. When a handsome man becomes an actor, all the women in the world transmogrify into apparitions before his eyes, ready to ravish the pure flesh of the T'ang dynasty Buddhist pilgrim Hsüan Tsang in their attempts to acquire immortality.

But to Julie, Yen Shan was like her first love, the one she had missed out on. Circumstances had changed by the time they finally met, making her feel even more melancholy and sentimental. She wished this moment would last forever. That too was exactly what he longed for, at least at the beginning.

Yen Shan had a gloomy side. His family was in financial straits because his father had died when Yen Shan was small. Yen Shan had the mind-set of a "salary man" through and through. In his profession, if you didn't know how to get along with people it didn't matter if you were the best actor in the universe. But he always felt insecure. He reached the apex of his career just over the age of thirty, and yet wasn't as remotely revered as a certain actor of Peking-style spoken drama who came from Chungking. His first attempt at directing was deemed a failure. Though at least *One Night Stand* didn't lose money— a fact Julie attributed to the deceptive name of the movie.

His father was a small-time businessman. "People said he had 'a commanding presence,'" Yen Shan crowed.

A petty merchant with an air of authority is how Julie envisaged his father. With an appearance a bit like Yen Shan—tall and skinny, large piercing eyes, high nose bridge, wearing a long gown and a wool hat.

"My only memory of my father is of him holding me as we sat in a rickshaw," recalled Yen Shan. "It was windy, and he wrapped my scarf around my face to protect me. 'Close your mouth tight! Close your mouth tight!' he kept shouting."

Yen Shan lived with his elder brother and sister-in-law. There were many people in the family who all depended on his earnings.

His married elder sisters frequently visited. Julie had been to his family home only once. A vintage black-lacquered, keyhole-shaped clock hung on the wall in the living room. Yen Shan told her it was an electric clock. Apparently his second-older brother worked in the electric-clock business.

Julie couldn't see the point of wasting electricity on clocks when windup clocks already existed. Staring at the round face of the clock on the wall, she didn't know what to say.

Yen Shan sensed it. "Lots of people buy them," he said, smiling apologetically.

"Oh," he said on another occasion with dawning realization, "you mean just the two of us?"

"*Yes*," acknowledged Julie with a smile.

"We still should live with your third aunt."

Chih-yung had also suggested they should one day live with her third aunt. Apparently both of them were terrified of living alone with her. She couldn't help smiling at this thought.

Julie never believed Chih-yung when he spoke of "our future," and she just couldn't imagine what the "love that endures to the end of time" that he wrote about in his letters would be like. She always felt a slight suffocating sensation when she tried, with much difficulty, to visualize what sort of house they would live in, and couldn't get very far with this line of thinking. Instead, when thinking of Yen Shan, she figured, "I must find a small room for myself, so it could be like going to work every day. I won't tell anyone the address, except Yen Shan, if he can be relied upon not to drop by. At night I'd return home, and then it wouldn't matter if anyone visits."

Occasionally, after they went out in the evening, Yen Shan would accompany her home but refused to go inside for fear of Third Aunt witnessing his middle-of-the-night visitation. They sat in the staircase instead. She wore a dark green, puff-sleeve coat made of rustic wool. The narrow-waisted overcoat flared out onto the faux-marble steps. They were like teenagers with nowhere to hide to be alone together.

"We should be called the 'Two Innocents,'" Julie said with an exasperated smirk.

"Yes." Yen Shan giggled. "'Two innocent childhood friends'—we should get a seal carved with the inscription: 'Two Innocents.'"

Julie smiled but didn't say anything. She had little time for the refined pursuits of scholars like seal carving. Besides, when would there be occasion to employ such a seal, unless they sent New Year greeting cards they signed together?

"You are made up entirely of defects," he mumbled, "save for, perhaps, frugality."

She smiled, boasting in her heart, "That's right, I'm like openwork gauze made entirely of defects."

Judy was always very reserved toward Julie and Yen Shan's relationship. One day, Judy chatted with Yen Shan for a while and then he left. "At least it's pleasing to the eye watching him sit there," Judy remarked to Julie.

Julie smiled but couldn't think of anything to say. "I fear I'm getting too serious about him," she finally confessed.

Judy shook her head slightly. "It's not at all like the way you were with Shao Chih-yung," she said in an almost contemptuous tone.

Julie was shocked but said nothing.

A Mr. Niu began to pursue Bebe. He was a university graduate from a rich family and around the same age as Bebe. He was short, with a fair-skinned face that resembled a puppy dog. Apart from appearing somewhat clumsy and stupid, there wasn't much more to say about him. Then there was the Cantonese Ah Leung, also a frequent visitor to Bebe's home. He was already in his thirties. Julie vaguely heard he worked as a machine repairman, which pretty much disqualified him in her mind. She had met him in Bebe's home. That day, Bebe directed him to the loose switch on the floor lamp. As she stood next to the light pointing out the problem, in an off-white pullover sweater, the light from the lamp formed a spotlight on her curvaceous breasts, which rose and fell as she spoke. Ah Leung's eyes almost popped out of their sockets.

Bebe told Julie that one day Mr. Niu and Ah Leung got into a fight that started upstairs and proceeded all the way down the staircase and out into the street. "I watched from the top of the stairs and laughed so hard I couldn't stand up straight. What was I supposed to do?"

"I just don't understand," Judy exploded one day, "why you insist on being so secretive all the time!"

Julie didn't respond. She knew a relative must have asked Judy, "Does Julie have any suitors?" Yen Shan wasn't a married man, but because they wanted to keep their romance secret Judy had to reply in the negative.

They had never actually discussed keeping their relationship a secret, but Julie knew that because of her own infamy—her reputation had already been tarnished for several years and the gossips were hungry for new ammunition—if word leaked out it would be a huge sensation and Yen Shan would certainly suffer. Two of his friends knew about them and probably didn't approve, but they kept quiet. He had a secretive personality anyway—very few people knew about his past.

Bebe telephoned. "That *Bolero* you like so much—I have a friend who has a recording of it. I'll stop by with him and we can all listen to it."

"I don't have a phonograph player," said Julie.

"I know. He'll bring one."

Bebe rang the doorbell and a thin white man carrying a large phonograph player stood behind her. He cautiously followed her in.

"This is Eugene," said Bebe. Julie never learned his family name. He was an Australian reporter with hazel hair, very handsome.

Julie stood next to the phonograph as the tango melody played, staring at the spinning record. When the song finished, Bebe asked, "Do you want to hear it again?"

Julie hesitated. "All right, let's hear it again."

They played it seventeen times in a row. The whole time Julie stood next to the phonograph player, leaning on the table and smiling.

"Do you want to hear it again?"

"No."

They chatted for a short while then Bebe said, "We should be going now."

From beginning to end Eugene didn't say a single word. Stone-faced, he lugged the phonograph away.

Bebe often talked about Eugene and showed Julie a chapter of a novel he was writing about a journalist in early Republican-era Peking who meets the daughter of a warlord—a delicate beauty of fifteen or sixteen who wore a rose-pink short jacket and black silk pants. They had a tryst in the library of the warlord governor.

"Eugene married Fanny," Bebe reported to Julie one day. "Fanny is twenty-one. He married her because she is twenty-one." As she spoke, Bebe smiled, pressing her lips together as if relating a marvelous tale. From her tone of voice it was obvious she was quoting him, meaning he must have told Bebe himself.

Julie saw Fanny once. She was a Chinese girl with narrow delicate eyes, an angular face, and a rigidly skinny body.

"At least he found something close to his ideal," thought Julie. Her family seemed wealthy as the wedding ceremony sounded quite lavish.

Bebe had seen Yen Shan at Julie's home several times. She hadn't heard any rumors about them, but Bebe had her suspicions. "All women who engage in serial intimate relationships," said Bebe one day, "quickly grow haggard."

Julie knew Bebe was deliberately provoking her, trying to trick her into defending herself, so she just chuckled indifferently.

Julie never told Bebe anything about Yen Shan, and Bebe never asked.

After Julie exited the cinema with Yen Shan one day, she noticed that he looked displeased. Later, when she peeked into the hand mirror she kept in her purse, she realized it must have been because of how she looked: her makeup had melted and oil seeped through the face powder.

"I love Ginger Rogers's insincere gaze," Yen Shan said, laughing.

Julie didn't know why, but she felt as if a needle pricked her when she heard that and couldn't think of anything to say.

Before Yen Shan visited, Julie didn't fetch ice cubes from the refrigerator and rub the ice on her face to tighten her skin, out of fear that Judy would see. Instead, she let the cold-water faucet in the bathtub run hard until the water was icy cold, but still Judy chanced upon her as she held her face close to the cold stream. They had both lived with Rachel and knew everything about the process of a woman past her prime, but Judy was dismayed when she observed Julie splashing cold water on her face.

It rained for days without end. "Rain. It's like living by a burbling stream," Julie wrote in her notebook. "Hope it rains every day so I can believe your absence is due to the rain."

Sprawled over a rattan recliner, an endless stream of tears flowed down her face.

"Julie," Yen Shan moaned, looking at her with gentle concern, "you crying like that makes me feel terrible." Yen Shan leaned forward in his seat with his elbows resting on his knees, hands clasped together.

"No one else will love you the way I do," she responded.

"I know."

But then she added, tears streaming down her face, "It's really only because of your handsome face."

He walked over to the large, round mirror on the wall, looked at himself somewhat curiously, then combed his hair back with his fingers.

Two months late again. She thought she was pregnant this time— *Why now of all times? Well, I'll have to tell Yen Shan.*

"There, there," he said softly with a forced smile, "we'll just announce...."

Julie gazed straight ahead and could see the road forward with him looked dismal; more tears streamed down her face. "To start our life together this way seems rather tragic."

"There, there," he said, in a comforting tone.

But he introduced her to an obstetrician, a Cantonese woman doctor, who examined her. It turned out Julie wasn't pregnant, but her cervix had been torn.

Julie thought it must have dated back to Chih-yung, as it had not hurt so much after him. She was a little startled to hear the news and didn't ask a single question.

The tiny, sallow face of the doctor's taut Cantonese visage dissuaded her from asking anything. Plus, these matters had always been taboo for Julie. She had always associated sex and fertility with the primitive origins of mankind, thus embodying all the mysterious and terrifying qualities of life.

Yen Shan came the next day for news. Julie had originally intended to say that it was only a false alarm and not mention the torn cervix, but since he knew the doctor and would sooner or later hear it from her, Julie had to tell him. *It will certainly make him think of me not only as a fallen woman, a withered flower, but as one who has allowed herself to be ruined and rendered useless, infertile.*

He was expressionless as he listened. Of course he couldn't show his delight at a lucky escape.

After the communists took over, Julian lost his job. One day he visited wearing a brand-new suit.

"I just had several new suits made," he moaned, "and now I won't be able to wear them."

Concerning current affairs, he said, "Of course now I'll have to go along with them. I've already registered at the neighborhood unemployment office."

"As if they're going to hand you a job on a silver platter," thought Julie.

Julian often indulged in wishful thinking. When he dropped out of school, before he had found a job, he told Julie, "If only I had a bit of money right now. The classified advertisements in the newspapers say banks are looking for investors, and I could be a deputy manager or even a section chief. Actually, a senior staff position would suit me just fine." He hemmed and hawed as he said the words "senior staff position," as though he knew he was a little too young to play the part. "Then later I could be promoted to be section chief of a branch, and rise up the ranks step by step."

When he began his "chickens produce eggs, eggs produce more chickens" sermon, after being taken for a ride by grifters, Julie laughed and couldn't refrain from crying out, "Stop it, please, I can't take it anymore!"

Julian looked at Julie, puzzled, but stopped anyway.

Then he continued, "Second Brother told me that when he was unemployed, he would force himself to keep his spirits up and go out and socialize every day."

Julian, having received his comfort and encouragement at the New House, obviously admired Second Brother.

Casually mentioning Second Brother in such a way meant that he had completely forgotten he had written a letter to Second Brother accusing Julie of disgracing the family's honor. Perhaps that damning letter had been a little premature. And of course it never occurred to Julian that Julie had seen the letter; otherwise, Julian wouldn't have visited Julie once in a while to "stay in touch," as he put it.

Julian stayed for a while that day. When he was about to leave, Yen Shan arrived. This was the first time Julian had bumped into a male at her residence, and a movie star at that, so he naturally burned with curiosity though sensibly didn't linger.

Julie had once told Yen Shan that he looked a bit like her brother when he was a little boy. Yen Shan thus paid close attention to Julian. "He really was born with a strange physiognomy," Yen Shan marveled after Julian departed.

Julie was taken aback, and said in her brother's defense, "He didn't look like that growing up." It was the first time she had looked at her brother through the eyes of an outsider. She wasn't sure when the transformation happened—as a teenager it looked like he would grow up to be quite dashing. But puberty passed and his neck remained thin, making his head appear to be too large and heavy, his nose protruding like a solitary alpine peak. If that nose were a chicken's beak, he would indeed resemble a tall chicken. He actually looked somewhat like a foreigner, an eccentric one.

Actually, it wasn't that bad—Yen Shan was just a little oversensitive. He had lost weight and appeared haggard. Naturally he was sensitive about a man's appearance, which served as a key asset in his career as an actor.

When Julian first arrived that day, he saw Judy. Later on, Judy burst out giggling. "I think little Julian will get picked up by an older woman looking for a bargain."

Julie acknowledged the comment with a smile but felt a bit sad that Third Aunt would still regard Julian with the same condescending eye.

Yen Shan became engaged to a young, pretty actress. Her mother kept her on a short leash. Before, she could only marry a famous owner of a theater in Shanghai at the very least—an actor like Yen Shan didn't have a chance. But nowadays they were all merely art and cultural workers.

Hsün Hwa became an official at the Cultural Bureau and grew rather plump. He had left the two women and married yet another. Yen Shan was close to him and invited several friends to a dinner party at his home in Hsün Hwa's honor. Julie was also invited, most likely because Yen Shan thought Hsün Hwa could help her out, given that they knew each other. But if Yen Shan really had such a purpose in mind, he never mentioned it to Julie.

At the dinner table Hsün Hwa said very little and not one word to Julie. After the meal, he immediately stood up, walked to the living room, and leaned against the piano with an air of desolation.

"*Is* he a Party member?" Julie asked Yen Shan later.

"I don't know." Yen Shan chuckled. "Didn't I tell you that already?!" He continued, "When I went to see a preview screening once, his first wife sought him out at the theater and made a huge scene. They weren't divorced yet and the new incumbent had just moved in with him. The woman rolled about on the ground and wailed, 'Let your friends be the judge!' Later Hsün Hwa said to everyone, 'Money's been handed over, the family visits are being made, what more can I do?'" Yen Shan smiled as he spoke, but it was obvious that he feared Julie would make a public scene like that when he married.

Yen Shan visited again. He seemed anxious as he paced the room in circles.

"When do you plan to get married?" Julie inquired solicitously.

"Already married," Yen Shan replied, and then smiled awkwardly.

A raging river immediately surged between them.

His expression also changed a little as if he too heard the sound of the river torrent.

The last "reformed" tabloid that remained after the communists came to power still occasionally carried society gossip about movie personalities. One report had the headline: "Newlyweds Yen Shan and Resplendent Autumn Snow Visit Our Newsroom." Yen Shan feared reports like that would upset Julie, so he asked a friend to pass on a request to the tabloid editor that he not publish news about their private life in the future.

Julie had only seen a blurred photograph of Resplendent Autumn Snow in costume. All women look more or less the same in costume, so Julie couldn't get much of an impression, other than her petite frame. Julie imagined his head snuggling up close to her chest, while she stood behind the woman's shoulder looking down, as if observing herself. Her pyramid-shaped breast in Yen Shan's hand looked like a little white bird with a red beak. The bird's heart fluttered. Yen Shan sucked its red beak. His eyes, like black mirrors, were shrouded in a layer of red mist.

Julie felt her heart burning.

Perhaps she was innately self-contradictory, as she had never imagined Chih-yung with other women like that.

Miss Su visited. And so did Yen Shan. Miss Su, who never frequented the theater, had previously met Yen Shan at Julie's residence. They introduced him as Mr. Feng, which was his real surname. After Yen Shan departed, Miss Su said to Julie, "Mr. Feng appears to have put on a bit of weight."

Julie felt as if a knife had stabbed her in the heart. Judy, who stood nearby, said nothing.

Mr. Niu invited Bebe and Julie to afternoon tea. He obviously knew about Julie and Chih-yung, and despised her. He merely bowed slightly when they met. It became dark early toward the end of the year, and by the time they emerged from afternoon tea it was already dusk. Mr. Niu accompanied them back to Bebe's residence, not far from the patisserie. As they approached the rear entrance, about to ring the bell, he stepped forward and, with obvious embarrassment, said in a low voice to Bebe, "May I see you again this year?"

Standing beside them Julie was overwhelmed. Three years earlier, Yen Shan had said the same thing to her over the telephone. At that moment, it felt to them as if not seeing each other until after the New Year was tantamount to not seeing each other for a whole year.

Bebe often laughed behind Mr. Niu's back whenever she talked about him. But this time she didn't. "Of course," she replied softly, looking up at him, "telephone me."

By the time Julie left for home it was midnight. Myriad feelings welled up in her heart.

Bebe's mother had insisted on giving her a big red apple. She held it in one hand while holding up her red scarf with the other to cover her mouth. Her dark green rustic wool overcoat billowed in the swirling northwesterly wind, like a broken lotus leaf covered with frost, floating on the water. On the familiar street, neon lights illuminated the footpath in red and blue.

The steel gates of the shops were shut. An Indian security guard sitting in the shadows suddenly called out, "Good morning, young lady."

Julie was thirty. She didn't turn her head but felt grateful for the greeting.

The red scarf covered Julie's mouth. She remembered Yen Shan's childhood story of his father using a scarf to cover his mouth in that rickshaw, exhorting him to "Close your mouth tight! Close your mouth tight!"

Mr. Niu inevitably had to be the one to ask, "May I see you again this year?"

Julie could deal with a vengeful, eye-for-an-eye, tooth-for-a-tooth, sort of god, but a god with an excessive sense of humor was really too much for her to bear.

And yet Julie never had any regrets about her relationship with Yen Shan; she felt fortunate to have had him at that time.

She had long stopped thinking about Chih-yung, though sometimes the pain from those times would reappear for no apparent reason. H. G. Wells wrote a science-fiction novel, *The Island of Doctor Moreau*, about a scientist who transformed animals into people, but after a short time, their original features reemerged, necessitating a bath in acid, which was called the Bath of Burning Pain, a phrase ingrained in Julie's memory. Sometimes while taking a bath, luxuriating in the hot water without a book, her mind wandered as she thought about nothing in particular, and then, with no warning, certain thoughts forced their way in, taking advantage of the vacancy. She wouldn't actually think of Chih-yung's name, but a familiar feeling that made her viscera seethe would spread over her entire body, searing her flesh, the excruciating pain rising and falling like the tide, totally submerging her again and again before finally receding.

Julie read a news report about air pollution giving stone cancer to the statues of Venice. "The end of time, when seas dry up and rocks crumble, comes quick," Julie thought to herself.

When she reread Chih-yung's works, she no longer felt admiration. They were suffused with the affected tone she had first sensed in his long letters sent from the countryside, and seeing him write "That too was ideal," she almost laughed out loud. When she read that it "wasn't ideal" for Miss K'ang to marry, she snorted but couldn't help frowning. It reminded her of when her compatriots reversed ideological positions, causing her to grimace with shock and wonder, "Why on earth are people still like this?"

Now there weren't any films in China to act in. Living overseas Julie saw an acrobatic troupe from China perform on television where one acrobat did a handstand on a bicycle with a ball balanced on her feet, among other amazing feats, far more impressive than a sea lion balancing a ball on its nose. Julie felt sad with the thought, "We Chinese are indeed very clever, cleverer than sea lions."

Julie never wanted any children, perhaps in part because she feared her children would be wicked and exact revenge on behalf of her own mother. Except once when she dreamt that she was in the color movie *The Trail of the Lonesome Pine*, which she had watched as a child. Based on a popular novel, the film starred Henry Fonda and Sylvia Sidney, though Julie had long forgotten the story, only remembering she didn't like it. The touching theme song added to the film's fame— she could still recall the melody. In those early days of color film, the reel progressed like a series of gaudy scenic postcards, depicting blue mountains with red log cabins against a turquoise-blue sky, shadows of trees swaying on the ground in the sunlight. In her dream, some children emerged from the pine forest, and they all belonged to her. Then Chih-yung appeared—elated, beaming—and took her hand to lead her back into the cabin. A comical scene. She blushed as their arms stretched out horizontally in a line, at which point she woke up.

A movie she saw more than twenty year ago; a man from ten years ago. Julie floated rapturously for a long, long time after she woke up.

She only had that dream once, yet she never stopped dreaming about exams. Nightmares, always nightmares.

Only the somber mood of troops waiting in the dawn before battle can compare with the morning of final exams, like the rebel slave army in *Spartacus* silently peering through the predawn mist at the Roman troops maneuvering in the distance—surely the most chilling moment in any war film—everything charged with anticipation.

CHARACTER LIST

AH LEUNG 阿梁: One of Bebe's suitors.

ANDREWS, MR. 安竹斯: Julie's university lecturer in Hong Kong. Died in Japanese invasion of Hong Kong in 1941.

ANGIE 安姬: Eurasian day student at Julie's university in Hong Kong.

ARAKI 荒木: Japanese military adviser. Shao Chih-yung's friend.

AUDREY SUN 婀墜: Julie's schoolmate in Hong Kong. Went out with Mr. Lee.

B

BEBE 比比: Julie's best friend. An Indian girl Julie met in Shanghai. Attended the same university in Hong Kong.

BOUDINET, COLONEL 布丹大佐: A French military officer. One of Rachel's suitors.

BROTHER HSÜ 緒哥哥: Uncle Chu's son. His birth mother was a servant girl of Uncle Chu's third concubine. Brother Hsü had a secret relationship with Judy but also had an affair with Brother Wei's wife.

C

CHAN 陳: A man who dated Bebe in Hong Kong.

CHANG, MISS 章小姐: Middle-aged woman from Rose's hometown.

CHARLIE YANG, DR. 查禮: Nancy's husband. A famous surgeon. Nancy and Charlie traveled to Hong Kong with Rachel. He once treated Julie's wound.

CHENG, MISS 蜜斯程: Administrator in Julie's university in Hong Kong. Nicknamed Automobile.

CHIEN-WEI 簡煒: See PI CHIEN-WEI.

CH'IEN, THE SECOND ELDEST 錢老二: A distant relative who Judy asked about at the dinner table.

CHIH-YUNG 之雍: See SHAO CHIH-YUNG.

CH'IN, MRS. 老秦媽: Judy's maid.

CHU, AUNT 表大媽: Uncle Chu's principal consort.

CHU, MISS 朱小姐: Hsün Hwa's girlfriend.

CHU, UNCLE 表大爺: Aunt Chu's husband. Likes to be addressed as His Excellency 大爺. Brother Hsü and Miss Su's birth father. Embezzled funds that Judy and Brother Hsü tried to repay. He was shot dead.

CHU'S PRINCIPAL CONSORT 竺大太太: See AUNT CHU.

COUSIN LÜ 呂表哥: An impoverished member of the Keng clan, a distant nephew of Jade Flower. Julie called him Cousin Lü. He later married a bank manager's daughter.

CRIMSON CLOUD CHANG 章緋雯: Shao Chih-yung's second wife. A former sing-song girl.

D

DAPHNE 黛芙妮: Julie's university schoolmate in Hong Kong.

DONALDSON, MISS 唐納生小姐: English spinster in charge of the women's dormitory managed by the American Methodist Episcopal Church in Hong Kong.

E

ELEVENTH MASTER 十一爺: A distant relative in the wealthy branch of the Sheng clan. A cabinet minister in the Peiyang government.

ELIZABETH 依麗莎白: Julie's schoolmate in Hong Kong.

ELDEST UNCLE and ELDEST AUNT 大爺大媽: Ned and Judy's elder brother and his wife. Eldest Uncle was twenty years older than Judy and Ned. He looked after them when they became orphans and embezzled their inheritance. Normally Julie would call him and his wife Eldest Uncle and Eldest Aunt. They verbally adopted Julie therefore she was instructed to address her birth parents, Rachel and Ned, as Second Uncle and Second Aunt.

EMMA 愛瑪: Julie's university schoolmate in Hong Kong.

EUGENE 艾軍: Australian journalist in Shanghai. Bebe's friend who later married Fanny.

EUPHORIA 愛老三: Ned's mistress, a former prostitute. Moved in after Rachel left Ned.

F

FANNY 范妮: A Chinese girl who married Eugene, an Australian journalist.

FAT NEPHEW and PIGTAIL NEPHEW 胖大姪姪和辮大姪姪: Distant relatives in the Sheng clan.

FEINSTEIN, DR. 范斯坦醫生: Famous lung specialist in Shanghai. One of Rachel's admirers.

FIFTH UNCLE 五爸爸/五爺: A relative in the Sheng clan. His younger sisters introduced Jade Flower to Ned.

FOSTER BOY 寄哥兒: Uncle Chu's adopted son. Nephew of a concubine.

FOURTH GRANDAUNT 四姑奶奶: A distant relative of Ned. A female younger cousin whom Ned greeted as Second Younger Cousin lived in Fourth Grandaunt's household. Second Younger Cousin was once a marriage candidate for Ned.

G

GOLDEN BOY 進寶: Auntie Han's son.

GOOD GRANNIE 好婆: Jade Flower's mother.

H

HAIRY BOY 毛哥: Julian's infant name.

HAIRY GIRL 毛姐: Julie's infant name.

HAN, AUNTIE 韓媽: Long-serving maid in the Sheng family. Julie's nanny. Mother of Golden Boy.

HENRI, SISTER 亨利嬤嬤: A Sino-Portuguese Eurasian nun in Julie's university dormitory in Hong Kong.

HONEST NEPHEW 誠大姪姪: Distant relative in the Sheng clan.

HSIANG, MISS 項八小姐: Relative in the Sheng clan. The eighth sibling of the Hsiang family. Julie called her Eighth Sister. Later married Mr. Pi.

HSIANG CHING 向璟: Writer and friend of Shao Chih-yung.

HSIU-NAN 秀男: Shao Chih-yung's niece. Looked after Shao's household affairs even after marrying Mr. Wen.

HSÜ HENG 徐衡: Painter and friend of Shao Chih-yung.

HSÜN HWA 荀樺: Literary editor who published some of Julie's writings. Taken away by the Japanese gendarmes for suspected communist activities. Shao Chih-yung used his connections to free him. After

1949, Hsün Hwa became a cultural official in the communist government.

J

JADE FLOWER 翠華: Ned's second wife. The eleventh daughter of the Keng clan.

JADE PEACH 碧桃: Part of Rachel's dowry. Rachel married Jade Peach off to the servant Yü-heng but the marriage did not last.

JADE PHOENIX CH'EN 陳瑤鳳: Shao Chih-yung's first wife.

JENNY 劍妮: Julie's university schoolmate in Hong Kong who was from remote northwest China. She dated Mr. Wei.

JORY 焦利: Judy's Eurasian colleague.

JOY 來喜: Servant girl in Ned and Judy's elder brother's household. Later became a concubine of Ned's elder brother.

JUDY 楚娣: Ned's younger sister. Julie's paternal third aunt. Sometimes was addressed as Third Mistress by servants. Traveled with Rachel to Europe. Had a secret relationship with Brother Hsü.

JULIAN SHENG 盛九林: Julie's younger brother. Rachel and Ned's son.

JULIE SHENG 盛九莉: Julian's elder sister. Rachel and Ned's daughter.

K

K'ANG, MISS 小康小姐: A nurse and Shao Chih-yung's young lover.

K'UANG, MISS 匡小姐: Daughter of a rich Cantonese businessman. She was murdered by her husband, Liao Chung-i, during their honeymoon trip to the Lake District.

KWONG 鄺: An overseas Chinese student who occasionally asked Bebe out. Later married Sally.

L

LEE, AUNTIE 李媽: Maid in Ned's family. Fired by Ned's second wife, Jade Flower.

LEE, DR. 李醫生: Malayan overseas Chinese in charge of student-relief work during the Japanese occupation.

LEE, MR. 李先生: Student from a rich family in Malaya, who dated Audrey.

LI, AUNTIE 李媽: Maid in Yün-chih's household.

LIAO CHUNG-I 廖仲義: A law-school graduate who murdered his wife, Miss K'uang, during their honeymoon trip to the Lake District.

LIN, DR. 林醫生: Rose's elder brother, a medical student. Accompanied Rose and Julie to safety during an air raid.

LING 凌嫂子: Respected maid in the Pien family. Bought infant Yün-chih from a famine refugee.

LIU, AUNTIE 劉嫂子: Maid in Yün-chih's household.

LLOYD 勞以德: British businessman and Rachel's longtime admirer. Died during Japanese invasion of Singapore.

LU, MISS 陸先生: Female teacher at the Liu Academy for Girls, which Julie attended in Shanghai.

LUKE, SISTER 路克嬤嬤: A nun in Julie's university dormitory in Hong Kong.

M

MARIE 瑪麗: Cantonese girl from an orphanage. Worked as a maid in Julie's university dormitory in Hong Kong.

MARK, SISTER 馬克嬤嬤: Acting dormitory proctor in Julie's university in Hong Kong.

MARSHA 瑪霞: Abortionist's assistant in the United States.

MARSHAL 馬壽: English teacher at Julie's university and one of Rachel's admirers.

MENG HSIAO-YÜN 孟曉筠: Involved in Uncle's Chu's corruption case.

MIKE 麥克: The dean of the Arts Department in Julie's university in Hong Kong.

N

NANCY YANG 南西: Rachel and Judy's friend. Dr. Charlie Yang's wife.

NED 乃德: The sixteenth child of the Sheng clan. Rachel's ex-husband. Judy's elder brother. Julie and Julian's birth father, though Julie was instructed to address him as Second Uncle. Sometimes called Second Master by the servants.

NIU, MR. 鈕先生: One of Bebe's suitors in Shanghai.

O

OLD MATRIARCH 老太太: Ned and Judy's mother.

OPPORTUNE JADE HSIN 辛巧玉: Concubine of Mr. Yü's late father. Some people called her Master Hsin. Shao Chih-yung's lover.

P

PHILIPPE 菲力: A law student, one of Rachel's male friends.

PI CHIEN-WEI 畢簡煒: Retired ambassador who was romantically involved with Rachel but later married Miss Hsiang. Also called Ambassador Pi 畢大使 and Mr. Pi 畢先生.

PURITY, MISS and MISS GRACE 純姐姐蘊姐姐: Sisters in the Chu family. Old Matriarch's grandnieces. Miss Grace was born to a concubine. Julie was close to Miss Purity, who later died of TB.

R

RACHEL 蕊秋: Julie and Julian's birth mother from the Pien clan. Yün-chih's elder sister. She was married to Ned in the Sheng family and sometimes addressed as Mrs. Sheng. Julie had been instructed to call her Second Aunt since childhood.

RESPLENDENT AUTUMN SNOW 雪豔秋: A female opera singer. Married Yen Shan.

RICK 雷克: Pathology teacher at Julie's university in Hong Kong. One of Rachel's suitors.

ROSE 柔絲: Julie's university schoolmate in Hong Kong. Dr. Lin's younger sister. Called the Belle of Penang.

ROUNDY 小圓: Julie and Julian's younger cousin. Julian's first love.

RUBY 茹璧: Julie's university schoolmate in Hong Kong. Reputed to be Wang Ching-wei's niece.

RUDY 汝狄: An American writer. Julie's second husband.

S

SALLY 賽梨: Julie's university schoolmate in Hong Kong.

SCHÜTTE, HERR 夏赫特: Principal of the German school in Shanghai. One of Judy's paramours.

SECOND BROTHER 二哥哥: A distant male cousin of Julie and Julian's from Tientsin. His father is one of Julie and Julian's paternal uncles from the well-off branch of the Sheng clan.

SECOND CONCUBINE 二姨太: Rachel's birth mother whom Rachel calls Second Concubine.

SECOND MASTER 二爺: See NED.

SECOND MASTER 二師父: A spinster in the Pien clan who later became a Buddhist nun.

SECOND UNCLE 二大爺: The nephew of Julie's paternal grandfather. One of Julie's paternal uncles. Julie called him Second Uncle.

SECOND UNCLE and SECOND AUNT 二叔二嬸: How Julie was instructed to address her birth parents, Ned and Rachel.

SEVEN, MISS 小老七: Euphoria's fellow prostitute.

SEVENTH MISTRESS 七老太太: Senior member in the family of Eleventh Master and Thirteenth Master from a wealthy branch of the Sheng clan.

SHAO CHIH-YUNG 邵之雍: Julie's first husband. Also romantically involved with other women. Worked for the Wang Ching-wei government during the Japanese occupation but had to flee after the Japanese lost the war. He usually appears as Chih-yung in the novel.

SISTER HSÜ 緒嫂嫂: Brother Hsü's wife.

SU, MISS 素姐姐: Uncle Chu's daughter from his first marriage. Miss Su and Brother Hsü were consanguineous siblings with different mothers.

T

TALL AND SKINNY 長子: One of two opium preparers in the Sheng household.

T'ANG KU-WU 湯孤鶩: T'ang the Solitary Mallard. A celebrity writer popular in the 1920s who established a new magazine to which Julie made some submissions.

TENG SHENG 鄧升: A longtime male servant in the Sheng household.

THIRD AUNT 三姑: See JUDY.

THÉRÈSE, SISTER 特瑞絲嬤嬤: A Cantonese nun in Julie's university dormitory in Hong Kong.

THIRD CONCUBINE 三姨奶奶: Uncle Chu's third concubine. Sold the servant girl who gave birth to Brother Hsü.

THIRTEENTH MASTER 十三爺: One of Julie's paternal uncles in Tientsin from the wealthy branch of the Sheng clan. He evicts Ned's mistress Euphoria.

V

VERMILLION, AUNTIE 老朱: Aunt Chu's maid.

W

WEI, MR. 魏先生: A man from Jenny's hometown in northwest China, who dated Jenny.

WEN, MR. 聞先生: Lumber merchant and the husband of Shao Chih-yung's niece Hsiu-nan.

WENDY 文姬: Literary editor who introduced Shao Chih-yung to Julie.

Y

YANG, DR. 楊醫生: See CHARLIE YANG, DR.

YEN MING-SHENG 嚴明昇: Overseas Chinese student. Julie's classmate in Hong Kong and former competitor.

YEN SHAN 燕山: Actor and director. Has a romance with Julie after Shao Chih-yung. Married Resplendent Autumn Snow, a female opera singer.

YÜ, AUNTIE 余媽: Julian's nanny. Came from the Pien clan along with Jade Peach as part of Rachel's dowry.

YÜ, MR. 郁先生: Provided refuge to Chih-yung in the countryside after the Sino-Japanese War ended.

YÜ-HENG 毓恒: A young male servant. Joined the Sheng household as part of Rachel's dowry. His marriage with Jade Peach does not last.

YÜ K'O-CH'IEN 虞克潛: Disciple of a famous contemporary writer. Shao Chih-yung's friend and colleague.

YÜN-CHIH 雲志: Julie and Julian's maternal uncle. Rachel's younger brother. The housemaid Ling bought Yün-chih from a refugee family when he was an infant.

TITLES IN SERIES

For a complete list of titles, visit www.nyrb.com or write to:
Catalog Requests, NYRB, 435 Hudson Street, New York, NY 10014

* *Also available as an electronic book.*

ALFRED DÖBLIN Bright Magic: Stories*
JEAN D'ORMESSON The Glory of the Empire: A Novel, A History*
ARTHUR CONAN DOYLE The Exploits and Adventures of Brigadier Gerard
CHARLES DUFF A Handbook on Hanging
BRUCE DUFFY The World As I Found It*
DAPHNE DU MAURIER Don't Look Now: Stories
ELAINE DUNDY The Dud Avocado*
ELAINE DUNDY The Old Man and Me*
G.B. EDWARDS The Book of Ebenezer Le Page*
JOHN EHLE The Land Breakers*
MARCELLUS EMANTS A Posthumous Confession
EURIPIDES Grief Lessons: Four Plays; translated by Anne Carson
J.G. FARRELL Troubles*
J.G. FARRELL The Siege of Krishnapur*
J.G. FARRELL The Singapore Grip*
ELIZA FAY Original Letters from India
KENNETH FEARING The Big Clock
KENNETH FEARING Clark Gifford's Body
FÉLIX FÉNÉON Novels in Three Lines*
M.I. FINLEY The World of Odysseus
THOMAS FLANAGAN The Year of the French*
BENJAMIN FONDANE Existential Monday: Philosophical Essays*
SANFORD FRIEDMAN Conversations with Beethoven*
SANFORD FRIEDMAN Totempole*
MARC FUMAROLI When the World Spoke French
CARLO EMILIO GADDA That Awful Mess on the Via Merulana
BENITO PÉREZ GÁLDOS Tristana*
MAVIS GALLANT The Cost of Living: Early and Uncollected Stories*
MAVIS GALLANT Paris Stories*
MAVIS GALLANT A Fairly Good Time *with* Green Water, Green Sky*
MAVIS GALLANT Varieties of Exile*
GABRIEL GARCÍA MÁRQUEZ Clandestine in Chile: The Adventures of Miguel Littín
LEONARD GARDNER Fat City*
WILLIAM H. GASS In the Heart of the Heart of the Country: And Other Stories*
WILLIAM H. GASS On Being Blue: A Philosophical Inquiry*
THÉOPHILE GAUTIER My Fantoms
GE FEI The Invisibility Cloak
JEAN GENET Prisoner of Love
ÉLISABETH GILLE The Mirador: Dreamed Memories of Irène Némirovsky by Her Daughter*
NATALIA GINZBURG Family Lexicon*
JEAN GIONO Hill*
JEAN GIONO Melville: A Novel*
JOHN GLASSCO Memoirs of Montparnasse*
P.V. GLOB The Bog People: Iron-Age Man Preserved
NIKOLAI GOGOL Dead Souls*
EDMOND AND JULES DE GONCOURT Pages from the Goncourt Journals
ALICE GOODMAN History Is Our Mother: Three Libretti*
PAUL GOODMAN Growing Up Absurd: Problems of Youth in the Organized Society*
EDWARD GOREY (EDITOR) The Haunted Looking Glass
JEREMIAS GOTTHELF The Black Spider*
A.C. GRAHAM Poems of the Late T'ang
JULIEN GRACQ Balcony in the Forest*
HENRY GREEN Back*

JEAN-PATRICK MANCHETTE The Mad and the Bad*
OSIP MANDELSTAM The Selected Poems of Osip Mandelstam
OLIVIA MANNING Fortunes of War: The Balkan Trilogy*
OLIVIA MANNING Fortunes of War: The Levant Trilogy*
OLIVIA MANNING School for Love*
JAMES VANCE MARSHALL Walkabout*
GUY DE MAUPASSANT Afloat
GUY DE MAUPASSANT Alien Hearts*
GUY DE MAUPASSANT Like Death*
JAMES McCOURT Mawrdew Czgowchwz*
WILLIAM McPHERSON Testing the Current*
MEZZ MEZZROW AND BERNARD WOLFE Really the Blues*
HENRI MICHAUX Miserable Miracle
JESSICA MITFORD Hons and Rebels
JESSICA MITFORD Poison Penmanship*
NANCY MITFORD Frederick the Great*
NANCY MITFORD Madame de Pompadour*
NANCY MITFORD The Sun King*
NANCY MITFORD Voltaire in Love*
PATRICK MODIANO In the Café of Lost Youth*
PATRICK MODIANO Young Once*
MICHEL DE MONTAIGNE Shakespeare's Montaigne; translated by John Florio*
HENRY DE MONTHERLANT Chaos and Night
BRIAN MOORE The Lonely Passion of Judith Hearne*
BRIAN MOORE The Mangan Inheritance*
ALBERTO MORAVIA Agostino*
ALBERTO MORAVIA Boredom*
ALBERTO MORAVIA Contempt*
JAN MORRIS Conundrum*
JAN MORRIS Hav*
PENELOPE MORTIMER The Pumpkin Eater*
GUIDO MORSELLI The Communist*
ÁLVARO MUTIS The Adventures and Misadventures of Maqroll
L.H. MYERS The Root and the Flower*
NESCIO Amsterdam Stories*
DARCY O'BRIEN A Way of Life, Like Any Other
SILVINA OCAMPO Thus Were Their Faces*
YURI OLESHA Envy*
IONA AND PETER OPIE The Lore and Language of Schoolchildren
IRIS OWENS After Claude*
RUSSELL PAGE The Education of a Gardener
ALEXANDROS PAPADIAMANTIS The Murderess
BORIS PASTERNAK, MARINA TSVETAYEVA, AND RAINER MARIA RILKE Letters, Summer 1926
CESARE PAVESE The Moon and the Bonfires
CESARE PAVESE The Selected Works of Cesare Pavese
BORISLAV PEKIĆ Houses*
ELEANOR PERÉNYI More Was Lost: A Memoir*
LUIGI PIRANDELLO The Late Mattia Pascal
JOSEP PLA The Gray Notebook
DAVID PLANTE Difficult Women: A Memoir of Three*
ANDREY PLATONOV The Foundation Pit
ANDREY PLATONOV Happy Moscow
ANDREY PLATONOV Soul and Other Stories

NORMAN PODHORETZ Making It*
J.F. POWERS Morte d'Urban*
J.F. POWERS The Stories of J.F. Powers*
J.F. POWERS Wheat That Springeth Green*
CHRISTOPHER PRIEST Inverted World*
BOLESŁAW PRUS The Doll*
GEORGE PSYCHOUNDAKIS The Cretan Runner: His Story of the German Occupation*
ALEXANDER PUSHKIN The Captain's Daughter*
QIU MIAOJIN Last Words from Montmartre*
QIU MIAOJIN Notes of a Crocodile*
RAYMOND QUENEAU We Always Treat Women Too Well
RAYMOND QUENEAU Witch Grass
RAYMOND RADIGUET Count d'Orgel's Ball
PAUL RADIN Primitive Man as Philosopher*
FRIEDRICH RECK Diary of a Man in Despair*
JULES RENARD Nature Stories*
JEAN RENOIR Renoir, My Father
GREGOR VON REZZORI An Ermine in Czernopol*
GREGOR VON REZZORI Memoirs of an Anti-Semite*
GREGOR VON REZZORI The Snows of Yesteryear: Portraits for an Autobiography*
TIM ROBINSON Stones of Aran: Labyrinth
TIM ROBINSON Stones of Aran: Pilgrimage
MILTON ROKEACH The Three Christs of Ypsilanti*
FR. ROLFE Hadrian the Seventh
GILLIAN ROSE Love's Work
LINDA ROSENKRANTZ Talk*
WILLIAM ROUGHEAD Classic Crimes
CONSTANCE ROURKE American Humor: A Study of the National Character
SAKI The Unrest-Cure and Other Stories; illustrated by Edward Gorey
UMBERTO SABA Ernesto*
JOAN SALES Uncertain Glory*
TAYEB SALIH Season of Migration to the North
TAYEB SALIH The Wedding of Zein*
JEAN-PAUL SARTRE We Have Only This Life to Live: Selected Essays. 1939–1975
ARTHUR SCHNITZLER Late Fame*
GERSHOM SCHOLEM Walter Benjamin: The Story of a Friendship*
DANIEL PAUL SCHREBER Memoirs of My Nervous Illness
JAMES SCHUYLER Alfred and Guinevere
JAMES SCHUYLER What's for Dinner?*
SIMONE SCHWARZ-BART The Bridge of Beyond*
LEONARDO SCIASCIA The Day of the Owl
LEONARDO SCIASCIA Equal Danger
LEONARDO SCIASCIA The Moro Affair
LEONARDO SCIASCIA To Each His Own
LEONARDO SCIASCIA The Wine-Dark Sea
VICTOR SEGALEN René Leys*
ANNA SEGHERS Transit*
PHILIPE-PAUL DE SÉGUR Defeat: Napoleon's Russian Campaign
GILBERT SELDES The Stammering Century*
VICTOR SERGE The Case of Comrade Tulayev*
VICTOR SERGE Conquered City*
VICTOR SERGE Memoirs of a Revolutionary
VICTOR SERGE Midnight in the Century*